THE MESSAGE

To Pam

Michael R Hon

THE MESSAGE

Dr. Michael Ritivoi Hansen

To order additional copies of this book, contact:
Xlibris Corporation
1-888-795-4274
www.Xlibris.com
Orders@Xlibris.com
96256

DEDICATION

This book is the product of my desire to understand what communism prevented me to understand all along: its nature and the reasons behind its doomed practices. It took me a long and lonely time to write it so, I dedicate it to those who, like me, want to understand where communism's failure originated, why and how.

I also dedicate this book to my American wife who encouraged and inspired me to undertake this work, and put up with my long hours behind the desk, fighting with the intricacies of the English language, the challenge of writing and the deeper meaning of communism.

CONTENTS

THE MESSAGE

THE HOME OF THE HOMELESS

THE MESSAGE

1. The Winds of War

I

I was born in Romania, in April 1943, one year and four months before the Soviet occupation. To me, that date bore a certain symbolism; it made me feel proud to have been born free. Freedom was a painful subject not only due to the Soviets, but to a chain of other occupations along history. There was a deep desire for freedom across the country. As a child, I thought that freedom is a basic ingredient of life—that not having it made us incomplete. I thought somebody could claim pride only if he were free. I remember freedom being often brought up in conversations, literature and classes. We had been surrounded by powerful empires. The Turkish, the Austro-Hungarian, the Russian—they all felt they deserved to have what didn't belong to them. And of course, a defeated country has defeated people who develop a psychology the occupier cannot even guess. I am sure there are books on that . . . few read them, however!

Regardless, this is my story. I would start it with a visit we had from an older friend of my grandfather, Ion Ritivoi. I never saw my grandfather, and my father barely remembered him. He died in the First World War. This was all we knew about him. The older man came to tell us what happened to his best friend, my grandfather, so we may remember him with as much regard as he did. I don't recall why it took him all this time to reach us, but my father was satisfied with his explanation.

My grandfather and his wife were small farmers from Transylvania's Sibiu County. At an age of big decisions, young and bold, they immigrated to Romania proper. At that time, Transylvania was under Austro-Hungarian administration, which pursued a compulsive assimilation of the Romanian majority to have a Hungarian minority's identity. The Hungarians used all possible angles to achieve this: Romanian under—representation in political bodies, absence of schools in Romanian, elimination of the Romanian credit structure, mandatory conversion to Catholicism in order to get a state job, forbidding Romanians from purchasing land, colonization of Hungarians, and so forth. It was unusual for a farmer to leave his land and take to the road, but for my grandfather, it was more of a burden to be humiliated by foreign authorities in his own ancestral land. He took his wife and crossed the Carpathian Mountains into *Regat* ("Kingdom" of Romania). Romania wasn't the land of milk and honey, but it was a place where they could start a new life, be accepted as Romanians, and be treated with dignity.

As what many of their kin had done before them, my grandparents settled in Bucuresti. There, through the recommendations of older émigrés, my grandfather got a job as a janitor at Carol Foundation (today University's Library), but his quiet life didn't last long. World War I started with Romania and Hungary in opposite camps. For my grandfather and his Transylvanian fellows, this was the time to put their money where their mouths were, and they created the first battalion of Transylvanian volunteers for the Transylvanian front.

The war itself was risky enough, but for these volunteers, it offered an additional risk: if taken prisoner, they would be hanged as deserters from the Hungarian ranks. In their late teens, these people had been drafted into the Austro-Hungarian army.

The creation of this battalion had a significance the king himself didn't ignore. He decided to show his appreciation for the volunteers' selflessness by reviewing their unit—a high honor. The petty officers in charge had been fired with excitement. Being locals from Bucuresti's outskirts they didn't connect with Transylvanians' heartache. For those officers, the King's arrival transcended many times over the symbolism and valor of the Transylvanian soldiers' decisions. The troop had to look great. This was all that their sergeants cared for. In my grandfather's case, after a rehearsal, the sergeant decided to assert himself by slapping every volunteer in the first line for not looking spic and span.

My grandfather was in the second line, but he perceived those palms on the face as a personal humiliation—an insult those men didn't deserve. In front of him was his friend Iacobul Dutului. Al Dutului, as they used to call him, said softly with pain in his voice:

"Ioane, this good for nothing is beating us."

This proved to be too much.

"Let's switch places," my grandfather told his friend, and he firmly stepped in the front line. When the sergeant came to him, he drew his bayonet and said with no hesitation, "If you touch me, you're gone."

The sergeant didn't touch him. Instead, he sent my grandfather to solitary confinement.

Time passed, and for the King's visit, soldier Ritivoi was groomed along with his comrades and sent back in line. Passing along, King Ferdinand recognized his former janitor and stopped to congratulate him:

"I am glad to see you among these brave ones, Ritivoi. Congratulations."

His Majesty knew him! The sergeant was overwhelmed. As soon as the King left, he fell on his knees and begged, "Ritivoi, don't report me. I'll do anything you ask but don't tell them," he said. He walked on his knees as my grandfather moved away.

"Don't worry, Sarge, but don't humiliate us anymore," he said with a low voice.

The older man who told us this story was Toma Stoisor, another one of the Transylvanian friends who all left their village together. When we heard the story, my grandfather wasn't with us any longer. He died in the war when my father was about three years old.

II

After a number of years, my grandmother married a man much bigger but less gifted than her son. To boot, the stepfather claimed absolute authority on his turf. He decided how much everybody, in particular my father, ate, how much they slept, and much of what they did.

Life drastically changed. Love and freedom faded into images from the past. The proverbial advantages of being the only child gave place to the disadvantage of being the only target.

"May I have another slice of melon?" my father would ask.

"What you had was enough. To-mor-row," the stepdad would say. He peculiarly stretched the word so that it hovered clearly in the air.

The reason for rationing wasn't financial. It was just how the stepfather was. Those were times my father didn't want to talk about. Only my brother's questioning skills could extract this melon story from him. Not all things were so bad. My father had the freedom to get as much formal education as he could, and he took full advantage of it. I assume that his stepfather proudly interpreted my father's success as a product of his stern education: "I made a man out of him," he used to say. With or without the guidance of his stepfather, my father was a top student all the way throughout medical school.

His success and gregarious nature helped him dream of success and freedom. His image of happiness held high a beautiful wife, a house in the middle of a ranch, many children, a happy family, horses, happy patients, a happy life, and of course, as many watermelons as his kidneys could handle. He always loved watermelons.

Despite my father's love for open spaces and interaction with people, he chose for his graduation thesis an indoor study pertaining to microbiology. The reason was rather practical: Professor Constantin Ionescu-Mihaiesti, the chairman of Microbiology, was the only professor who didn't require a fee for his advisory role. It was understood that no matter what medical field the thesis was in, after graduation my father would be able to freely choose the place to practice and go on with his career. So it came with no surprise when Professor Ionescu-Mihaiesti, who recognized my father's abilities both as a medical doctor and as an organizer, offered him a position in his Microbiology Institute in Bucuresti, my father declined. He set his eyes on a rural clinic at Ionesti, Vilcea County, a picturesque place that won his heart. Professor Ionescu-Mihaiesti gave his selfless support to his best student. He used his great influence to provide my father with the entire inventory he wanted for his ideal clinic. This included a well-supplied medical lab and several hospital beds, an uncommon feature for a *dispensar* (territorial clinic for ambulatory patients).

Things were falling into place. My father persuaded an Ionesti landlord to donate to the *dispensar* a piece of adjacent land, which conferred open access to the highway and a great front lawn. Meanwhile, he achieved an even bigger success. He met a beautiful girl with whom he fell in love head over heels. This girl, in due time, agreed to marry him, and they both got on the train steaming toward Ionesti.

III

However, life has its own unpredictable ways. World War II (WWII), which had recently started, proved to be a vortex stronger than Romania's desire for neutrality. The neutral countries of Europe started to fall either to the Germans or to the Soviet Union, while both eyed Romania. For Germany, Romania was important for its central location, for its agricultural output, and for its oil reserves. It also had the advantage of offering those resources next door, sheltered from British attacks. For the Soviet Union, Romania was an old target of its Western expansionism.

From 1711, when the Russian troops first stepped on Romanian soil, until 1944, there were recorded twelve Russian invasions (Ion Constantin: Romania, Marile Puteri si Problema Basarabiei, p. 16). Nevertheless, the first Russian occupation took place in 1812 when, at the end of the war between Russia and Turkey, Turkey gave Russia the Romanian land between the rivers Nistru (spelled Dniester in Western literature) and Prut called Basarabia. This gesture didn't cost Turkey anything since it didn't own it but satisfied Russia. Since then, Basarabia, where Romanians are an absolute majority, has changed hands several times, depending of who prevailed. Every Russian takeover brought in more Russian civil servants, business people, and Russian military. Many of them made Romania their home. A common practice of Russian imperialism Basarabia didn't escape was the relocation of large groups of people across borders to weaken national identity in occupied territories. Still, Romanians remained an absolute majority in Basarabia, a majority which always dreamed of rejoining the rest of Romania.

In line with those inconsiderate practices, before WWII started, on August 23, 1939, Hitler made a pact with Stalin (the Ribbentrop-Molotov Pact) which, among other provisions, allowed Russia to retake Basarabia any time it wanted. In June, 1940, Stalin made good the treaty and demanded the "return" of Basarabia and the "transfer" of the northern part of Bucovina, a Romanian province never before administered by Russia, as a "modest compensation," according to Soviet Foreign Minister Molotov, for the losses Soviet Union had suffered during the last period of Romanian rule in Basarabia (Keith Hitchins, Romania 1866–1947, p. 446). Molotov gave the Romanian government twenty-four hours to reply. King Carol II, taken by surprise, sought international support, but Germany, Italy, Turkey, and several Balkan states advised Romania to succumb to Soviet demands. Taking advantage of this difficult situation, two other Romanian neighbors, Hungary and Bulgaria, both German allies, pressed immediately for their own territorial claims against Romania. The Romanian King consulted his generals. The report from the chief of the army general staff indicated that the Romanian army could not survive an all-out attack. The King attempted a dialog, but Molotov summarily rejected any negotiations, and on June 28, 1940, began to occupy Basarabia.

Things became further complicated when on August 23, 1940, Hitler signed the Vienna Award, through which he transferred the N-W section of Transylvania to Hungary. This way, he satisfied Hungary, which was committed to its German alliance and, at the same time, preserved Romania as a functional state which, even if neutral, still offered a recognized strategic and economic value to Germany.

The Romanian government tried to maintain the country's territorial integrity by seeking the Allies' protection but to no avail. The repeated requests to have its neutrality guaranteed didn't go any further either. The Allies constantly avoided such dialog, thus leaving Romania isolated in the middle of the European continent full of powerful alliances and treaties. Then Germany started to occupy country after country, no matter if neutral or not. At this point, ignored by the Allies and concerned over Hitler's success, Romania thought that the only way to preserve the rest of the country was to have closer ties with Germany, which, in the end, brought us into an alliance with it. The general opinion was that if we don't, Hungary could have had all of Transylvania (slightly less than half the size of Romania proper) awarded to it for its allegiance to Germany. Once the alliance with Germany ratified, on June 22, 1941, Romania proclaimed war on the Soviet Union in order to free Basarabia. Then Great Britain declared war on Romania on December 4, 1941, for its refusal to withdraw from Basarabia, which was, as I mentioned before, traditionally Romanian land, with a Romanian population willing to be part of Romania. The people's desire didn't matter much in the face of British interests, and so Romania found itself fully involved in WWII.

IV

The consequence for my parents was that only one month after the opening of his beautiful Ionesti clinic, my father was summoned to military service. To his bad luck, General Antonescu, the Leader of the Romanian State, decided that my father's class be the first contingent of medical doctors enrolled as soldiers with no pay. Both before and after that decision, the medical graduates had been enrolled as lieutenants.

Under those circumstances, my mother took the train back to Bucuresti to live with her parents, while my father was put through a brief military training before being sent to the Russian front. His only recourse against the system that shattered his dreams was to exasperate his sergeant with his "inability" to understand that the rifle was made of two parts: one of wood and one of metal. He persisted in answering:

"The rifle is made out of three parts."

"What three parts, soldier? There are only two. One of wood and one of metal," the sergeant would say.

"What about the strap?" My father would ask.

"That doesn't count."

"How come it doesn't count?"

Obviously the subject was open to debate, a debate which only belittled those involved. To my father's class, this proved that the sergeant was an idiot, and to the sergeant—that higher education was a waste. This is probably one of the reasons why this oversimplified description of the rifle was dropped shortly after. Once trained, my father was shipped to the Russian front. Instead of serenading my mother, he was serenaded by the Russian children outside his tent:

"Mamaliga malako,

Romania daleko." (Polenta with milk, Romania is far away.)

If he had reported this repeated occurrence, the German allies would have executed those children as combatants involved in psychological warfare. In my father's opinion, this execution would not have changed anything other than bringing more death. Morally, he felt that this was his problem to deal with privately.

He diligently took care of his wounded soldiers amid rain, mud, relocation, freezing cold, occasional enemy attacks, and all the other miseries of war. Yes, there were Russian attacks against the tents with the big red cross on the top. Somebody from a Russian utility plane tried to drop bombs by hand. The amazing fact is that he never managed to hit any target. Nevertheless, my father found it unsafe and appealed to his superiors to lend him a cannon for a week or so. Once he fired a shot, the plane turned around and never came back.

My father's war assignment lasted several years—far beyond its scheduled limit. Replacements were ordered, but the new appointees from back home managed each time to evade actual deployment. My father's petitions got nowhere. With passing time, the army's policies changed, and he was elevated to the rank of lieutenant and was paid. After a while, he even got a leave to come home and see his wife but no replacement was found.

Then a miracle happened. In the middle of the war, my father got the news of my birth. Imagine his joy. His first son! This was his victory over the death around him, his statement to the world, and a big step toward his dream of a fulfilling life. From then on, most of his precious rations of chocolate and the chocolate he got in exchange for his ration of cigarettes became mine to suck on through a piece of gauze. Back home, chocolate was a rare luxury only the privileged few could afford.

It is worth noting that by giving away that source of pleasure and energy, he acquired the happiness of doing something special for those he loved, which in turn gave him more energy and satisfaction than all those chocolates could.

My birth qualified my father for another leave to go home. This time, he had to ride in more precarious conditions. The war wasn't going well, transportation suffered, and the weather on the Ukrainian steppes was freezing. He stowed away on one freight train after another, huddling against the bitter winds the best he could, and at times risking to be shot for stealing coal from locomotives to warm up. Eventually, he made his way back to Bucuresti, which seemed to him an oasis of civilization. My mother appeared more beautiful than ever, and I came across as a picture perfect baby.

He enjoyed his family, but he didn't lose sight of having an audience with the health minister in an attempt to get to the bottom of the lack of replacements. The health minister received him with all due respect:

"Dr. Ritivoi, I cannot agree more," the minister said while shuffling his file. "We have called for your replacement several times. All have found reasons not to perform their duty. I don't know what to do anymore. Give me the name of a doctor who hasn't served, and I will see to it myself that he will replace you."

"I know that Dr. Portocala, the son of Professor Doctor Portocala, hasn't," my father said without hesitation.

The health minister wrote a note, attached it to his file, and got up from his chair. He stretched his hand and said, "All right, I will follow up on this. You did more than your share, Dr. Ritivoi."

In a couple of months, my father was replaced and was allowed to come home. This happened toward the end of the war, when a far worse change loomed over Romania. Communism broke its Eastern confinement and started to spill westward. Nobody in our country knew much about communism. We only knew that not much good comes to us from Russia, and that communism meant an end to our way of life, a departure from our democratic values.

2. Politics at Its Best

I

After my father's return, Romania started to prepare for the reversal of fortune created by the defeat on the Eastern Front. The Russian army, supplied by the United States and helped by a gruesome winter, started to prevail. Also, the Allies opened a new front in the West thus stretching the German defense. All these events made it obvious that Germany would lose the war and that Romania could face the dour perspective of a Russian invasion.

Sandwiched between two superpowers, the Romanian government tried again to do whatever it took to save the country. It sent messages to the British and American governments stating that the Romanian army, which had been about 1,000,000 strong (Third Axis Fourth Ally by Mark Axworthy, p. 214 and Rumania 1866–1947 by Keith Hitchins, p. 471), could change sides as soon as they guaranteed the country's territorial integrity. As previously stated, Romania got involved in this war for the purpose of self-preservation. National integrity was the reason why Romania sought unsuccessfully the Allies' protection before turning to Germany for the same reason.

In response to the King's message, the British Foreign Office stated that the boundaries of postwar Romania would be drawn in accordance with the British recognition of the Soviet Union's security interests along its western frontier (Rumania 1866–1947 by Keith Hitchins, p. 491). The American general Henry M. Wilson, commander of Allied forces in the Mediterranean, in his turn, instructed the Romanian government to capitulate immediately and to offer no resistance to the advancing Soviet armies. He later added that they should establish direct contacts with Soviet high command to arrange cooperation between Romanian and Soviet armies against the Germans (ibid., p. 494).

This would be all right if the Soviets were reasonable and trustworthy. Since Romanians knew their neighbors to be otherwise, they pressed the Allies to offer guarantees of territorial integrity and the preservation of democracy throughout this process. No success.

The Soviet Union, on the other hand, in order to hurry Romanian capitulation, announced on April 2, 1944, that they did not seek to acquire any Romanian territory or to change the country's social order. Feeling the pressure, Hitler informed the Romanian government that Germany no longer recognized the validity of the Vienna Award (the unilateral transfer of NW section of Transylvania to Hungary). This attempt to secure Romania's loyalty came too late. Romania opted to receive the Soviet Army peacefully rather than have the country ransacked.

Nevertheless, at the last moment, the Romanian government tried to involve Western powers in the process of negotiations—as full partners in the agreement or in bringing Western troops to Romania as a guarantee that the Soviet Union would respect its promises. None of these attempts worked. They couldn't. In May, 1944, Winston Churchill negotiated with Stalin the so-called Percentage Agreement, which gave the Soviet Union 90 percent influence in Romania in exchange for 90 percent British influence in Greece. President Roosevelt endorsed it, and on June 10, 1944, the Romanian government reluctantly accepted Soviet conditions.

Changing sides was upsetting for the Germans. In response, Hitler ordered the occupation of Bucuresti and set up a pro-German government run by a general. However, the plan proved to be unrealistic. The Germans staged several attacks on Romanian targets, with no serious consequences.

Romania was not alone in changing sides. After the Allies took over Sicily in July, 1943, Mussolini's Fascist regime collapsed, and Italy sued for an armistice. Two other Axis satellites that benefited from German largess with Romanian territories, Hungary and Bulgaria, went the same way. The Hungarian regent Miklos Horthy asked Hitler to let Hungary withdraw from the war. Hitler refused and ordered the German High Command to execute the prepared Operation Margarete (the occupation of Hungary). The operation was effected by March 19, 1944 (The Barnes Review. May/June 2007, p. 38). In the spring of 1944, the other German ally, Bulgaria, which adhered to the Rome-Berlin-Tokyo alliance in March, 1941, (The Columbia History of the World by John A. Garraty and Peter Gay, p. 1064), tried frantically to negotiate a deal with the British and the Americans (The Other Europe by Garrison Walters, p. 306). Both advised Bulgaria to talk with Stalin, and Bulgaria was occupied without a struggle. Neither Hungary nor Bulgaria had common borders with the Soviet Union and didn't loose territories to it. Romania did.

II

On August 23, 1944, five years to the day from the Ribbentrop-Molotov Pact (August 23, 1939), which allowed the Soviet Union to incorporate Basarabia, and four years from the Vienna Award (August 23, 1940), which transferred NW of Transylvania to Hungary, the Romanian King broadcast a proclamation announcing the break of diplomatic relations with Germany and an armistice with the United Nations. (The term United Nations was originally used by the Allies during the WWII denoting the states that were allied against the Axis powers. Only after the war was this name assigned to the international forum we know today.) The King declared that Romania had joined forces with the Allies against the Axis and would relocate its army from the Soviet border to Northern Transylvania to liberate it from Hungarian and German control.

Soon after, on August 31, 1944, the Red Army occupied Bucuresti. The armistice, which was drawn up by the Soviet Union, provided that the Soviet High Command in Romania would alone supervise the fulfillment of the terms of the armistice. The Allies objected, but this didn't have much effect. In response to these objections, Soviet Foreign Minister Molotov agreed to the creation of the Allied Control Commission for Romania (Rumania 1866–1947 by Keith Hitchins, p. 502 and 505), which included American and British representatives, but they had no power to make important decisions concerning Romania and no permission to deal directly with the Romanian government, which could be done only through the Soviet authorities (ibid., p. 502). As expected, the commission proved to be an impotent forum used by the Soviet officials to their advantage.

Thus the Soviet occupation began, and with it, the installation of the communist system. To add insult to injury, August 23 became a communist national holiday, the day of our "liberation from under the Fascist yoke" by "the glorious Soviet Army." Later on, under Ceausescu's regime, it was stated that as a matter of fact, Romania had liberated itself. The Soviet Army came in as an allied force, facing no opposition.

In the beginning, Romanians were concerned but held hope for international protection. After all, the Romanian Communist Party was insignificant (only one thousand members) and unpopular due to its disproportionate number of minorities and its support for the disdained Soviet annexation of Basarabia and Northern Bucovina. People still hoped that the Soviet statement of intent not to change the country's social order as Molotov had said in May would hold, and they trusted that the United States and Great Britain would honor their position as guarantors of free elections.

Stalin, instead, had his own simple and efficient five-pronged strategy:

1. Dismantle the Romanian army and take control of what was left of it.

The 380,000-man Romanian army at the disposal of the Soviet commanders had been used in the heavier fights in the north of Transylvania, through Slovakia and Moravia into Bohemia, with losses of about 30 percent killed or wounded (ibid., p. 503, 504, 520). They were credited with taking over 100,000 prisoners (Comunismul in

Romania by Ghita Ionescu, p. 120, 121) and making an important contribution to the Soviet success. That area offered a particular challenge for being a German back yard familiar to the German Army, having a moderate climate, and being of primary importance. At that point, Germans were more concerned about the Soviet advancement in the East than of the Americans in the West. On the Eastern Front, Germany not only lost the support of the sizable Romanian army, but that same army was added to the Soviet side. This, in addition to allowing free passage through Romania, contributed significantly to the Soviet success on the Eastern Front. Nevertheless, the Romanian contribution was never recognized by the Allies and certainly not by the Soviet Union

Shortly after August 23, 1944, on the Moldovan front, over 100,000 Romanian solders had been disarmed by the new Soviet allies for no valid reason, and all their equipment was captured. About the same time, the Romanian Black Sea military fleet had been confiscated by the Soviets. The army as a whole was drastically reduced, with the result that from a total of fifty divisions with 1,100,000 soldiers on August 23, 1944, it was left with seven divisions or 138,000 soldiers in 1947(Sub Povara Armistitiului by Alesandru Dutu, 1944–1947, p. 9).

Military factories were dismantled, the aeronautical industry eliminated, military repair shops closed, warehouses emptied, military as well as civilian equipment confiscated, and in reality, the country went through a period of sheer plunder in complete disregard of the armistice provisions.

The Soviet Union annexed Basarabia—which is half of Moldova proper—and Northern Bucovina to their empire and called it the Moldovian Socialist Republic of the USSR. It is not clear why they chose to call it Moldova and not Basarabia. Did they have the rest of Moldova in the back of their mind?

Meanwhile, the unsympathetic officers had been discharged. At the same time, political officers with no military experience had been appointed to all units to take charge of political indoctrination of the troops and to scrutinize the political correctness of all military decisions. Many generals were sentenced for no valid reason, and the funding for the army was reduced to the level of starvation (Sub Povara Armistitiului, by Alesandru Dutu, p. 12).

2. Destroy the country's infrastructure.

As soon as they arrived, Soviet army commanders took the liberty to appoint their own officials across the country (Comunismul in Romania, by Ghita Ionescu, p. 118) and to gradually create their own communist institutions, which paralleled the existing ones and rendered them ineffective. In the process, members of the existing political class had been gradually eliminated. Particular attention was given to the legal system, whose professional standards were an obstacle to the Soviet intentions. The communist ways required courts to be run by loyalists with no legal training, which overstepped the existing system and allowed communist-inspired groups to impose a new and terrifying type of justice reminiscent of the French Revolution.

Meanwhile, in the communist press and through public rallies, the Romanian government was under constant attack. Direct political, diplomatic, or military threats were constantly used to pressure political bodies to implement one change after another. Each such change meant an advancement of Soviet interests and the appointment of Soviet-chosen persons to higher and more responsible positions.

A particularly important event took place in the middle of February, 1945, when Soviet authorities sent Andrei Visinsky to Bucuresti to coordinate the communist drive for power. His first move was to impose a drastic reduction of Romanian police, gendarmes, and army in and around the capital city, Bucuresti. Then on February 24, a large demonstration was organized by a coalition of leftist parties, advancing towards the office of the Minister of the Interior. Shots were fired by unidentified persons, and several were killed (Rumania 1866–194, by Keith Hichins, p. 514) by bullets proved not to be the kind used by the Romanian Army (Comunismul in Romania, by Ghita Ionescu p. 136). The chief of the Romanian government, Radescu, accused the communists. This gave the Communist Party and the Soviet authorities an opportunity to brand Radescu as "fascist" and an excuse for Soviet officials to summon the Allied Control Commission, where he was asked to explain this accusation. On February 28, Andrei Visinsky had an audience with the King, were he demanded the replacement of the head of the government, Radescu, within two hours, with a non elected leader of a leftist party, Petru Groza. "Visinsky let it be known that unless the King accepted a Groza government he could not be responsible for the maintenance of Romania as an independent state" (Rumania 1866–1947 by Keith Hitchins, p. 515).

Tension was built up through mass demonstrations organized by communists (still a minority but amply able to excite the mob). Communist squads of armed men were set among demonstrators. Meanwhile, Soviet military commanders moved Romanian army units, some already disarmed, away from Bucuresti. As a trump card, Groza sent a message to the King stating that, "Soviet officials had promised him a substantial improvement in Soviet-Rumanian relations upon the formation of a Front [of leftist parties] government, including an easing of the armistice terms and a return of Northern Transylvania. Lacking any promise of significant Western help, the King could no longer resist Soviet pressure and announced the formation of a government held by Petru Groza on March 6," 1945 (ibid., p. 515), which included members of a leftist group of parties. This government was named the National Democratic Front.

Just weeks before the appointment of Petru Groza as Prime Minister, the United States, Great Britain, and the Soviet Union signed the Declaration on Liberated Europe (Yalta, February 12, 1945), which precluded such pressure tactics but played no part in determining Soviet policy toward Romania. The notion of broadly representative and democratic governments established through free elections and responsive to the will of their citizens, which the declaration called for, was the furthest thing from Soviet thinking and practice.

The Western Allies' reaction to the creation of the Petru Groza government was a protest with no consequences. With the war still going on, the Allies probably felt they should restrain their criticism of the Soviet Union. However in May, 1945, Germany was defeated and, at the ensuing Potsdam Conference (July 17–August 2), "The Americans and British denied the legitimacy of Groza government on the grounds that it did not represent the will of the majority of the

Romanian people. When the American delegation pointed out that the Yalta declaration on the future of Eastern Europe had been ignored in Romania, Stalin complained about high-handed British action in Greece . . . "In later discussions Stalin categorically rejected the idea of free elections in Rumania because they would most certainly bring to power an anti-Soviet government" (ibid., p. 520).

Encouraged by the Potsdam declaration, which required a genuine democratic government in Romania, the King asked Petru Groza to resign. Petru Groza refused, which was in violation of the Romanian constitution. At the ensuing London Conference (September 11–October 3, 1945), the constitutional impasse couldn't be resolved. Among the many issues defying a solution was the definition of the term "democratic." For the Soviet Union, "democratic" meant communist, while for the Western Allies, it meant elected by the majority of voters. Soviet Foreign Minister Molotov found it hard to understand how the Americans and British could see a Russian-friendly government and free elections in Romania at the same time.

This stalemate couldn't be brushed off. A new conference was scheduled in Moscow on December 16, and an arrangement was forged. The Soviet Union agreed to the inclusion in the Petru Groza government of two representatives from two mainstream political parties (subsequently demanding them to be rather unknown names) and to set the date for early elections. The Petru Groza government would guarantee all democratic parties complete freedom of association, assembly, and freedom of the press. In return, the United States and Great Britain promised to recognize the new Petru Groza government (ibid., p. 524). The recognition of that undemocratic government, signed on February 4, 1946, was a political blunder, a defeat for democracy—for the Romanian people, for the major political parties, and for the West. American and British words suddenly meant much less than expected. Practically speacking, the Petru Groza government had been the organization needed by the Soviet Union for the manipulation of the upcoming "democratic elections."

Each such political squable had been used by the communists as an opportunity to constantly improve their position. The Groza government appointed communist prefects and communist-dominated councils with extensive executive powers in every village and every city of every county, thus rendering the mainstream political parties ineffective. For the same reason, it sponsored local "vigilance committees" which took over the duties of law and order. There were also created workers committees and peasant committees to wrest control of the factories and to expropriate the land from large estates. Those organizations didn't have legal authority, but they did undermine the existing political and economic structure, created fear, and paved the way for further and more drastic changes to follow.

All civilian servants and officials who had served in the government and the military between September 1, 1940, and August 23, 1944 (ibid., p. 528), were purged and could not be hired at any level of public service, including by scientific and professional organizations. This drive to marginalize and intimidate people unsympathetic to communism was continually reinforced by additional legislation. The details of this process are too cumbersome for this synopsis. Two examples are the abolition of the Association of Plastic Artists and "cleansing" the Association of Architects of so-called anti-democratic elements. "Revolutionary restrictions" were applied on the admission of new members, meaning that only a supporter of the communist trend could be accepted. In March, 1945, the Ministry of Propaganda was created for the control of all information available to citizens. In April and May, the Ministry of Arts and the Department of Cults had been founded to control the country's cultural and spiritual climate. People had to be alienated from the way they used to think and feel. New values, new understanding, and new attitudes were needed for following the new direction.

On April 21, 1945, the earlier definitions of "war criminal" and "war profiteer" were considerably broadened as to include former politicians, bureaucrats, and businessmen. Then People's Tribunals had been established to prosecute those defined as such. In those "Tribunals," the usual legal procedures could be ignored. "Arrests began, at once, of former ministers and other high officials in the Antonescu dictatorship and of former prefects, police officials, and functionaries of all kinds" (ibid., p. 529). On June 1, General Ion Antonescu, the government leader during the war years, who among other things introduced a rare law in December, 1942 that prohibited the deportation of Jews to German concentration camps, was executed along with his brother, Mihai Antonescu.

On July 13, 1946, a law introduced by the Petru Groza government abolished the senate, whose members had mostly anti-communist views.

3.   Bring the feeble Romanian Communist Party to a state of health.

That was quite a task. Nevertheless, Stalin knew how to do it. After all, in the beginning, the Communist Party had been a minority in Russia too. The plan was rather simple: excite the mob with slogans, use brutal force against those who didn't follow the new trend, and encourage others to sheepishly join the winner.

For this task, three communists who trained in Moscow were brought in and put in positions of leadership in the Communist Party. It didn't help the Party's image of serving foreign interests, that they came from Moscow, that two of them were Jews (Teohari Georgescu, Ana Pauker), and the third was Hungarian (Vasile Luca). In addition it didn't help that the Communist Party supported the Soviet annexation of Basarabia and the North of Bucovina. Nevertheless, the process began.

The first priority was to expand the party. One effective way of doing that was to create a union with other leftist parties. Later on, these leftist parties would find their leadership infiltrated by Communists and then incorporated in a festive way under the communist banner. Intimidation and propaganda would do the rest. Another way was through encouraging the formation of splinter groups from major parties and incorporating them in a similar manner.

It goes without saying that the few communists found in prisons were freed and used as leaders.

The success of the move to increase the Communist Party membership and improve its image rested on the message of assimilation and appeal to a broad range of the population. There was no mention of revolution or abolition of private property—just civil rights, political freedoms, the expanded right to vote, land reforms, promises of credit on easy terms to small businesses, etc. The leftist group of parties, named the National Democratic Front, was still short of gaining the needed popular support, but what they had instead was the continuous behind-the-scenes Soviet backing that ranged from advice and plots to threats and brutal force. Unfazed by the lack of followers, the communists pressed ahead with a range of measures meant to increase their power and to cripple the opposition.

In an effort to become a mass organization quickly, the Communist Party opened its membership to a variety of characters, in fact to everyone who might be beneficial to their goal. At the same time, to show its effectiveness, the Front demanded immediate land reform and proceeded with the expropriation of land from all individuals holding more than fifty hectares. In doing that, they had been careful to spare the properties of respected landowners like the Church and the Royal House.

Then in mid-October, 1946, the unelected Petru Groza government posted November 19, 1946, as the election date. Days later, the Communist Party announced the formation of the Bloc of Democratic Parties, which would present a single list of candidates in the elections, representing all member parties. The Communist Party had to display decency and fairness in order to get credence and support at this point in the game. No matter how much decency it displayed, this move showed that the Communists had control over the group and assimilated the other group members' supporters. The Bloc's platform was designed, again, with the intention to appeal to the public at large until the election. It reaffirmed its respect for individual private property, guarantees of democratic liberties to all citizens, improvements in the standards of living for the mass population, the development of heavy industry as a basis of a general economic recovery, the mechanization and rationalization of agriculture, a progressive income tax, etc. The platform also included "a dutiful promise of friendship and co-operation with Soviet Union" (ibid., p. 530), which said enough to scare a lot of people away.

4. International isolation of Romania and its capitulation to complete Soviet control.

For the Communists, isolation wasn't just a defensive measure like a fortress. It was also an offensive device in their war against the people's value system. In order to introduce the new communist mentality, Western influences had to be eliminated and people had to be cornered and indoctrinated. It is said that, once, Lenin refused to finish listening to a piece by Beethoven because "if I listen to it to the end, I won't be able to finish my revolution." For communists, traditional values are a threat, a cultural resistance, and an ideological weapon able to undermine "our Regime of Popular Democracy."

Soviet communism was set to prevent western influence, particularly because our country was already disposed to it. Romanians believed in eternal morality, which had been a stabilizing factor in their lives, while Lenin didn't: "We don't believe in an eternal morality, and we expose as falseness all the fables about morality." He also said, "Our morality is entirely subordinated to the interests of the proletariat's class struggle. Morality is what serves to destroy the old exploiting society and to unite all the working people around the proletariat, which is building up a new communist society . . . We do not believe in an eternal morality, and we expose as falseness all the fables about morality" (Marxism and Morality, by Steven Lukes , p. 22). This was the point of communism's founders: "Morality has always been class morality . . ." (Engels 1877–78, Marxism and Morality, p. 13). Whatever serves the communist interest in its "class war" or otherwise is defined as "moral". This kind of understanding justifies the need to redefine our values and to eliminate the Western influences in the process.

An important role in this process was played by the Churchill—Stalin Percentage Agreement. "British intervention against Communists and their supporters in Greece in December, 1944, Soviet leaders may have reasoned, justified their giving Rumanian Communists the go-ahead to install their own government in Bucharest. In any case, this meeting [Moscow, mid-January, 1945, between Gheorghiu-Dej, Ana Pauker, and Soviet leaders] proved to be fateful for Rumania, for Gheorghiu-Dej and company were assured of the support they needed in their drive to seize power" (Rumania 1866–1947 by Keith Hitchins, Professor of History at University of Illinois, p. 512).

Using negotiations, conducted mostly through ultimatums, the Soviet Union took control of Romanian natural resources and the economy. In addition to the imposed heavy war reparations, the Soviet

Union required reimbursement for the cost of maintaining its occupation troops, and Romania had to endure the unofficial Soviet confiscation of equipment of all kind and various other demands (Comunismul in Romania by Ghita Ionescu, p. 121). Also, in addition to war reparations, in May, 1945, Sov-Roms had been created (Romanian companies with Soviet CEOs) in all main sectors of the economy, primarily raw materials, as a means of transferring them to the Soviet Union. To complete the picture, the Soviet Union refused to return to Romania the National Treasure given for safe keeping to the Russian government in December, 1916, due to the uncertainties of the WWI. But then on October, 1917, the Russian Communist Revolution happened.

In February '48, a long-term treaty of friendship, cooperation, and mutual assistance was signed. In the same year, a Soviet-inspired constitution was adopted, and the communization of education instituted. "Starting from kindergarten, the children have to be prepared for a collective type of life," said the education minister and, soon to be Romania's leader, Gheorghiu Dej. That approach included the presentation of the Soviet Union in the most favorable light, mandatory Russian language training starting in the fourth grade, Marxist studies, minimization of Romanian traditions, and the emphasis of slavish influences in all aspects of the Romanian cultural life (ibid., p. 207). Romanians had always been proud of their Latin heritage.

Connections of any kind with Western countries were gradually reduced to nothing. Western radio broadcasts for Romania were jammed and declared illegal. Anybody caught trying to beat the jamming could be sent to the newly created forced labor camps. Also, the newly created Ministry of Propaganda took control of all information available to the public. Its purpose was the imposition of a new political and cultural environment, a new way of thinking that set allegiance to communism above friendship, family ties, and love. Our non-communist role models were debased, prosecuted, and frightened; religion was ridiculed as ignorance, superstition, and a tool of capitalist oppression. The Greek-Catholic church was closed, its priests forced to switch to Greek-Orthodox, resign, or be jailed. Interpersonal relations were marred by fear and suspicion. Because we were isolated from the world and from each other, we could be controlled.

5. Win the "democratic" elections by any means.

In the middle of October, the unelected Petru Groza government set November 19, 1946, as the election date. This gave other parties about one month of preparation time, and even that was full of obstacles: their meetings were disrupted by groups of brawlers, distribution of their papers prevented, while intimidations and irregularities abounded (ibid., p. 154). Meanwhile the communists prepared for this moment since the Soviet invasion more than two years earlier. The communist head of the Ministry of Interior and a member of the team brought from Moscow, Teohari Georgescu (born Burah Tescovici), was appointed to run the election.

As a prelude to the elections, the government released a decree which "allowed the government to appoint its own functionaries as heads of all electoral boards, which, among other tasks had the responsibility of registering voters" (Rumania 1866–1947, p. 530). The decree also "disenfranchised numerous, vaguely defined categories of persons such as those who were guilty of 'crimes against the people' or who had 'positions of responsibility' during Antonescu dictatorship" (ibid., p. 531). "Leading Communists were dispatched to all parts of the country to take charge of the election campaign. A formidable administrative apparatus was thus mobilized to promote the candidates of the Bloc and, especially, to prevent the opposition from mounting an effective campaign. Police and other officials interfered with the circulation of opposition newspapers and pamphlets and, together with specially formed squads of Communists and their sympathizers, they broke up the National Peasants and the Liberal Parties [the main opposition parties] meetings" (ibid., p. 532). The opposition sent protests to the Soviet officials and to the Allied Control Commission, but they were ignored.

Nevertheless, the majority of Romanians opposed communism and deeply resented Soviet interference in our national affairs.

3. FROM FRONT LINE TO HOME FRONT

I

On my father's return from military service in the spring of 1943, the Ionesti clinic wasn't available to him any longer. After being fully equipped and closed for a while, it was assigned to another doctor.

Glad to be back in civilian clothes, my father made a tour of Bucuresti and paid a visit to his respected professor, Dr. Constantin Ionescu-Mihaiesti, who again offered his help. He proposed that my father lead the section "Nicolas Favre" of the Bucuresti's Institute of Microbiology, which he chaired. As he did after graduation when he chose the open air of Ionesti over the enclosure of a lab, my father declined the offer and recommended his colleague, Dr. Atanasiu Pascu, for the job. My father wanted to deal with people, not with lab equipment. He wanted versatility and freedom and so, he took instead a government appointment to the medical office of *Gaz Metan* plant on Marasesti boulevard, which was close to home. At *Gaz Metan*, it took him no time to become everybody's friend and to get familiar with all the technologies employed throughout the plant. He felt unrestricted. Seldom could he be found in his medical office, but he found ways to diligently service everybody in need, even if it meant home visits (not part of his job description).

Meanwhile another opportunity came my father's way. The Institute of Microbiology had received one offer of scholarship to the Pasteur Institute in Paris. Professor Ionescu-Mihaiesti offered it to my father. This was his last big opportunity to achieve a larger freedom before the clanging drop of the Iron Curtain, but, my father refused it. Again, he recommended instead his colleague, Dr. Atanasiu Pascu. Dr. Pascu took the offer, married Professor IonescuMihaiesti's daughter, and never returned to Romania. It was said that in time, he took a leading position at the Pasteur Institute.

My father's refusal of this scholarship was motivated by a moral distaste for abandoning his country while it was in peril. The general elections were scheduled, and this was the last opportunity for the historical political parties and for Romanian democracy to survive the red tide. There was fervor all over the country to reject the communist candidates, a fervor my father couldn't miss. While I have no doubt he felt that way, my mother disclosed later that he was also afraid to accept the challenge of an unfamiliar environment. He would feel like a fish out of water. Having a family to support, forced into a structured life he could not control, deprived of his safety net of friends and relatives, no familiarities . . . , it seemed frightening.

When the general election came on November 19, 1946, the country experienced one of its most tense moments. Romania's future was at stake again, threatened by those we feared the most: the Soviet Communists. Neighbors on the street were discreetly exchanging signs, which symbolized one historical party or another, in an emotional determination to reject communism. I assume my father was all over the town that day.

The day after the election, on November 20, 1946, the government was expected to announce the results, but for unspecified reasons, there was a delay of forty-eight hours. On November 22, when the results were published, the Bloc of Democratic Parties was proclaimed victorious with over 70 percent of the votes and a solid majority in the newly created National Assembly. "It appears that when Communist leaders realized the extent of their impending defeat, they had the reporting of returns suspended as of noon on 20 November and sent instructions to all prefects to 'revise' the figures in order to show a victory for the Bloc" (Rumania 1866–1947, by Keith Hitchins, p. 533). It was also reported that Ana Pauker (Robinsohn), one of the leaders of the Romanian Communist Party and a member of the team of communists trained in the Soviet Union, consulted her boss in Moscow and got the go-ahead to falsify the election results.

In his *Confessions* printed in 1996, Corneliu Coposu, secretary of the National Peasant Party, gave a detailed description of the events: "Dr. Titu Onisor, who took part in the process of centralizing the results, disclosed the manner in which the vote outcome was decided: the reversal of the real count" (Corneliu Coposu, Confesiuni, p. 63). The votes of the winning National Peasant Party had been transferred to the Block of Democratic Parties. The National Peasant Party was the true winner, with 72.6 % of the votes, and not the Block. Concerned, the leaders of the National Peasant Party summoned copies of vote results from each voting place in the country and reached the same bewildering conclusion.

Aware that at the Yalta Convention, the Western victors guaranteed free elections in Romania, people confidently expected the signatory countries to honor their commitment and invalidate the election results. Instead, the Western powers were more interested in photo opportunities and in appeasing the Soviet Union. Iuliu Maniu, the leader of the National Peasant Party, sent vigorous memos to both the American and the British governments, in which he didn't hesitate to call them liars. The British government didn't even bother to answer, while the Americans, apparently more out of touch, accused Mr. Maniu of insolence. Maniu then sent documentation to back up his previous statements, and now the American government chose also not to answer. The guarantors of our democratic process, the United States and Great Britain, denounced the election as unrepresentative of the Romanian people and held the Groza government responsible for reneging on its promise of free elections, but neither was prepared to go any further than that.

In mid-May, 1944, the British and Soviet governments agreed to divide southeastern Europe into spheres of influence. The agreement was approved by President Roosevelt on June 12. After that, there was little else that could be done. France, the world's fourth major war victor, had no desire to say anything on that matter, and so Romania's fate was sealed.

On December 1, 1946, a new Romanian government, which kept the appearance of a coalition, was formed, with communists holding the key positions (Rumania 1866–1947, p. 535). By that time, the massive Soviet economic penetration of Romania, achieved through large-scale removal of assets and products in total disregard of the country's output, was secured by a series of long-term economic treaties (ibid., p. 536). The Soviet grasp was so tight that by 1947, Romanian ties with the West seized to exist.

"Dominant in internal political life since the reorganization of the government on December 1, 1946, and freed of any effective Western intervention by the Paris Peace Treaty, the Communist Party set about in earnest to eliminate what remained of the opposition. In March and again in May, 1947, the Ministry of the Interior carried out mass arrests of opposition politicians, including Social Democrats [Socialists] and of intellectuals and workers, perhaps 2,000 persons in all, and held them in prison or sent them to concentration camps recently built for this purpose. These waves of arrests represented only the beginning of what was to follow in the next four or five years. Evidence suggests that Soviet authorities in Rumania were deeply involved in this campaign and may even have initiated the action on direct instructions from Moscow" (ibid., p. 540).

With the elections won, the Communist Party moved to eliminate its fellow election partners, members of the Bloc of Democratic Parties, and assimilate their members. Thus, on January 9, 1947, the Communist Party decided to "improve" the social composition of the Plowmen Front by removing its "bourgeois elements" and then united both parties into one larger Communist Party. The next step to power took place during a Joint Congress on January 21–February 3, 1948, when the sizable Social Democratic (Socialist) Party was united with the much smaller Communist Party under the name of the Romanian Worker's Party. The independent splinter of the Social Democratic Party, which had resisted being part of the communist agenda, disappeared when its leader, Titel Petrescu, was arrested in May, 1948, and imprisoned without trial.

Gheorghe Tatarescu and his faction of Liberals, which had previously joined the Bloc, were the only significant political grouping in the government not yet controlled by the Communist Party. He was kept free for as long as necessary to keep the appearance of a coalition government. The problem was that Gheorghe Tatarescu, who joined the Bloc under the condition of respect for private enterprise and maintaining the middle class, remained committed to those principles as initially stated. However, once the communists felt free from pre-election restrains and image building promises, they revealed their real intentions. On December 5, 1947, they brought a vote of no confidence in Tatarescu. He resigned as Foreign Minister and was replaced by Ana Pauker. His party had promised close cooperation with the Communist Party in building a new society, and now, in all practicality, it was no longer significant.

Then the actual winner of the election and the most respected Romanian politician, Iuliu Maniu, the head of the National Peasant Party, was accused of treason for attempting to create an independent Romanian government in exile. He was sentenced to life in prison along with some of his close friends. This way, the only political party left standing was the previously insignificant Communist Party.

The last casualty in the communist power grab was the monarchy. On December 30, 1947, the Communist Party forced King Mihai to abdicate. The same day, the country's name was changed to The Romanian Democratic Republic; democratic as communists understand democracy.

From there on, we got expropriations, collectivization, nationalizations, confiscation of the properties of German-speaking Saxons in Transylvania and Swabians in Banat, deportations, intimidations, further deepening of Soviet control, and everything else the Communists desired. In 1948, Russian language became mandatory across the country starting with the intermediary schools. Casa ARLUS (Asocitia Romana pentru stringerea Legaturilor cu Uniunea Sovietica / Romanian Association for closer Ties with the Soviet Union) was set "in all localities." The Soviet army, which was supposed to be withdrawn from Romania within three months of the peace treaty on February 10, 1947, was kept in place until 1958.

Romanians were left with the regret that General Patton, who wanted to continue the WWII eastward advancement in Europe until the Soviet troops were driven back within Soviet borders, didn't have enough credence and conveniently died on December 21, 1945, twelve days after a car accident, reportedly of a broken neck. While the cause of the accident was clearly a three-vehicle collision, the investigator Ladislas Farago couldn't conclude its lengthy search because the official probe "was not thorough and left questions open," Daniel W. Michaels, who researched this case, said. The strange car accident, in fact, didn't kill General Patton, as generaly known. He was transported, with serious but not life-threatening injuries, to a hospital where only doctors had been allowed to see him. There, he died of a heart attack when he began to recover.

General Patton was convinced that sooner or later, the United States would have to confront the Soviet Union, an assertion the American politicians didn't want to consider. He antagonized General Eisenhower (primarily a political soldier), who stopped the advancement on the Western Front, where the German opposition had ended, and waited for the Soviets to occupy Berlin. General Patton could also have entered Prague ahead of the Soviet army, but he was stopped by General Eisenhower (The Barnes Review July/August 2008, p. 42). Expectedly, Joseph Stalin disliked General Patton, but his pointed anger erupted when the General opposed the repatriation of a large number of Soviet refugees and POWs. When repatriated by the orders of President Roosevelt and Winston Churchill, they were executed. Concerned about General Patton's opinions, Stalin pressed that he was secretly preserving Waffen-SS units to later attack the Soviet Union. Reportedly, Stalin ordered him murdered, while U.S. officials looked the other way. Also, General Patton upset Jewish avengers with his mild treatment of the defeated Germans already going through terrible times (The Barnes Review July/August 2006, p. 50).

On September 25, 1979, Douglas Bazata, a former agent of the Office of Strategic Services (CIA precursor, responsible directly to President Roosevelt), said in a conference in Washington: "I know they wanted him [General Patton] killed because I am the one who was hired to do it. Ten thousand dollars. General William Donovan himself, director of the O.S.S., entrusted me with the mission. But I could not do it. Another man confessed to me he did it and was paid to do so." (TBR July/August 2008, p. 43)

General Patton's opinions could not prevail at that time, when the whole world desired to see the war end. Nevertheless, his opinions were validated by subsequent Soviet expansionism: declare war on Japan on August 8, two days after the disastrous nuclear attack on Hiroshima. In 1946, Winston Churchill acknowledged the creation of the Iron Curtain—a de facto occupation of Eastern Europe. In 1947, the communists threatened Greece and Turkey. In 1948, Czechoslovakia fell to communism, and the Soviets implemented the first blockade of West Berlin. In 1950, South Korea was invaded by the communist North. In 1954, French Indochina fell to communism, and the list goes on.

It is sad to see that after an enormous sacrifice of lives and means, an ailing American President, Franklin Delano Roosevelt, concluded WWII by removing a despicable dictator (Hitler) only to uphold a worse one (Stalin) and by freeing Western Europe only to have Eastern Europe and most of Asia enslaved to Soviet communism. As a consequence of the faulty WWII peace agreements, the appropriate conditions were created for the start of the Cold War and the division of the world into opposing camps with the subsequent "hot wars" of reunification and independence, the alienation of the Arab world, guerilla wars, and untold suffering. In a way, the conclusion of the WWII replicates the conclusion of WWI when the utopian Woodrow Wilson presided over another faulty peace agreement, which set the stage for WWII.

Isn't it strange? WWII started because Germany invaded Poland and it finished with allowing the Soviet Union, not only to do so instead, but also to mutilate Polish borders and subject its people to indescribable human rights abuses. F.D.R. biographers claimed he was more interested in the votes of Polish-Americans back home than in the fate of Poland, while Winston Churchill didn't care much about either. To make things worse, on its own, the Soviet Union occupied part of Finland, the Baltic Countries, and Basarabia (Moldova) with no opposition from either the U.S. or Great Britain. Also, the Soviet Union occupied parts of Asia and became instrumental in spreading communism abroad. As a matter of fact, the Soviet Union was the only country (besides Bulgaria) that extended its borders as the result of WWII.

A less-publicized casualty of the way President Roosevelt conducted the war was the truth about communism. Presumably because Stalin was our ally, the news about his crimes and about the nature of communism was downplayed then and continued to be under publicized. Compare the extent of publicity around the six million victims of the Jewish Holocaust and the extent of silence around the two hundred million victims of communism world-wide, about sixty million by the Soviet Communists alone.

II

Once in power, the only remaining obstacle the communists saw ahead was the people's cultural identity. Without a new and unifying value system to its liking, communism could not claim legitimacy and hope to be implemented. In order to install a new culture, the old one had to be removed first, and this couldn't be done through coercion alone.

Communism was envisioned by Marx as a new world order, in which working people would transcend national and regional differences through a higher understanding and achieve a state of "unprecedented development" united by common goals and ways. The problem was that the unique way envisioned by Marx wasn't agreeable to too many others. The communist mentality didn't seem right to people in general; not enough to be accepted. So, he acceptance standards had to be changed.

Words started to get strange new meanings. To exemplify, for communists, "art" meant to glorify communism in impressive ways; art for the sake of beauty was considered a waste, even a deterrent. One time, my brother submitted for an art show a painting with flowers against a wooden fence. His submission was rejected by political watchdogs because the wood in the background loosely resembled a cross. In other instances, the beauty of art was downplayed because it could divert attention from revolutionary goals. Freedom, peace, democracy, and so forth suddenly acquired different meanings. Value was that which fit their purpose: Lenin created the Gulag but had no use for Beethoven! The communist government proceeded with all its means to instill values of its liking.

Dynamic times and a country full of concerns! My father couldn't miss all the debates and emotions involved. Nevertheless, his impetus didn't affect the situation one bit. Professor Ionescu-Mihaiesti, who got his postgraduate training in the U.S. at the University of California in Los Angeles, started to get himself into trouble. He was regarded as politically unreliable because of his training abroad and was tolerated only because he restructured Romanian microbiology to match modern standards. Among other things, he made Romania one of the first countries in the world to vaccinate its entire population against poliomyelitis, but professional dedication was not enough. His intelligence, his education, and his value system were all distasteful to the new leaders. Things got really hard when the communists asked him to publicly condemn the United States for its use of germ warfare in the Korean War. He couldn't condemn something which he didn't believe had happened. As he knew the Americans, they would never commit such crimes. Not to mention that there was no proof of microbiological weapons having been used. On the other hand, it would be suicidal to buck communist propaganda. When the time came, professor Ionescu-Mihaiesti cautiously said,

"If the United States used microbiological weapons in Korea, no doubt it has to be condemned."

For this "if," Professor Ionescu-Mihaiesti was replaced as the head of the Microbiological Institute with Dr. Bilbiie. Under this new leadership, the institute had a chain of setbacks which, after a while, brought about the reappointment of Professor Ionescu-Mihaiesti.

While still influential, Professor Ionescu-Mihaesti tried again to help my father get started in a project dear to him—a university career. He recommended my father for a position as assistant professor and laboratory doctor at Coltea Hospital, in the department of microbiology, of course. From there, he could later obtain a transfer to a similar position in his desired clinical field. But my father preferred to avoid those temporary solutions, which he was afraid may become permanent. Thus, he went to his appointment with the chief of Microbiology at Coltea and asked from the start for access to the clinic.

"Dr. Ritivoi, you can go in the clinic any time you want, but your employment is for Microbiology Lab," the chief of the Microbiology said.

With no further comments, my father took from his pocket a prepared written statement to decline the offer, put it on the doctor's desk, and left the room. I guess he felt proud of himself. Once this business was finished, he returned to *Gaz Metan*, where he was well known, well loved, and where he had complete freedom.

The last kind gesture Professor Constantin Ionescu-Mihaiesti made for my father, as I remember, was to become the godfather of my youngest brother, whose first name thus became Constantin, according to a Romanian tradition.

At *Gaz Metan*, after becoming familiar with all the technologies and procedures used in that institution, my father started to miss the prestige and the professional challenge of a hospital, which was also the recruiting ground for university careers. Unrestricted in his isolated industrial medical office, he clearly saw that that wasn't the picture of success he had envisioned. Then a new opportunity came, where he got the attention of another medical celebrity of his time, Professor Dr. Baltaceanu from Brincovenesc Hospital. This time, my father accepted a position at Brincovenesc in the clinical department, the place of his dreams, at least for the time being, with no university affiliation. According to the new communist law, he was paid less in the hospital than in his previous industrial office. He also had less freedom, and his work was more structured. But nobody could stop him from walking throughout the hospital and making friends and acquaintances.

Unfortunately, Professor Baltaceanu died of a heart attack a year later. He was replaced by Dr. Dinculescu, who was regarded as a political appointee with minimal professional skills. In his new position, Dr. Dinculescu needed to boost his sketchy credentials, and he found an ideal opportunity in my father due to his detailed knowledge of professor Baltaceanu's work. It hadn't gone unnoticed that of late, my father had become Professor Baltaceanu's private secretary, and in this capacity, helped him organize the materials for a comprehensive publication. It didn't take long before Dr. Dinculescu got in touch with my father and proposed a deal: my father was to write the book and sign Dr. Dinculescu as coauthor. In return, Dr. Dinculescu would make sure the book would be published and get attention.

III

This type of arrangement was common under communism. It replicated the communist takeover, the unskilled confiscating that which had been built by the able. Stealing intellectual property grew as communism advanced. It reached its peak twenty years later when the first lady, Elena Ceausescu, authored a comprehensive publication in chemistry, whose true author wasn't even mentioned. To add insult to injury, she was not even a chemist. I mean she had the title but not the education and the knowledge to match. How could she? Elena had quit school at the age of fourteen, when she flunked nearly all the subjects in her curriculum except singing, gymnastics, and needlework, according to a school report kept hidden by a retired schoolteacher. Nevertheless, she surfaced as a doctor in chemistry after her husband, Nicolae, became the First Secretary of the Romanian Communist Party and the undisputed leader of the country.

There was no record of any degree in chemistry that she held before becoming a doctor. All she had were a couple of evening classes speckled with absences (*Kiss the Hand You Cannot Bite* by Edward Behr). For a communist First Lady, that was enough to get her admitted for a doctorate. At the final examination, during the written test, a young and inexperienced assistant professor caught her cheating. The oral examination, which by law is public, supposedly took place one day prior to its scheduled date, in a private setting, and no member of the commission ever agreed to talk about it. From the recent testimonies of informed experts, most of them coworkers, Elena's ignorance in chemistry had been astounding, but this didn't stop her from being a doctor and a member of the Romanian Academy.

For my father, the kind of arrangement proposed by Dr. Dinculescu was out of the question. It rubbed him the wrong way. He perceived it as unfair, not to mention that he saw in this proposal the system's attempt to incorporate him into its corrupt ranks. As emotional as he was, my father not only refused the deal, but he also promised to break Professor Dr. Dinculescu's legs if he would cross his path again. From that day on for several months, I remember him carrying a stiff cane. He felt victorious. His story of the event was freely shared with all those willing to listen, notably with Brincovenesc Hospital's doctors and pharmacists. The stiff cane became his baton in his march for fairness.

With the passing of time, his crowd cheered less and less, and he got tired of carrying that cane. A couple of years later, my father lost his position in the hospital and was transferred to the territorial clinic called *September 13*, where he spent the rest of his medical career. Not long after, he lost his recently acquired part-time university employment as assistant professor.

The book deal my father turned down seemed a fair deal to many others but those many others didn't have his big dreams, his big anger, and his deep insecurity. He had what it took to rise to the top, and he had what it took to waste it. The time to fly was gone. According to the new system's dynamics, he had to fit into one of the available slots and stay there. No more dreams of open spaces, creativity, or making a difference.

One last opportunity came when a position of inspector in the Health Ministry was offered, but again, this would remove him from healing the sick and would bring him into the communist bureaucracy. He let the chance pass, and with it, the opportunity that might have catapulted him to the position he wanted. Thus, he was left to watch the sky like a bird caught in a wire.

IV

My father's troubles didn't stop here. He and a group of friends used to meet every so often and freely exchanged political opinions. They felt great in their small display of independent thinking. In a symbolic way, they defied set boundaries, claimed their abilities and the freedom to think and express it. What they did was practically harmless but, under communism, thinking outside the official doctrine was unacceptable. The system could last only if people believed in its theoretical model, and so their theory could not be touched. No alternative thinking could be tolerated. In its permanent state of vigilance, after a while the system discovered my father's group's little crime and, one day, picked them all up in *Securitate*'s [Secret Police's] cars.

What happened after that is anybody's guess. My father didn't discuss this subject for the rest of his life. My brother, who spent more time at home (I was attending school in the city of Brasov), told me that for a couple of weeks, my father was picked up by a Securitate car every morning on his way to work and brought back to the same spot at the time when he was supposed to return from work. Meanwhile, his salary was paid on time and he became more pensive than ever. It takes a lot to make a man like him sit on a chair for more than ten minutes and be silent, but it happened. We became concerned. Securitate is not known for civility. For a while, I thought that he had been blackmailed with the safety of his children and thus, forced to defile his principles.

I don't know what he went through but after that I noticed drastic changes in his behavior and opinions. His exuberant idealism dried up and he became a silent materialist. His deep rejection of communism gave way to a philosophy of submission. His new wisdom was:

"If somebody wants to help his fellows, he has to do his best within the boundaries of the existing political system. To fight the system is foolishness from which nobody can profit." Or: "The change of kings is the joy of fools."

Something broke him to become that "good citizen." Soon after, he became a Communist Party member and a Neighborhood Representative in the local government. He also became withdrawn, critical, and selfish. His love for us, his children, took backstage to personal concerns. It is not that he loved us any less. No. His personal concerns got bigger.

Sadly, he never expressed his love. There is something irreplaceable about putting it into words. Words have power, can set things in motion, and can make things happen. He sent us his precious chocolate from the Russian front, he traveled through the freezing weather on the eastern steppe to be able to get a glimpse of his wife and his son, he wandered by bicycle through the villages around Bucuresti for food staples in the lean years after the war—he did provide us with the best available, but he never verbally expressed his love for us. I assume that for him, love simply existed, and that was enough. Possibly, he adopted the communist opinion that showing softness of heart is a display of weakness. His inner struggle seemed to be for thoughts he couldn't have muster, not for feelings of which he had plenty. My father chased his thoughts with passion until the passion was yanked out of him and replaced with an old fear he tried to evade for so long. He probably missed that those who fear cannot love at the same time, or he didn't have the drive any longer to do anything about it. Fear is a silent killer. Nevertheless, love was there, waiting to be acknowledged, however neglected, under a mound of concerns.

4. MY FRESH START IN THE BIG MESS

I

As I mentioned, I was raised during the Soviet occupation and came to awareness in the midst of the events described above. My earliest memory was the fear of the sirens marking the change of shifts for the factory workers (a reminder of the American aerial bombardments of Romanian oil fields, called Operation Tidal Wave, with all its panic and destruction). My father even built a makeshift bomb shelter in our backyard, just in case. I also remember my fear of anybody in military uniform and of gas masks. Put such mask over somebody's face and the whole meaning of existence changed for me. As the bombs from the sky had been replaced with the Soviets on the ground, things got worse; the terror turned from occasional to constant.

Stories were told with low voices and shifty eyes to trusted people. The popular comedian Constantin Tanase appeared one evening on the stage of his theatre with wrist watches strapped to his body everyhwere possible. Without a word, he turned around and behold, a pendulum was hanging on his back. Then he quietly sauntered off stage. This was the last time he had been seen. No investigation of this case was ever made. The Russian soldiers had the habit of robbing people on the street of their watches, and they were supposed to be our allies!

In time, soldiers had been withdrawn from the streets and an invisible army of communist loyalists and Securitate agents took their place. People had been encouraged to report on others: employers, neighbors, friends, or family members. My father was coming home at times with angry eyes and breathing heavily. He would say, "They picked up professor X or Mr. Y," and I felt each time, the enormity of having a distinguished man sent to a forced labor camp only because he was a distinguished man in that sea of brutality. How could that savagery match their claim of superior social order? How could I love this system, which demanded a kind of love logically justified and narrowly interpreted but never felt? Their slogan was, "who is not with us is against us." "With us" meant to surrender who I am and become who they want me to be. I couldn't do that, I didn't want to, I shouldn't. This set me from the beginning among those who are against them and qualified for political prison.

My aunt Zoe owned a small pharmacy on Splaiul Unirii. One day, she came through our kitchen door and, without a word, sat on a chair, pale with her wide eyes fixed on something she couldn't see.

"Are you okay?" My mother asked concerned.

Aunt Zoe kept looking at the same lower and insignificant spot.

"Don't scare me Zoe. What happened?" My mother asked.

"They took it away," she said without moving.

"What did they take away?" Mother came closer to her.

"The pharmacy. Two men came in and asked me to put the key on the counter. I was so scared, I didn't even ask them who they were," she said.

My mother didn't need any further explanations. She stood transfixed for a moment.

"They have a way of being so frightening! They look at you like you are a criminal, totally unemotional," Aunt Zoe murmured. "They asked me to pick up my coat and my purse and leave. They told me the pharmacy was now nationalized. That simple! What could I do? I complied," she added.

"I am glad you did," Mother said, pulling a chair, "If you wouldn't have, it could've been far worse."

"I had some groceries in the back and the income from the last two days. They're all gone . . . What do I do now? How we will live?" Aunt Zoe asked.

"I've just cooked something. Let me give you a plate," My mother offered.

"I cannot. Thank you Nina," Aunt Zoe said, pausing with her arms in her laps. "How do I feed my family now?"

My mother suddenly became aware of my quiet presence.

"Mihai go and play with your brother. I'll call you when lunch is ready," she said and watched me go.

I didn't want to hear any more of what my aunt had to say. I heard enough. I could vividly picture those who confiscated her small, one-room pharmacy: two well-built men in civilian cloths, with inconsiderate, angry eyes, proud of using their limitless power of doing something they considered important. They were incapable of understanding the significance of their acts, but eager to side with the political power and accuse those "selfish bourgois" who did understand. I saw these types of men on the streets. They hated everyone who preferred the old democratic system, regarding them as "class enemies" that should be treated mercilessly. Should my father or my aunt be regarded as an enemy? Were the communists any better?

All my uncles where demoted based on suspicion of disagreement with the new political system. The fact that all of them came from low-income families also called "healthy social origin" didn't matter vis-à-vis with their higher education and independent thinking. The hardest hit was my Uncle Constantin, who got reassigned from practicing law to being a factory worker based on a denunciation from one of his Jewish friends, who apparently wanted to secure his own standing with the system.

The most vivid memory from my preschool years was trying not to fall asleep at night before my father would finish listening to *The Voice of America* and fall asleep first. Then I would get out of my bed and change the station. I reasoned that in case of an unexpected Securitate night raid, which was a rather frequent occurrence, the radio station wouldn't show my father's interest, and he would be safe. If caught, he could be sent to a forced labor camp or a political prison. Of course,

I took care to be tight-lipped about anything meaningful that could endanger my family. I hoped my younger brothers could be more aware.

With such a start, it shouldn't be surprising that I entered my first grade marked by fear. I feared my teachers . . . all teachers as a matter of fact. Their faces were always sober and burdened by unknown thoughts. I suspected they had to watch their students and report any non-communist traits. As a matter of fact, I still believe they were instructed to do so, even if only a few truly complied. But was my teacher one of the few? At times, the school had to run surveys of students' social status. Periodically, we were asked of our parents' previous professional and political affiliations. They were certainly hunting for any mismatch with other statements. I invariably struggled to find ways to defend my father from being labeled as "small bourgeois" based on his medical credential. The bourgeoisie were the enemy, which communism wanted to eradicate. According to Karl Marx, the bourgeois, big and small, were meant to disappear.

I remember my father coming home at irregular hours, seldom in time for supper, huffing and puffing, updating his wife on the latest communist abuses. When he had something to say, it didn't matter to him if we, the children, were around or not. I certainly got the message. The new system seldom sentenced somebody to death for political reasons but often killed them in the newly created forced labor camps; implied less liability and provided free labor. The outside world was a dangerous place. I couldn't be part of it. I felt much more comfortable with the world of my mind, clean of death and deceit. That seemed fine, but the reverse of the coin was a degree of separation from the world around. The two didn't have much in common. The first obvious consequence was my academic performance. To make things worse, my father became thoroughly unhappy that I, his first born, didn't come close to his performance at my age. He expected me to be equal or better.

He came from a simple family, while I had two educated parents. He had nobody to introduce him to art and fine intellectuals, while I was walked through all the museums and art shows in the city. I was exposed to the company of Professor Dr. Ionescu-Mihaiesti; Professor Dr. Baltaceanu; the poet Tudor Arghezi; sculptor Gh. D. Anghel, who later asked me to pose for his well-known statue of Mihai Eminescu; Master Schveitzer-Cumpana Rudolf (professor at Bucuresti Arts Institute); and other top professionals. I had a house full of books and art. I should perform better, he thought.

What my father didn't see is that at my age he had had more autonomy, confidence, and courage. He had lived in a free country with a loving mother who relied on him and who didn't micromanage his activities—true luxuries. Instead, I was afraid that at every turn, I might upset somebody and provoke unforeseeable consequences. After several years of my average performance, my father came to the conclusion that I don't have what it takes. He was disillusioned, and I was hurt to disappoint him.

In my fifth or sixth grade, an extended family meeting was summoned by my mother to discuss the problem. In her opinion, my father had failed to deal with me in a proper, more thoughtful way.

"What can I do if he is stupid?" My father defended himself in the big room, while everybody thought I was asleep in the room next to it. In fact, I was asleep until the party grew loud. Emotions had been high. My aunts were accusing my father of lack of patience and understanding, and he was accusing them of planning to estrange his son by removing me from his presence and taking charge of my instruction. I was caught between those two camps, squashed and diminished.

"Mihai cannot be more than what he is," he exclaimed. I understood that I wasn't much.

These words fell on me like a ton of bricks. Trying not to wake up my brother sleeping next to me, I quietly cried until the tiredness took me with it. Meanwhile, that meeting concluded with the decision that I would live with one of my aunts in the city of Brasov. She and her husband, a university professor, were a childless couple who could offer the quiet order and supervision, which were impossible in my father's house. It was not only that my father couldn't follow any rules, but at the same time, my two brothers were in a permanent state of rivalry, and my mother was overwhelmed with work and concerns.

II

So I spent my intermediary and high school years in Brasov. Time passed slowly. Besides the firm, well-intended, and unemotional supervision, I had to deal with some impossible subjects in school like Russian Language, Scientific Socialism, and Political Economy.

The Russian language was the tongue of the occupying power, introduced in 1948, at the height of communist terror and declared mandatory. For me, at least in the beginning, this subject had the meaning of a dark omen and its teachers seemed political bulldogs. When the teacher of Russian came in, I would feel like I was in Securitate's custody. Obviously, the Russian language is just another language, good to know, but for me, having to learn it seemed humiliating.

As for political studies, when we first started them, the class was impressed, and we paid so much attention that the teacher got excited. She told us a couple of years later that she had published a study on our great scholastic performance. Apparently, we had been good above and beyond our usual selves all because we were overwhelmed by the crucial importance of the new ideology. The system had been eager to indoctrinate us, and we had been eager to comply. A perfect match like that could be only successful. Most of the insights I share with you here come from those classes.

As difficult as it was, I passed all the tests and grades. I had to. I wanted to finish school and I also wanted to avoid any appearance of resentment or resistance to those politically sensitive subjects. Such resistance could be interpreted as political opposition and would have negative effects on my family and even on my own future. By then, I was well aware of the importance of our secret Securitate files filled with remarks from all kinds of people, usually the most unexpected ones.

My uncle in Brasov once lost his professorship at the Institute of Silviculture, where he was the chairman of Forests Management, because a technician reported him. The technician said that during a field trip when they had to mark trees for a class project, my uncle expressed that the forests were being cut at a higher rate than they should have been. The son of a peasant, my uncle had more trust in a simple man like that forester than in a professional whose promotion hangs on political points. The forester choose to report my uncle's statement and my uncle was fired on the spot. In those times, truth could be deadly. It didn't mean a thing that my uncle's professional assessment was accurate; it mattered that he was politically incorrect. The Soviet Union, through the much-hated *Sov-Rom Woods*, demanded so many logs from us, and we had to deliver them regardless.

His ousting was reversed by his foreign students; the only ones who could afford to take a stand with no fear of punishment. They informed their embassies that if they lost their most valuable professor, they had better pack and go back home. Their embassies passed the information to our communist visionaries, and my uncle was reinstated. The Romanian students showed their appreciation for my uncle, Professor Dr. Niculae Rucareanu, the coming Christmas, when they gathered under his study's window at three o'clock in the morning and sang a beautiful carol. Unbeknown to them, they sang those songs to me. In their two-bedroom apartment, I was sleeping on a sleeper chair placed in my uncle's study. That night, I was slowly awakened by a soft angelic choir. When I finally realized that the choir was real, I ran to wake up my uncle. However, by the time he was ready to see them, his students had quietly disappeared in the dark. The next day (we didn't have days off around Christmas), my uncle addressed the class:

"It was brought to my attention that some of you tried to reach me yesterday. I am sorry I missed you. I would appreciate it if you would come to my office at the break."

He waited behind his desk, but no one came. In those times, the students could be expelled from universities for singing Christmas carols.

In the eighth grade, if I remember correctly, I was myself one step from *exmatriculare* (expelled from school) for political reasons. At that time, I was attracted to girls strongly enough that when one of them from a parallel class asked me to write in her private book, I felt more than privileged. That book proved to be something disappointingly innocent. It had one generic question on every page, for about fifteen or twenty pages. Some boys were then invited to take the book home and fill in brief answers. No question was as intimate as I had hoped, but the whole thing was nevertheless a sign of attention, which meant a lot to me. Then the book fell into one of the teacher's hands, and he took his time to attentively read it all. On the page with "What dance do you like the most?" one of the boys answered, "The dance of Romanian Socialist Republic's anthem." I had never even noticed that stupid answer. Even if I had, I wouldn't have paid much attention to it. But that teacher did, and on the top of that, he brought the issue to the School Council. All professors felt compelled to show political vigilance, which made me as well as all who wrote in that book, eligible for *exmatriculare*.

After a due display of loyalty, the Council expelled the student who wrote that stupidity but voted for the next lighter sanction for the rest of us who didn't write anything politically connected: a grade above failing the class on social behavior. Any other transgression on my part, no matter how small, would mean unconditional *exmatriculare*. Quite silly. After this, I was regarded by our political watchdogs, for the rest of my life, as a person with questionable political convictions.

A couple of years later, I had to write an essay about a prominent Romanian mathematician. For the hard-to-find biographical data, I looked into a collection of Mathematics Magazine my uncle had. Many volumes were from before the communist takeover and had uncensored articles. There I found that our renowned mathematician had held some political seats with one of the so-called historical parties (older, main stream parties, with wide recognition). The truth is the truth. I mentioned it and I finished harshly criticized for not being more selective in my research. The most vocal was our French teacher and the school's Communist Party's secretary, Mrs. Ana Lupu, who kept her eyes on me throughout high school. A couple of times she even found it appropriate to comment in front of the class on my political reliability. I thought then that by displaying her political dependability, she would guard to some degree her good stand with the party and the future advancement of her only son, a privileged piano student in Moscow. From her perspective, I could be used.

Toward the end of my high school years in the early sixties, political studies and the Russian language became routine classes, no longer intimidating. This state of affairs was paralleled by the general compliance of our countrymen to the new system. The political terror subsided behind the scenes, based on the assumption that the public had gotten pretty much educated. The political apparatus liked to see itself as successful and misread people's compliance for conviction. Along with a better understanding of the new system, the public got less fearful and more proficient in dealing with it, meaning able to play it to their advantage.

The sixties were the best years of Romanian communism.

III

High school was the time when I began to want to know that which we were prevented from knowing. What was wrong with communism? What kind of thinking could aim for social justice through social abuse? How could it pursue general happiness by using general repression, and how could it predict general fulfillment while preventing it? What was the thought that doomed the communist project? Something at its foundation was terribly wrong. I managed to point out some obvious shortcomings, but the deeper I searched, the fuzzier the answers I could come up with.

Grasping the truth was for me a matter of self worth. I could not claim intelligence or awareness as long as I couldn't understand what was taking place around me. The whole communist phenomenon was a bundle of contradictions and failures. It was obvious that the information available to us had been filtered, monitored, and interpreted. All right, but then how much was the information doctored? What was the truth about the whole matter?

The system venerated the new man, visionary and selfless, and yet closed to any non-Marxist thought and closed to any non-materialistic understanding in the name of higher understanding in and of its self ! A Romanian saying says, somebody is not truly stupid until he is proud of his stupidity. This is communism in a nut shell! A visionary who is oblivious to the spiritual dimensions of life is basically unable to be a visionary; he is limiting himself. Also, communism, which promoted selflessness, is built on a materialist philosophy that leads to selfishness.

So there is a problem here, but what is it? Where and why did Karl Marx go astray?

I didn't know. From our Marxist studies, I could detect at that time only a couple of inconsistencies. First, Marx claimed that the value of an object is given by the amount of work invested in it. All right, but we have land, trees, and scenery, whose value is not related to any work. More than that, if a highway is built next to a piece of land, that land's value increases with no work invested in it.

Second, while Marx was full of resentment against those who make an income from exploiting those who in fact willingly accepted the terms of their employment, he had no quarrel with those who made an income from not working at all but engaging in speculation, usury, gambling, charging interest, acquiring inheritance, donations, and such. He was happy to get free money from his or his wife's family and from his friend Friedich Engels. Was this his idea of fairness?

We innocently asked our teacher these and other questions like "Is communism the end of social evolution? Is it the perfection that cannot be improved any further? If so, is stagnation possible?"

Our Marxism teacher came up with some explanations, which didn't seem to make sense and which I didn't have the courage to contest. I suspected she was unable to offer a better reply . . . you don't beat a dead horse. Also, if I were too insistent, I would appear to be a doubter of the system, so I faked satisfaction.

Besides the teacher, there was nobody I could talk to. People were either too scared to speak their mind, too ignorant (many by choice), or too willing to elaborate on the system's behalf. Even my father preferred to dodge the subject. I believe there were Marxist publications available for those interested, but I couldn't afford to spend time with those hard-to-read books, which were biased to begin with. They were designed to embellish rather than to openly debate; otherwise, they wouldn't have been published.

I knew for a fact that very few took the communist dogma seriously and even fewer bothered to study it. It doesn't help that Karl Marx had a heavy-handed style. I believe he wrote as he thought: convoluted and apparently overly concerned that he may not be convincing enough. His biographers describe him as a "blatant" megalomaniac who lacked confidence. (Frank E. Manuel, A Requiem For Karl Marx, page 214) Guided by a "deep rooted aggressiveness" (ibid p. 218) and "deep rooted aggressiveness" (ibid p. 218) and "lust for absolute power" (p. 209), he had "no much sympathy for human beings" (p. 214). For him, rural life was idiotic (p. 135), women had been treated in his writings as "lesser beings" (p. 44), and "had no appreciation of the uniqueness of native cultures" (p. 135). He even "lived in constant denial of being a Jew" (p. 21) and "mocked the 'Jewish' character of rivals for revolutionary leadership in the communist or working-class movement" (ibid P. 15) As a reaction to his own insecurity, Marx loaded his writing with explanations, specialty wordings, self-satisfying satire and mockery, side remarks, and foot notes, the full understanding of which required more erudition than a blue collar worker could ever muster. So the vast majority of communists were incapable of reading Marx.

More telling were the results of Marx teachings. His claim of absolute righteousness restricted independent thinking throughout the communist system. During his life, he didn't get the support of the working class so he claimed that the working class should be led to its destiny regardless of workers' acceptance or lack thereof, which legitimized the ensuing communist heavy handedness. Because he couldn't accept cooperation, he demanded the elimination of the capitalist partner in his social struggle so that proletarians would proceed unopposed. Thus he justified the bloody revolution. He was judge, jury, and executioner, and so were all of the communist leaders after him. These guidelines had brought us straight to this new communist system based on submission, suspicion, fear, ignorance, and survival tactics.

IV

Mrs. Lupu's vigilance followed us all the way to graduation, when she prohibited our class to have a yearbook. No reason was given. I suppose it was the communist paranoia about uncontrolled associations or loyalties. We didn't deserve that. We had been one of the best classes in academic performance that old school ever had. In the end, my colleagues had to put up with the photos I took with my uncle's camera.

Mrs. Lupu also conditioned the approval of our graduation party upon organizing it in association with the parallel classes and in the presence of two observers designated by the Municipal Union of Young Communists (UTM/Uniunea Tineretului Comunist). We agreed, of course, and made arrangements with Hotel Aro, decided the menu, collected the money, and started the show. We had been assigned two "good comrades" who observed, looked after the girls and, for lack of better political issues, they criticized a boy who brought his guitar, for not being more "progressive" with his songs. This boy had a penchant for light Italian and Spanish music that we all appreciated at the time. He was asked why didn't he emulate the "local elements" and emphasize our country's recent achievements rather than play simplistic love songs. The boy stumbled, softly played some notes, and our small musical fun withered. We had to rely on the official hotel's orchestra.

Nevertheless, we had a good time. There is something special about graduating from high school. We were about to have our lifestyle dismantled. No more daily gatherings at school. Our friends were to go different ways, take charge of their lives, and practically disappear in mounds of personal concerns. Some started already to assert themselves—lighting cigarettes or indulging in an extra glass of wine. After a while, the room got too heavy with smoke, the dance steps appeared too repetitive, and the conversations reached a saturation point. Still, I didn't feel like abandoning my pals, and I stepped outside for a breath of fresh air. I rested on a rail and enjoyed the quiet night. The darkness on the ground, sparkling with electric bulbs, seemed to continue seamlessly with the darkness of the sky, sparkling with stars.

A girl came to rest on the rail next to me. She was a year younger, soon to be a senior, but occasionally invited to our celebrations.

"Hi Iulia! It's getting stuffy inside," I said, unmoved.

"It's a beautiful night," Iulia said. She stood pensive for a short while then raised her eyes to the sky. I turned my head. Her lips stood fresh, slightly open, and her eyes reflected the stars. What did that mean? Like attracted by a magnet, I slowly got closer. She closed her eyes, and the stars in her eyes hid under her eyelids. I bent my head and touched her lips with mine. She let her lips savor the moment, long and tender.

"You taste like fresh strawberries," I said, fascinated. My hand lingered on her slender neck.

She smiled.

"I never thought we would get so close. We've always been watched by some adults," I slowly disclosed my frustration from the last couple of years.

"Don't apologize. I wanted it," Iulia said, looking in my eyes with the softness of clear water.

"It was more than I deserve."

Iulia smiled again. I wrapped my arms around her, and we stood so for a long time. Maybe it wasn't that long but having so many feelings and thoughts could fill a long time.

"Tomorrow, I have to go back to Bucuresti," I said, suddenly concerned.

"I know . . . I waited all this time for you to make a move. Now, when there's no more time, I had to come to you before you disappear," she said.

"I didn't dare to ask you for a date. Silly, isn't it?" After a pause, I added, "It's probably better that I didn't."

"Why?" She asked.

"I probably won't be able to hold my horses," I admitted.

"You mean pregnancy?" She looked along the street with a mysterious smile on her face. "This is the least of my concerns," she said.

We stood quietly side by side, lightly rested on the rail. Then Iulia said calmly, "I am a virgin. I want you to be the one," and looked in my eyes.

I felt there was nothing that could separate us, that my decision would irreversibly impact her, and that conferred on me a huge responsibility. "It's very romantic, how can I say no. Nevertheless, I'll be going away to the university if I can succeed at the admissions competition. I don't want to take advantage of your affection. I will be gone from this town, maybe for good. This is a big decision, please think twice. I will leave tomorrow for two weeks. Then I will return for a short while. I have to go . . . I plan to compete for the medical school in Bucuresti."

"I won't change my mind," Iulia said with confidence.

"No matter what happens in two weeks, you already gave me the most precious gift I've ever received. The biggest compliment! This is my true Graduation Party. Thank you Iulia," I said.

Iulia looked in my eyes and let all her love flow through. I wrapped my arms around her. How could I repay her? No, it cannot be a repay. If I do, that cannot be a gift; it becomes a transaction. I cannot do that. What can I do to rise to the occasion?

The two weeks passed amid excitement and expectations. Initially, my return to Brasov had to be for a formal good-bye to all my friends, a restricted get together, more like a farewell to our good old times. Each one of our five friends had plans to go to a different university in a different part of the country. We would be left with memories only, so we decided to make this moment memorable! But then, there was Iulia, and the future had already begun. It came so fast! What do I do if she gets pregnant? With no sexual education, which fit so well into our government policy of increasing the birth rate, the happy time I highly expected seemed to be a Russian roulette. But then, Iulia was prepared for this possibility somehow.

On my return to Brasov, Iulia stood firm on her commitment. The following day, we were both naked, next to each other, ravished by emotions of all kinds and totally dedicated to our project.

"We're safe. My parents won't be home before five," Iulia said with a serious face and wide eyes.

I caressed her face and neck. My featherweight touch was enough to guide her lower and lower until she laid on her back. I followed her until we couldn't get any closer. Mesmerized by her touch, everything else disappeared from my awareness. I started to float in a blissful parallel existence that didn't have anything in common with what I used to know. We sailed through beautiful dreams until our boat slowly returned to the reality of our surroundings.

The following days, we met as often as we could, pressured by the awareness that I had to leave the city, pursue my goals and find my way. I could not stumble on my first step or any other step. So after a week of dreamland with Iulia, I returned to Bucuresti and got fully involved in the challenging task of winning the dreadful competition for acceptance into medical school. I had two and a half months to prepare; not much in my opinion, about two weeks and a half for each subject.

According to my uncle who had supervised me all along, I should have gone to a trade school. In his opinion, it was preferable to be a good mid-level technician than a poor high-level professional. Obviously, he didn't think too highly of me.

But then, if I didn't pursue higher education, I would prove him and my father right and, more importantly, I would fail to prove to myself the worth I knew I had. This was my time to crow or get cooked. While aware of all this, I also had to decide what career I would like to embrace. Our universities had very specific orientations. Once you chose a class, you were set for a certain profession. Which one?

In high school, the only concern was passing the grade. Nevertheless, I tinkered with several ideas, all biology related, until there was no more time to tinker. My choice became clear: medical school. It was the most difficult one to get admitted to, but to me, it was a fascinating field with the added bonus of providing a rare independence. As a medical doctor, I would be my own boss, make my own decisions, and be solely responsible for them. There would be no room for the kind of political interference I saw in other professions.

V

The biggest hurdle in becoming a medical doctor was the admission. The competition was fierce. Twenty candidates for one place was a common occurrence. Moreover, there was always the fear of the unfair, unknown political files, behind the scene interventions, connections, and influence. It could be nerve-wracking. Everybody threw in everything they had.

In the face of this challenge, I felt a little insecure and, as a precaution, I decided to apply to dental school, which didn't seem to have as much clout as the medical school and which offered at least the hope of a less stringent competition. As it turned out, I made an inspired decision. The country was in short supply of dentists and, in typical communist style, somebody decided to fill the void in a one-time, big, patriotic push. A couple of years earlier, our government sent Dr. Ovidiu Statescu to search the market for a suitable, modestly priced dental unit that could be copied and manufactured internally. Dr. Statescu recommended a German unit that was later replicated in IOR (Industria Optica Romana) factories under the name of DENTIOR. With the production line set, the dental schools got their equipment, and the largest class in the history of Bucuresti's Dental School was created. Of course, this large unforeseen admission significantly decreased the level of competition.

To my advantage was also the fact that in the previous year or two, around 1960, the communists abandoned the provision that a high percentage of those admitted to universities—about 75% if I remember correctly—had to have a "healthy social origin" (come from working-class families). The ban of those from the "enemy's class" (clergy, former politicians, former business owners, and such) was also dropped.

In 1963, I met in Bucuresti a student in a nursing school called *Scoala Tehnica Sanitara.* Her name was Sherg Asta Ingeborg. She stood in my memory as soon as I found out she was the daughter of the former owner of Sherg textile factories in Brasov. She had everything she needed to become a doctor— the will, the abilities, the family support—but she missed the communist approval due to her "unhealthy social origin."

This discriminatory policy didn't prove to be beneficial. It didn't produce neither a healthy political group of intellectuals nor quality professionals. According to my cousin, who got into medical school six or seven years ahead of me, this practice had been a failed experiment, the scholastic difference between the motivated students and the promoted ones being too hard to bridge. I assume, this failure, in conjunction with an improved sense of power and control, prompted our communist system to abandon its quota.

Good education was a thorny subject for the system. On one hand, quality professionals were needed to carry the party's economic plans, but on the other, they were regarded with suspicion: trained minds were better equipped to see communism's shortcomings. During the pre-communist times, the professionals had been classified as "petty bourgeois,": a group considered by Karl Marx to be history's "fools," "clowns" of the social order, and victims of self deception due to their aspirations of improving their material condition and joining the upper class. The foolishness was, according to Marx, their inability to see that the upper class was destined to disappear. So, join it if you so desire and see how far you can go.

In time, this attitude toward professionals changed. The mocking attitude of old became a mixture of dependency, mistrust, and control. No matter how hard the system tried to bring the professionals to the income and awareness level of the working class, it didn't work. The professionals still had a wider horizon and wanted more from this life than communism could offer. In fact, they should, but this otherwise very human desire put the system on the defensive. To want more than the system was set to give was a destabilizing threat, an open challenge to Marxism. As a result, the system regarded the professionals, the middle class, the petty bourgeois of Marx' time, as potentially unreliable and made them their main object of attention. To make things worse, the uneducated communists propelled to power were instinctively uncomfortable with those with trained minds.

"We respect our intellectuals, comrade doctor, but I don't know why you always have to be kept in line. You always manage to complicate our simple, straightforward policy line. I don't understand what you find so difficult to comprehend. We just cannot rely on your education and let you loose. We cannot relax our political education in the field. We never know with what uncalled-for utopian ideas you may come up with next," a political activist, proud of his role in society, told me once.

General Secretary Ceausescu, a primary school dropout, appointed to his cabinet several equally underschooled individuals. He simply disliked intellectuals. When appointed Major General (political officer in charge of the indoctrination and political oversight of the armed forces) in the Communist Romanian Army, Ceausescu was still unable to write even a simple report without major mistakes. It was in the late fifties, shortly before his appointment as First Secretary (a title later changed to General Secretary) that he started to improve his "near illiteracy." Once in power, he got a university degree under special circumstances, but this didn't change his mistrust of authentic intellectuals or his proverbial bad taste, which a good education could at least have softened. Of course, if he was right—no one dared to say otherwise—and the others were wrong, then, this conviction empowered him to fight the Romanian culture and the country's cultured people. Formal education was a challenge to his own abilities and, in order to eliminate this challenge, he promoted across the country a kind of culture he felt comfortable with. We cannot get into the details here, but this is how the country's creativity dropped to an embarrassing low, and why the able ones who felt stifled dreamed to emigrate. Like Marx in his time, if Ceausescu couldn't fit his existing environment, he promoted a new one to fit his comfort level.

Another factor in communist disrespect for intellectuals was Karl Marx' opinion that personalities don't make history, but history makes personalities. Intellectuals would spring from the woods when needed. As a quirky result of this belief, such things as genetics and upbringing must not matter that much. Their importance was, in fact, dismissed until the mid Sixties, when the West made big strides in the field. At any rate, Marxism regarded people as peons on the table of history. It was inconsequential if they wanted to comply to Marxism, which was considered a window to historical truth, or not. The natural laws would force them do.

Communism had a special package for intellectuals: to be closely watched, indoctrinated, kept fearful, and dependent. This way, their creative potential is reduced, and of course, the system feels safe. As for technological achievements, they can always be bought or stolen from the West. There is a plentiful supply of "useful idiots" out there. The morality of stealing is not a problem by communist standards. According to Marx, morality is class related. If stealing benefits the working class, it is moral.

VI

A combination of improved chances and diligent preparation got me into dental school. With this, a new chapter opened up to me:

responsibility, independence, higher understanding, the perspective of creativity . . . this is life! The abstracts of high school were replaced by specific studies, deeper and more interesting. I had a sense of growth I never experienced before and the excitement of advancing into my own professional life. The memories of the previous years disappeared in the face of a wave of dreams and challenges. My high school friends lost some of their importance as they lost some of mine. Iulia remained the brightest, but even she slowly gave way to my new challenges. The present had been a vortex that got all my attention.

Of course, our political system made its odd presence known as it always did. We, the students, were summoned one day to attend an Extended Communist Party Meeting, where Professor Eugen Costa, Chairman of Prosthodontics, was called to purge himself of past political sins through a thorough self-criticism. On a podium, in front of a quiet crowd of faculty, clerks, technicians, and students, Professor Eugen Costa painstakingly minimized the importance of his membership to one of the former political parties and of having had a private dental practice. The audience listened dutifully as the poor man proceeded to humiliate himself. As if it had never happened, once this meeting was over, nobody mentioned it. We all did what we were supposed to do so the school would continue to function unshaken. Nevertheless, Professor Costa retained that apologetic, meek attitude. Years later, I read a small newspaper article about him, a retired professor and a neighborhood deputy, trying to appease everybody in a small incident. I saw again in his attitude the kind of humility he displayed in that meeting. Apparently, he was still trying to convince people that he was a good person.

Such were the times. People had to be taught who, why, and what was right so we all could follow one path, under the guidance of one Communist Party. To make sure we followed that one required path, we had to attend Political Education and Political Economy classes. These were not intimidating any longer. It seemed that a crack quietly appeared between what we had to do and what we were meant to do. The leaders were willing to take our right motions as signs of right convictions. In later years, it became apparent to me that those in charge truly believed they had succeeded in instilling the communist mentality in the country; while in my experience, few really believed in communism. It was only that everybody understood that that was the environment we had to live in and formally complied with the requirements. I did too.

The communists took care of their things in their places, and I pursued my interests in school. For the time being, our goals coincided: to become a good professional. I felt free. It had been so fascinating to study the human body and go into the fabric of life, see intimate details, and understand their workings. I would recommend to anybody to carve a tooth before his next step in life. That is an adventure in a different world, perfectly organized, so close, and also so poorly understood, where everything follows its meaning. Isn't this interesting? A living tissue guided by meanings! If a living bone is not used, it will diminish because its meaning is gone. Don't use a muscle, and it will diminish. Each tissue has its purpose. That purpose runs its existence like it has a mind of its own. Look at the heart. It pumps non stop for eighty years a thick liquid called blood through 100,000 miles of blood vessels, most of them of microscopic size. How is it possible? Imagine then interfering in the life of tissues! Drilling the first live tooth was an emotional moment, more sobering than I expected. Talk about responsibility, respect for nature, and concern for the patient! I have practiced dentistry for forty-two years now, and I still see every case like the first: unique and interesting. Otherwise, I wouldn't have lasted this long.

Such enthusiasm helped me achieve an early reputation. News moved fast and eventually reached my father too. No doubt he was pleased with my advancement, but didn't actually say anything in that matter. I had the feeling that he perceived the six years I spent in Brasov, against his will, as more than a physical separation. It seemed to be an emotional setback he couldn't overcome. I came home for all vacations, but, seemingly, the developement I achieved appeared too foreign to him. At the big family council, when the decision was made that I should do schooling under my aunt and uncle's supervision, he accused them of wanting to estrange me from him. At the time, I thought it was only one of his rhetorical statements. I probably misjudged him; he did perceive my departure as a personal loss he never recovered from and, he lived his self-fulfilling prophecy. Far from being estranged, my more organized and less outspoken nature seemed, as a matter of fact, inherited from my mother.

The fact is, I didn't know what was in his mind. Instead of opening up to us, he would rather run around the city for deals and connections. I remember him deeply involved in a crusade to provide natural gas piped to the house of Schweitzer Cumpana Rudolf, the most talented artist alive in Romania and professor at the Plastic Arts Institute in Bucuresti. No doubt that my father, who was in a perennial shortage of funds due to his expensive tastes and low income, expected a couple of paintings from the maestro in return. Since his student years, he saved for art, and it seems he couldn't stop doing that, sometimes to our detriment.

I also remember him cultivating relations with Gheorghe Anghel, Tudor Arghezi, Iorgu Iordan, and other artists whose names I don't remember. He treasured like gold a letter from Tudor Arghezi. His relation with the latter started to fade away when the writer decided to succumb to communist pressure and write politically correct poems like *Pe Razatoare.* The association with celebrities gave him a high like no other situation could.

Those priorities left my father with little funds for his family. As I recall, during high school into my second year in medical school, I spent winters without an overcoat, and I never received pocket money. Probably, my brothers didn't receive any either. Once in dental school, I started to make my own money with injections and later with dentures and denture repairs. At times, I could even help my brothers.

I was the oldest of the three brothers, two years between each. My middle brother was a pediatrics student and in love with a colleague that could not be any other but the best-looking girl in the class. They married soon after graduation. My youngest brother, inspired by Maestro Schfeitzer Cumpana, made a couple of brilliant oil portraits that convinced my father of his talent and encouraged him to join the Plastic Arts Institute. My brother spent one of his vacations with Gheorghe Anghel at Pasarea Monastery, where the master worked in quiet seclusion. There, my brother learned the trade, and among other things, posed for the statue of Mihai Eminescu in my stead. I had to focus on my final exams.

In the last year of school, when most of my work was clinical and when my middle brother had just started his own hospital training, we both received a bunch of telephone calls, all asking for Dr. Ritivoi. This was too much for my father, who felt sidestepped:

"In this house, there is only one Dr. Ritivoi," he said and left the room more hurt than furious.

5. A Communist Professional

I

After licensing, I was appointed to work in a rural office in Sibiu County, close to the town of Copsa Mica. I didn't know that Copsa Mica was the most polluted town in Europe, but what difference could it have made? That was my assigned office. The Copsa Mica hospital was the territorial supervisor of the medical facilities in my village and the place to see first.

It was the early morning of October 2, 1968, when the commuter train from Sibiu, where I had reported to the county's medical director, arrived in Copsa Mica. I got up from my seat, sleepy after the monotonous ride in the overheated and stifling compartment. My freshly pressed suite had lost some of its dignity and my face some of its freshness, but once I stepped on the platform, the crisp air made me forget all those small inconveniences. A soft and cheerful sun made the morning fog appear surreal like in an impressionist painting. Leaves in fall colors were gleaming playfully against the hazy background.

"How late does the fog stay around here?" I asked a man who stepped down next to me.

"The whole day. It will get clearer in an hour or so but never as bright as you may expect. This is mostly smog from the factories. There is a lead factory, but most of what you see is black soot from plastics.

They produce there a hard-to-contain black pigment. You will notice, nobody dries their laundry on outside lines. They hang it inside." The man made a good-bye sign and went on his way. I assumed he had to go to work in one of those factories.

It didn't take long to discover that soot claimed every exposed surface. This is probably why all the homes around had been painted in shades of gray. Better not touch anything. I noticed also a peculiar faint smell in the air. What could it be? I stepped outside the train station holding my luggage. I looked up and down the road, trying to pierce the fog. No way to get a hint. A man came slowly from behind me, probably from the same commute.

"Excuse me please, can you tell me which way is the hospital?" I asked.

"Take the main road to the right. You cannot miss it. It's a five-minute walking distance," the man said casually and glanced to his right.

I intended to introduce myself to the hospital's medical director as the county office had instructed me. I had to receive the keys to my office if nothing else.

The hospital's outline started to take shape behind the first corner. If it wasn't for the smog and fog, it could be seen from the train station. I crossed a small front lawn and I entered a single-story building, sitting like a purgatory between the street and the hospital itself. That was the polyclinic (multi-specialty ambulatory offices) customary in every town. Typically, it included the dental offices.

The dentists were just arriving for their morning shift, slowly and seemingly unmotivated. With no patients in the waiting room, there was little they could do other than arrive on time. A dental assistant proposed coffee and crossed the hall to the dental lab to boil water on a Bunsen burner. I introduced myself; we shook hands. The two dentists seemed intimidated by my presence, trying to appear busy rather than getting engaged in a conversation. I sensed I appeared to them too challenging, coming straight from the capital where all the availabilities are, loaded with fresh professional knowledge. Bogged in their small routine, they probably forgot a lot from what they had been taught in dental school years before. Cluj graduates (in that area, they must be from Cluj) had been always proud of their university town while always aware that Bucuresti is the capital. Slightly embarrassed, the two dentists looked around the office, studied the appointment book, and sat down absorbed in their thoughts. Work or no work, we were paid the same.

"Can you tell me when will Dr. Micu come?" I asked one of the dentists.

"Comrade Director is probably in the hospital by now. He is always early. As a matter of fact, I believe he was on duty last night, wasn't he, John?" He asked the other dentist who was casually flipping through the appointment book.

"Pardon me, what did you say?" John asked.

"Dr. Micu, where can he be found at this time? Dr. Ritivoi wants to meet him."

"Well, he probably is doing his hospital round now. After that, he goes into surgery," John tried to be informative beyond his usual self.

"When may be a good time to see him then?" I asked. "This is the day when the new graduates are coming."

"Ye . . . I don't know. He is probably aware of that. His secretary may know," John extricated himself.

"Good idea," I said and took a step toward the door. "Where is her office, if I may?"

And the secretary said, "Comrade Director is seeing his patients in the hospital now."

"I was told in Sibiu to present myself to the Comrade Director at eight o'clock. Today. Was Dr. Micu informed of this appointment?" I firmly asked.

"Comrade Director reads all his messages. As I said, he is doing his rounds now," the secretary insisted.

"Once done with this round, will he return to his office?" I pressed.

"I don't know. I cannot promise," said the secretary.

I assumed he would. That seemed logical, but Dr. Micu didn't return.

"He probably went back to surgery," the secretary explained.

"May I see the chief of the dental service then?" I said.

"Dr. Farben? She was on duty last night. She is probably home now," she said.

"Wasn't that Dr. Micu's duty?" I asked, perplexed.

"Well, they help each other when necessary," she explained.

After several more hours of waiting, I concluded that the Director had forgotten about me. An unusual situation. It was also unusual that nobody offered to remind him of my presence or pay any attention to me like I was a nonentity. No use to linger around. I took a later commute to my village on the banks of the Tirnava Mare River to see my office. Local officials probably had the key.

The office to which I was assigned was a true test of dedication. I asked everybody—the local M.D., the mayor, the local nurse, all answered that there was no dental office in the village. None had ever been. There were other problems too. The village was in the way of the main draft of polluting lead and black soot from Copsa Mica along the river. Everything I touched blackened my hands. Local peasants coming from their work in the fields were blackened like chimney sweeps.

If this were not enough, there were other stringent issues as well. The village had no store where I could purchase food. In that rural economy, people were self-sufficient. It meant that the existing rural store had stocked only staples and alcohol. Also, the village didn't offer any lodging. The local M.D. asked me to talk to the mayor about all these, and the mayor raised his shoulders powerlessly. Few people I asked about lodging, didn't want to be bothered. Nobody believed I would stay long enough to make their effort worthwhile. I assumed that to them, I was too much of a stranger who didn't fit in.

If this were not enough, the local medical doctor put a little too much interest in explaining that not only there was no dental office, but there was no reason for one. Copsa Mica is next door. My appointment there must be a mistake the county director would certainly fix. I got the feeling he was afraid that I might actually stay there. His sizable dispensary was a logical choice for a dental office, an intrusion he couldn't easily accept. He couldn't even accept to let me sleep overnight in the private room he seldom used, certainly not that night. I thought he didn't want to establish a precedent, or maybe he didn't trust me with his things. What a reception I had! I was basically left in the street with the deeming daylight. No doubt that nobody wanted me there.

Worrisome, but if so, they made the wrong assumption. No matter why the locals wanted to see me gone, that office was my God-given place. I was not going to go back to my father or to my uncle with my tail between my legs. Oh, no! I was supposed to have an office there, and I would.

In order to get what was legally mine, I could raise hell, complain to the higher-ups against underlings, claim to be victimized, and ask for what the country and the party had promised me and others took away. It would work, but I hated the idea. Crying foul in front of Party leaders was a relatively common practice at that time. Our political system did it to itself; with all power comes all responsibility.

Even if I would accept this charade, claiming my office meant to accuse people, to knock on doors, to look like a whiner, to wait idle until somebody could find me another office, and eventually to be moved from one office to another. No, this couldn't be my way. There must be a solution to this problem. Tomorrow morning, I have to discuss it with Dr. Micu.

It was getting late, and for the first time, I was tired and hungry in a strange place . . . not to mention rejected. The sun itself was placidly going to its rest, behind the horizon.

I took a deep breath and started to walk the main street of the village, from house to house, asking for a rental until somebody thought it would make sense to empty his storage room of bacon, sausages, onions, and whatever else and rent it to me. I took the offer with no hesitation, and while the man fixed the place for me, I walked back to the dispensary to pick up my small suitcase.

On my return, that empty room looked more like a crypt: dark gray, cold, narrow, with the door and a slender window cramped on one of the small walls. As I opened the door, a bulb sadly dangled on its wires, in the middle of the ceiling. It was cold, and I felt drained. My mind still tried to figure out how to have built a dental office then and there, where everything had to be planned and approved years in advance.

The landlord knew I hadn't eaten all day but didn't feel any desire to offer food. He had brought in a rustic bed with a huge sack filled with straw, serving as a box spring and mattress combined, and had set it next to the far wall. In the middle of the room, a little on the side, he placed a small iron stove. Under the small window, next to the door, he had set a small square table and one chair. He took a responsible glance around the room. Before leaving, he casually pointed to a nail in the door for a coat hanger, and with this, he felt he had done enough.

The dawn found me awake and freezing cold. The iron stove, which I heated red before going to bed, looked as if it hadn't been used since its inception. I stayed in my bed, on the top of that sack of straw, unwilling to venture from under that blanket on which I piled all my clothing. The sun was the only thing that could tease me out of that hole; it had been known to sustain life. As it rose, my perspective on life gradually brightened until I found the motivation to come out of that bed and face the new day.

With a surge of optimism, I took the early commute to Copsa Mica. I assumed that Copsa Mica Hospital, as our territorial administrator, should help me with the office. When I arrived, Dr. Micu was again unavailable, and nobody could give me an appointment or tell me when he would be able to see me—disheartening. He owed me at least some professional courtesy. Anyway, he couldn't avoid me forever. No matter what I intended to do, I couldn't do it without his help. He was the man, and it seemed that the only way to see him was to keep trying until he won't be able to avoid me any longer. For a while, I walked around that polluted town searching for anything of interest. There was none. Particularly noticeable, no eating place. All I could find was a poorly supplied small grocery store, where the best available was lower-quality salami and bread.

At that stage in my life, any food was good. I took that greasy paper wrapped around a chunk of salami and the bread, and I sat on the only public bench in sight, placed along the main highway, which also was the town's main street. Occasional cars and trucks passed by in a cloud of smoke and dust. Not an ideal place to eat but better than nothing. Luckily, I had a small folding knife in my pocket to cut the greasy pieces of salami and slices of bread. When finished, I got back to the dental office to wash my hands and try again to see the medical director.

Dr. Micu was still unavailable. I lingered around and tried to see him a few more times, each time feeling more and more like a pariah. Nobody wanted to give me any attention. Dr. Farben, the Dentist in Chief, declined any involvement in this matter. It was all between me and Comrade Director.

Waiting to be received didn't bring me anywhere. I decided then to pay a visit to the hospital's storehouse. The keeper allowed me to check her dental inventory, which surprisingly had enough to equip a full-fledged operatory. I compiled a list of available items that I needed for my office and left it with the keeper to present it to Dr. Micu for approval. The only problem with that inventory was the antiquated dental unit, which had missing parts. The unit was foreign made, probably before World War II, by an unknown manufacturer—a model probably long discontinued. The chance to get spare parts for it was practically non existent. In our bureaucratic system, even if available, the parts had to be included in a hospital's allotted budget a year in advance and approved by Dr. Micu, the county, and the officials in Bucuresti. This in itself would be an impossibility due to the low budget and more pressing necessities. Ideally, I should receive a new unit, but that was also impossible on short notice for such a small village. There were more important centers in need. My only chance was to fix that old unit using local means.

I thought a simplified version of the main missing part could be manufactured in the local factory. The way I imagined that part was simple and doable in any lathe shop. I would lose some versatility, but I could still perform all phases of dentistry. This was my best hope to have a working dental unit. I borrowed a pen, a ruler, and a piece of paper from the storage room keeper and drew that part with all its specifications. Then I took that drawing to the mayor of Copsa Mica who, by communist rules, was also the local Secretary of the Communist Party and had authority over all the economic units in town. He received me right away, listened to my plea, and after an official pause, agreed to help. A couple of days later, the storage keeper received Dr. Micu's approval for transfer of the inventory, providing I got the office space.

Things were taking shape. I was already searching for a location. What else could I do there? After investigating the few state-owned buildings in my village, with the mayor dragging his feet all along, I set my eyes on the school's library. This was a small, free-standing, one-room brick building located in the school yard. The room was of about ten by twenty feet and could hardly be called a library. About thirty used and abused paperbacks on an improvised shelf, guarded by a full-time librarian, was all there was. Probably, I wasn't the only one who had noticed that waste. When I suggested moving the library into one of the empty rooms in the school's main building and make the small detached building available for the dental office, the mayor agreed with uncharacteristic ease but added in the same breath that he could not help with any improvements or renovations. The village had no funds left for that year.

I didn't count on him anyway. With a lot of persuasion, promises of dental rehabilitation, and some money from my own pocket, I managed to have my office up and running in a couple of months. Many things had to be improvised, but I had a place where I could perform a full range of dental procedures—from fillings to root canals to prostheses. My schedule was erratic. People came whenever they felt like it, but in the beginning, it was acceptable. I wanted to treat as many patients as I could before I had to go off to military training in another couple of months. I reasoned that while I was in the service, my patients would have plenty of time to debate my work and spread the word. Then when returned from the military, I would have a full and more orderly schedule.

When the time came, I went off to duty as required. The army was a whole new experience but otherwise of little consequence. My most vivid memory is that of our commanding officer, a good man with a peculiar way of expressing himself:

"The barrel is the part of the rifle that conducts the bullet along the barrel."

Or:

"Comrades, I already told you these things, and if I didn't, I repeat . . ."

One time, later in the day, he brought us back to the dormitories after a field exercise and said,

"Comrades, be quiet when you get up there because it will come out an amalgam." In other words, don't disturb those already resting.

Another time, the officer admonished us:

"Comrades, I heard that some of you sleep with your feet in the bed." The fact is, some went to sleep with their boots on. In order to sharpen our vigilance, the officer spread through his underground network the news that we might have an alarm that night. In our experience, the most frustrating garment to bring up to standard in an alarm were the boots. Some figured out a shortcut.

The good thing about our commanding officer's statements was that they didn't require replies.

II

On my return from the army, I was summoned by the County Medical Director for an interview. I had no idea what the subject could be, but I didn't expect anything good. From my experience, an authority never calls to congratulate you. Maybe he was informed that my office was not up to snuff, or maybe he didn't like my erratic schedule. Who knows? The village's medical doctor wasn't too happy with the kind of freedom I had. Possibly, he had complained that I didn't work eight hours a day as required. I arrived at the appointment a little tense. The Medical Director received me with no expression on his face. He was busy with his routine, reading and signing papers. From behind his desk, he raised his eyes from the papers in front and said with no introduction:

"Dr. Ritivoi, we want to give you the opportunity to work in a better place. We have an opening in Medias. Are you interested?"

Now this was a surprise! Who wouldn't prefer a city to a village? On the other hand, in that village, I had the independence I couldn't have in a bigger place. Professionally, I could perform in my village the same procedures I would in Medias. In addition, I had started to like it there. I had gotten a better room in a better place, I resolved the food problem, and I knew people who respected me and whom I respected. I felt welcomed and I loved them. Even the weird ones had something likable. Then there were those surrounding hamlets, a couple of hills away, which because of their remote location and type of terrain, had been considered inappropriate for collectivization. Collectivization was the mandatory process of putting together the private plots in a certain area in order to create a single large "collective farm" that would be serviced by a technical unit and monitored by a certified agronomist. The stated idea behind the collective farms was a better, more advanced agriculture.

The unexpressed intention was to industrialize the countryside, bring the notoriously independent peasants under communist control, and in fact, transfer their private properties to the state as what had been done to the private industries in the cities. Certainly, there were differences between the nationalization of industries and the collectivization of land. To begin with, nationalization was done through confiscation, while collectivization was done through "convincing." The small farmers were "enlightened" by teams of communist activists about the advantages of large farms, mechanized and professionally run, over small individual ones. If the farmer resisted, it would be explained to him that if he didn't understand to help the country's progress, the country would not understand to help him either. Civil services would be denied to him, his children would be denied schooling, the older children would do their military service as unpaid laborers, local authorities would deny him the release of legal documents, and so forth.

If he resisted further, the farmer would be led to understand that his life would be an unbearable misery. That meant frequent threats, temporary imprisonment, unbearable taxes, occasional beatings, and if centrally located, his land would be confiscated anyway. He would receive in exchange a less productive parcel out of the way. Further pressure often included mocked or real deportations and other measures that escaped my awareness. It is reported that about 80,000 peasants who opposed the land reform were arrested, and about 30,000 were tried in public as an example for those who didn't understand yet what was good for them (Dennis Deletant: Ceausescu and the

Securitate, p. 9). In the end, everybody joined. The proudest suffered the most—another lesson in life that pride doesn't pay. Obedience is the way to survive. "The sword doesn't cut off a bowing head," some used to say.

Deprived of property, removed from decision making, and kept in perpetual poverty, the rural population was broken down psychologically, lost its bond with the land it tended, and became dependent on handouts from the only owner in the country—the communist government. The government decided what to cultivate, how to prepare the fields, how much to produce, and how much the state should take from what had been assumed it would produce. The peasants received what was left, which invariably was too little. The government always collected what was forecast to be collected, while the production never reached the forecasted volume. Through this process, dignified, independent owners had been denied the creative involvement, the decent rewards, and the pride of ownership with its intricate understandings, emotional attachments and control over their own lives. In their condition of servitude and poverty, the only way out was, as in any other communist sector, that of abusing the system: women and the elderly showed up to work with no intention to exert themselves. They would come mostly to claim the meager pay for a day in the field, while able men worked in the nearby town for wage. When in need, they stole products from the fields and so forth. In a word, the collective farms never performed as projected. At times, army units, high school students, or city employees were brought out to help, frequently in soggy areas, where the peasants refused to go.

Collective farms had a hard time on fertile, flat land. In those hills, a couple of miles from my village, collective farming would have been an economic disaster. Left undisturbed instead, life there was so peaceful and well-balanced that it felt like a fairytale. People were self-sufficient, open, and happy, glad to see a passer-by, giving and trusting as I knew them from my childhood, from the stories of those who had remembered, and from the literature of that past time. I felt at home there. Thus when asked if I wanted a transfer, I said,

"Comrade Director, this is a hard decision. I like my place. Why should I move?"

The director barely moved behind his desk: "If nothing else, because you will have amenities. You can take a shower."

Here he touched a sensitive point. But again, why did he want me in Medias? What was the hidden agenda?

"A shower counts; nevertheless, I would move to Medias if I could be appointed to the town's central clinic. I won't accept a factory office or an out-of-the-way place."

"This is exactly what we have in mind." The director put his pen down and rested his back on the chair. "I know that if we leave you in that village, sooner or later you will look for a transfer. We offer you this position because we want to keep you in our county. Take it. It is a good move."

Medias was a town with about one hundred thousand inhabitants, the second largest in the county, where I could benefit from the company of educated people and enjoy the charm of a medieval downtown. Not a bad choice after all. The Medical Director was right: it was a matter of time before civilization would call me back. I accepted the transfer.

III

It was all good except the job didn't come with living quarters. The Medias Hospital didn't receive from the government enough apartments for all its employees. Some had to commute from surrounding villages, and the others had to find shelter any way they could until their turn on the hospital waiting lists would come. As a doctor, I had some priority, but there were hospital nurses, ambulance drivers, and mechanics with families on the list for years. I couldn't be placed ahead of them. Besides, for the moment, there was no living space available. I had to figure something out. Well, what worked once would work the second time, and I took to one of the main streets on foot, door to door, looking for a room.

Housing has always been a problem in our communist state. In its attempt to rapidly industrialize the country, the system moved large numbers of people from villages to towns but never succeeded in building enough apartments for them.

The designed communist economy was set to unfold through a succession of five-year plans. Every five years, the leadership would come out with a comprehensive economic plan for the next five years. The presentation of each such plan was celebrated as a national event, a victory for our political system, in a festive manner. The General Secretary would get up on his high podium in hours-long, high-profile meeting, broadcasted unabridged on radio and TV. Later, the plan would be "debated" in political meetings across the country, in all workplaces. Some liked to hear that the General Secretary was aware of our problems, and the solution is under way, even if it never arrived. Unfortunately, all the numbers and statistics the General Secretary presented from his podium were inflated and based on already inflated reports from the field.

Consistently we were told that Romania's industrial development would increase 13 percent a year or even 15 percent, a rate comparable with those of Taiwan and Japan. I believe Western countries took note of this and saw communism as viable and thriving. All sounded good, but few of the promises and predictions, if any, ever materialized—pretty much like the communist concept itself.

I didn't place much trust in what the government would do for me. It was mostly concerned with itself. Besides, my life was my responsibility. Medias was a city all right, but there was no advertising available. This gave me no choice but to walk the streets and knock on doors as I did in the village. The private homes used to be small, economic ones, most with two bedrooms (in Romania called three rooms as it takes the living room into account) designed for specific needs. No spares. Even if it were possible to lease one of those rooms, doing it felt like the desecration of a holy place.

People were considerate, as always, but I had to cover about half of that long street before I found an older couple willing to give me a bed in their small, one-bedroom house. The bed was in fact a sleeper couch in the living room, and it came with some restrictions: home at a certain hour, lights off at a certain time, and no girls.

Then the word got around, and about a month later, somebody came to my office and offered to rent me a whole room in their three-bedroom apartment. A year later, the hospital informed me that it had an available three-bedroom apartment (four rooms) to share with a newly appointed dentist. Having been awarded an apartment on arrival made me believe my colleague had some kind of Securitate affiliation. Soon after, my suspicion grew when this new colleague who didn't display any professional qualities above average was "elected" Communist Party Secretary for the hospital's Dental Service, and several years later was transferred to an important position in the Bucuresti's prestigious Center for Continuous Stomatological Education. (Getting a position in Bucuresti, the capital city, particularly for someone who didn't have a Bucuresti ID, as it was his case, had been a near impossibility at that time.) There, he was again "elected" Communist Party Secretary. This cohabitation of ours wasn't a happy affair. After a year of sharing the same front door, kitchen and bathroom, my colleague and I each received separate one-bedroom apartments. After five more years, I managed to buy my own house.

Things were going pretty well. As a matter of fact, my life went through rather rapid changes ever since my graduation. On my first vacation as a certified stomatologist (in the U.S. known as a dentist) after I received my first job assignment from Sibiu and before I had to start my employment, I took advantage of a special offer for an off-season stay at a popular resort. The weather turned out colder than expected during that Fall, with shorter days and brisk bouts of wind. I walked throughout the town and saw all that could be seen before I started to feel lost in a sea of insignificance.

There I saw a pretty girl enjoying her time off, apparently not interested in any outside interference. My clumsy attempt to converse didn't go well. But then, short of inspiration, I mentioned I was a recent graduate of Bucuresti dental school. After that, a conversation appeared possible. With some perseverance on my side, we met again and found we could get along pretty well. We saw each other daily for the duration of my stay. In our cozy meetings, we discovered common concerns and common goals. She didn't have any appreciation for communism which thwarted her family's attempts to improve their life. The business her parents started was nationalized, and left with no means, they couldn't afford their mortgage and got evicted from their home. They had to endure the pangs of hunger and a winter on the

84

streets. Her father died. Her lonely mother finally got a low-paying job and a room in somebody's nationalized apartment. That was too little too late for them to love the Communist Revolution. Communists were right to assess that those they ruthlessly persecuted would never appreciate what communism had done. Based on this judgment, the communist leaders considered their victims as enemies in the class war. Nevertheless, they were mistaken to assume that those persecuted would fight them back with the same ruthlessness they themselves displayed. Unlike the communists, the "class enemies" only wanted a better life. This girl, Adriana, didn't believe she could build a fulfilling life in our communist Romania and wanted to emigrate.

The fact that she had the confidence to tell me all those things on our third date seemed extraordinary. Usually, that kind of openness was a Securitate trap to pry into someone's intimate opinions, but this time, all that she had said had a ring of sincerity. As an added bonus, she wasn't fazed when she found that I was appointed to work in a village. Most girls take the life in a village—removed from urban perks, culture, and social interaction—as a personal drama. Not Adriana! She broke the mold; she had the freshness I was looking for, and within days, we felt we knew each other for ever. The time together became a step into another dimension. Her strength and clarity of convictions made me feel confident that together, we can succeed in facing whatever challenges this life would lay ahead of us.

We spent as much time together as we could. Once my employment started, I used my freedom to run from my village to Bucuresti almost every week for about three days. In turn, Adriana didn't hesitate to ditch some classes and come, from time to time, to see me in the village, freshly coiffed, wrapped in an airy cashmere shawl, with a box of fresh chocolates from Capsa in her hand. After all that fun and closeness, it seemed normal to want to get married. It was the right time. And we did it as soon as I got a decent room to live in.

Meanwhile, my middle brother and his girlfriend graduated as M.D.s and enrolled in internship programs: he for Ear Nose and Throat and her as an Anesthesiologist. They married soon after Adriana and I did. Her parents did all they could for their only child to have the greatest wedding party possible. My father played his best disks, my mother cooked her best recipes, our friends and relatives had been smiling and happily conversing. The wedding party went well until Adriana started to feel sidestepped and even looked down on. She compiled a collection of smiles, steps, and other small signs that indicated to her she was disliked, even scorned.

"I cannot stay here and endure this treatment one moment longer," she told me angrily.

"What are you talking about?" I asked, concerned.

"Don't tell me you don't know. You're probably a part of it. Of course you are part of it. Don't tell me you don't notice how they look at me," she said.

"They will certainly look at you if keep acting this way. Everyone is having a good time. It's my brother's wedding! Whatever you feel, can you put it aside for their sake?"

"Did you notice your mother didn't say a word to me?" She said unabated.

"Did you notice how busy she is? Don't make a scene now, Adriana. The newlyweds don't deserve this," I told her.

"Sure, you're concerned about them and not about your wife. Who is discriminated here, me or them? Who are you supposed to protect here, me or them? I could never imagine I would step into such a sick family. Let me tell them what I believe about their unfair behavior, your mother in particular. Everybody believes she is the Second Coming of Christ while, as a matter of fact, she manipulates everybody with a smiling face. She cannot fool me!"

"You have a point. Sure, we have to deal with this situation. Let us leave and talk it over. We can put things in order by discussing them privately. In the middle of this celebration, we cannot resolve anything." I placed my hand on her back compassionately.

Adriana agreed with a small nod, and I went to my brother and my sister-in-law to apologize for having to leave earlier. My father noticed our small commotion and decided to throw his credibility into the fray to save the moment.

"You are my daughter now, part of this family. Bestow to me the favor of celebrating their wedding. I promise to make sure nothing will be denied you. Stay for my sake if for nothing else!" My father said.

"Thank you father, but this doesn't change the situation," she said, looking modestly at the floor, with a sad face.

"Dad, it is better that we leave now," I intervened. "We have to talk it over, in the quietness of our home."

We returned to our room, my former living quarters in my parents' home. I hugged Adriana and let her empty her bag of anger. Listening to her protracted speech, I wondered how she could accuse those innocent people with such impunity for things never obvious to me. Even if she saw something, shouldn't she be more mature about it?" Didn't she know that by doing what she did, she damaged her own stand rather than helping it? What kind of mess did I step into? For a moment, I panicked at the idea that I married a psychopath. Before anything else, I had to calm her down. I wrapped one hand around her shoulders, and I caressed her face and neck.

"I am on your side, Adriana. I won't let anybody hurt you. Tomorrow, we will be on our way to Medias and will leave all those things behind us. When we meet them again in more quiet conditions than that wedding party, I will be able to talk to them and settle things out," I assured her.

Adriana wasn't too convinced, but her anger had enough time to run its course. Slowly, she accepted my suggestion, and we hugged and set up for a due night's rest. Nevertheless, her antipathy for my mother never died, and I could never effectively appease her.

For a while, we, the brothers, followed our ways with little interference. My middle brother and his wife got busy with their internship, at the end of which they got their specialist degrees. They got appointed to the Galati City's Pediatric Hospital. My youngest brother graduated from the Plastic Arts Institute and received a job at the National Museum at the art restoration department.

Meanwhile, I pursued my goals in Medias. Two years into our marriage, we had a beautiful daughter. This and my rapid professional advancements gave me enough reasons to overcome Adriana's bouts of complaints and hoped for a better future. I achieved early popularity. I got my specialist degree as soon as the rules allowed, and for the first time in town, I finalized several dental research projects which led me to present three studies at different interregional conferences. With this, my reputation grew, and I also earned some time off for presenting my work.

The time off was a big reward in itself, keeping in mind that our work schedule was six days a week with a one week vacation per year. The party even set its eye on our seventh day by organizing all kinds of "works for the community's benefit," usually construction cleanup, agricultural, and such. My schedule was further loaded with a part-time job at a newly opened Pay Clinic. I had been willing to push myself in order to speed up the purchase of my first car, Dacia 1300, a replica of Renault 12. Having the car, my appreciation of a day off increased tremendously.

To help my progress, I willingly became a Communist Party member. The General Secretary's denouncement of the Soviet invasion of Czechoslovakia set the party in a better light. Also, since my father joined the party, the idea of me doing the same didn't seem as bad as it had previously felt. For some reason, communism wasn't a stigma any longer but a particular condition we had to live in. If I wanted a successful career, it didn't make any sense to stumble over this Communist Party membership formality. As an earthy person once put it, "You don't want to pee against the wind."

IV

This was a dynamic period, but under communism, dynamism has narrow limits. My growth, be it professional, general knowledge, or material, started to meet obstacles unlikely to go away. From a professional viewpoint, there was not more that I could accomplish. In due time, I could attach another degree to my name and do more research, but I would still be limited to performing the same bottom line procedures as always, in the same way, with the same limited and deficient supplies, which were becoming more deficient every year. My repeated attempts to compete for a position in the capital, Bucuresti, failed each time. With each failed attempt, I doubted my abilities more than before. After all that daily studying and with all my local success, I still failed. I was always a runner-up but never a winner. Meanwhile, the colleague I shared that apartment with, who didn't display any aptitudes, got a position in Bucuresti on his first attempt. I thought, maybe I was nothing more than a small town success, unfit for a major city. Maybe I wasn't good enough after all. It seemed, by being unable to get a job in my birth city, Bucuresti, I would never be able to return there for more than visiting.

From a material point of view, I was stuck also. All my resources went to the maintenance and improvement of my two major investments, the house and the car. Even if I were able to save, by our rules, I had reached the limit of what I was allowed to have. With our fixed income, we could justify only so much buying power. Anything over that limit was, obviously, coming from illegal sources, according to communist legality, and was punishable. In a relatively short period of time, I had already achieved more than most in our country did in a lifetime. This drew attention. If the government were to decide to play hardball, it would be of little consequence that my home was only 25 percent paid, with 75 percent still owed to every acquaintance in town (home loans were non existent in communism). If I would have to defend myself in court, it would be an uphill battle. The courts regarded private loans with suspicion because of their uncontrolled nature. In addition, I couldn't bring my lenders to testify. They didn't want their private affairs exposed in that environment of suspicion, envy and fear. Nevertheless, friends warned me that I was being watched, and, eventually, I could be brought under investigation for illegal gain.

Some patients preferred to pay me in order to take them after hours with no waiting in line, no time pressures, and a speedy resolution. I considered I earned that money; nevertheless, these earnings were considered illegal for the same reason the market economy was considered illegal . . . it was a non communist way. Not to mention, I was using state facilities for personal gains. What could I do? No private facilities had been permited under Marxist rules. To a certain extent, the system would let the unrecorded gains pass. They were too widespread to punish them all. Besides, people needed additional income to augment their low salaries and to be able to accept the system as it was. I heard on different occasions that medical wages were as low as they were (about even with those of machine workers and one fifth that of a middle Securitate officer) because it was assumed that we received private supplemental income from patients.

So the gifts, the under-the-table money were allowed to some extent, but that extent was always personalized. The General Secretary, who didn't receive a salary, could use the country's treasury for private reasons, at will. He even traded Romanian citizens of German descent with West Germany for German Marks deposited into his personal account. Then, it was the "nomenclatura," and the party's "active," who "earned" the right to be rewarded in ways not available to common people. Securitate officers had special privileges too. To an extent, I thought I deserved some allowance for my professional expertise and proficiency. I knew for a fact that most of my colleagues dragged their feet on quality as well as the volume of their work. Our chief was a prime example of laziness and incompetence. Anyway, how much slack was tolerated and who was overlooked was anybody's guess.

To complete the picture, the limit set by the communist system on my abstract needs was even more stringent. The material comforts I built so diligently failed to provide both the expected peace of mind and the opportunity for quiet reading and reflection. The house required constant work amid a chronic lack of supply and reliable workers. It was a continuous drain on my funds and energy. Even if I had had time to quietly read, we didn't have access to the kind of information I was interested in.

There were a few good books available. Our system was mostly interested in classics that displayed what Marx called "essential contradictions" generated by the capitalist system (in fact, human dramas prone to happen in any kind of society). The modern foreign writers were closely scrutinized to support some leftist points of views. I had heard enough about social injustice to have waned my interest in this issue. For a good show, complete writings of Marx, Lenin, Stalin for a while, and of Ceausescu since his rise to power, could be found in all book stores. Indigenous contemporary writers were politically correct and of lower quality in my opinion. Of course there were few professional books, mostly by Romanian authors, and this was pretty much it. Nothing unorthodox.

Understandably, we had to be kept away from anything promoting independent thinking because it would erode the monopoly of Marxism and dispel the communist illusion. The abstract was communism's worst nightmare: intangible, uncontrollable, and able to overrun the official dogmatism. It couldn't be tolerated; not even something as simple as meditation. For this reason our government created the Department of Agitation and Propaganda in charge of keeping us permanently "educated," i.e., having denied access to other points of view and fearful of exchanging nonconformist ideas in case we thought any. The result of this policy was fear, self-censorship, isolation, suspicion, miscommunication, and everything these entailed. I was frustrated by the inability to discuss anything of substance.

One of my uncles, who had returned from his doctorate at the Sorbonne shortly before the communist takeover with a whole collection of interesting books, had his library raided several times by Securitate and left with only a handful of lesser publications. He was also demoted from his ministerial position. It didn't matter that he was the son of a laborer. It mattered that he was educated abroad. Everything was supposed to agree with Marxism, or it would be regarded as hostile. "Who is not with us is against us."

All those frustrations wouldn't mean that much to me if I could have been able to have a fulfilling family life. We had everything we needed to be happy: common goals, common ways, and mutual support. We both had a kick when we found that Pierre-Joseph Proudhon said, "Property [capitalism] is the exploitation of the weak by the strong. Communism is the exploitation of the strong by the weak." We preferred to be exploited under capitalism than treated "fairly" under communism.

In Romania, food started to get more sparse, more difficult to get. The media presented the whole world being in trouble. In these circumstances, we felt more united in our determination to build a safer life. This had been reassuring but, was that love? I thought so. I had nothing to compare but, looking around, yes, it was pretty good—common goals and supportive of each other . . . We improved our home because if our attempts to emigrate won't work, we would still have a place to live in. On the other hand, being involved with the house would give authorities the confidence that our heart is there and we won't run away if they would approve our request for a short trip abroad. Even if we emigrate, we would still need each other, probably even more than before.

As long as we had dreams for our future, we could cope with our problems. Apparently, everybody has issues. It's part of life. As Adriana hated my mother, I kept them away from each other. As she hated every presentable girl around, particularly if educated, well, it was still understandable and I didn't give her any reason to complain. She prevented me from having friends, I could still understand her insecurities and I avoided them. I was busy enough working two jobs and as much overtime as I could, not feeling as if I was missing something. As for tenderness, I never had, except from my overworked mother. I always had a task to fulfill, and its fulfillment was my source of satisfaction. Despite everything we had in common, and all my efforts to appease her, Adriana saw me as the reason for her deep unhappiness. I had no idea why. She also hated most of the females in my side of the family, my mother in particular.

As we advanced into the 1970s, things changed for the worse. Procurement of food became a constant concern due to shortages and longer lines. I had to bribe more and build more connections for a piece of meat or a gallon of gas. Propaganda became more absurd and more intrusive. The television news, jokingly called Nicu's adventures because of its ceaseless praise of every move General Secretary Nicolae Ceausescu made, became a source of irritation. Every week, we had some kind of meeting to attend under a never-ending political pressure to believe what our system wanted us to believe. Busy all the time, indoctrinated, and separated from knowledge and from each other, I didn't make any progress in my search for meaning. To the contrary, with my increased desire to know came an increased awareness of what I didn't know. All my material possessions in the end proved to be nothing more than flaky crusts over an empty pie.

V

Not knowing where I am makes it impossible to know what path to take to reach my goals. With no opinion of what life is for, I couldn't formulate clear goals for the future. The lack of access to facts and opinions made it difficult to evaluate the life I was living and find a good reason to be proud of myself. Meanwhile, the system made sure I could not find any satisfying answers outside its Marxist creed which, itself couldn't provide of what I needed .

I didn't ask for much. A glimpse into another perspective, a word of wisdom, or a valid opinion would have done so much for me. But this was not possible. Dreaming outside the mold was prohibited. Dreams defeat fear, and fear was the way to corral us around the only dream allowed. Marxism is based on materialism as you probably know. To look beyond materialism means to look beyond Marxism, which means to doubt communism. Like anyone who is insecure, communism promoters cannot accept doubt and cannot accept responsibility for their actions. They hide behind "the most advanced philosopher of all times," Karl Marx, and hold him infallible.

Once the Marxist foundation is established, the official answer to any further search for answers becomes: Why lose time with this kind of nonsense and not do something "constructive" instead? Be a dedicated professional, be part of our leaders' effort to build the country and save energy. It's better to help your own people rather than ask futile questions, thereby disrupting your and others' lives, or run the border looking for an easier life in other countries. Stay and work selflessly. This is character. The answers had been already found for you by those much better suited for this job. You must simply accept them; don't try to beat the professional, particularly when he is a genius. Don't pursue your own answers; don't think for yourself. Do what you are told.

Understandably, if you search for personal identity in communism, which is centered on collective identity, you introduce a distance between "me" and "us" and soften the system's unique goal, unique way, and unique motivation. You soften the system itself.

I have no doubt that uniformity offers stability. Different political systems try to achieve it in different, more or less subtle ways. For communists, the unifying force is Marxism. More than that, Marxism is Communism's only claim of legitimacy, which makes upholding it and proving its own Marxismness the single most-important preoccupation, regardless of how valuable or damaging this dogma may be. From my perspective, Marxism is plainly counterproductive. Take the entrepreneurs for example. They are good for the economy but cannot be accepted in communism because they are independent thinkers, poor followers, and they create business for personal profit, all of which are incompatible with Marxism and therefore are prohibited.

Marx saw communism as a relation "between persons without any sense of self-interest conflicting with that of others or with the public or collective interest" . . ."as a state in which man's private interest is made to coincidewith the interest of humanity." He doesn't say who's supposed to assume this insurmountable task of making private interest coincide with collective interest. This change cannot happen spontaneously. Marx's materialism entails private interest and not the interest of humanity. Materialism supports selfishness, which is incompatible with altruism or compassion on a consistent basis.

For materialism, mind and spirit are secondary and dependent upon matter. If this is true, the mind is not free because it is subservient to the matter, which produced it. At the same time, matter's purpose is self-preservation. Its concern with others is limited to the extent to which the others can benefit oneself. In other words, the interest of humanity becomes attractive to individual only if it serves his self-interest. The engine is the self-interest. The interest of humanity that has to coincide with the private interest and not the other way around as what Marx stated.

In order to make self-interest coincide with the interests of humanity, one needs a mind free of material bonds, a mind which follows higher reason, not subjected to individual interpretation and selfishness. That higher reason that supports such attitude is love, the one that Marx and Marxists discredit. Love is the only motivation that doesn't require a payback; its pay is love itself.

Self-interest coordinated with public interest is thus feasible only along a non-materialistic and consequently non-Marxist line of thinking. Keep in mind that materialism recognizes the accumulation of goods and means as formula for success. All right, but the accumulation of goods and means doesn't provide peace, love, or happiness, which are the true indicators of success and are immaterial. So Marx's theory doesn't apply again.

It is hard to believe that Marx missed such simple truths. As a matter of fact, I believe that Marx was a materialist only up to a certain point. He didn't deny God out loud. He only claimed that life is a quest for material goods like food, shelter, and clothing before anyone can pursue higher goals. He blamed religion for deceiving people; he believed that morality is class related and consequently temporary, relative, and worthless. He believed in Darwin's theory of evolution (even if his communism was consiered as the end of social evolution) and in man's ability to control nature, but he didn't deny God. We don't know how he regarded God, but he didn't shut the door. This ambiguity is illustrated by his mixture of materialism and spirituality.

Materialism is his belief that social evolution is run by people's desire to have things. In his perfect communist society, he foresees things produced in abundance and shared freely. "From everybody according to his deeds, to everybody according to his needs." But he falls into spirituality when he assumes that people will automatically work to capacity and share selflessly. People are seldom inclined to work to their potential and share freely. They work to their potential only when motivated by either love or profit. The same applies to sharing. Someone shares either out of love or for profit. Love is spiritual, doesn't require pay, and is selfless. It's rewarded by the help it provides. My father's reward for sending home his ration of chocolate during the war was his happiness to provide for those he loved. Profit, on the other hand, is the product of materialistic reasoning; it requires a payback, the higher the better. It is selfish, and its reward is personal gain.

As we know, Marx doesn't accept love, which leaves him with profit as the motivating factor for both work and sharing. But because profit is a disgusting capitalist practice, he changed its name when applied to communism to *plus-value* and defined it as a kind of profit, which is spent on behalf of the society rather than given to a single business owner. All right, but is this kind of fairness compatible with materialism? We come to the same question and the same answer as before. Materialists work and share for material gain, while consistent and predictable fairness in such deeds can be achieved only through a non-material reason: love. Love is the only state of mind that consistently generates compassion, fairness, selflessness, and so on.

Marx blames capitalism for going wild with its profit, but at the same time, he dismisses love, which is the only guarantor of fairness:

in communism there "will be no more 'principle of love'" (Marx and Engels, 1845-46). He assumed that everybody will think as he did and will willingly abandon the desire to gather for the desire to share because it makes sense. At this point, I am not sure that if put in the position to freely share, Marx himself would. He had the makeup of a taker.

By dismissing both profit and love as motives to work and share, he has to offer an alternative. And he offered his logic as the third possible motive. He assumed that logic would motivate people to earnestly produce according to their capability and to freely share according to others' needs. But is this so? Logic is conditioned by deeper beliefs in either love or profit. Logic only blurs the difference between the two. Marx and the Marxists believe that their discarded love will, as a matter of fact, kick in unnoticed, under the disguise of camaraderie and fairness, and save the day. If not so, the selfishness will came into play, and the old reviled capitalist way will prevail like never before. With no love, sharing is never free. Thus, it remains to conclude that Marx hoped that his communism, even if based on materialist presumptions, would succeed due to higher, non-materialistic values.

Subsequent communists in turn chose to take into consideration only the extreme materialist interpretation of Marx's theory: atheism with its consequential reliance on human intelligence as the highest intelligence there is and its ensuing social engineering, coercion, selfishness, etc. As I experienced communism, their camaraderie and fairness were mere slogans. Enough to look at the kind of fairness the communist leadership displayed, at the selfishness needed by people to survive the hardships set for them and the abuses met at every turn! It is only normal for communism to apply a different mantra than advertised: from everybody as requested to everybody as directed.

The *abilities* and the *needs* are confusing terms anyway. Who is supposed to decide what those are for each person? It was obvious to me that the best qualified to know someone's abilities and needs is the person himself. But then, can the person be trusted to provide accurate information about these attributes? The answer depends upon the person's awareness, willingness, and fairness, qualities which, in my experience, are rapidly losing importance in communism instead of being sharpened. Even if they were sharpened, is the political system willing to take them into consideration as such? Can the system provide everyone with what he needs? I didn't think so.

Until they find an answer, I decided to take the matter into my own hands and worked to my ability to fulfill my needs. Then, once I bought my car, after five years of practice, I was informed by different people that I might be investigated for growing too fast—disappointing news. After another three years, I bought that home, and this was the end of the road—nothing else to look forward to. I had to slow down and obey, hoping that I will be left alone. No matter what might happen, I figured that my own expectations for my own life could not be fulfilled in communist Romania. All that stress with personal loans, long hours of work and study, high professionalism, tight savings, special attention to local authorities' dental needs, and painstakingly building connections and bribing people in order to obtain basic necessities had been motivated by an illusion. The system outsmarted me. It used my abilities for its needs. What a fool I was! Materialism is by its nature a taker.

VI

To fulfill dreams and grow was as impossible for the whole country as it had been for me. People's living conditions were deteriorating. The system found it more profitable to sell its food and energy abroad for hard currency than to give it to its own citizens for subsidized prices. We paid a high price on what was left over: chicken claws for soup, chicory blended with chick pea, oat, and 10 percent or 15 percent coffee for "coffee"; a mixture of blood, bone meal, and fat for salami; and, if lucky, poor quality meat, often from diseased animals. For better products, we had to pay much higher prices, under the table, to those who handled them. A butcher could very well do better than a doctor.

The apologists say that nobody died of starvation in communism. That may be true, but there certainly was malnutrition, depression, inability to raise children as needed, and a suicide rate higher than in the free world and much higher than our country had had before communism. Dr. Stancu, the Medias psychiatrist and a friend of mine, reached this conclusion at the end of a private research, which was understandably kept confidential. People were broken into submission, but this came with a price. The acceptance to say and do what one doesn't believe he should, does mess up the mental gears. Interestingly enough, this submission was interpreted by some in Western democracies as a sign of success, an expression of a better system—less chaotic than theirs.

Self-improvement was in big trouble for the whole country. The highest level of awareness allowed was the assimilation of Marxism and support for the party's line. That's it. The irony was that Marxism, with its intention to unleash human potential as never before, was the biggest obstacle in achieving that very goal. This potential could not be unleashed in our environment of restriction on information, isolation, and fear. As already mentioned, Marxism has a materialist foundation. Matter is by definition limited in size, shape, number, quality, and durability. These, in turn, entail selfishness and aggression in order to get access to that which is limited, and those are the antithesis of cooperation and fair share prophesized by Marx. For a major philosopher, he relied too much on wishful thinking.

Selfishness and aggression is also the end of love. Love didn't mean much to Marx. Nevertheless, love is what makes life worthwhile. If we dismiss it as being a part of class-related morality, meant to change or disappear along with the "exploiting" class, or for any other reason, then we are left with selfishness unopposed. There is nothing between love and selfishness.

6. A LOGICAL SPIN ON LOVE AND PEACE

I

Truly, communism had been a flashy display of selfishness. It confiscated for itself, in country after country, all important possessions and then went on to confiscate people's value systems. In order to incorporate the new communist mentality, people had to change their prior beliefs. The traditions were reinterpreted, and the new artistic productions were channeled to comply with the newly invented Socialist Realism. Religion was presented as an elaborate superstition, while knowledge was molded to comply with Marxism. Free thinking was curtailed, and we had to assume all those new standards as our own, or pretend we assumed them, or at least don't criticize them.

The shortage of goods and the fear of repression were excellent levers for manipulation. People switched from living to surviving, with little concern that mere survival implied a lower-quality life. Kickbacks, bribes, servitude, denunciations, stealing, and lying were all useful tools for making it through the day. Moral lapses were losing their demeaning significance. They were just survival tools, and survival was necessary. In order to please the rulers, people avoided all signs of independent thinking. Demagoguery was also a hot item. It was good for an agreeable political image, and physically, it costs nothing. The psychological cost could be overlooked. Integrity was a luxury few could afford.

It is not a secret that compromised integrity takes a toll on our mental processes and, with compromised mentality across the board, the communist goal of perfect, happy society is an imposibility. Communism is incompatible with fairness. Nevertheless, it claimed fairness all the way to the end. Meanwhile we, the people, drifted toward low self-esteem, pessimism, miscommunication, fear, mistrust, stagnation, moral relativism, and so forth. Selfishness, which Marx assumed would disappear along with love, flourished in direct proportion with love's repression. Egotism became the reality of the day, the means to success, and a socially acceptable tool.

In this process, love was safely pushed away from real life into fiction. The initial altruistic view of love for the communist cause was gradually replaced with love for the "enlightened" leader. The general secretary claimed that the country owed him love in a fashion similar to owing taxes. Niculae Ceausescu started to be presented as the Carpathian Genius, the kind that is born on earth only once every five hundred years. He was also presented as "the beloved son of the people." Needless to say, nobody gave him that much love. He simply assumed they did after having received servile and obsequious praises and adulation for so long.

It is possible that Ceausescu never understood love. Nothing in his biography suggests otherwise. In his hampered emotional development, the distinction between love and sex was blurred beyond usual. From a materialistic perspective, love is an instinct meant to promote sex. Materialism, however, needs to requires a physical purpose for whatever we think or do so; sex has a strong political advantage over the ethereal love, primarily due to its physical aspect but also, it is affordable and keeps people busy and away from trouble. Good for social stability too. Equally important, sex provides a highly desirable demographic growth, which went well with Ceausescu's push for a compulsory increase in the nation's birth rate. He even introduced the award of *Heroic Mother* for women with more than four children.

Love, as concern for others' well-being, tapped into a dimension the party couldn't control and preferred to avoid. It is eternal, which

Marxism cannot accept, and independent of any dogma. Love could also cast doubts on communism's legitimacy due to so many loveless performances in its resume. Communism is built on reason-propelled materialism, which can justify a lot of loveless and cruel acts but cannot change the truth uphold by love. It is no accident that Marx and his subsequent communists related love with the exploiting capitalists but not with the fair proletarians.

With such kind of signals from the very top, love's meaning deteriorated among the citizens from being a blessing to being a liability. Yes, liability. Love means sincerity, and sincerity leads to transparency and vulnerability. In those abnormal times, people did their best to hide their normalcy, their thoughts, and feelings. They had to appear politically correct, not the natural selves. We couldn't afford any more hurdles, and thus, love became impractical, most likely a mistake. In our society, to love meant, to a large extent, to be naïve, unfit for survival, faint hearted, and poor fighters . . . a liability. You don't let your emotions confuse your judgment! A successful life was thought to be based on cold judgment and suspicions, certainly not on kind emotions. The whole of communism is a cold judgmental construction that could not allow feelings to deter it from its path. If you have to love something, love the communist ideal and its promoters, which, was assumed, will bring a positive outcome.

II

For us, the Romanians, communism was a misconception carried out by poorly educated and contemptuous people. Meanwhile, to my confusion, communism in the West was gaining credibility. How was this possible? Didn't they know? They had intelligence and all kinds of means to find out what was happening inside our system, didn't they? Nevertheless, President Franklin Delano Roosevelt thought he could charm a genocidal criminal like Joseph Stalin. He actually said while getting ready for the post WWII peace treaty, "I think that if I give him [Stalin] everything I possibly can without demanding anything in return, then *noblesse oblige*, he will not attempt to annex anything and will work to build a peaceful and democratic world." Winston Churchill wasn't too far behind. He said on the House of Commons in February 27, 1945, "I know of no government which stands to its obligations . . . more solidly than the Russian Soviet government." He also said at Yalta in 1945, "My hope is in the President of the United States and in Marshall Stalin, in whom we shall find the champions of peace, who after smiting the foe will lead us to carry on the task against poverty, confusion, chaos, and oppression." This was said at the dinner table, where politicians usually praise each other; but still, it seems over the top.

The post-WWII leaders were not so complimentary toward their Soviet counterparts. President Roosevelt acknowledged two weeks before his death [12 April 1945] that Stalin "has broken every one of the promises he made at Yalta" (John Lewis Gaddis, *The Cold War*, p. 22). I am surprised he expected anything else. Following presidents were aware enough of the danger represented by communism to start the Cold War. Nevertheless, no postwar leader openly emphasized the facts, with the exception of Ronald Regan, whom media vilified for that. Those leaders had to appease a growing leftist movement in their own countries. People mainly from the universities, media, Hollywood—usually the independently wealthy white upper middle class—found communism appealing and the Cold War an embarrassing American overreaction. While America was blamed, the Soviet Union undemocratically and often violently spread communism in other countries without much criticism. The Soviet Union was prized in the West for its economic achievements, while its economy was in shambles. Communism was credited with social justice, while it established a new form of social injustice and while its population was depersonalized and forced to accept lower human standards. Some professionals even claimed that if communism wasn't satisfactory, this happened because we, the victims, didn't accept being further victimized and refused to let communism show all that it could do.

Marx's prediction that capitalism would be hanged with the rope that it produced itself seemed more real than ever. The Western powers had already given Stalin extended borders and Eastern Europe as an added bonus. Securitate General Ion Mihai Pacepa, who defected to the United States in July 1978, related in his book *Red Horizons* that Leonid

Brezhnev, through "his personal messenger" Nikolay Shehelokov, asked Niculae Ceausescu for "help in supporting the 'nuclear freezers' and the international peace movement as a way to disarm the West." Meanwhile, communism got a lot of support from the West through preferential media coverage, money, smuggled classified information, and advanced technological data. Many in the West believed that communism might not be such a bad thing after all. They preferred to let communists continue their activities, advocate the Western unilateral disarmament, and push the "make love not war." Of course, nothing is wrong with making love but don't confuse it with wisdom.

III

Peace is a beautiful concept, but peace at all costs is an idea floating between immaturity, demagoguery, and cowardice. Regardless, we got a strong peace movement demanding unilateral disarmament under the assumption that by doing that, the Soviets would do the same. This thinking reminds one of Franklin Delano Roosevelt's "if I give him [Stalin] everything I possibly can without demanding anything in return, then, *noblesse oblige,* . . ." Did anybody really see any *noblesse* there? Did anybody knew that for communists, morality is relative and self-satisfying?

Still, under the peace movement's pressure, the United States reduced its military spending, cut some military projects, signed the damaging SALT I treaty in 1972, and engaged in the negotiation of the SALT II and ABM treaties. As expected, this *noblesse* didn't oblige the Soviet Union to do anything. On the contrary, they violated most of their military agreements, took advantage of the Western's weakness and tilted the balance of power in its favor as never before.

While outwardly supporting the doctrine of mutual assured destruction as a deterrent of nuclear war, the Soviet Union was quietly engaged in a massive civil defense buildup described by Leon Goure, director of Soviet studies at the University of Miami's Center for Advanced International Studies, as "extremely comprehensive." I remember during the high school years having to attend ALA classes (Aparare Locala

Antiaeriana/Local Defense against Attack from the Air) which mostly dealt with protection against nuclear fallout. "They [Soviet leadership] intended, if there is such a [nuclear] war, to win it." While flashing appeasing numbers for public consumption, it used approximately 25 percent of its Gross National Product for military spending (*A History of the Soviet Union second edition*, by Peter Kenez, p. 233). This change gave Leonid Brezhnev the confidence to say in 1974, "The general crises of capitalism continue to deepen. Events of the past two years are convincing confirmation of this." Between 1974 and 1980, ten new nations, most notably Afghanistan, fell to communist expansionism. Ironically, these events were made possible by the peace movement. All ten nations fell through undemocratic ways; as a matter of fact no nation has ever chosen to be communist through free and fair elections.

IV

In his quest for peace, President Gerald Ford signed in 1975, along with thirty two other world leaders from both sides of the Iron Curtain, the "Helsinki Final Act." Through this pact, the post WWII European frontiers were recognized as "inviolable" regardless of how they had been achieved. This was, in fact, a gift to the Soviet Union, which had extended its borders by force at the end of the war. In exchange, the Soviet Union and its Eastern European satellites agreed to "respect the human rights and fundamental freedoms, including the freedom of thought, conscience, religion or belief, for all."

From the Western perspective, this pact which represented the formal end of the Second World War, was a big relief. Those temporary borders had to be finalized sometime either by accepting them as they were or by contesting them. If the borders were contested, the Cold War would have heated to a boiling point, and nobody wanted that. We should remember here General Patton's advice to restore the Eastern borders before finishing the WWII. It would not only fairly resolve this borders issue but would avoid so much suffering!

Obviously, it was practical to accept those borders as permanent no matter how unfair, and thus eliminate a point of contention. None of the big powers would lose anything, only the small countries like Poland, Romania, Czechoslovakia, and the Baltic Republics would. Make love, not war! On the other hand, human rights, if applied, would destroy the communist system, which was built on anything but individual rights.

From my perspective, the Final Act couldn't have been more upsetting. First, it legalized brutal Soviet takeovers. Second, it is unjust for others to decide the fate of lands over which they didn't have any jurisdiction. Third, we can only question the wisdom of exchanging something obvious and concrete for something unverifiable. Land for human rights? Did anybody really expect human rights under communism? Marx wrote, "The recognition of the rights of man by the modern state has no other meaning than the recognition of slavery" (Marxism and Morality, by Steven Lukes p. 63). Consequently, communism is based on dismissing human rights. They mean the dissolution of communism and the return to democracy. Would communist leaders self-destruct?

Agreements work among people of integrity, but here we are dealing with different characters stemming from different philosophies. For Marx, ethics were "phantoms formed in the human brain." In the Soviet communist paper *Krasny Mech* from August 1919, was written, "Our morality is without previous models, our humanity absolute, because it is based on a new ideal: to destroy any form of oppression by force . . . For us everything is permitted . . . only blood can transform the black banner of piratical bourgeoisie into a red flag" (The Barnes Review, September 2008, p. 18). When V. I. Lenin dissolved the Constituent Assembly, where the communists were a minority, he argued, "The interests of the Revolution stands higher than the formal rights," and this remained a communist standard. The communists take everything they can and give little, if possible nothing, in return.

V

Faithful to his beliefs, after he signed the Helsinki Final Act, Comrade Ceausescu, the General Secretary of the Romanian Communist Party, didn't lose any time in setting the record straight. In a public speech, he declared that in Romania, human rights were better respected than in

Western Democracies. In other words, in Romania there was no need for more human rights. "We will change when the poplar tree produce pears," he said. One of the general secretary's earlier speeches shows his consistency, "We do not understand democracy in its bourgeois meaning of babbling, lack of discipline, and anarchy. We understand democracy as the active participation of the citizens in formulating and implementing the party's policy." Things were fine by his standards. He wasn't the first communist leader to make this claim. Lenin said that Soviet government was "a million times more democratic than the most democratic bourgeois republic."

7. A Crack in the Rock

I

In the middle of this circus, a little known writer, Paul Goma, came up with an open letter to General Secretary Ceausescu, in which he asked for the recognition of certain human rights. *Radio Free Europe* published the letter, introduced the writer, and made known his invitation to everybody interested to cosign. Mr. Goma's letter fell like a bombshell in the pool of endless adulation for our leader. It was the first open public criticism of our communist system since its inception and, like any first time, had an added symbolic importance, probably even more important than that otherwise cautious criticism itself.

The fact that a common citizen could break the fear barrier had to be bottled up. If people were allowed to bring up their grievances and complaints, the whole communist myth would be shacked up. People could easily connect the idea of human rights to lack of food and fuel, chronic hunger and chilling cold in their homes and work places, darkness in their homes and on their streets, and chronically, lagging public projects. From here, there might be only one step to exposing communist mismanagement, abuses, repression, coercion, and crimes. No, Pandora's box should stay closed.

The system was well versed in handling public discontent, but this time around, its past experience was of a little use. In its infancy, communism was in a delirious display of power. After Helsinki, with all the power in its hands, it didn't have any longer the same freedom to use it. While in its beginning, the communist camp was isolated and indifferent to what the world had to say, this time, Romanian communists discovered they needed capitalist money and technology. If Paul Goma had published his open letter before the Helsinki Final Act, he would have been removed from the records in no time along with anybody who had ever talked with him or even thought of him. But after Helsinki, reluctantly and raising all kinds of obstacles, the system let him be.

Paul Goma had the wisdom of publishing his open letter in the West, thus making himself known to those whose business was to know. His freedom became a proof of compliance with the Helsinki Final Act, and that compliance granted Romania the Most Favored Nation status in trade with the United States. I have no doubt the Comrade (Nicolae Ceausescu) wanted to kill Paul Goma from the bottom of his heart, but he couldn't afford the consequences.

II

So the Romanian communists became more flexible. The General Secretary went on TV with a rather nervous speech targeting Goma but avoiding his name. As the number of cosigners increased, threatening phone calls started to pour over Goma's telephone number, and the police encircled his building. Only residents were allowed through. Several days later, a member of the Central Committee summoned Mr. Goma to a meeting, where he tried to protect the general secretary's image as a man above and beyond the trivial issues in the letter. He also tried to bribe Mr. Goma with promises of employment. To substantiate his benevolent tone, the government official released the tight access to Mr. Goma's building, but then more people came forward to sign the letter. Some of them had reputable names. This surge made Securitate raise the ante by sending Mr. Horst Stumph, a Securitate major and former boxer, to thoroughly beat Mr. Goma in his own flat, two or three times, only days apart. For a while, Mr. Goma's telephone had the incoming calls blocked. I don't know what other means of intimidation were used, but I know that Securitate refrained from killing him outright until a more suitable time. The Most Favored Nation Status as well as the General Secretary's image had to be protected.

Paul Goma's name was never mentioned in the communist media and probably not in the American liberal media either. Nevertheless, many Romanians knew about him even if only a few had the courage to sign his open letter (about two hundred, according to Mr. Goma). The rest bent their heads in fear and focused on groceries. Most Romanians didn't even know what human rights they were entitled to. Weren't we free? Many were confused over the importance of those human rights. Were they worth fighting for? They were afraid. An opposition would upset their frail balance and plunge them into an even harsher life. People had been happy that they could make it through daily difficulties—that they had a place to call home no matter how small. What else did we need?

III

Seen from the outside, the quietness on the streets could be mistaken for a sign of normalcy, while in fact, it merely showed a defeated people. The terror had been eased because the system was in firm control. Censorship had been formally abolished in the previous years because people had learned to censor themselves. In fact, control was never removed; it had been merely receded behind the scene. The whole system was wobbly but still functional. Between the people and the government, there was a sick interdependence. They both ran in a vicious circle, where each side plundered the other as a means of survival. Communism confiscated anything of value for itself, and people responded with abusing the system in return.

The consequence of communism's guaranteed employment was the employee's lack of motivation. Many times people went to work to rest, "They pretend to pay, and we pretend to work." No fear of punishment existed. Once dodging work became a widespread practice, there wasn't much the communist authorities could do about it. That was the working class's state, and because of that, no worker could be roughed up unless singled out for a major sin. They couldn't be reprimanded as a group. It was a sort of power in their number, except that this time around, the power worked in reverse to how the founders of communism thought it would.

From this perspective, what Paul Goma offered us was a break in this chain of moral decline. For the first time in Romanian communism, he proved it was possible to claim one's dignity. His letter to the general secretary was proof that fear is a self-defeating mechanism that cannot be justified. Fear was inspired by the tools of power and the illusion of strength, but the tools of power are not the power and the illusion of strength is not strength. Power resides in everyone and is subjected either to each one's courage or to each one's fear. Courage prompts someone to use his own power, while fear motivates him not to use it. The choice is personal. What Paul Goma showed me was that power comes from knowing yourself and dignity from being true to it. Paul Goma was the victory of spirit over matter. His message did redeem our nobility if we only could act on it.

But could I? It wasn't that simple. My financial condition was secure, my path of peaceful cooperation with the system was well trodden, and I knew rather well what could happen to me if I choose confrontation. As my father used to say, "The worse enemy of something good is something better." If you pursue something better, you may lose the good you already have and gain nothing instead. Yes, after making all those efforts to secure my life, I could lose everything. It would be safer to continue in the same rut like everybody else.

On the other hand, if I missed this unique opportunity, would I be able to live with myself? Could I afford to let go my biggest chance to become the one I thought I could be? I had to seize the moment! I couldn't let my possessions become my priority. They had never been more than means for a higher end after all. As it was, the means had been too burdensome, and the end didn't seem any closer. Making money the way I did didn't make me that proud anyway and didn't bring me any closer to the higher standards I always wanted.

I better break my dependence on communist benevolence; stop pleasing those I despised. I took a deep breath. The only risk I saw was the risk of doing nothing. Next Sunday, my wife and I got in the car, our daughter with us, and drove to Paul Goma's.

IV

I collected all the needed information about Goma from *Radio Free Europe*: his address, phone number, along with his appearance, his wife's and even his dog. To disguise ourselves, my wife and I thought we should appear like a relaxed family coming home with groceries. We had no doubt we would be expected; I set the appointment by phone, knowing well that his was bugged. The only thing Securitate didn't know was our identity.

I parked the car in the neighborhood, and we walked the next two hundred yards slowly, keeping a careful watch for street signs and numbers. As we came close to his apartment building, my wife started to tell a short story to our five-year-old daughter and made her laugh. In front of the building, I spotted several adult males who could be Securitate officers—all well built and all involved in simple activities, in which they didn't show too much interest. From time to time, they glanced casually around. Slowly, we passed them, and with a sigh of relief, rang Paul Goma's doorbell. We recognized his prematurely white hair, his beard, his heavy eyeglasses, his red-haired wife, and his dog. I had no doubt we had the right person in front of us, but I allowed Adriana the time to get comfortable with her identification too. After a short exchange, both my wife and I signed the open letter. We also handed him our own explanatory letters, which were supposed to be sent to *Radio Free Europe* through his connections. Those letters were meant not only to emphasize our reasons for signing Mr. Goma's letter, thus eliminating any confusion, but also a measure of personal protection. People in the West, had to know our names, or I was afraid we could quietly disappear into the Romanian prison system.

We had been probably the last signatories of the open letter. After we signed, for about a month, *Radio Free Europe* stopped giving any information about Mr. Goma and didn't acknowledge our letters as it would normally have done. Before, Goma was the radio's daily topic.

After a month of waiting in a vacuum of data, the first news of him was about his temporary arrest followed by his emigration to France. Under those circumstances, it was probable that neither our signatures nor our letters reached the West. Securitate conceivably got those letters, and with that, our future no longer looked secure.

8. All That We Control Is Our Choice

So from waiting to hear our names and our letters on *Radio Free Europe*, we began waiting for Securitate's call. I didn't expect leniency. They killed people for much less. With no way to know what would happen next, my imagination had free range. The system had us in its hands, lonely and unknown to everyone but them. No one else had been aware of our political problem that, as a matter of fact, filled our minds to the exclusion of all other concerns. We didn't find it fair to share our thoughts with those who seem not interested in the matter. If we would, we would do to them a disservice they didn't deserve. On the other hand, by talking to others about our human rights stand, we could be seen as spreading propaganda against the state—dangerous—and we could be more harshly dealt with. Frightened and lonely, Adriana and I kept following our routine in that vacuum of news, waiting for the system to make its move. Time rolled by incredibly slowly. I saw nothing that I could do but wait in that deafening stillness. Did fear block my mind? I found it prudent to wait, keenly aware of eyes and ears following us constantly. I felt as though we were two fish in a bowl, being watched, naked and powerless.

Our isolation was self-imposed, obviously. We said what we had said, and now that things didn't go as predicted, it was prudent to refrain from adding anything to it. Anytime we felt like talking about anything politically related, we had to drive away from the house and out of the car to the banks of the Dezna River and almost whisper. I didn't want to be accused later of meaning more than what we had disclosed in our well thought-out letters. The knowledge of what communism could do to insubordinates like us, the emigration of Paul Goma, and the lack of support among peers all left me feeling isolated in the face of pending doom. I was afraid for my family and for myself, but still, if I had had to sign that letter again, I would have.

I believe it was in November 1977 when, after eight months of tense waiting, Securitate finally made its move. One evening, my wife and I were summoned to the local Securitate office. This unusually civilized approach was in itself alarming. I didn't know whether after that interview, we would be allowed to return home or whether we would be retained and run through their works. We quietly walked the streets in that late hour, not knowing if we'd see the light of day again.

"If they jail me in one of their cold cells, they will finish me really fast," Adriana said with her eyes fixed to the pavement like there was something important at her feet. "Take good care of our daughter."

"Sure. Goes without saying. But let's not assume anything before we see what they have in store for us. It may be a simple interview, as they said. Who knows?"

"Who knows . . . Anyway, just in case . . . Why did they fix this appointment so late?"

The interview was non threatening, just a deposition on how we got to know about Goma, how we had found him, and a lot of questions about Goma's behavior. Did he promise us anything? Then the Securitate's major let us go home. Obviously, this didn't mean anything else other than for now, we could return home. Something more serious was bound to happen to us. We had crossed the line.

I didn't have any doubt that one way or another, we would pay for our defiance, but for the time being, I was relieved. It seemed that the Helsinki agreement protected us. We openly expressed reasonable opinions—no reason to be indicted. The ice was broken. The story had been told, the news was out, the legitimacy of our attitude was recognized, so I felt free to speak.

II

My first concern was to protect my parents and my brothers. There wasn't much that I could do, but I could show that they didn't have prior knowledge of my intention to sign Mr. Goma's letter and that they had nothing to do with my dissidence. I also wanted to inform them of what had happened before anybody else could come with false information and try to confuse or trap them.

Knowing well that their telephones were bugged, I thought the best way to do this was to give them a call. They were all living far from my Transylvanian town. My youngest brother and my parents lived together in Bucuresti, and my middle brother was in Galati, next to the Soviet border. A personal visit was impossible to fit into our six-day-a-week work schedule, so that a phone call would appear a logical choice and would allow everybody interested to hear loudly and clearly what I had to say. My father's and my brothers' expected surprise would work in their favor also. I counted on their awareness that when faced with this unexpected news, they wouldn't say anything out of line.

My sister-in-law (my middle brother was not home) listened quietly and, after a brief break, said, "Mihai, I always thought you were smarter than that."

My youngest brother was earthier, "So you stepped in a big pile of shit."

My father sided with philosophy: "It is your life. What can I say now that things are done?"

After that, my brothers cautiously kept their distance for a while. I had no doubt of their affection, and I don't doubt they understood my motives very well. They simply planned to make a living in our country, and this required a peaceful coexistence with the communist system.

My father was the only one who felt that nothing more could be taken from him, and he came from Bucuresti to stay with us for a while. He knew firsthand what the system could do to us and, just in case, wanted to be at hand. Again, there wasn't much he could do, but he could offer moral support and be a witness to what could eventually take place. Also, he could take care of his granddaughter if we would be taken away. He certainly wanted to provide us with some protection and comfort, but I also thought that he wanted to feel part of the stance he couldn't take himself. It broke my heart to see him quiet and pensive as never before. He could have been afraid for us. I would never know what was in his mind.

III

Securitate decided to use my father's presence to its best advantage, against my wife and me. In our neighborhood, there was a man who had spent his childhood in the same village as Adriana. This prior camaraderie conferred on him a specialness he wouldn't have otherwise had. On one of those days, while I was at the office, this neighbor paid Adriana a visit. He expressed his concern for our political implication, but things being as they were, he wanted her not to be held responsible for more than her fair share. A well-connected friend told him privately that one morning, after dropping our daughter to school, my father had gone to the local Securitate office to ask that I should be treated with clemency in the Goma case because I had been pushed to get involved by my conniving wife. If left up to me, I would never have done such a thing. It was implied that she should carry most of the blame for siding with Paul Goma.

Under normal circumstances, such news would have given Adriana plenty to say but, this time around, she related the information with an objectivity rarely seen and left it there. We both knew our close relationship was one of the few assets we had in our confrontation with the system. Regardless of whether the information was true or not, this was not the time to argue.

IV

Things didn't go the way we thought they will. Goma was gone, our letters were safely in Securitate's hand, and we had been powerless on the government's black list . . . what would be next? Who knows? I would occasionally watch the dark night sky full of stars moving across the universe with total indifference. Certainly, this is how it should be except, I thought, my fear was big enough to reach up high and make one give me at least a blink. Foolish me! We too keep moving along our path, unaware of other's pains. Where our path may lead? I knew how ruthless the communists can be.

Once I started speaking my mind, I found it hard not to go all the way and empty the box. But then, if I would criticize the General Secretary directly or the communist concept, I would be moved into a higher tier of dissidence, with unpredictable consequences. I saw the jail's gate open in front of me and slamming behind, then beating, malnutrition, all kind of psychological abuse, and who knows what else. I decided not to add wood to the fire. We only had each other to openly express our thoughts, and we kept going on the bank of the Dezna River and tried to sharpen our justification of what we did. We expected to face trained professionals, who could easily confuse or intimidate us.

Besides the love for our stubborn little daughter, this fight was probably the only bond between Adriana and me. Our success depended on our unity. We had made a good team so far. We achieved a lot but, if I check carefully, I never felt the love I expected. As a matter of fact, she probably didn't truly appreciate me; sometimes I felt I was seen as a rather naïve fellow. I even suspected she started already to look around for someone different. Anyway, I was sure she couldn't forgive me for not scolding my parents, my mother in particular, for being unfair with her according to her idea of fairness. How could I? They didn't show any disrespect for her. Their only sin was that of seeing her for what she was.

One of those days I took the train to Bucuresti to attend a dental conference. The train stopped briefly in Brasov, my high school town. While watching the familiar platform, my heart skipped a beat: Iulia serenely slid in the first-class coach. She looked great. The train released a short signal and took off slowly before increasing its speed and cruising along rivers and ravines. With my heart awaken, I raised from my seat and advanced slowly to her wagon. Iulia was alone in her compartment, comfortable next to the window. I slid her door open.

"Iulia?"

"What a surprise! Back to Bucuresti?" Iulia threw a surprised and mysterious look.

"That is my town. I guess the fact that I was born there qualifies it to be called mine. More importantly, how are you?" I prodded.

"Fine, thank you. I am a nurse now, if this is what you want to know," she answered.

"I would like to know a lot of things about you but, I probably don't deserve this privilege," I said cautiously.

Iulia smiled while looking forward.

"May I sit? Bucuresti is not that far away."

Iulia showed me the velvety bench, still smiling seemingly more so for herself.

"It seems so long since I saw you last," I said, looking through the window to the changing scene.

"True."

"I am married now. I work in Medias," I nervously tried to unload those important and also meaningless details. "I have a daughter. She will be six pretty soon."

"Congratulations," Iulia said politely.

"It is so nice to see you again. There are about ten years."

"Time goes fast, doesn't it?" she said.

"You look fabulous. Are you married?"

"No, I am taking my time," Iulia said in a way that lightly veiled a story.

"Julia, you may not answer if my question is too bold. I often asked myself what it would happen if you would get pregnant then, ten years ago."

"It's all right. At that time, I wanted to get pregnant. I planned to go to my grandmother, in her pretty village and give birth unknown and undisturbed. I wouldn't mess up your career." She looked straight forward, determined and still maintaining her softness.

"I guess I was too young and too stupid."

"We all go through that."

"Gracious for you to say that. I'll go to my seat now. Being close to you is getting dangerous. We keep meeting at wrong times."

Iulia looked forward again. "Time is never wrong . . . and neither right. We made it seem so."

"Yes, time is nothing more than time, and we are what we are; never what we were and neither what we will be. Well, so much for wisdom. I better go now. I am so glad to see you again," I said. I slowly got up and slid the door.

"Good by, Mihai," she said looking square in my eyes

I looked at her one more time with a warmth that flew out of me like a river. Than, I closed the door and smiled from the other side of the glass before pacing away.

I kept that smile on my face for a long while. Away from Adriana, I felt free to smile and dream. No need to control my expression for a change. Instead, I had to control my renewed feelings for Iulia. Was I a fool to forsake her?

V

Securitate was unexpectedly professional this time in comparison to the "good old days." It methodically explored all our weaknesses and gathered all its data before crafting its next move. They made another attempt to separate Adriana from me. It didn't work for the immediate future as they probably hoped, but it did its damage years later. This side story is beyond my present purpose.

Friends known and unknown told me that Securitate agents came in town and collected any kind of information they could find on us. As I found later, people inside the dental clinic as well as some regular visitors from outside were assigned to observe and report my words and deeds. Others had been assigned to frighten us with how dearly we could pay if we kept going our independent way. They advised us on the friendliest terms to recant and save our skin. I believe Securitate figured out the isolation and the fear that we experienced because it did everything possible to exploit them.

Obviously, we didn't know the details of Securitate's works. Nevertheless, we expected close surveillance. Then, after so many months of agony, I started to think it had been foolish to hide. They got what they needed anyway. The more defensive Adriana and I would be, the more clever, persistent, even suspicious they would become. I thought then that it would be beneficial to show more openness, providing I refrain from further political opinions. I picked a couple of professionals my age, which I had reasons to believe were in good terms with Securitate, and I extended my friendship to them. My overture was warmly received. From there on, my main concern was to show moderation when talking about Goma and communism. It was so tempting to go a step further! After all that years of submission, I finally raised my little voice only to stop short. It was hard but wouldn't be wise to do otherwise. The Helsinki Agreement could protect a tactful criticism expressed privately on limited number of occasions, but our system would find ways to go around Helsinki's guaranties if I were to go to the root of the problem or to win a wider audience. Nibbling around the edges and blaming insignificant people for significant lapses was a common practice used even by the General Secretary himself. Well, I was out of favor, but physically safe for the time being. As for the more distant future, no doubt I had cooked my goose. I had no more future in Romania.

9. THE BITE OF THE RED DRAGON

I

After about five months from our depositions, the system finally dropped the other shoe. An old-style Extended Communist Party Meeting was organized. Traditionally, this meant an all-out attack, a display of communist power, and a sublime unleashing of the faithful against the one who dared to think outside their box. In the beginning years of communism, Extended Communist Party Meetings were nothing more than a vulgar form of a modern inquisition. Their purpose was to legitimize political crimes: "people" expressed angry condemnation, and the system answered with harsh punishments. Since then, these meetings mostly capitalized on their frightening past and were used to scare people back into submission. In the aftermath of the Paul Goma affair, several Extended Communist Party Meetings were organized.

The most noticeable was the one against Ion Negoitescu, a distinguished literary critic and a prominent signatory of Mr. Goma's letter. From what I learned from *Radio Free Europe*, a mob was set to express "sincere indignation" pointed with spiting, calling him names, accusing him of homosexuality, and so forth. In the end, someone demanded a harsh reprimand for his betrayal of the trust the working class had invested in him when promoted to be a university professor and a published writer. The vocabulary used, the level of insults, and the frightening accusations were crude reminders of the deadly meetings of the not-so-distant past. For the older Mr. Negoitescu, that vulgarity and those threats were too much to bear. He balked and withdrew his signature from Mr. Goma's letter. Then the party showed magnanimity and didn't formally punish him (something it couldn't do anyway due to its international obligations).

The party didn't treat all Goma's followers the same way. Less prominent signatories of the letter were given their passports to see the world, knowing that they would not come back. Some were mistreated, and some disappeared into isolation but not imprisoned. What kept them free was having their names communicated to *Radio Free Europe*. Our names had not, so I didn't know what to expect. They kept all choices open.

The day came when all hospital employees, including those from territorial offices, were gathered in the conference room. I never saw that many people there. I quietly took a seat in one of the front rows. Nobody made eye contact with me, and I didn't attempt any. I had plenty to think about. It seemed to be rather quiet.

Soon, Dr. Danciu, the hospital's medical director, opened the session. A presidium had been elected, for the first time since I know, with no political activists from the county among them. No doubt they had their observers mixed in the crowd. The director was chosen to preside. He announced only one topic for that meeting: "The case of Dr. Ritivoi, who contacted suspicious elements with connections abroad, in an attempt to solve an ordinary matter." After a brief presentation, people were invited to comment.

A couple of characters I never met before took the stand and spoke in what seemed a typical early 50s-style.

"Comrades, I have no words to describe the shameless counterrevolutionary attitude that Dr. Ritivoi had. We paid with blood for this democratic system. We sacrificed to give him the free education he got, to offer him the facilities he works in, to give him a decent piece of bread, and for what? For him to spit on us, to go to that homosexual, whatever his name is, looking for justice. What justice could that man offer? To boot, he tried to send a letter of complaint to the West. What does the West has to do with it? What justice is he looking for? We have justice, comrades. This is what our system is all about, justice—the best justice somebody can get—people's justice, not fancy interpretations of some books, which benefit special interests and big money. We stand behind our honest, hard-working people and give them everything in our power, wholeheartedly, justly, in a communist way.

And then, we get people like Dr. Ritivoi, who come and put a stain on our reputation for not doing what he wants us to do. In case he doesn't know yet, this is a democracy, not a dictatorship. He is not the one to decide, the people are, through our elected leaders. He went instead to a shady character, out of touch and out of luck, for help! What does this attitude tells us about Dr. Ritivoi? Instead of contributing to our advancement, he makes a mockery of our system. It is shameful that we still have such people among us."

The audience was quiet. I peeked around. People pensively looked down at their hands or at the floor. The speaker continued for a while but didn't miss to mention:

"I have served the party faithfully, comrades, and I wasn't treated in return with the consideration I deserved, but I didn't complain. I am a faithful servant of our noble cause, not like Dr. Ritivoi here who, in fact, hates our revolution. Do not be mistaken, he doesn't look for human rights, he wants to destroy our communist system."

I found later that the speaker was a pest control employee who, in his hay day, had been an appointed judge in the feared People's Tribunals of the late forties and early fifties. Once the country was purged of "dangerous elements" like former politicians, senior state employees, and business owners, he had been given the opportunity to get a law degree in special evening classes, but he failed to follow the rules. After ruining so many lives, he perceived himself important, deserving a lifetime seat as a judge based on his record alone. He stood proud on his imaginary pedestal until downgraded to pest control. When the system needed someone like him, it used him. That's all.

A couple of others spoke along the same lines. I was described as "unable to understand," having "suspicious convictions," serving "foreign enemies," and so forth. According to our unwritten rules, once the dust had been stirred up by the designated faithful, others willing to display their own political reliability would get up and support what already been said. Some tried to do so, but their tone lacked conviction. They seemed more willing to understand my frustration rather than condemn it. At this point, the director decided to avoid any further deflation. He didn't wait for other, slow-to-come, voluntary speakers and asked me to respond to the accusations.

I got up from my chair in that quiet room. I didn't fear any longer. I said, "I thank everybody for your interest in my action. From what I have heard so far, I have received a lot of insults, I have heard a lot of slogans, but there were no comments on the issues I raised in my letter. I did expect a point-by-point discussion, but it didn't happen. Nobody showed me where I was mistaken or what statement of mine is inappropriate. Consequently, I have nothing to respond to. I am the first one interested in the correctness of my beliefs. I am willing to adjust my opinions, but you have to convince me this is necessary. Until then, I don't have any reason to believe I erred."

I sat down in that silent room. No chair crackled. I felt an indescribable peace. The director got up from his chair and said that he himself didn't find flaws in my character, but I was wrong in the way I had tried to address my disagreements. Going to Paul Goma had been a mistake. Our system offers all the necessary tools to correct any deficiency I had complained about. All I had to do was to use the democratic institutions at our disposal, and justice would certainly prevail. We were a Popular Democracy. He asked me then to comment on his suggestion, and I said that I would do as advised if another situation arose before looking for other options.

The meeting concluded with the unanimous approval of a *vote of blame with warning* for improperly addressing my concerns—technically, a slap on the wrist. People started to move, got up from their chairs, mingled, and slowly walked out. A side door opened, and the mayor slid inconspicuously toward the director and started to talk with a low, indistinguishable voice. I felt the audience had been satisfied with the way all had ended, even if nobody dared to even look at me, not to mention talk or make a sign. I appreciated their silent concern, but still, the best way to show my gratitude was not to personally address anybody. I was a marked man after all. Let them decide if we should talk.

The fact that the system didn't mop the floor with me couldn't mean peace. It only meant caution for the time being. I had no doubt that what they would like to do with me was different from what they did. All that "human rights rubbish" I brought up couldn't stand. Something had to be done. After another four or five months, the county's leaders decided it was the time to put a different spin on my case.

II

One sunny day, toward the end of August 1978, when the air was full of romantic memories of summer, a city clerk came to my home.

"Comrade Doctor, a group of comrades from the county have asked me to bring you to the City Hall. They want to talk with you. I'm only supposed to accompany you there."

This group of comrades had been conspicuously absent at the Extended Communist Party Meeting in the spring. All those officials gathered in a private meeting could mean the real thing. Privately, they could say and do what they didn't dare to say or do in public. I changed out of my yard clothes and walked to the City Hall. The clerk followed me at a distance.

In the conference room, a long table was set at one end of the room and a lonely chair in dead center of the empty space in front. Eight officials in a row sat at the table, facing the empty chair—my chair. I recognized the Chief of Police, the Securitate major who took my deposition, and somebody else from the city. The others were introduced as county officials with imposing titles. I was ready for anything. Only one man from the table spoke; the others stood with solemn faces, obviously attentive. He started with some general questions, but soon he came to what I thought was a rather transparent trap.

"Comrade doctor, let's be honest. We know you want to emigrate, and all that hoopla with human rights was only a pretext. If this is what you want, than let's deal with it in an honest and proper way. You want to emigrate? All right, write down a request, and we will answer you with no delay. Fair enough? I am the president of the Commission for Emigration Approvals, and I promise to take care of your case personally."

He didn't even promise to let us go. I had no doubt that he never intended to approve our emigration. They never let go of a good professional who could be used and abused while safely under control. Only undesirable characters, trouble makers, thieves, Christian fundamentalists, some spies in between and retirees whose pensions would be cut off once they cross the border, had been let go. This policy had the added bonus of showing openness to the world. "Our people are free!" I didn't belong to any of those. The trouble I created to the system was minor, easy to contain. Any way, Securitate got it right. We truly wanted to leave that mess. After what we had done, more than ever before, we couldn't see for us a future in Romania. I wanted so much more for my family!

"Comrade, this is an unexpected proposal that involves my family too," I said. I cannot give you an answer now without consulting my wife."

"We understand. Look, tomorrow is my day of audience at *Consiliul Judetean* (County's Council). You go home, talk it over with your wife, and tomorrow come to the *Consiliu* with your application so we can resolve this problem once and for all."

The county official had touched a sensitive point. It wasn't hard for anybody to figure that I would like to go. Half of the country wanted to emigrate. Besides, no doubt Securitate had detected my preparations to run the border.

Again, I didn't believe the system wanted to free me. In my town, I was practicaly isolated. I had no followers or supporters, couldn't present a serious political risk and, I could be prevented from moving into a bigger city. The local people weren't interested in political opposition. They won't jeopardize their hard-earned comfort for what most of them considered a pie in the sky. Beyond them, there was nobody I could relate to, much less confide political opinions in. In fact, I could be kept there indefinitely and put to work.

I also suspected the officials would use the proposed request for emigration to discredit my human rights stand. If I were to file that request, in all probability, I would be accused of using human rights issues as a cover for my intention to emigrate and not for its own merits. The party's attitude at the time was that emigration was a kind of desertion, a moral failure. Obviously, as a failed person, I couldn't claim to be principled. Then I would have to defend and expose myself to more accusations. On the other hand, if I were to refuse the offer, I would lie to myself. I wanted to get out of that never-ending mess.

Adriana didn't have this kind of problems. The moment I mentioned their proposal, she slapped her palms and jumped from her chair:

"Mihai, those idiots just gave us the passports with visas to go," she said.

"Well, not yet . . . ," I said.

"They did. Listen to me," Adriana insisted.

III

The next day, Adriana and I went to *Consiliul Judetean* (County's Council) but not to the man who expected us. We went to the highest county authority we could reach and complained that the proposal to apply for emigration was unbecoming for a Communist Party activist.

"We hereby request that all those comrades who spent their day in that meeting to be penalized. Their workday should be annulled. They should be ashamed of their deed," Adriana said firmly. "If those undeserving officials who summoned my husband the previous day to City Council continues to harass us, we would write another letter about the violation of our human rights."

It worked. Somebody with authority decided it would be better to let us go on a trip abroad. Thus, the following day, we got an approval to our two-year-old application for an organized tour of Turkey, the only democratic country on the government list of available trips at the time.

"You see," the officer who handed us the passports said, "you didn't have to create all those complications. You want a visa, you apply for it, and when the time is right, you get it. It's that simple."

Obviously, the organized trip we had applied for two years earlier was history, but who cared. We got our visas. Such tours through democratic countries had been almost synonymous with running away, and because of that, they were rare, staffed with Securitate officers, and reserved for hand-picked people.

Well, what a change of fortune! We were already planning to leave the country against all odds. For lack of a better idea, we had made preparations to cross our heavily guarded border on foot. We had been aware of the danger. Some of those who tried had been caught and severely beaten, some had been shot, but some succeeded. I thought that if well-planned, it was worth the risk. If we couldn't live in Romania while on good terms with the system, we certainly wouldn't while on bad terms.

This unexpected visa found us prepared. It took only days to put our affairs in order and hit the road.

10. The Free World

I

From Turkey, we took a cruise to Italy, and from there, we continued our westward migration till the end of the world: California. We went unabated by our first love, Western Europe. Its leftist movements, the popular slogan "better red than dead," all spelled trouble. What was in their minds? Were they afraid, uninformed, or had they different values than I expected? What did they believe communism is? I had no time to figure those things out. It's only that the west had been such an ideal for me that this kind of attitude came as a disappointment. Regardless, we chose to leave these questions behind and go to the United States, where the backbone of anticommunism was.

II

From the safety of the United States, I subscribed for a while to Romanian language newspapers and followed up on developments back home; but then, the news started to weigh too heavily on me, and I stopped reading them. I had a new life to build.

A new beginning in a new country, with no knowledge of local customs, of local language, with no money, no credit, and no right to practice one's profession is not an easy task. But at the same time, this new beginning gave us tremendous optimism and determination. We were in good health, and we felt unrestricted. No shun or disapproval. We felt free to achieve all that we wanted. In due time, I could practice dentistry at the highest level, I could achieve the comfort and security needed to study everything I wanted, and I had all the information on earth at my disposal. Yes! I could reach my dreams.

While the United States appeared to be the great place I wanted to live in, it also surprised me with what I thought was an abuse of decency, which nobody seemed to mind. How that bottled Mountain Spring Water could be called so while taken from the city pipes? How could it be priced higher than gasoline? Something is not right. I was also impressed by those large billboards along the freeways suggesting so boldly that you may be happy if you purchased what was advertised. Was this possible? As far as I knew, happiness could not come from any object. It comes from people. If somebody's happiness depends on owning something, then that person is in a pretty bad shape.

Obviously, materialism doesn't need the communist door to enter people's lives. This shouldn't be a surprise. It is only that it tarnished my ideal image of the country of my dreams. I took a deep breath. Give somebody the illusion of happiness due to owning an object, and that person goes for that object like a mouse in a trap full of cheese. Was Marx right after all? Will capitalism self-destruct? If I have to compare the two systems, in capitalism, materialism is offered on a golden platter, while in communism, it is shoved down your throat. The only difference is in the way it comes.

I thought I had made a good comparison, and I came to share it with Adriana. I thought she could build upon it, or provide a feedback, and have an inspired conversation. Instead, she was unimpressed:

"Shut up and don't belittle yourself with these stupid remarks. We just arrived, and you already want to teach them something. Forget it. We came to them, not they to us. You know something? They don't need you and your enlightenment! This country is full of professional philosophers well beyond your abilities. Nobody needs your ridiculous opinions. You know the Roman saying, 'If you stay quiet, you may look like a philosopher.' So better be quiet. You embarrass me. Don't forget we came here to build a better life for ourselves. This is what you have to keep in that mind of yours."

How could I forget? I was only trying to make sense of so much novelty. It was overwhelming! It was amazing how the Americans achieved so much while we, in communism, badly trailed behind. If I were to live the life of a welfare recipient with no further achievements, I would still have been better off here in the United States than as a dentist under communism. Just thinking back of the difficulty of getting decent food or firewood, of the endless chain of connections and bribes needed, was enough to make me feel I had left behind a nightmare.

Here instead, everything seemed so easy. You start working on a project, and the consequences would show up seemingly unobstructed. Things will work out. The feared lack of credit had no significance to me. I didn't even know what credit is. I knew I had to work toward my goals, and I started almost upon my arrival to learn English and to read medical books in preparation for the National Boards. In between studies, I did some part-time work here and there. After a few months, I found that the kind of work that fit our needs the best was janitorial. Office cleaning had to be done after hours, which gave me the whole day for study. When tired of reading, I would go out for a couple of hours looking for new business. Then I would study some more, and in the evening, I would grab my vacuum cleaner and drive around town, from job to job.

III

From the day we left Romania, I kept my parents informed of our achievements. Nevertheless, my father didn't stop being concerned. Obviously, he didn't believe what I was telling him. Not that I was a liar, but we had lived in the communist world were the ends pardon the means. No abuse made in order to achieve the communist goal is to be condemned. On a personal level, no lie delivered for a good cause is deplorable. By those standards, abuse is not necessarily bad. Truth and lies were merely interchangeable conveniences. A lie meant to relieve my father's worries was justifiable. In that case, he shouldn't trust me, and at the same time, he should see nothing wrong with his mistrust. On the contrary, his mistrust was proof of wisdom on his part, and my lie, a proof of thoughtfulness on mine. Weird, isn't it?

I felt from the beginning that he suspected I tried to make him happy, while in fact, I was facing difficulties and humiliations. From his perspective, his son, a doctor, having to clean restrooms in a foreign land, was degrading. This saddened me, but this was his belief, and there was little that I could do about it. Communist propaganda was full of dismal stories of humiliated émigrés, too proud to recant. I had reasons to assume most of those stories had been fabricated in order to prevent other people of falling into the same "mistake." The state itself sponsored honorable lies (allowed by Marx's class-related morality).

Nevertheless, I believe my father saw me as vulnerable, lost among insensitive strangers, doing menial work, and perhaps lured by glittering novelties, unable to realize that my licensing in California might be so difficult to achieve that it would never happen. After all, I didn't have what it took. I'd been a pitiful average student in intermediary school. I'd failed three competitions for a dental position in Bucuresti, and I chose a less-than-ideal wife. The writing was on the wall. What possibly could be expected of me in that foreign land, in the most difficult American state, to get licensed?

Particularly because I had been an immigrant, in my father's opinion, a support system was essential. He perceived friends and acquaintances as safety nets, a soothing reassurance. People to whom I could brag or complain were a necessity, particularly if well off. A good connection is always useful. He couldn't accept that I didn't need to brag, complain, or ask for help. Concerned, he got in touch with an older country woman from Sibiu who had a son in America and asked her to ask him to help me. Her son, Mr. John Halmaghi, the chief librarian at University of Pittsburgh, didn't hesitate to call me right away.

"Dr. Ritivoi, my mother called me on behalf of your father, Dr. Niculae Ritivoi, and asked to offer you the help you need. I understand you are preparing for the National Dental Board. Following up on this call, I would like to know how I can help. What I can do for you?"

My father had told me about Mr. Halmaghi years before. I had even seen a picture of him in the audience with the Pope, but I didn't need any help. The money we made was enough to keep us going. Why couldn't my father believe me?

"I appreciate your kind response, Mr. Halmaghi. Certainly, my father is overly concerned despite everything I wrote home. The fact is, we manage to cover our needs. Obviously, it will take some time before I get my dental license, but things are advancing pretty well. All I need is God's help."

God was new in my vocabulary. On my way to America, somebody gave me a Bible and, having plenty of time on my hands, I started to read it. What a surprise of how easy to comprehend it was! I thought it would be one of those ancient documents you had to be a scholar to figure out. Even more surprising, it emphasized a new understanding of life so different from what I was taught all those years and so much more satisfying.

IV

Of course, I'd heard about God since my childhood, but besides His name and His esoteric goodness, I knew almost nothing. The communist system discouraged us in every possible way from going to church. It prohibited spiritual initiation, ridiculed religion, and emphasized it as superstition, naivety, and fear of the unknown. It prohibited Bible teachings outside of regular sermons during the service, limited printing and distribution of Bibles or related materials, and infiltrated and controlled church activities. People were free to attend religious services, but most didn't want to be known as church goers or giving up to superstition. My mother, and later my uncle, took me to church on special occasions, but to me, the services were too long and hard to follow. Most of the time, the congregation didn't convey the deep emotion that I assumed opening to God would inspire. Besides, standing up for an extended time was so tiresome that I would lose all my attention. Not to mention that the sermon at the end seemed too abstract to comprehend. In a nut shell, despite my good will, I didn't get it.

Only after leisurely reading that Bible at my quiet table did I see its beauty. What a revelation! Its emphasis on love was like a breeze of fresh air after a lifelong forced feeding with class hate, political vigilance, prejudiced attitude, criticism, sacrifice, class warfare, self-denial, and intransigence. All those constantly promoted attitudes were so oppressive that they sucked the life out of me. No wonder when I read about love being the perfect connection between people, I felt my psychological cuffs falling. Love is an emotion with no negative side effects. Love is the union of the whole creation. Love is the awareness of each one's value, of each one's innate beauty regardless of what mistakes he made down the road. It is the best thing there is. "God is love." I much preferred to "know the truth" than to know Marxism and "see the plank in your own eye" than look at "the straw in the eyes of other's" and accuse them. Is there anything better than that?

V

Alternating medical and dental studies with spiritual reading and janitorial work, I made the best use of my time, and I mustered all the motivation I needed to pull through it. About two and a half years after my arrival, I got my California Dental License. I had dreamed of this moment for so long that dreaming itself had become a fixture, a fixture in a world where nothing is fixed! I looked at that piece of paper I got in the mail, and I wondered what novelties it would bring. I had known that that moment of change would come, and still, it came so surprisingly sudden.

In Romania, despite my daily studies and thorough preparation, each time I competed for a position in Bucuresti, I narrowly missed. In the end, I started to doubt my abilities. I never excluded the possibility that my Securitate file barred me from entering the capital, but I couldn't be sure of the real reason of my failure. Now in this foreign land, where other dentists I knew with much better credentials than mine needed double or triple that time, I had passed without flinching!

Before I even finished reading my license, I felt the big void of not having to practice different dental preparations or studying any longer. Suddenly, I had so much time on my hands that I started to feel unproductive. Then from out of nowhere, I asked myself if when I would start working on patients again, would I still be able to drill in reverse, looking through the dental mirror? After almost three years of physical work, would my fingers regain their light touch? I hope so . . . I had done it once before.

More unsettling still was the thought of higher demands than I had ever had. In front of me was the unfamiliar must for top professional performance and responsibility. Yes, unfamiliar. In Romania, as in any communist giveaway, we practiced bottom line dentistry with minimal responsibility amid low public expectations and dismal peer competition. My desire for excellence was optional. This time around, everything had to be close to perfection in a much more complex environment.

The skills I had to update for licensing with the California State Board were only the tip of the iceberg. To practice dentistry, I had to master much more than that. In addition, I had to face the big challenge for which I was totally unprepared—that of setting a business. With no previous idea of how to accomplish the task or what was available, what the laws and customs were, and not the least, a heavy accent and a limited vocabulary, the challenge was considerable. It was one thing to learn the language by reading medical books and practice English on my vacuum cleaner and another to properly communicate with patients, colleagues, and suppliers. I was painfully aware that at my level of preparedness, trying to look professional would be a challenge.

Learning had just started. In order to familiarize with the local ways and trends, I considered two options: seek temporary employment in another office or open my own office from the start. The first, to my still-communist mind, meant exploitation. Not a cruel exploitation as Marx described, but I assumed I would be asked to perform selective procedures, probably the most simple and repetitive ones. The ownership of an office, on the other hand, would expose me to a wider variety of challenges and force me to learn the trade faster. The choice became clear: an office of my own.

The challenge was considerable. I had to get a business loan, find a location, select equipment, and decide on leasehold improvements to fit the equipment. I had to choose instruments, materials, dental forms, and advertise—all of this being my first-time experience. To make things even more difficult, I didn't know the dynamics. It didn't cross my mind that there are such persons called contractors. The situation got further complicated when I managed to upset my dental dealer. He had anticipated so many sales on my account, but then, I found a dentist who had closed his practice and sold a lot of inventory at lower prices. Of course, I took the opportunity. In retaliation, the dealer provided faulty guidelines for the location of hookups to water, vacuum, and sewage, and later on, he settled on another dental office across the street from mine and asked that dentist to give me his regards. I assumed he didn't mean to be complimentary.

A new beginning has a lot of unpredictable, never-thought-of pit holes. I never took English classes, and I didn't anticipate this to be a problem. I'll learn. But then, how do I ask a patient to sit on the dental chair? "Sit down" seemed blunt, impolite. How do they do that and make it flow? Also, while I knew my medical terms, I was unsure of how to pronounce them in English. So in the beginning I kept away from professional interactions. Also, I feared I was not a match for dentists born and groomed in America, raised having everything they needed at their fingertips. I didn't have their confidence, their relaxed, articulate ways. Certainly, that surety has to come from solid professionalism. They probably were more qualified than I was.

Obviously, I had to improve in all directions. One can improve himself only as much as he realizes he needs to improve, and there was so much I didn't know I needed. How could I? Traits acquired during my communist past like insecurity, miscommunication, fear, and mistrust seemed normal. Also, I had no idea how rudimentary my social abilities were. Small mishaps and challenges gave me as many reasons to doubt myself and feel embarrassed. My father, my uncle, my wife, my country—all doubted my abilities, and now, I added myself to the list of doubters. How sad! In the end, I saw in front of me the two old choices: either move ahead or fail.

VI

I couldn't afford to fail. I couldn't accept to fail. More expertise would probably be the answer; it is always a good idea. I read dental books, and I participated in what I considered to be the most appropriate seminars. Then I incorporated new techniques in my practice, and I strived for preparations of a dental board quality. I offered the best service I could to my patients. Nevertheless, I continued to feel vulnerable, hurt by my own critical thoughts and by any suggestion. A suggestion, even a question, meant that something had to be improved. It implied criticism, and in my experience, criticism could be only demeaning.

I shied away from social activities mostly because I felt odd. When I wanted to impress with a deeper understanding of a subject, I would suddenly feel unprepared for the task. Either the subject unexpectedly appeared too basic to deserve attention or more complex than I had thought. It had been pretty bad. Strangely, I hadn't had this problem in Romania, and I saw no reason why it should be any different in California. But it was. Also, I soon discovered the number of subjects on which I could appear informed were embarrassingly limited to my communist experience, a field in which I slowly started to discern the inner workings.

While these gradual discoveries had been exciting to me, they didn't seem to excite anybody else. Communism was a kind of bad thing, period—unpleasant and pretty much of no interest. Who wants them? The Americans at large don't believe that that reality has anything to do with them. Not to mention that the subject may be divisive. Some believed that communism, in an improved form, is a valid way toward social equity. Also, it didn't help that once started on this subject, I tended to become too emotional about it. My hands would turn cold and many times I would quiver, probably my face would become intense. In conclusion, I was unable to create flowing conversations. Adriana could be right, I was a social dud.

My old dream of in-depth readings and thinking had been still on the back burner. Business demanded a lot of my time; dental readings were still a priority, while other readings were slow and interrupted by frequent checking of the dictionary. I mostly read short articles. Besides, even if I would have liked to venture into longer writings, the book stores didn't seem to have the kind of specialty books I had been looking for. No matter, one step at a time. They should be somewhere.

11. There Is More to Freedom than Democracy

I

I wanted so hard to be at least as articulate as I had been back home but, my progress was hampered by worsening marital problems. The time spent at home became a nightmare. One year before getting my license (one year and a half since our emigration), Adriana refused to help me with the business's weekend work any longer. She complained of a myriad of symptoms and concluded she did enough for the family. From there on, it was my duty as the man of the family to provide. I just passed the National Board, so I had more time in my hands to go out and work alone. I had no objection, and I did just that. I even expanded our business to the point when I had to hire help.

Nevertheless, all that progress failed to bring us peace and happiness due to the fact that Adriana was displaying an ever-increasing hate for me. She accused me of being underdeveloped because I couldn't stand up to my parents, of being an unaware gay because one proposed to me when coming out of a spa, of being borderline stupid because I couldn't support some of her preposterous statements. It seemed it bothered her that I was too considerate, which to her, equaled unmanliness.

"If I hear one more person saying that you are delicate, I will explode. I want you to be a man, not a sissy," she would say.

"Is there even a single instance when I didn't perform my manly duty?" I asked.

"I am not talking about sex, you stupid asshole. Everything in your mind is sex. There is so much more to manhood than that like be firm and stand for your family," she spat out.

Be firm! Blasting everybody around wasn't my way. Besides, she expected plenty of tenderness for herself. In that respect, she didn't consider me tender at all. Coming home after a day of work, I had to massage her back for half an hour so she could sleep, which she wouldn't do anyway. She would watch TV until late and wake up late the next day. She also expected me to listen to her protracted speeches about what I don't do right and how I should be, and of course, how I am like my mother—a failure. She considered that I became an American only because of her. For that alone, I owe her a lot. I would listen patiently for as long as I could, and then I would fall asleep, tired of work, worries, and of her tirades.

She constantly blamed me for everything not to her liking, and she didn't like a lot of things. In my willingness to be fair with her, I accepted she may have some points, but accepting a little opened the gate for accepting more than my fair share, which added to my list of difficulties and to my poor self-image. I'd always been the object of her anger, but lately, her anger had reached a level I had never experienced before.

It is never a good time for marital trouble, but the worst time is when you have a chance to take off and build a professional life. It may sound strange, but I thought she purposely sabotaged this process. The life I had been building was for the whole family, but she seemed uncomfortable with my success. In a way, it was one-sided; I thought she felt left behind so I offered to support her with a profession of her own.

"After I damaged my health helping you? It's too late now. I don't have any longer the energy after I have invested everything in you. Now it's your turn to take care of me, and you better not slack on it," she answered. For communists too, it was easier to blame their capitalist partners than rise themselves to the occasion.

I didn't know how to normalize our situation. I had enough to deal with without the additional stress of confronting Adriana. Her constant criticism actually prevented me from building the much-needed confidence, and of course, I couldn't show to others the confidence I didn't have. I couldn't fight on two fronts. Keeping my domestic turbulence low seemed to be the way, but was it? It hurt me so much to see Adriana indoctrinating our daughter with how bad of a man and husband I was and how low my family in Romania had been! I basically watched her committing a psychological crime, but I believed that once my daughter grows and becomes able to see the truth for herself, all Adriana's charges will disintegrate.

Will they? For some time, my daughter was distant to me, and I couldn't figure out if this was her nature, if Adriana succeeded to estrange her from me, or if I truly was so awkward that she couldn't find anything appealing in me. At times, she even took her mother's side and used her mother's words to her mother's pride. Those times, I rather let her be:

"Alice, this is not your problem," I used to say.

"Sure, this is your problem, so better show more respect for my mother," she answered.

"Alice, I didn't say anything which is not respectful. Don't do this."

"Don't tell her what to say and not to say," Adriana jumped in. "Even a child like her can see through your so-called peaceful attitude. She can see the evilness in you. Don't do to her what you did to me."

I wondered what I did to her that was so bad, and I quietly drifted away.

Coming tired from work, I would go early to bed, and slowly fall asleep with Adriana deliberating non stop about how miserable I was and easily manipulated by my crafty mother, all to Adriana's vague detriment, of course. Then I would get up early in the morning, and in the quiet and sunny living room, I would open a book and read for an hour. A pen and a notebook were at hand for new words. Those were the most peaceful times.

In some of those moments, I would remember Iulia. My life would be so different if I was with her! I probably won't be here in California but still in Romania fighting for decent food, decent heat, decent clothes, and decent access to knowledge and higher thoughts. Since we left Romania, the life there deteriorated to unprecedented and unforeseen levels. I married Adriana for her boldness, and her boldness helped us get out of there. Still, it would be so good to have on my side a loving and thoughtful woman.

II

After living for a while under constant verbal attack, I decided to seek the help of a psychiatrist. While I believe I did the right thing, this attempt didn't go anywhere due to the fact that Adriana built around herself a wall impossible to penetrate: her self-righteousness. If she was right, then she didn't have to change, and no psychiatrist could do anything about that. The only reason she agreed to attend those sessions was the hope that she would be able to convince the psychiatrist of how rotten I was and get her righteousness endorsed. I also believe that Adriana had figured out that I would rather put up with her than to pick a fight, and she stood her ground.

Of course, we could separate. This undoubtedly would lead to a divorce, which would mean major emotional and financial stress. I knew Adriana. She would go for the jugular. Even more importantly, a divorce would mean to break my marital vow, which was meaningful to me. I believe the words have deep significance, that they are something which shouldn't be abused. I needed time to see if anything could get better with improved cooperation and care on my part. I needed more time to come to a decision I could live with.

I took more time. I treated my family with more weekends in fun places, and I showed more understanding and submission, but nothing could appease Adriana. Anything could ignite her anger, and anything became a daily occurrence. I remember a typical scene when, one day, we took an evening walk. People passed by, when she unexpectedly said, "Do you see how ugly that girl is?"

I wouldn't answer. To me, that girl wasn't ugly, but to say that meant disagreement and probably another wave of accusations. With a little luck, something else would attract her attention, and we would get over that girl's appearance.

"Can you answer, or are you suddenly dumb?" She snapped.

"Sorry, I don't see her as that ugly . . . ," I said, my voice trailing.

"You're more tasteless than I thought. How can you say such a thing? You know something? I believe you said that only to irritate me. Otherwise, I have to believe you're an idiot. You see how you provoke me without even saying a word? God forbid that you open your mouth! This is pure evil. There is something in you that upset me only by you being around. There is nothing that I can see in you that makes me proud. Maybe your dentistry, and this is a maybe because I don't know what the hell you're doing there. It wouldn't surprise me if somebody would tell me one day that you messed up his mouth. Then what would be left to respect you for? Your father was right. You're stupid. You're like your mother, quiet and stupid. What a family! And I had to get in it. I helped you get out of that country, I helped you open the office, I did everything for you. Without me, you would still be in Romania doing extractions. Truly, what would you do without me? Tell me! I made a man out of you and look what I get in return! I tell you, there's something fundamentally wrong with you. Get out of my sight! How could I ever accept to live with you is beyond me."

I saw my marriage as being a replica of communism. Communism imposed its ways as the only right ones, and so Adriana imposed hers. Communism claimed to be devoted to the working class, and in the name of that devotion, ruined the whole country. Adriana claimed she had sacrificed her life for me, and in the name of that sacrifice, had brought incredible stress and damage to the whole family. Both Adriana and communism had a destructive love, for which they both claimed in return something which was never enough, never clearly defined, and always mandatory. Also, they were both unforgiving if their expectations were not met, and they were both on the wrong track. I know I cannot blame communism for everything. Nevertheless, most of its ways were adopted by its subjects. It provided a template for success and showed people what success means. Of course, success meant to them possessions and control.

My attempt to save my marriage resembled my attempt to build a happy coexistence with the communist system. In both cases, I made the effort to fit in, and I received instead constant criticism, suspicion, self-aggrandizement, distorted facts, and denials. In both cases, the partners' goal seemed to be to break me down and then reconstruct me as they saw fit. In both cases, I endured. I worked harder and tried unsuccessfully to please. In both cases, I resisted being deconstructed, and this had irate them both. I keenly kept the marriage going for a few more years until I finally understood that my marriage was already broken. It was a dead-end street, just as my life in communism had been. In both cases, I lost all my material gains and gained instead some experience and some freedom.

In one quiet moment, it came to me that my marriage had been an extension of my entire Romanian past, not only the political one. Adriana's personality resembled my father's and my uncle's strong characters. All of them had been dissatisfied with me. For them, I fell short of the mark. I have always believed that I am much better than they thought, and I have always struggled to reach my own level. I left my parents' family and built my own. I left my communist country to embrace new values, and I left my abusive wife to build a new life. Of all changes I ever went through, the divorce had been the most painful.

I frequently asked myself why that step was so difficult. People were divorcing around me in almost a casual way. Why did it have to be so hard for me? What made it so difficult?

III

After the divorce, Alice decided to stay with her mother. I didn't object. She was 17, old enough to make her own decisions, and strong-willed. In my opinion, she made the wrong choice, which was in fact the logical consequence of so many illogical developments—Adriana's last victory. Several months later, Alice changed her mind and moved with me. I just started to feel comfortable in the privacy of my rental studio—quiet, sunny, and facing a flowery slope. Alice's arrival made me happy for the opportunity to improve her life in a peaceful environment and to provide better guidance. That meant to leave that beautiful studio and set in a two-bedroom apartment on the street side, where I let her have the master bedroom. I bought bicycles so we could cruse together along the beach, we made time to discuss career opportunities and dined together. Nevertheless, a close connection couldn't be established, and soon after, she married without even introducing the man.

The divorce put me in the position of eligible bachelor, a fact that was easily noticed in a Romanian community. This proved to be a mixed blessing: I was thankful for the attention but embarrassed by my inability to respond properly. How surprising! When I was free to meet the world, I found myself completely unprepared to do so. I had been so burdened with my problems that I couldn't carry a decent conversation and couldn't show any humor. The time for joy was long gone. I had to figure out too many things for myself before being able to be a reasonably good companion. I am sorry I disappointed some people.

One thing I realized by then was that I didn't want any more Romanians in my private life. I didn't want anything that could bring back old memories and old trains of thought. All those had to be changed. I couldn't be truly free if subjected to old patterns and constant reminders. I wanted a new life, so let it be new.

12. One Thing Leads to Another

I

The news from Romania showed a constantly deteriorating standard of living. The country was mercilessly saving energy, food, and money in order to pay back foreign loans contracted to build large and unproductive industrial projects. The general secretary found that Romanians eat too much and, to save them from obesity, introduced food restrictions called the Scientific Diet. Government semantics never ceased to amaze me. In order to prevent public unrest, official propaganda was raised to new heights and the Securitate upgraded its vigilance. General Secretary Ceausescu criticized the shop managers for lapses that didn't belong to them, and of course, none of them was punished. Nobody cared any longer. People got so depressed that they even stopped telling jokes, a perennial Romanian trait. They walked with their heads down, in their gray garments, on gray streets, looking for any store that could sell a bit of decent food, the kind refused by other countries.

Among other things, Paul Goma briefly came to the attention of the Western European media. After he settled in Paris and his human rights movement lost momentum, Ceausescu decided to assassinate him.

Goma's courage could not go unpunished, and the time was ripe. He was on foreign soil, fading into anonymity but still being remembered in Romania, where the people had to be taught a lesson. Fortunately, Matei Haiducu, the Securitate officer sent to execute the plan, had a plan of his own. He disclosed his mission to French Intelligence, got a political asylum, and the whole affair was publicly disclosed. President Francois Mitterrand cancelled his scheduled official visit to Romania, and the incident became a major embarrassment for Ceausescu.

As expected, Ceausescu didn't feel guilty. He was angry with the officer who had ruined his plan. But guilty? The decision was based on certain reasons and those reasons precluded guilt. As mentioned before, for communists, morality is relative. Goma had attacked him, the country's best hope, and questioned his ways, which, in Ceausescu's opinion, were the best for the country under the existing circumstances. He considered that Goma deserved to be severely punished and made an example for other lunatics who may be inclined to follow his example.

In his isolation among servile and self-serving people, Ceausescu became a psychological case. It happens to all dictators sooner or later. Nobody could make any important decision but him. He couldn't accept any ideas but his own. This situation convinced him that he was the only enlightened mind around, surrounded by idiots. Some of the idiots had been handpicked as such by Ceausescu himself, but most were so careful not to upset the boss that they appeared idiots. Despite the massive effort made by communists to convince the population of their righteousness, the best response they could get was a lip service. The two traveled on parallel lines: the communists, didn't realize that their goal was unattainable, and the people didn't care about the goal; they kept focused on their daily bread. Marxism had set everybody—from leaders to manual laborers—on the wrong track. All the troubles along the way were but a consequence of wrong assumptions, wrong tactics, wrong morality and wrong priorities. All power is wasted if misused. For that reason, power doesn't mean having the tools but having a mind able to use the tools constructively. Communism didn't have that. As Maxim Gorky noticed, one cannot be communist and intelligent in the same time, unless dishonest. If communist and honest, one cannot be intelligent.

Ceausescu could see his subjects' faults, but not his own, nor the faults in the communist concept. Consequently, he got angry with the people for the failure of his economic projects. "They don't deserve me" was his conclusion. Probably, this contempt made him insensitive to the indescribable hardships he imposed on people. Or maybe he was insensitive to other's hardships regardless. One cannot be a communist if he doesn't see people as expendable.

II

The Communist puzzle preoccupied me enough to maintain an interest in it after I left the country. It's always good to be informed, except that every time I looked back, I felt my that emigration reversed. Every sentence from Romanian papers transported me back to a world of sadness. Every sentence revived thoughts and feelings that should have been left behind where they belonged. When reliving the Romanian drama started to weigh too heavily, I decided to minimize any interference from that quarter. I stopped the papers, and I reduced my social interactions with Romanians. I made a much better use of my time working instead on my English, reading good books, and living my new life. This cutting of the cord brought me a certain degree of freedom, but there were still communications with friends and relatives back home.

A person cannot sterilize his life. Even if possible, neither should he. The fact is, I wasn't only running from the influence of the past. I also wanted to protect those back home from having a red mark on their Securitate files. Ideologically, I was probably considered infectious. If my friends and relatives decided to stay there, then I did not want to make it more difficult for them than it already was.

The communists knew that even the most innocent exchange between any of their subjects and an outsider was harmful to their cause. Such an exchange would typically leave the outsider unimpressed with communist achievements and its own citizens craving what the outsider represented. The outside world had so much of what we had been missing. As a logical consequence, in the beginning, the system curtailed all exchanges with the outside world by dropping what was known as the Iron Curtain. But things changed. Ceausescu needed the Western support, and this required him to show openness to the world while he couldn't afford to lighten the tight control over his citizens at the same time. Thus, the Iron Curtain started to change from total isolation to a discriminating one. In practical terms, all contacts with the outside world had been carefully selected and monitored.

For the average Romanian, receiving a visit from a friend or relative abroad became possible but associated with the subliminal fear of retribution. Visitors from the West were prevented from sleeping over in their friends' or relatives' homes unless their kinship was of the first degree. The hosts, on the other hand, had to report to the Securitate what had been discussed during those visits. This rule wasn't always enforced and gradually lost its importance; nevertheless, it got the people's attention, which was no doubt its main purpose. Behind the scenes, the Securitate could monitor anybody, anytime, any way.

People were always reminded to speak what was politically correct, guard their thoughts, fake emotions, moderate their signs of appreciation of any Western achievement, and talk uncommitted. We didn't need much persuasion. Miscommunication was already a learned survival tool. But of course, the communists couldn't censor the nonverbal communication.

Simple letters and phone calls fell into the same category of ideological interference. The system preferred not to have them. It even used to spread the news that the person who hadn't written for a long time was either in a bad shape or prematurely dead. To make sure they won't be caught lying, those in charge would prohibit the return of the targeted ones living abroad. In my case, they withdrew my Romanian citizenship. It is easy to guess that not writing protected the communist system more than the poor Romanians back home.

At that stage in my life, my concern for everybody back home made me keep the communications to a minimum. I kept in touch with my parents only. The others could know about me and my family through them. However, while my reasoning was considerate, my willingness to protect them as well as myself didn't tell the whole story. The fact (I am embarrassed to admit it) is I was unable to open up and express anything intimate. Truly, I was a poor writer and a lousy speaker.

After much effort, I wrote stale letters and had awkward phone conversations. No words flew freely from me. I'd written inspired love letters in high school, but that was then. I didn't feel love any longer—just duty and concerns. Under communism, I had to watch my words. Then I met Adriana, who greatly increased my need to self-censorship. She too had the strong desire to isolate me from friends and family, to remove any support system I might have had, and depend on her. Any sign of independent thinking on my part meant her failure to control me and increased her need to further isolate and brainwash me.

My relatives couldn't be dismissed for any reason. Because of this awareness, Adriana used every means she could think of to discredit them and nudge me away. For the sake of some resemblance of peace, I complied while I kept my true feelings and thoughts to myself. This more or less worked for the duration of our marriage. But then, when Adriana and the communists were no longer in my life, I discovered that with all the freedom in my hands, I couldn't open up to them. If I pushed myself to be personable, I would feel embarrassed as if I'd behaved in an unnatural way. Strange . . . I had to control my emotions practically all my life. I thought the emigration and the divorce had freed me, but that inhibition became a part of me. I couldn't shake it off.

More disturbingly, I felt unable to correct the problem. My only solace came from the knowledge that deep inside I loved my family even if I couldn't express it. I made gestures that showed love even if I couldn't open my inner world's doors—they were stuck shut. Of course, my parents had to hear from me to make sure that I made it and that I was healthy and reasonably happy. For them and for my own dignity, I had to prove I could function, and that I could communicate.

III

Easy to say. I had lived for too long in a world where I had to hide. There, political correctness had been mandatory, and what was considered correct was faulty. It was quite messy. To maintain this abnormal situation, our system didn't tolerate objections. Then, I married Adriana who demanded her own kind of political correctness enforced by repression.

I remember, while in dental school, I attended a social event organized by the student's club. There also came a western journalist accompanied by, of course, a translator, undoubtedly a Securitate watchdog. The journalist picked a student from the crowd and asked her some questions. She did answer, but when the questions became more focused, she panicked and started to cry uncontrollably. We who witnessed understood her well and slipped into a respectful silence. She couldn't lie, and she couldn't tell the truth. The translator understood as well, but he knew how to cover it up with a seemingly reasonable explanation. The only safe way to communicate had been to miscommunicate and to be able to come with an acceptable reason for every lie enunciated. Otherwise, one had better shut up.

Then in California, I discovered that miscommunication was no longer a necessity. On the contrary, it was an impediment. A clear and on-point presentation is the picture of confidence and professionalism, not the double talk, lies, or embellishment. At the time I opened my new office, my English wasn't that clear, and I was more concerned with covering for what I thought might deter a patient than informing him of all the pluses and minuses. What can I say? When insecure, one tends to be defensive rather than straightforward. Miscommunication had already been a part of my way. What I didn't feel comfortable with had to be hidden and, most importantly, I didn't feel comfortable with myself.

Hiding meant crippled self-love, ruined inner peace, and hampered ability to deal with whatever life brought my way. By hiding my thoughts and feelings, I could never be as straight as I wanted to be with anybody, including my parents. Moreover, what I didn't bring forward I couldn't face and resolve. To make things even more difficult, because I didn't show affection particularly to my parents, I felt guilty for doing them injustice. They were entitled to enjoy what they already had sheltered in my heart. To make a long story short, my communication with those back home was a difficult task. Especially difficult was the communication with my father.

Of course, I tried to circumvent my shortcomings by using intellectual escape routes. Presenting interesting things could deflect attention from not being affectionate, but you cannot replace one with the other. My only comfort was the fact that I gave my parents the equity from the sale of my house in Romania, and that I used every opportunity to send them money through acquaintances that traveled back home. I wanted them to be financially safe, but at the same time, I secretly hoped every time I sent them something, my father would see me in a better light. I guess "Mihai doesn't have what it takes" was still resounding fifty years later.

Sending money, labor-intense letters, and phone calls were the best I could do. I was aware that this was the equivalent of whipping the saddle so the horse would get the message, but this is how it was. My only true asset was that I knew I loved them and that they loved me regardless. So I continued in the same way. It wasn't a bad situation after all, I reasoned. In time, it might even develop into something better.

13. The Return

I

At that time, the future seemed to be an extension of the present, with minor variations added. In reality, the future was to be full of surprises. In December 1989, communism, with all the power it had accumulated in its hands, couldn't sustain itself any longer and collapsed. In Romania, President and General Secretary Nicolae Ceausescu, who was called by his media "the most beloved son of the people," was executed in a popular uprising, and this eliminated the possibility of communist resurgence.

Ceausescu had taken care that nobody under him could take control of the country in his stead, and nobody did. A communist official, Ion Iliescu, came up from obscurity and tried to implement in Romania what Gorbachev attempted in the Soviet Union: revitalize the ailing communism through "glasnost" and "perestroika" type reforms. Nevertheless, the tidal wave of radical reforms that wiped out communism altogether proved stronger than him as it was stronger than Gorbachev. It was believed that Securitate, under Iliescu's directions, created a ridiculous number of bogus political parties in order to discredit the newly proclaimed democracy. Then, when a couple of parties started to gain traction, he mobilized the so-called miners, who, in a well organized manner, ransacked those parties' offices. Then in small groups, they acted in professional ways beyond the abilities of real miners as, armed with clubs, patrolled the streets, and attacked suspected supporters of those parties. Any way, Romania managed to change its status to democracy and, with this, came a change in my status, from being a former citizen to a reinstated citizen.

In practical terms, I could safely return home. The so-far inconceivable and long-buried hope of seeing again my family, friends, and places surfaced with unexpected vigor. I wanted to revisit my dental school, see some of my colleagues, and walk again the streets of my old neighborhood. We had been raised in a house built by our maternal grandfather on a street with only two homes in the middle of a strawberry field. Now, our street is a busy downtown where those two old homes seemed lost among larger buildings. I can tell a lot of stories connected to our street! There, I started my medical career by stitching together my brothers' cuts and dressing the wounds they sustained in our wild play. Our father had a surgical kit in the attic, a leftover from the time when he thought he would open a private office. Then, once out of universities, my brothers and I got pinned down on different jobs in different parts of the country. Each built his own family and defined his own personality, but we always cared for each other. It would be so good to meet them again after eleven years abroad and exchange notes. My parents should look older. I didn't realize how much I missed them. In fact, I missed everything from before I got married, the date when my personal Iron Curtain dropped, and, I bought a round-trip ticket to Bucuresti.

II

My brother Constantine met me at the Otopeni Airport with a unique mixture of emotion and seriousness. We hugged, and he earnestly grabbed my heaviest bag. I don't believe he smiled, but his joy was undeniable. Talking more than usual, he tried to be as useful as possible by filling me in with all the news in town.

"After the revolution, all rules collapsed. You know how strict they used to be. Well, now people park on the sidewalk, cross the continuous lines any time they feel like it, make illegal turns . . . everything goes and the police has nothing to say."

The biggest news of all was the Revolution. He was right there in the street when everything started. He saw Ceausescu boarding his helicopter from the rooftop of the Central Committee building after his failed attempt to address the crowd. He told me of the unusual things he had noticed in town. Some of them seemed significant, and I asked him for details. Then, he suddenly stopped.

"You know, I shouldn't say those things."

"They seem to be hardly a secret. Don't you have freedom now?"

"Well, things have changed, but it is a long process. You know, the more things change, the more they stay the same. I don't want any trouble. It's just not safe to talk about anything beyond trivial."

"Don't you believe in the value of truth?"

"Truth or not, it doesn't change anything other than make my life more difficult. My kids are too young . . ."

"Sorry, I understand. How are things at home?"

His speech had a hard time to come back to its original exuberance. His face was more tense, and he used more brakes in his speech. Poor man! I loved him. He parked the car in front of our parent's house, with two of its wheels on the sidewalk.

Our house was lit inside and out, as I hadn't seen since my childhood. On special occasions, all my aunts and uncles would put their resources together and organize a party until late in the night. My mother and my aunts were cooking special dishes together in our full-of-life kitchen. My father was running around joking, laughing, playing pranks, taking Aunt Maria's blood pressure, and reassuring her that 170/100 won't prevent her to have a happy life. He was the connections man, the one able to procure all kinds of rare and enjoyable things. His most appreciated gadget was a modern turntable, which could feed ten or twelve records one after the other. He had also managed to purchase a set of rare foreign records with waltzes, the lovely *Eine Kleine Nachtmusik*, and other great classical pieces. At the time of my arrival, my aunts and uncles had vanished in the land of memories. My only living aunt could not walk beyond her front door. Things were different. The lighting was not as bright as before because of a ban set by Ceausescu on bulbs more powerful than 40 watts. A younger crowd was filling the house: my brothers and their families.

They came from the front door but let my father go through and be the first to greet me. He was smaller than I remembered and slower but still in control. A man of few words, we hugged, and leaving no room for opposition, he picked up my luggage and brought it inside the house. Then I got to my brothers and sisters-in-law and their children. My mother, with her glimmering eyes, let everybody else come to me first. Watching the others' joy multiplied her happiness and rewarded her loving patience. She hugged me tenderly and then moved away to take care of something and wipe a couple of tears. Everybody was happy.

Once past this welcome, we had a moment of hesitation and slight embarrassment. From within me came the thought that we'd probably displayed too much affection. Communists don't get soft—they are always vigilant. None of us endorsed communism, but still, this was our environment. After so long, it rubs on you and seems normal. Nevertheless, I was surprised I was still under the spell of that kind of normality. Shouldn't eleven years of freedom and democracy prevent me from falling back into that mental frame?

This hesitation was quickly dispelled by the children with their curiosity—always genuine and lovely. Besides, half of my bags had gifts for them, enough to keep them busy for a while. My mother, with a sense of timing that could only be acquired through raising three boys and a husband, brought us all to the big room where the table was set for a four-course dinner, just like in the older days. At this time, she moved slower but surprisingly efficient from one task to another. She seemed even frailer and alone in that dimly lit cluttered kitchen. Her sisters didn't share the load any longer. My middle brother had provided seafood and other rarities acquired through his connections, but still, she had to cook alone. My brothers and their wives had been full time employees and had their hands full with their own households. So my relatively lonely mother put up a brave fight with the pots and pans and pulled it through.

There were other changes too. The abundance I remembered was not there any longer. It had vanished along with the exuberance of my aunts and uncles. My father firmly took his old seat at the head of the table, ahead of anybody else. He either forgot or didn't want to plug in his turntable. He waited quietly for all others to take their seats. When my mother started serving, he asked with patriarchal concern. "How many years do you still have to pay for your mortgage?"

"About twenty-five."

"You have to pay for it as soon as possible."

"I do the best I can, Father."

I took my old place at my father's right. My brothers got pretty much theirs next to their wives and constantly moving children who wanted to squeeze all the benefits from my unusual presence. From them came all the smiles and inquiries, and to them went most of my attention. Nothing is more beautiful than innocence. My mother took her place at the other end of the table, the closest to the kitchen, where she run any time she felt something was needed.

Her effort had been impressive given her age and her unmistaken willingness to see me wanting for nothing. I noticed that the room wasn't as warm as it used to be. The gas pressure had been so low that burning it in full throttle the whole day still couldn't do the job. The lighting had a wimpy yellow tint, and the food wasn't that plentiful. My mother, aware of the skimpy supply, kept running ceaselessly between the dining room and the kitchen to prevent the table from running too low. I wanted so much to take care of that table myself and see her comfortable, but of course, this wasn't possible.

The dinner didn't last as long either. My brothers and their wives had their own schedules and children to prepare for bed. Nevertheless, they didn't leave before all the dishes had been washed.

III

The next day, I took on one of my goals. I walked the route from our home to my elementary school through the same streets I had strolled forty years ago. Every home along those streets gave me a distinct feeling. Each had a story to tell. Could I recapture that? I sauntered along and observed those homes with their small yards and fences to match, most of them unchanged. I felt again their individual mysteries, the same way as in my youth. Was my memory bringing back those old feelings? Or did those homes preserve their old individuality? It was so intimate. At the end of the street stood my school, which was unchanged down to the pieces of damaged mortar on a corner. In the main hall, I saw the same clock the teacher sent us to read the time. Back then, I was scared that he would send me too and I would make a mistake. What should I say when the minute hand was between two lines? My first day in the first grade was so memorable that I remember every detail. During breaks, an old lady, with only two teeth in her mouth, would come and sell lollypops through the fence. I would buy one because others did. Otherwise, I didn't trust her; those unwrapped lollypops looked suspiciously shiny. After a good look through the grounds, I continued my walk along the streets where my friends lived and where we played up until the sixth grade, when I moved to Brasov with my uncle. In one of those intersections, my father had laid his hand on a couple of good-for-nothings who had grabbed my youngest brother's new beret and run with it. They had stopped to enjoy the trophy when my father caught up with them.

When my mother was in preschool, her father had a small warehouse on Marasesti Boulevard at the end of our street for his leather-tanning factory. On those shiny leather sheets, my uncle Constantin (the one who had been a lawyer before the communists downgraded him to a machine worker) had practiced his fighting skills to prevail against his nemesis: an older boy living two streets down. That small warehouse serves a different purpose now, but the construction looked unchanged. Close by was the Methane Gas Enterprise, where my father had managed a medical office in his younger years. The place had undergone a face-lift and a name change. It became *Distrigaz*. "There is money in gas," some say.

I walked further down Marasesti Boulevard to Carol Park, built by King Carol the First sometime before World War I, around a well-preserved natural lake. Two rows of trees much older than the park itself lined one of the park's alleys. That alley was an old route for vendors bringing in their big oak barrels mounted on carts, freshwater from the springs on Silver Knife to downtown. I believe those mounted barrels where called *sacale*. How funny that forgotten name sounds now! We, the children, organized serious fieldtrips to that park. We were irresistibly attracted to a huge grotto with waterfalls and giants carved in stone by an artist called Paciurea. From there the water slowly glided toward the lake and its several small meandering creeks. In one of the creeks, I launched the only submarine I had ever built. I liked building small boats; it carried my imagination to mysterious places. I had once even wanted to become a shipbuilder in my adult life. Two larger canals, the preferred routes for rowboats, encircled two attractive islands. One of them used to have a fascinating small mosque with an equally small minaret. The sanctity of that mosque embodied so many beliefs and dreams unknown to me that it seemed it had descended from a forgotten fairytale.

I loved that park. Then came communism, a master of destruction and a lousy builder. This centrally located park needed a new face worthy of the new political system. One by one, accidental fires destroyed the park's two pavilions built by the king. Then the mosque closed. One day, it disappeared, and its foundation was covered with sod. Then the whole park was remodeled to accommodate a Soviet-style mausoleum for the heroes of the communist party. This meant, among other changes, the disappearance of the cave and its waterfall. The cave became an underground refrigerated storage for the mummified body of Gheorghiu Dej, the communist party leader before Ceausescu. Communists loved to mummify their leaders and expose them for generations to come. The elevator built to bring Gheorghiu Dej's body for display in the mausoleum above vibrated more than it should due to a miscalculation, so the officials decided not to use it. Also, with the advent of Nicolae Ceausescu as the new communist leader, the interest in Ghorghiu Dej waned quickly, and the display was abandoned before it began. Along with those changes came the change in the park's name to the Park of Liberty—the liberty to build communism, of course.

IV

During my walks, I found some of my childhood friends and neighbors still residing in their old homes. From them I learned that after I left Romania the careers of my two brothers had been brought to a halt. My middle brother was forced to give up a university calling in Bucutesti. His professor, who was grooming him for the position of successor as chairman of the ear, nose, and throat department, found the goal unattainable because of me, a political dissident and a U.S. émigré. My brother had been left to practice medicine in the provincial town of Galati for the rest of his career.

My youngest brother, who had worked as restorer to the National Museum, was harassed for not having security clearance any longer. The museum was located across the square from the communist party's central committee, where Ceausescu had a private quarter. By communist standards, I was a traitor and a source of unwanted political ideas, which made my brother unsafe within such proximity. His boss harassed him with questions, lamentations, and insinuations until one day, my brother had had enough of it and resigned. No alternative employment was given (under communism, the state was the only employer). This way, the system couldn't even be blamed for firing him, as it couldn't be formally blamed for thwarting my middle brother's career. As usual, in these situations, our government had made my family pay for my defiance. It enticed them to despise me for what was considered a logical reaction on their part, to my disloyal and selfish. With the same move, it prevented my family from appearing as vibrant and successful as they should and showed to others what may happen to their families if they choose to defy our political system. At least, the system could show that my dissidence came from a family of average means, nothing that deserves consideration.

You cannot keep a good man down. My brothers were prevented from occupying the professional positions they deserved, but they couldn't be prevented from showing their abilities. My middle brother became a Hero of the Revolution (tax exempted for life) and a personality in Galati. My younger brother made more money than ever before by manufacturing designer leather goods and later on by doing private restorations for churches and art collectors.

Still, nobody in our family reproached me; nobody, except my father.

A couple of years earlier, I purchased for my parents a television set. One of my acquaintances who traveled back home and offered to see them called from Bucuresti to let me know that their thirty-year-old black and white TV was on its last leg. He offered to buy them a new colored one with a remote if I would reimburse him upon his return. I agreed, and he bought for them the biggest set available. As my father got older, he spent more and more time in front of the screen. It actually became his window to the world. During my visit, he thanked me several times for this television set more often than necessary and a little too rhetorically. It didn't make sense, but I thought he wanted to make sure his thankfulness came across. Thanks seldom came easily from him. I understood him better only toward the end of my visit when he once said,

"All those who immigrated to America have enriched their families back home. Only you haven't."

I silently took the blow. He did not expect an answer, only cast the blame that disquieted him for some time. It hurt. I wouldn't accuse him of any of the things I could have. He did what he thought he should and this is all that was. Who am I to ask him do anything against or beyond what he was willing to do? Still, why did he feel that way? It also hurt that I assumed the blame, as I did so many times before. Rather than seeing his injustice, I chose to share his point of view and feel his anger. He certainly thought I was better off than I really was and assumed I could do more for him. He thought I should do so because I was *his* son. Since he thought he was right, then I was wrong. Again, I wasn't good enough. Saddened to be seen as stingy or ungrateful, I chose to accept the indictment. After all, I could squeeze more money for him from my credit. I took the hit with no attempt to defend myself, as I always did, and tiptoed out of his sphere of attention saddened and back to my quiet world.

I felt again as though I had never left Romania. "Mihai doesn't have what it takes" sounded again in my ears. The communist mantra "who is not with us is against us" pushed me out into the cold again, looking inside, hungry for love. Once again being "with us" meant surrendering who I was so I could satisfy the other's requirements. My father, my uncle, the political system, my wife—all of them had criticized me so often—and I had tried to please them so often that I had forgotten how to hold out for myself, if I ever knew how. My human rights stand seemed a distant island in an ocean of appeasement.

14. "Know the Truth and the Truth Shall Set You Free"

I

I returned to California humiliated. I thought I was free only to find myself a slave to old doubts and fears. I thought I had a new life when only my environment was new. I had come to America, but I had brought my shackles with me.

Was there any hope? There must be. I had acquired the belief that life is a meaningful experience, a path to self-discovery and improvement. This means it offers answers. If only I could figure them out. Why was I not free, not even after I had run to freedom and paid for it?

II

After a long introspection, I concluded that freedom doesn't belong to a place or an external condition but to somebody's reaction to it. The physical environment is limiting and consequently not conductive to freedom. Freedom must be a feeling, a mental condition rather than a physical one. It is rather the ability to think 360 degrees in the best way you can. Sure, if one loses his physical freedom, he will probably develop a mental obsession with that loss, which is the true lack of freedom. Someone else may overcome his fixation with loss of physical freedom and be free. Through this perspective, freedom is a personal choice.

The well-known physical freedom is always limited. One may be free to go to the next town but not to the next country or planet. The mental freedom instead is limitless. So which one is the true freedom?

Think of oppression—the utmost expression of lack of freedom. Oppression is so annoying and intrusive that it captures someone's mind and thus limits his freedom of thought. Truly, the more limiting external conditions are, the more they capture one's attention and induce his loss of freedom. In a communist dictatorship, understandably, the chance for one to lose his mental freedom is much higher than under democracy. Still, no external condition, no matter how oppressive or how unobtrusive, can warrant freedom of the mind or the lack of it.

I remember a Romanian dentist whose behavior I could never understand. He had no ambition for promotion of any kind and he did apparently senseless things. For a time, he wore ribbons with the Romanian flag's colors in place of shoelaces. What kind of nonsense was that? Regular laces were handier and sturdier. Besides, he drew unwanted attention. As expected, the mayor, who by communist rules was also the communist party secretary of his area, called him.

"Comrade Doctor, we have been informed that you're wearing our flag's three colors for shoelaces."

"Yes, Comrade Mayor, and I am proud of it," the dentist said while slightly raising his chin.

"You may be proud, but other people take it as an insult to our country." The Mayor moved a pen on his desk from the right to the front.

"They are idiots, Comrade. If everybody wore these colors with the same pride as I do, this country would be a much better place," the dentist continued in a jovial demeanor.

"Yes, I know. But there are some rules here," the mayor replied in a neutral voice.

"Those rules have to be revised. I love my country, Comrade. No rule is greater than that."

"Well, it is good that you love your country, but show it in less questionable way. You may upset some people, you know. Be more political." The mayor smiled paternally.

"Can you see, Comrade?"

"Of course."

"This is very important. I can see very well. It is such a blessing to see. All right, I'll see what I can do for you." The dentist turned around before the mayor could formulate a conclusion.

A month or two later, the mayor was interrupted by the dentist in the middle of a meeting:

"Comrade Mayor, I came here to ask you to reappoint me in the most remote village in the country. Yes, send me in the Danube Delta somewhere. I want to serve my country, Comrade."

The mayor patiently took a moment to reply. "Comrade Doctor, we appreciate your zeal, but you better stay where the party appointed you. The comrades from the health department knew what they were doing."

"No Comrade, this place is too comfortable. I cannot stay here when hundreds of people suffer toothaches in isolated places," he said with a slightly dramatic accent.

"It is wonderful that you want to sacrifice your comfort for them. I will take it into consideration. Now let us continue our work here."

"That is the spirit! Thank you, Comrade. Please continue."

As expected, the mayor, who told the story with a compassionate smile, never bothered to do anything in this case. It wasn't his prerogative to reappoint a doctor, but he could convey the message to his superiors. Without a doubt, he would have beaten the drums if my fellow dentist had shown disrespect to the system, but not for a weirdo who otherwise did his job. Why the dentist had done this became apparent to me only after my visit to Romania: he bought his freedom. The officials accepted his unusual behavior, and this gave him the freedom to express more than us, the submissive ones, ever thought of. He could speak his mind to a larger extent without the fear of being taken seriously and punished. He got his ticket to a broader and bolder thinking. In fact, he fared through communism better than I did.

Freedom is personal. I lost mine during childhood when I became afraid of soldiers and authorities. That was the time when I started to hide my feelings and thoughts. Eventually I became so proficient in doing it that I became unable to show them when I should have. Pathetic, isn't it? It didn't help that during my thirty-five years under communism, I had no good role model. Everybody was hiding his true self, and by doing that everybody gradually regressed. In the middle of this mess constantly upheld through propaganda and fear, I thought I kept myself above the trend, and yet I had been as damaged as all the others. Once I freed myself from that abusive system and my abusive marriage, and after living for a while in the uninhibited California, I expected to be more like a Californian only to discover during my brief return to Romania that my expectations had been unrealistic. I was pretty much the same old Mihai. The difference was that this time, I had known uninhibited people I could to compare myself with.

III

Why couldn't I stand up to my father? Why did I feel guilty for not giving him more? I didn't owe him anything other than respect, and he certainly got from me more than that. On the other hand, I felt blasphemous for even having those thoughts. The more I pondered, the more I found my solvency to be legitimate. But then, if I didn't owe him anything, why did I feel guilty?

The answer came to me slowly and timidly: because, in front of him, I never stood up for myself, always avoided confrontations. I did that because I was afraid . . . I never put it that way before. I was afraid . . . With fear came the unwillingness to set things in motion, to disclose anything, to take charge. This is why I behaved the way I did! Gosh, I thought I was better than that. Fear prohibited me from expressing affection and thoughts. The added fear of further disappointing my father, the most important male figure in my life, made it particularly difficult to express my affection. I had a lifelong hurt for disappointing him.

If I can summon the strength to break my fear of standing up to, and being honest with my father, I would be able to break all other fears and get the chance to be as wholesome as I always wanted. If I overcome my most difficult challenge, all other challenges will become manageable. The key to any other relationship was in fact my relationship with my father.

I considered this from all angles, but the simplicity of this thought didn't entail its easy assimilation. The change of one thought brings the change of other thoughts and the demand of a whole new understanding and a new attitude. The task seemed monumental. Nevertheless, this was my only way out. I either change as I thought or stay as I was. Nobody could do it for me. So I decided to go back to Romania and do what I couldn't do before.

By the time I reached this decision, a year had gone by.

When I sat across from my father again at the dinner table, I tried to create a bonding conversation. I asked him about his beginning years as a doctor. He answered my questions with no enthusiasm. Then I changed the subject to our ancestors, but again, his replies where brief and uninvolved. His patience with my inquiry didn't last long at all. After a few questions, he put a stop to the whole thing:

"You will find all these in my files, when I'll not be around any longer."

By then he was in his early eighties. I put down my silverware and looked in his eyes. This was my time to break free:

"Dad, soon I will have to return to California. Before I go, I want you to know that I made this trip only because I wanted to be with you and Mom. I want to tell you what I wanted for a long time. I love you, Father and I love you, Mother. I am proud of everything you did for us in difficult circumstances."

My mother's eyes couldn't hold a couple of tears. My father sat unmoved in his chair, and without raising his eyes from his dish, said,

"Eat your food."

I had no doubt he meant "You eat my food."

This time, I didn't let his feelings overwhelm me. I gave him what I thought I should, and as a matter of fact, I was generous. To this, there is nothing to add or subtract, and in that moment, we both knew it.

My father got preoccupied with his dish, less confident than he wanted to appear, and I gave him the peace to do that. If I would reply, I would only hurt him with no avail. Everything had been said.

Those words marked a turning point for me, and another big step toward freedom. The spell of "Mihai cannot be more than that" dissipated. I became "more than that," and from there on, slowly and surely, I turned more like I wanted to be. I felt like I got a new lease on life, with courage and joy. My insecurities diminished, my confidence increased, and my mind seemed to sharpen. I don't believe I became all that I could have been if I would have lived under normal conditions, but I got enough in order to be happy with my progress. I regained the confidence and sense of humor, my relationship with my patients became relaxed and open, my communication with those back in Romania gradually got stress-free, and I remarried a beautiful girl.

She came as a patient, deeply concerned with a sore tooth whose symptoms nobody could explain, not even a couple of reputable specialists I personally knew. I was her last hope due to my advertising, which emphasized training abroad. She thought that I may know something those trained locally don't. Her symptoms truly seemed contradictory, and still, they must make sense. I let her speak and used that time searching for an answer until I remembered one sentence from one of my Romanian professors from long ago. That answer allowed me to relieve her pain with the simplest procedure possible in less than five minutes.

Since then, she had believed I am the best dentist there is. I didn't subscribe to this opinion, but I couldn't convince her of the contrary ither. She actually saw my heaviness, but also she felt I have a pure core buried deep inside, overwhelmed by doubts and misconceptions. She even felt she can weed out all those obstacles and invested all she had in bringing me up to par. She is my gift from God who thought I am God's gift to her.

A couple of years after that visit to Romania, my father had a stroke, which greatly reduced his mobility. He couldn't leave the house by himself any longer and lost control of some bodily functions. Then I went back in Romania and brought what I thought would make their lives easier. As I remembered, those items couldn't be found in their market. Undoubtedly, the plastic tubes, attachments, and other aids helped my mother more than anybody else. She assumed without a flinch all new duties created by my father's condition. During this visit, I also arranged for a maid to come twice a week and help with the chores, and I introduced them to a dental school classmate, then professor, to take care of their dental needs. My brothers pledged to share responsibilities, and not the least, I made sure I expressed my love for them again.

Several years later, my father had another stroke. This one came a couple of days prior to the visit of a friend of mine from California, who offered to see my parents, give them news and some money, and answer questions. When my friend arrived, Father could barely articulate his words. My friend took a digital camera from his bag.

"Dr. Ritivoi, would you like to send a message to Mihai? I can record it here if you agree."

My father couldn't say much. He approved with a small move of his head and said as clearly as he could: "Tell Mihai I love him."

By the time I received this tape, my father had gone from this world, but he didn't go before sending me that beautiful message. I took the first flight to see him one last time. From next to his coffin, I took a long look trying to match the face I saw with the man I knew, but with no luck. His features had collapsed over an empty body. He wasn't there any longer. He had been in the message recorded on that tape, filling my heart. When the time to choose came, his bitterness over unfulfilled dreams made room for that which makes life worthwhile—his love. All his life he struggled to surround himself with quality things—tools, paintings, books, carvings—only to find quality elsewhere. In the end, the matter didn't matter. What is outside of us stays outside.

If truth is that which doesn't change, then matter is an illusion and materialism a misconception. What doesn't change is the immaterial.

I love you, Father.

THE HOME OF THE HOMELESS

1. A Visit to an Old Friend

It was October 18, 1998, when during a mild and romantic Romanian Fall, I went to see my old friend, Marin Voicu, in his Bucuresti apartment. He was in his eighties by then and in poor health. From pieces of information acquired on different occasions, I had put together a picture of a weak heart helped by a pacemaker, which occasionally ran out of power, and diabetes he didn't consider to be that bad. Nevertheless, the two conditions combined made his walking difficult. These and a sense of insecurity made him give up getting out of his building in the last couple of years. There could be other issues involved he didn't consider worth mentioning. He was very particular about his self-image. He saw himself as the one who has solutions for most, if not all major social and personal problems across the world and, of course, was convinced of his righteousness. If right, why change? Changes are a nuisance. More than that, changes, in his opinion, were proof of a weak mind. Faithful to this convictions, his opinions were as inflexible as the Rock of Gibraltar. This is how I have known him for twenty years, and I have reasons to believe he had been equally inflexible for the forty years before that. In our communist past, the lack of flexibility had been a virtue.

Since no thought can leave the thinker unaffected, Mr. Voicu protected his righteousness by finding reasons to reject most of the other opinions that he had encountered throughout his life. However, he loved to be confronted with new ideas, the more the better, in order to dismiss them all and thus prove again how right he had been all along.

He had plenty of opportunities to experience the most diverse situations and opinions, and yet, they failed to move him. He went from poverty to wealth, from communism to capitalism, from tragedy to success and back. He met interesting people all along, but throughout, he maintained the same set of opinions.

This lack of flexibility was the main reason for my visit. Mr. Voicu used to have an opulent lifestyle in California before he had retired in that modest apartment in Romania four years earlier. This big change could have made him see certain things differently. If he had, it would mean so much for both of us. For him, a sign of flexibility would mean a huge step forward. For me, I would be happy to see him break that sound barrier. Also, deep in my heart, his change would be a satisfying defeat of a communist trademark—self-righteousness.

Karl Marx, the communist founder, was the ultimate self-righteous. His combination of leftist extremism, philosophical reputation, and lack of flexibility attracted like a magnet like-minded characters who upheld Marxism as the highest justification for their propensity. Marxism is communism's legitimacy. For this reason, it is held as an unfailing, absolute truth. In order to match this vision of truth to real life, the communists changed the definition of rights, freedom, love, democracy, and in general, moral values, in ways that would fit the Marxist meaning. Then they started to vehemently demand that everybody under their control accept their revised definitions and their self-righteousness as justified. We were all supposed to believe what the communists believed so that shoulder-to-shoulder we would all march toward the same utopian future. In front of this terrible steamroller of compulsory changes, advanced by indoctrination and fear, people retreated to their personal and lonely citadels: their own minds. There, they resisted the continuous and concentric brainwashing attacks for as long as they could.

Our lonely resistance worked for the short term, but in the long run, isolated and confused, we started to drift into personal versions of reality. For those who don't know, in order to consolidate its power, communism frightened and isolated its subjects. Afraid to talk, unable to trust, and brainwashed, we, the subjects, were unable to validate our ideas and consequently started to slip either into insecurity or into our own self-righteousness or into any combination of the two. Few had the ability to resist. I wish I were one of them, but I was too unprepared for the task and too young to know. As an adult, I immigrated to the United States, where gradually I started to reach my potential. In the end, I was left with disdain for self-righteousness. I assume this is why I always wanted so much to see others breaking free from this condition.

The taxi stopped next to his apartment building of a standard, unimaginative design, typical of the communist era. In front of the building was a small square park, poorly maintained, of which Mr. Voicu didn't fail to praise every time he mentioned his residence.

It started to get dark, and I became concerned that I might not be able to read the list of residents usually posted at the bottom of the staircase. The lighting on the stairs was a perennial problem in these buildings, as it was never enough and never predictable. I should have had the foresight to bring a flashlight.

I passed the building's main door, and I looked around the small landing at the bottom of the stairs. No tenants list was posted. I warily had to rely on the directions Mr. Voicu gave me on the phone, which were so detailed that they impaired clarity. Carefully feeling the stairs, I walked to the second floor and rang the bell to the first door on the left.

Mr. Voicu's unkempt hair and unshaven beard appeared in the crack of the door. When he saw me, he smiled and opened it all the way.

"Dr. Ritivoi, you've made it!"

"A victory over darkness! Glad to see you after such a long time." A broad smile flew across my face. "Did anybody consider some lighting on this staircase?" I pointed with my thumb over my shoulder at the darkness behind.

"Yes, they did. Occasionally somebody steals a bulb; otherwise, it's okay. If you press this button, the light comes on long enough to get into the street." Mr. Voicu pointed to a button not far from his doorbell and not too different looking either.

"I didn't see it downstairs. Maybe I confused it for a doorbell," I said while stepping inside.

"Unlikely. We don't have one downstairs, only from the second floor and up. Downstairs you have to rely on the light from the street.

It's for the kids so they won't play there. Let them go outside . . ." Mr. Voicu locked the door behind us and fastened his robe to keep it from sliding off his protruding belly.

"You have a nice place," I said as I stepped from the vestibule to his unusually large living room.

"It came out well. I knocked down a wall between two smaller rooms. This is where I spend most of my time. I have a bedroom there," he pointed to the far wall, "and a full bathroom next to it, and a kitchen. This is all I need," he said, avoiding my eyes.

"It is a good arrangement. Nevertheless, it's not like what you had in Los Angeles, on Mount Olympus."

"Nooo, that one was too big. I sold it long ago." He took an inquisitive look around the room. "Do you know what I'm writing now? I am translating this book about communism from English to Romanian. I know you don't like it, but this book poses a very interesting angle. Sit down, please." He showed me a couch on my right and pulled a chair for himself. His right shin had a rather large ulcer that didn't seem to heal.

"I've had this for a while." Mr. Voicu noticed my glimpse and looked inquisitively at his wound. "I keep it uncovered so it can crust over. I've got this frinch crème now. It is supposed to work well."

"Medication is improving all the time. Now use it as recommended, or you may not reap all the benefits." He wasn't good at following instructions; probably my advice wouldn't change a thing. He was still a dreamer: a crème can't dry it out. It may help in other areas, but it doesn't dry anything. I switched my attention from his troubled leg, and perking my tone a notch, I said, "Well, I assume that you have finished your memoir. I would like to buy a copy."

"No, not yet. Now I am excited about this translation. It's an interesting book." Mr. Voicu moved his hand in the general direction of his desk.

"But communism is dead. I was informed that Romanians don't like to look back." I couldn't refrain from objecting.

"It may be dying, but it's not dead. It survived in East Asia, and it is favored in Latin America and among the poor. Even the academic circles consider it as feasible, you know . . . it's not eliminated as a valid ideology. People still look for an alternative to capitalism. You'd be surprised how many are still interested in it. This book I've started to translate is a classic," Mr. Voicu said without any concern for communism's failures. If the idea were interesting to him, he assumed it should be interesting to others. "It has some excellent points. Look at what this so-called freedom has brought to our country. It is worse now than it was under Ceausescu. People are really suffering . . . They have to know what they are missing."

"I would rather show them the beauty of what they will be getting," I said.

"What beauty?" He raised his shoulders in hopelessness. "There is more poverty now than there was before."

"There are more opportunities too . . ."

"Oh, sure! Opportunities for charlatans ." Mr. Voicu's eyes lit with anger.

"Charlatans bred under communism." I said and looked him straight into his eyes. "A change in a political system doesn't automatically bring a change into people's mentality. It takes time. People here still want to be told what to do, are still afraid of taking charge, still hoard everything they can put their hands on, and still don't trust anybody. They still bribe and steal. People survive now the way they learned to survive then."

"You cannot overlook that communism reduced the disparity between the rich and the poor. This already solved one of society's problems."

"Mr. Voicu, I don't know what problems Karl Marx wanted to solve, his or others'. He was a misfit. But let's admit he was concerned with social equity. What I saw was the communist leaders' attempt to artificially level the lives of people who had different needs and abilities. This uniformity was achieved while the leaders retained all the privileges for themselves. Ceausescu surpassed any king in history. The principle of equality was applied to others only. Isn't this a denial of the very goal they claimed to pursue?"

"Dr. Ritivoi, you don't see the forest because of one tree. He generated a system where the difference between the highest and the lowest income was no bigger than five times. This generated a lot of peace."

"The highest paid being the security and repression apparatus," I added.

"The highest paid in the United States are the football players. So what's the difference? Neither are scientists."

"I thought the highest paid are the money lenders." I tried to lighten the situation.

"This is besides the point. The goal is still fairness."

"All right, and what did this fairness accomplish? Make those with lower skills feel psychologically better? From my observation, it frustrated those who were not allowed to advance as they could have and it undermined the motivation of those who were supposed to create and produce. So what should the goal be, then? To allow people to create and enjoy the benefits of their abilities, or to level their income? Maybe communism should concern itself with growth instead of uniformity."

"Growth requires guidance," Mr. Voicu said quietly.

"Fulfillment has other sources than guidance. Someone doesn't need government control nor financial uniformity to love or be happy."

"Love and happiness are personal matters. Social matters are different; they require government, laws, and resources," Mr. Voicu answered promptly.

"And did communism provide those resources? It just collapsed because it couldn't provide them," I said.

"This is a young system that needs time to perfect itself. Social fairness still can be achieved."

"Mr. Voicu, you are an idealistic materialist. How you combine the two, only you know."

"If social engineering cannot fix our social problems, what can?"

"Love."

"And how can people be made to love?" He asked and stood transfixed for a moment with his eye wildly opened.

"They cannot."

"You see . . ." he finally moved.

"People on their own, can. Social solutions are the sum of personal solutions. A successful society requires members with a wholesome value system, healthy mentality, spiritual awareness . . ." I said slowly.

"Sure, let's wait now until all get enlightened! I know your opinions. We have discussed these before. You see things differently. Many do. Nevertheless, I believe our country missed a good opportunity," he said while looking at his bad leg.

I didn't come to let him escape using that kind of argument. I bent forward while resting my elbows on my knees.

"Good opportunities come from good judgments and a healthy value system." I directed at him. "Communism, meanwhile, didn't excel in either one. It's basically a misjudgment, and it pursues contradictory goals. If you remember, morality is relative to them, it is class-related. So, whatever decisions the communist leaders made, they were assumed to be in the working class' favor and consequently considered moral. The communists were, supposedly, on the right side of history. Whatever serves their interests is considered good; lying, cheating, and killing included. This made the use of coercion and the reformulation of values not only possible but also necessary in order to justify all their abuses and create an illusion of hope." I caught his attention, and then I continued, "Once you accept that morality is relative, nothing can stop someone from believing that it is not only class-related but individually related as well. Along this line, whatever someone can justify, from his perspective, is moral. Correct? You see, it's getting chaotic; and this requires coercion in order to maintain an appearance of normalcy. As a matter of fact, the communist system runs in a vicious circle: it uses coercion to succeed and succeeds because it uses coercion. True normalcy is out of question in this condition. It's quite obvious that we built our country on one's questionable rationality. This being said, what outcome could be expected from this mess? Do you truly believe that communism could prevail over western democracies?"

"If done right, it could. I know you don't like the word 'right.'" He rearranged himself in his chair and pulled his housecoat forward.

"Remember how you used to live in California? The lifestyle, the quality of information, the opportunities . . ."

"Well, I know . . ."

"You always praised Romania over the United States. Fine. Now that you are in Romania, do you really believe this is a better place?"

Mr. Voicu laid back in his chair. His housecoat slid sideways again. After a moment of introspection, he said slowly. "My neighbors believe there is something wrong with me because I came here while most Romanians would like to be in the United States. I know, but they don't know what I know."

"You don't know what they know either."

"We all have our understanding of things." Then, he suddenly changed the subject. "Let me give you my own blend of drinks." He got up and took a couple of steps toward the refrigerator then stopped after a couple of steps and turned towards me. "Tell me if you like it. It is orange juice with *tsuica* [Romanian prune brandy] and *Fanta*. Fanta is a carbonated drink they sell here—a little sweet." He took a plastic bottle from the refrigerator, filled two glasses with its yellow liquid, gave me one, and watched with interest as I tasted it. "It's pretty good, isn't it?"

I had hoped that, by comparing his former rich life in the United States with the modest one he had in Romania, I would get from him a rare appreciation for the former, but I didn't.

"Yes, it is very good."

A spark lit in his eyes. "It has everything in it: vitamins, carbonation, and taste. You want more?" He tentatively raised the plastic bottle.

That crude comparison of his life in Los Angeles versus what he had in Bucuresti was the strongest argument I had. If that one didn't work, none would.

"Oh no, thanks. It's good, but I have a heavy day. I couldn't take too many days away from work back in California, so I overloaded my schedule." After a brief break I continued. "Mr. Voicu, I have always found your life experiences very interesting. Would you have any objections to use any elements from your stories for my own writings? I'm contemplating to write about the impact of communism in our lives."

Mr. Voicu moved uncomfortably in his chair. "I don't want you to suck the air out of my own memoir. Let me publish mine first. After that, you may feel free as long as you take only bits and pieces."

"Of course. This is only an intention so far. I didn't write anything yet, so you have plenty of time to publish yours. I need only some supporting events from your life."

Mr. Voicu showed me the bottle with an inviting gesture, and when I refused with a slight rise of my hand, he poured another glass for himself. Looking at his glass, he finally said. "The way I know you, you are going to criticize them . . . They weren't that bad, you know. Anyway, I shouldn't tell you what to do."

We discussed for a while the subjects of his choice: his attempt to get back his family's properties, his health served so well by the Romanian doctors, his routine, etc. He didn't ask anything about Southern California, where he used to live. With that, I concluded my visit. I didn't know that would be the last time I would see him. He had a heart attack a year later, before he could publish his memoir.

He didn't publish anything. I believe he never intended to. His true goal was to prove his point to himself. Others could come with observations and criticisms and spoil the image of pristine righteousness he wanted so hard to uphold. I believe his self-esteem depended on being right.

2. A Side Effect

An old saying says, "Moderation is the key to success." We want to be free, and at the same time, we look for firm guidelines. We want to be right but also open to new discoveries. We want to explore, but we love a place to call "home." With these in mind, the key to success seems to be a fine balance between opposing values. When we lose this balance, we slide toward extremes, which often leads to fundamentalism. The less educated, the more chances exist for someone to miss this balance and become a fundamentalist. Fundamentalism confers a soothing sense of surety after all; false, but reassuring.

The one fundamentalism I am quite familiar with is communism. Karl Marx, its founder, was an obsessed self-righteous. He guarded his theory to the last detail with everything he had: fits, accusations, ridicule of those who dared to differ from his opinions, arguments, writings, manipulations, etc. It is apparent to me that this vehement self-righteousness is was what Lenin and other like-minded revolutionaries shared wholeheartedly. In their state of being semi-educated young men animated by political fervor, all they needed was a philosopher who supported their preexistent revolutionary impulses in a seemingly scientific way. Then, they found Karl Marx, who offered all the above plus the endorsement of their rage to boot. A philosophical quality had thus been cast over their violent tendencies, and the world never looked the same since. Rebels of all kinds adopted this newly found superior authority to justify all they did and called themselves communists, Reds, Maoists, or any other related name. They took over the shaky Russian empire, and from there, communism was abusively spread over large parts of the world. Along with this authority came the newly legitimized self-righteousness. Every communist leader, from the national party secretary to the last guerilla commander, used it as a prerogative.

From the leaders, self-righteousness spread to the communist apparatus known in Romania as the "party's active." It proved to be a trendy little trick that justified its user's doings, enhanced his sense of security, and helped him elbow his way around. Being used by the leaders, such a questionable practice achieved recognition, and it didn't take long before the public found it useful too.

We shouldn't underestimate the attraction this easy way of gaining an illusion of confidence can have over the tedious work of self-improvement. This cheap substitution had been facilitated in communism, as mentioned before, by its moral relativism and the lack of proper guidance. For total domination, our communist system systematically compromised all available support systems: family, church, traditions, unbiased publications, friendships, and organizations. All we had left to rely upon was self-reliance, which, under those conditions, also led to self-righteousness.

With everything crumbling around, the only person someone could rely on was himself. The lonely citizen who couldn't trust anybody had to be right in order to resist his own deconstruction, survive the indoctrination, and claim his embattled uniqueness. In communist thinking, the only personal value comes from the obedience to its doctrinal rules. For communists, willingness to obey is proof of enlightenment and reliability. It means the assimilation of Marxist principles—the understanding that society is run by "objective" historical laws—external to humans and thus out of human control. Individual actions in disaccord with these laws are simply temporary inconveniences that everybody should better avoid. Moreover, these temporary inconveniences hold the whole country back, and this makes them national crimes.

A major counterproductive effect of this theory is that it takes away our importance as unique individual human beings and deprives us of our freedom of choice. Nevertheless, the communist kind of political correctness demands the acceptance of that diminished importance, to settle for being robots of history. In Marxist interpretation, personalities don't make history; history makes personalities. Of course, Marx argued that in communism, we will have the freedom to create and achieve our highest potential (a striking reminder of the 1960's drug culture's claim). As it turned out, our reduced importance did matter after all: it prohibited our highest potential to materialize.

Communism doesn't only reduce our importance; it also decides who we should be and what the communist prototype of "advanced" citizens should look like. We tried to look acceptable for the photo ops, some more than others. Because we had been treated as someone we were not, we instinctively searched for what we had been denied: our identities, dignity, and importance. People hunkered down during the Stalinist terror. But afterward, as the system perfected its grip on power and started to show some flexibility, things changed. Individuality started to assert itself. People pursued personal goals. If this required lip service, so be it. It was barely noticed that, in time, the appearance of compliance led to real compliance and to a strange bond with the power they hated. Also, by living within the system for a while, people became more familiar with its workings and learned how to use it to their benefit. Thus, a new lifestyle was born.

In Romania, I was annoyed by people's desires to explain everything, to show their personal understanding of all kinds of petty matters. It seemed to me they did that in order to overcome their rubberstamp image. Obviously, nobody was foolish enough to tangle with communist fundamentals. By stopping at subliminal hints, people prevented themselves from developing a deeper understanding of their condition.

While the communist system required submission and adoption of communist ideology by all, those actions were damaging to communism itself. The state of "unleashed human creativity" foreseen by Marx could not be achieved as long as people's access to information was curtailed. Quality intellectuals and motivated people needed for economic success were impossible to groom as long as they were subjected to fear, suspicion, abuse, and regimentation.

Even under ideal conditions, the communist centralized, bureaucratic economic structure was too rigid to successfully compete in the global market. Still, the communist goal, as stated in its bylaws, was to be spread worldwide. The solution for its international success was the same one that had been used in succeeding internally: the elimination of the competitor. In the class conflict between the working class and the business owners, Marx' solution was the elimination of the latter. In the wider conflict between communism and capitalism, the solution should be similar. Take out the opponent and there's no conflict any longer. It's obvious that this vision requires a large dose of self-righteousness.

In its relentless pursuit of control the communist system, as I mentioned earlier, carefully removed any support system that could aid individual resistance. People had been conditioned to hide their most meaningful thoughts. They greeted each other, exchanged simple messages, and went on their way, alone with their thoughts and beliefs. Naturally, the consequence of this isolation was stagnation, mistrust, misconceptions, miscommunication, lower productivity, psychological problems, and everything related. To prove this point, all Romanian celebrities manifested their abilities either before communism or in exile and none within the system.

To me, the communist sinister legacy doesn't lie as much in how many people it exterminated, but with what it did to those left alive. All the fear, psychological manipulation, deprivation, indoctrination, denial of knowledge, glorification of brutal force, and so forth drastically minimized people.

3. MR. VOICU

In December, 1978, when he greeted us at the Los Angeles airport, our American sponsor gave us a list of successful Romanians whom we might want to meet. Among them were a couple of practicing dentists, who could introduce me to the licensing process, and Mr. Voicu, whose name struck a chord with me. A few years earlier, a man named Voicu fled Romania in a utility airplane. We had few such vehicles since, at the end of World War Two, the Soviet Union prohibited us from producing airplanes any longer. The Mr. Voicu I had in mind made an arrangement with the pilot, who also took his own family on board before taking off. It was the first such border escape that we had heard of, and it drew attention.

Romania was surrounded by communist countries at that time. The shortest route to reach a Western democracy went through either Yugoslavia or Hungary, which implied risks. The pilot flew low over Hungary to avoid radar detection; nevertheless, the Hungarian defense was alerted. It dispatched a MIG (a Soviet-made fighter jet) to control the situation. Voicu's pilot was asked to land, which meant they'd be returned to Romania and face the consequences. The group preferred to take the risk. There was the chance that Hungarians would figure out they were fugitives with no interest in Hungarian affairs and let them escape rather than shoot them down. The Romanians' desire to flee communism was common knowledge at that time. With the MIG flying in circles, they crossed into Austria and, out of gas, landed in a potato field.

There were so many unexpected and creative ways our countrymen used to run away that someone could make a new book with stories like the One Thousand and One Nights . If nothing more, we could look forward to sharing some good stories with Mr. Voicu.

"He made a fortune on real estate," our sponsor said. "Some made good money buying rundown homes, fixing and reselling them at higher prices, or renting, of course. It's a good idea to see him; you may get a job. I paid your rent for one month. I cannot afford more than that. So you're responsible from next month on. I talked to somebody to bring you to the Welfare Office, but you still have to figure out what you want to do. This is a free country!"

All those from our sponsor's list had been known for their willingness to help, with Mr. Voicu topping them. We were told that the newcomers had been for him an irreplaceable source of fresh news from back home and an opportunity for an exciting debate on trends and events.

Within days of my arrival, I was through with sampling America by exploring all the stores and streets in the neighborhood and was ripe for expanding my horizons. What better way to do that than to use my sponsor's list? Anxious to get started with my new life, I made my first calls to the Romanian dentists. They had been extremely helpful in getting me started on the path to the National Board exams. Before meeting them, I had no idea whom to call and what to do to achieve my California dental license.

Then I called Mr. Voicu. He showed little need for an elaborate introduction.

"You know what," he said after the first round of talk, "come Saturday with your family for dinner. We will have plenty of time to share notes."

The following Saturday I was looking for his residence on Mount Olympus Drive. For the ancient Greeks, Mount Olympus was the residence of the gods. I found it a little too bold to simply apply that name to a residential street, but this was America. When I rang the bell a heavyset man in his early fifties, with medium height and thinning hair, opened the door with a smile. The feature that first caught my attention was his lips, which were of average width but with little consistency.

"Mr. Voicu?"

"Dr. Ritivoi? Mrs. Ritivoi, I assume. Welcome!"

He showed us to the living room where a huge window on the left, taking most of the wall, overlooked the city of Los Angeles. In front of the window and about six feet awaywas a long coffee table with several crystal bowls filled with nuts and crackers. At each end of the table a large armchair inspired comfort. Behind the coffee table, on the right, a couple of couches faced the window. Behind the couches and three or four steps higher stretched the second half of the room with its massive dining table of carved wood, cushioned chairs, and several pieces of assorted furniture. Within easy access from the table, catered food kept warm in an inviting display spread its discrete aroma through shiny covers. The room's upper level could be accessed from both the near and the far end of the lower section, whose last obvious detail was a well-supplied bar set against the far wall.

Mr. Voicu showed us to the couches and took a seat in the armchair closest to the entrance.

"When did you arrive in California?" He lay back, leaning to the right with his legs crossed and fingertips touching across his belly. He seemed so comfortable that he could have been born in that position. From that angle, he could comfortably carry his conversation and glimpse the panoramic view virtually at the same time.

"Not long ago, about a week," my wife Adriana answered from her armchair at the far end of the coffee table in front of the bar. She sat erect on the edge of the chair with her hands clasped in her lap.

"You probably stayed in one of the European refugee camps before coming." Mr. Voicu briefly searched our faces.

"Yes, we spent about three months in Traiskirchen. I guess this is a standard procedure," Adriana said.

"Yes, Austria is popular. I came through Italy. They had a refugee camp at Latina, close to Rome. We had a lot of freedom there," he said, sketching an open gesture.

"Once we got our IDs, we could get out of the camp anytime. Mihai worked as a bus boy in Baden," Adriana added.

"We've all had a humble beginning in the free world. I walked dogs, something I had never dreamed of in my life." Mr. Voicu arose from his chair and walked to the bar. "Mrs. Ritivoi, what can I tempt you with?" he asked. "This Grand Marnier is appreciated around here. You may like to try it. Dr. Ritivoi, this is a great cognac, unless you prefer something else, of course."

All those brand names were as exotic to us as they were unknown, so we accepted what was offered. Mr. Voicu then filled a glass for himself and relaxed back in his armchair. "How do you like California so far?" He savored a sip of cognac.

"I believe it is a great place. The weather is the most impressive," Adriana said.

"So far we have spent most of our time in different government offices and meeting people." I felt I should be more specific. "Other than that, I mostly checked out the neighborhood on foot. Walking is a wonderful way to feel the town. My first surprise, if you want, was how many cheap products there are for such a wealthy country."

"Mihai, you cannot say that." Adriana interfered. "They have everything for everybody. I am sure you can find the quality you want in better neighborhoods at higher prices."

"I'm sure. I only thought that in capitalism everything is better than what we had."

"You haven't seen anything yet," Mr. Voicu said placidly.

"I have in mind some overly ornate sofas in a furniture store on Pacific Boulevard. When you sit on them, you sink too low. You can even feel the wooden frame."

"Well, some people prefer this combination." Adriana interrupted me impatiently.

"I understand, but nothing is more pitiful than the combination of pretentious design and low quality. This intrigues me. How can a professional furniture maker consent to such a compromise? Of course, inexpensive items are necessary as well," I said, uncertain of the quality of my reasoning.

"Your standards are not everybody's standards. This is America. You are one of many, not the voice of authority. You're not even a dentist. You are nobody. Don't tell people how to do their job now. Romania is far away, *capisci*?" Adriana nervously tried to conclude the subject.

"Here they produce everything that sells—pompous or not. Good taste is not an issue. It's not even politically correct to mention it," Mr. Voicu said, lowering the corners of his mouth with disapproval. "There is more to find, Mrs. Ritivoi. This is a country of contrasts; a lot of times it is hard to make sense of it. I apologize for my impatience, but can you give me some news from Romania? I am still interested in how the life is there. Tell me, please, how you got out to begin with. That is never easy." He savored again the cognac from his glass. I politely did the same and set my glass on the coffee table.

Among Romanian émigrés, the story of how somebody managed to *get out* is always interesting. People had to be bold and imaginative or they would never escape our communist grasp.

"It was a long struggle, in which Adriana played an important role. Before we begin, tell me, are you the Voicu who fled the country in a utility plane?"

Mr. Voicu smiled. "That is quite a story, but no. That is another Voicu. I didn't have to go to that extreme. I drove. I'll tell you later, but let's hear your story first. It seems to be much more interesting."

This was an ideal opportunity for Adriana to indulge in the long version of our fight to get out of the country, the most important event in our life and Adriana's preferred subject. It was her boldness that got us out in the end. She moved back in her chair and started telling how we came to sign Paul Goma's letter to General Secretary Ceausescu, demanding what we assumed had been our human rights, and everything that followed.

II

"Paul Goma is a weird character as far as I know," Mr. Voicu said when Adriana's tale came to an end. "No offence, but what normal person would challenge such a sturdy political system like communism?" He raised his shoulders in disbelieve.

"We have been accused of Don Quixotism before," Adriana answered promptly. "If you don't stand for what you believe, then what do you stand for in this life?"

"I don't underestimate your courage, but your signature on his letter couldn't change anything. It is not enough to matter there. You're lucky you got out, but you also could have easily gotten into deep trouble for nothing. I wouldn't risk my life for that signature. Again, you're lucky you got out. In regard to Goma, well . . . he is a controversial figure. I wouldn't trust him in such a delicate matter as political dissidence." Mr. Voicu got up from his armchair. "More liquor, Mrs. Ritivoi? Dr. Ritivoi?"

"No, thank you. I'd like to finish this one first." Adriana accompanied her refusal with a slight gesture.

"Maybe later, thank you," I said, and raising my voice a bit, I added, "You have to trust somebody. In certain instances, you have to trust even those you don't trust. Certainly, what we did implied a risk, but it was a risk worth taking. Of course, we took precautions."

Mr. Voicu refilled his glass, took a sip, and said satisfied, "Sorry to disagree, but no precautions are enough in this situation."

"Precautions are not the issue here." Adriana could barely hide her irritation. "Making a difference is. We didn't hope to change the system with our signatures, but we proved that subjection is not the only viable choice we had and that fear can be overridden. This matters!"

It was obvious that Mr. Voicu didn't see what difference we'd made with those signatures. He used the short pause that followed to get up from his armchair and show us to the dining table. We dutifully took our half-empty glasses with us and sat where shown in the elevated half of the room. From up close, the food in the warmer smelled most tantalizing. Raising the shining lids was suggestive of the emotion in raising the curtain in a long-awaited play. There were dishes I had never seen before, all fresh and delicious. I filled my plate and I kept thinking of the Paul Goma episode.

To this day, I have never heard a Romanian acknowledge him. People either avoided the subject or complained of some flaws in Mr.

Goma's character, ways, or writings. What a pity. Even if Mr. Goma were flawed, which was never apparent to me, couldn't anybody recognize the value of this first public criticism of the communist system in our country? Why could no Romanian acknowledge his merit?

How deeply communism had affected our minds! The communists justified their claim to power by criticizing anybody who challenged them. By putting everybody else down, they could stand up. I felt that people applied the same cheap tactic to Goma. Was he too high? Let's bring him down, or at least ignore him.

People would prefer to prove their righteousness in any imaginable way rather than admit they didn't rise to the occasion. At that stage of the game, we got so accustomed to communism that as a whole, we preferred to cope rather than challenge it. This accommodation had been considered a form of wisdom . . . certainly a survival skill. To no one's surprise, physical survival is all that matters for a materialist.

I returned to my seat with a dish full of steaming exotic Chinese food and started to diligently enjoy it. "It's very good." After a couple of bites, I looked at our host and said, "Going back to Paul Goma, he signifies an historical moment. He had the courage to do what nobody could do before him. He was the precursor to bigger oppositional movements. Did you hear about the massive coal miners' strike in Valea Jiului?"

"I did. But they didn't change anything, did they?" Mr. Voicu said, unabated.

"Not yet. Even if we assume they never will, I believe it is a huge personal accomplishment to break the chain of fear and speak your mind. This is freedom," I said as I resumed eating.

"Well, the miners had several days of feeling great. After that, they had the noose tightened. They have been relocated, isolated, and closely monitored. None of the promises given under duress have been kept."

"This is the Marxist morality. What's good for their system is good, period." Adriana interfered casually.

"Their leaders disappeared," Mr. Voicu continued unabatedly, "and their workplace had been flooded with Securitate. Did they achieve anything? Did the miners continue to feel great after that? I don't think so. As a matter of fact, they may now regret the strike." Mr. Voicu said while holding his fork still with its tips up .

"No one forgets the taste of freedom. As for their achievement, that is proof that the system is vulnerable, that fear is not justified." Adriana looked at him, red-faced.

"I lived there through hard times, and I was never afraid," Mr. Voicu said. "I didn't feel chained. It is true that I got out, but I am not quite sure this was a good decision. I had a pretty good life there."

"If you had a privileged position, you could feel pretty good, no doubt. You probably didn't live through the austerity period," I said as I pushed my chair aside to refill my plate.

"No, Dr. Ritivoi, but I didn't live in constant danger of lawsuits that we have here either. Wait until you open your dental office and you'll see. Every patient stepping into your office is a potential lawsuit, no matter how well you treat him. Everything you'll do to him will aim at preventing legal problems. Professionalism becomes a side effect of your legal concerns. What kind of life is this? Isn't this living in constant fear?"

III

"Don't you idealize life under communism?" Adriana asked.

"Not at all. I am aware of their mistakes. They confiscated my family's property. We had a lot of good agricultural land . . . they confiscated a way of life as a matter of fact. My father was the unofficial leader of the town of Tuza, if you remember. It was more like a large village with some stores on the main street. Only later, they built some economic units, a small factory, repair shops, and so forth. It used to be an idyllic place . . . I mean, before. Anybody who had a problem could come to my father for help and advice. He earned enough not to need anything from anybody. He was well respected for that.

"When the communists came to expropriate us, the whole village surrounded our house and didn't let them come through. My father advised people to go home because they could not prevent it from happening. Moreover, if they resisted, the communists would come back with re-enforcements and make it more painful for everybody. But people didn't want to go. It was their value system at stake too.

Obviously, the people couldn't win. What they could do under the King couldn't be done under the communists. One day, about three o'clock in the morning, a couple of cars came from the dark and picked up my father from his bed. He never returned.

"They sent him to forced labor, without trial. There he had to dig dirt at the same rate as a healthy laborer in order to earn his food. But he was older and physically unfit for this type of work. The common communist attitude was that those who belonged to the upper class should be subjected to the same conditions as the working class so that they could see for themselves how unfair they had been. That was pure hate . . . , a thinly veiled assassination.

"How can I idealize communism? I don't, but capitalism is not any fairer. It doesn't kill, but it squeezes out of people everything that can be squeezed before letting them die of natural causes." He looked through the window at the warm evening colors shrouding the city. His face had a younger glow, like stepping back in time.

"We don't expect to have it easy," Adriana replied. "We just don't believe in communism and don't want to live as they want us to live. There is so much more available here. If you don't like it in this country my advice would be to make up your mind and choose one of the two systems. There is no other system available in the modern world."

"Mr. Voicu, how can you appreciate communism after everything they did to your family?" I asked, impressed by his story.

"I don't appreciate them for the harm they caused, obviously. I only recognize the good they could accomplish with all the means at their disposal. I appreciate the principles they upheld."

"We are dissatisfied with what they did too, so we may conclude that we agree on this point," I added before Adriana could say something. "As for communist principles, I believe they are deeply flawed."

"It is what they can do that drove us out of that land of *Popular Democracy*," Adriana said, nevertheless. "In my opinion, everybody should take a stand against communism's abuses."

"Mrs. Ritivoi, you ask for too much. Everyone is a potential killer. If given the proper opportunity, anyone could revert to violence in order to achieve a goal he considers worthwhile, be it communism or not. You know, Nazi Germans killed millions of Jews because they thought they should, and communist Jews killed tens of millions of common citizens of the Soviet Union because they thought they should too. The only difference is that in the Soviet Union nobody had been held responsible."

"The difference is that communists have crime and violence written into their instructions." Adriana set her silverware on the table and rested back with the most serious look. "It is a calculated way of governing, empowered by resentment and justified by self-righteousness. This is the only way they understand it to be. Stalin directed the massacre of about sixty million people, Mao is responsible for another seventy million, the Khmer Rouge killed about one-fourth of the Cambodian population in four years, and so forth. The information is still available. We are living in a world disappointedly resilient to the truth. Communists couldn't do and will not do any better than they have already done. This is the limit of their understanding, of their abilities."

"I know those things, Mrs. Ritivoi, don't misunderstand me. I am only saying that with so much power they could do better. If I admire anything, it is their pursuit of social justice. That they didn't achieve it as they thought they would is a different issue."

"How can they succeed with such idiots at the helm?" Adriana continued.

"I wouldn't call Karl Marx an idiot, and neither Lenin or Trotsky or even Ceausescu," Mr. Voicu said. His eyes left the scene of the city and looked across the table at Adriana.

"Do you believe that such a monstrosity as communism is the product of intelligence?" Adriana said, playing with a crease of her napkin. "I would assume that the results are the reflection of the mind that produced those ideas. The whole thing is a misconception of a misdirected mind."

"Well, they had good intentions and good reasoning, but they went terribly wrong along the way. That was a tumultuous time, no doubt. Then we had the Russian occupiers who ran the show their way. But once the Russian advisors and the Russian army withdrew, things gradually improved and could still improve. You don't know this, but the communists killed my innocent wife, and I am still not angry with them. It may sound strange to you . . . I loved her. Before I tell you the story, would you like to go back to the couch downstairs? It is more comfortable, and we can enjoy the view better. In the evening it gets beautiful."

Adriana and I took our glasses and moved back to the coffee table in the lower section of the room in the seats we had before. Mr. Voicu offered new drinks. We declined and said we'll finish what we still hve, so he filled a glass for himself and returned to his armchair. With the brandy in hand, he let his sight get lost in the horizon, then started:

"I always wanted to be a medical doctor," he said, "but it didn't turn out that way. I got admitted to medical school back in '48. One day, in the beginning of my freshman year, I attended a basketball game between the IMF [the Institute of Medicine and Pharmacy] and the Polytechnic Institute. We had a strong woman's team hopeful of winning the University Cup. The Polytechnic team had been our main opponent, so we all went there to support our girls. This is when I saw the girl I could never forget. She was the captain of the Polytechnic basketball team and the chief of her class . . . the best and the most beautiful. From that moment on, I had never wanted anything from this life other than to be with her. At that time, it was possible to take some tests and get transferred from one school to another, provided you had high grades upon admittance. I hit the books like never before. She was a freshman too, and when I got the transfer, I landed in the same class as hers.

"You cannot imagine my happiness of being able to see her every day in school. Simona was her name. I don't think my presence had mattered to her. In my eyes, she was as high as the ancient gods: beautiful, busy, organized, intelligent. I floated somewhere outside her interests. My greatest achievement was to have her accept my offer for a ski trip to Predeal. Simona skied much better than I, useless to say. In the evening upon our return, we found the door of her flat sealed and a note posted for her to come to the Securitate headquarters as soon as possible. She rang the doorbell, hoping against all odds that somebody would answer. No response. No doubt the Securitate had detained her parents.

"Being picked up in the middle of the night had been the fear of any successful person at that time. Those who had done well under our former democratic system were considered class enemies. You have certainly heard of former officials, politicians, and higher officers being sent to detention and labor camps. The communists wanted no physical or ideological opposition, be it real or only possible. They didn't take any chances. You probably heard of these things from your parents."

"Of course," Adriana said, stone-faced.

I quietly approved with a move of my head.

Mr. Voicu continued. "Her parents hadn't been politicians. Simona's father had been a professor of economics, but still, intellectuals were regarded with suspicion; the more refined, the more mistrusted. At that time, an anonymous note to the officials stating that somebody showed a lack of appreciation for anything communism upheld, or that someone had noncommunist opinions or listened to the Voice of America radio station, or criticized the conduct of Soviet occupiers would trigger a pickup from his bed. Anxiety was high. Simona knew her parents were not inclined to pay lip service. They had tried to keep their mouths shut, but they couldn't hide their convictions that well either.

"Simona froze in front of her door. Such a note could make anybody see his life pass by. She suddenly realized she didn't have a home to go to. Her face lost its color and her eyes searched around, confused. Instinctively, I offered to let her stay at my place until she could come up with a plan. I had rented a studio downtown, outside the campus. My father still retained his properties, so we could afford this privilege.

"On the second day, we found a new note on her door asking her to report immediately to the Securitate. Something was terribly wrong. Her parents must be in trouble. After two days of fear and uncertainty, Simona concluded there was nowhere to run and that she had better face up to the challenge. She knew she was innocent. This didn't mean much at that time, but it was all she had. Hiding wasn't an option. Set to help her parents, she decided to do what the note on the door required.

"Then, I proposed to her to get married. If we were married, she wouldn't be alone. I would have the authority to protect her . . . as much as this was possible. So we married that same day, and she went to the Securitate. There, she was arrested on the spot. For years, I didn't know where she was or why she was detained. Nothing . . . nothing about her and nothing about her parents. Much later, I learned that she had been arrested because her phone number had been found in the address book of one of her volleyball team members. That teammate had been involved in some form of anticommunist activity, and everyone associated with that girl was considered a political threat and arrested. She had been deemed guilty before proven innocent. Her innocence couldn't be proved, and neither could her guilt. This made her hang in limbo in one of the country's prisons.

"During her detention, I had graduated and became an engineer. My dissertation dealt with building a hydroelectric dam on river Bistrita. The Soviet Union commissioned the building of dams on any workable river in the country, and what the Soviet Union did, we all had to do. However, since Bistrita was a good river to dam, my project came at the right time. The communist officials found the idea very attractive and got me involved. I was put in charge of the project, and from there, I advanced quickly. I was promoted to a lot of responsible positions. You know, 'a young, dynamic element with progressive ideas . . . ' and all that stuff. Meanwhile, I tried to find my wife. I wrote several petitions to the authorities. Every time, the answer was that the government didn't have any record of anybody with her name in the Romanian prison system."

"They probably booked her under her maiden name. The communists could be, at the same time, shrewd and incredibly dumb," I said. Adriana gave me a sharp look, meaning, my interruption was both inappropriate and stupid.

"I have no idea of what they knew or did. Anyway, I used both names, of course. From their stonewalling attitude, it became obvious that I could not get anywhere through legal channels. I needed inside information. Therefore, I carefully built connections within the Securitate. Even so, I had to be careful. Because of my good standing with them, I believe, I got promoted to higher and more responsible positions. Among those, I became the head of Earthquake Readiness Commission, which oversaw the prisons' structural readiness too. This gave me a foot in the door. I could check any prison in the country for structural safety, but I couldn't just go and check them all. That would generate suspicions. I still had to find the prison in which she was kept.

"Only a year later, when I mentioned in a casual conversation that my wife had been the chief of her class when mistakenly arrested, the officer I was with said that they had in Jilava prison a female who had been chief of her class too.

"I could barely control my excitement. Right away, I organized an inspection of earthquake safety at Jilava. I asked for all the prisoners to be taken out into the yard so that we could inspect the construction. I looked across the yard, and there she was: hiding behind others so I wouldn't see how dirty and humiliated she looked. I saw no spark in her eyes. More importantly, she didn't show any joy in seeing me. Nevertheless, to me, she was as beautiful as ever. If only given the opportunity, everything could be fixed, including the spark in her eyes.

"After this visit, I took the risk and inquired with the prison administration about her charges. Of course, I got a song and a dance about security, secrecy, ongoing investigations, enemies of the revolution, and so forth. To this, I answered that I loved the revolution, that I selflessly supported it in my capacity, and that I intended to take the personal responsibility of watching her. You know about this politically correct nonsense. They had had her in custody for eight years already. If they couldn't find her guilty in eight years, they wouldn't be able to find her guilty from then on. I declared that if, by any chance, she was to be found guilty of counterrevolutionary activities, I would turn her in myself. They loved this type of demagoguery. Meanwhile, I said it was more practical to integrate her as a productive member of society than keep her locked up at public expense.

"The papers moved quickly from then on, and she was released to my care. She had never been charged. No connection with any anticommunist activity could be found. There was no apology either. Anyway, her release didn't help her recover. She couldn't recapture her dreams. She had been released with bad teeth, falling hair, an abused body, a vanished self-esteem, mistrust, no hope, and, I am afraid, no love. The years in prison had brought her down to the extent that she didn't want to live any longer. Six months after her release, she committed suicide."

IV

His eyes lowered from the horizon to the floor in front. Emptiness beyond words crossed his face.

"No doubt it had been hard for her, but at least you're still young. You can build a new life." I warily expressed the first encouragement that crossed my mind.

"I did, as you can see, but it is not the same. I couldn't remarry, if that is what you mean." He made a vague gesture.

"Yes, marriage is part of it. I mainly mean a fresh start, any start." I scrambled for an attractive solution.

"Marriage here is a transaction, not a romance, as we knew it." Mr. Voicu dropped the corners of his mouth.

"I am sorry Mr. Voicu," I said, fighting a sense of powerlessness.

"Marin. Call me Marin. Everybody calls you by the first name in this darned country."

"I noticed. But to me it sounds awkward; it makes me feels disrespectful. Does addressing you as Mr. Voicu bother you?"

"How could it? I am only trying to get you Americanized. Honestly , the formal way is a good habit. It provides dignity to both sides."

"Forget about all this European politeness." Adriana interfered. "Do as everybody does. You are not going to change their ways, so it's better to change yours."

"That is a practical approach," Mr. Voicu said cautiously. "Whichever way you choose is a good one. It is not the word that counts, but the meaning behind it."

"Truly, what you mean is who you are, while what you say is what you want the others to know you by," I said, animated by what seemed to be a bright idea. "It is hard to argue with that. On the other hand, what you want others to know reflects who you are. Somebody cannot avoid showing his face no matter what. Same with the communists: the more they say what's politically correct, the more they come across as either dishonest or as unaware. Meanwhile, they cast the blame on those who are honest and aware. Why? To make them feel guilty and to dominate them. Fearful people are easy to control. Isn't it sick?" This rare outburst of thinking made me feel terrific, and my attention perked up for more ideas to come.

"No, communism may have its flaws," Mr. Voicu lightly shook his head with a worried look, "but I can't blame it for everything going wrong there. Despite all individual abuses and mistakes, communism as a concept comes with many good ideas. As a matter of fact, you can find more justice there than here. I mean once established, communism pursued the common good, which in capitalism is left up to the mercy of merciless individuals. You don't expect the quest for profit to generate fairness, do you?"

"As a matter of fact, the quest for profit is a stimulating practice and consequently more productive than the controlling and inhibitive communism," I said, animated by this new thought. "As it is, capitalism has a way to generate more fulfillment than all communism put together." I moved to the edge of the couch and turned toward Mr. Voicu. "You know, communism professes freedom, but this freedom is pursued through regimentation, which in turn is the end of freedom. It is a self-contradicting system."

"Doesn't seem that contradictory to me," Mr. Voicu said with a placid voice, looking in the distance. "It's still fairer."

"Communism tries to create equality by forcing diverse people to be alike. Now, how fair is this? Capitalism, meanwhile, is based on agreements. Which one is better then? Which system offers more freedom?" I asked.

"Mihai, the issue is not freedom as an abstract notion. Don't float in the clouds now. The issue is the freedom to make it, to achieve your goals. If this is tough, then too bad. Is it better to give up hope?" Adriana said firmly.

"Freedom! Everybody talks about freedom like it didn't exist in communism." Mr. Voicu insisted. "Mind your business and you were free. I didn't have any problem there with freedom, and I was from a so-called bourgeois family."

"Then how does this freedom explain the killing of your wife, your father, and other innocent people?" Adriana moved impatiently.

"Obviously, that was an abuse, but you have to understand those times. The communists where suspicious of everybody, and as a matter of fact, they should have been. Not too many liked them. People don't take change too easily."

"If communists were not wanted, what they brought about could not be called democracy," I said, looking Mr. Voicu in the eyes. "As a matter of fact, the communists shouldn't be in power. They didn't even represent the Romanian people. Before the Russian occupation, if you remember, the Romanian Communist Party had only one thousand members and a disproportionate number of minorities, who, among other things, wanted to donate *Basarabia* to the Soviet Union. Could such a party be a legitimate leader of Romania?"

"Not at that time, obviously, but later it grew to be accepted. It became the most numerous party in the communist bloc, percentage-wise," Mr. Voicu said.

"Sure, pure survival tactics from both sides," Adriana grumbled. "The party wants members as a show of acceptance, and people want party membership for protection against discrimination."

"Well, you cannot deny that at least the founding members joined it out of conviction. There was no incentive for them to be communists other than their belief in the goal," Mr. Voicu said, unmoved.

"As a matter of fact, they could very well have had nonpolitical incentives." I braved. "They could have had a desire to get out of the anonymity of being poorly paid, uneducated laborers, and the easiest way to achieve that was to get in the streets and cry foul. Ceausescu didn't read a book in his life, and he could barely write a report. In fact, his education was limited to primary school before rising in politics. The Romanian historian Ghita Ionescu wrote: 'he swallowed the Marxist ideology whole.' No need to study it. Even the few educated communists, mostly liked the idea without getting too deep into the details. Any way, they wanted social justice achieved through them, their way, with them at the helm."

"No . . . you've pushed it too far. Who else can implement communism than a communist? As for material benefits, we all have material needs. The communist idea is rather simple; you don't have to read Marx to get it. All you need is some compassion," Mr. Voicu said.

" That's an interesting remark. I've been thinking about that recently," Adriana said from the comfort of her seat, bathed in reddish sunlight. "They seem to be motivated by compassion, yet compassion never enters their vocabulary. The Communist Revolution itself was everything but compassion. Marx' focus was not on building a better society but on the destruction of the existing one. This, in and of itself, reveals more hate than compassion."

"I can see you don't like them." Mr. Voicu slowly rose from his armchair, went to the bar, and poured wine into a new glass. He looked inquisitively to Adriana and me while holding the bottle, but we declined silently. He put his bottle back and returned to his place. "You have to admit that many communist leaders simply believed in the idea. I was not a party member, yet I agree with many of their principles."

Adriana, relaxed in her armchair, was looking in the distance. "They're either idealists or self-seekers . . . ," she said without moving from her contemplative position, "or idiots."

"Communism used everyone for its own purpose," I said. "I am confident you were never been out of their sight. Everything about you begged for their attention: an 'unhealthy social origin,' a wife suspected of counterrevolutionary activities, your high employment status . . . everything. You became an Inspector General only because of what you could offer them and nothing else. In fact, you were suspected and watched all the time. This is probably the reason why you ran out in the end."

"You don't know that." Adriana intervened, visibly upset. "Would you stop teaching everybody! You don't know what happened and why it happened. You are not God, you know."

" It's okay, Mrs. Ritivoi. Dr. Ritivoi has raised a legitimate argument. Yes, I ran out. I only wish I had never come to this country. These people are weird. They always declare wars, none for self defense."

"This issue is probably more complicated than it seems." I checked my watch. We had spent more time than anticipated. "Adriana, I believe it is the time to go. We have a meeting with our sponsor too."

"Why are you looking at me? Take charge, you are the man."

I understood that I was not man enough, but I had heard worse from her mouth.

"Sorry, Mr. Voicu. It has been a very pleasant evening, but all things have an end. Thanks to you, the free world looks already great to me."

"You Americanize fast. In Romania, we used to spend long hours around the dinner table. You're ready to go only after a few hours."

"Yes, I remember those days. Nevertheless, I seldom managed to stay to the end."

"Didn't stay?" Adriana came to correct me. "You didn't talk, period."

"It seems that today I broke my record. I had a great time. Thank you."

"Well, in two weeks I will have dinner here for a group of Romanian friends. Why don't you join us? They are older but educated, pleasant people. You'll like them."

V

As soon as we left the front door, Adriana said angrily, "Did you notice he didn't invite me? He looked at you only."

"It's understood we will come together. You means both of us. He is not the type to make such blunders. I am sure the other guests will come with their spouses. It's not a bachelor party."

"I wonder. They may bring younger nieces and daughters with them. They are not stupid. Only you can be so naïve. Don't even think of going alone."

"Of course not. On the bright side, it's nice to see that you care so much about me."

"Oh, shut up."

The visit to Mr. Voicu had been the most exciting event I had attended in a very long time. Such an uninhibited expression of unexpected opinions had been a dream come true for me. Even his support for communist ideas seemed exciting because for the first time that I had remembered, they hadn't been politically motivated. They were most intriguing. For those who lived under communism, it was quite obvious that that political system was a dead horse. But not for him.

"What made him believe like that?" I asked myself. "He wasn't that simple-minded to hold the system in high regard because it gave him a high job, or was he? In Romania, he had built a hydroelectric plant and managed hundreds, maybe thousands of employees. In California, he improved homes using several workers. The power he used to have could have been mesmerizing to him. With as much power as the communist centralized system offered to its leaders, much could be done. I believe he anticipated how he could fix many social ills if . . . But he brought himself to California, a state were despite more money and freedom, he had less power and recognition.

"All right, providing this assumption is correct, it cannot explain all that criticism of the United States. What could generate it? Was it the old communist mistrust of everything that wasn't by them, or the habit of criticizing others to uphold themselves? Maybe, in order for him to be right, the Americans had to be wrong. Who knows?

Whatever it is, the free world proved already exciting. It would be interesting to continue the conversation with Mr. Voicu and find more answers."

Two weeks later, Adriana and I drove again to Mount Olympus.

"Mrs. Ritivoi, Dr. Ritivoi, thank you for coming," Mr. Voicu said at the door. "I want you to meet some of my friends."

In the upper section of the large room with the panoramic view of Los Angeles, several people sat patiently around the dinner table looking in our direction. The food warmer, placed in the same spot as before with its covers removed, generously released its enticing aromas.

Mr. Voicu stopped next to the head of the table and said, "Friends, this is Mrs. Ritivoi and Dr. Ritivoi. They arrived in California last month from Romania. Dr. Ritivoi is a dentist preparing to get his American degree." Then he introduced his guests. Mr. Dumbravescu had been an attorney thirty-five years earlier, before communism. He had been disbarred afterward due to his high profile and high clients, and after a period of unemployment customary for those suspected to have hidden savings, he had been given a clerical position. His friends in the West paid for his release, a noble gesture he was never able to repay. His wife, a Romanian he met in California, was about ten years younger and full of energy.

Mr. Filip used to own a factory that was nationalized, like all other factories, once the communists took over. He was then hired in a different place as an engineer. After lying low for a while, he crossed the Yugoslavian border on foot and walked mostly at night all the way to Austria. Mrs. And Mr. Moraru chose to be quiet about their past. They seemed unwilling to look back.

"It's gone," Mr. Moraru said. "We've heard enough lamentations to last a lifetime. I see no reason to add to it. It is enough to say that it had been great before those animals got the country. What can I say? Not even the animals kill to display power!"

Mr. Bumb, the last guest, had served as a colonel before the army had been cleared of "exponents of the bourgeois-fief owners' regime." After that, the only job he could get was that of a machine worker. Like the others, with the exception of Mr. Filip, he had emigrated legally, after retirement.

It seemed that the discussions had been well underway when we came because Mr. Voicu, once back in his chair at the head of the table, picked it up with vim and vigor from where they had left off. "Don't give me that. Our single candidate system is much better than the messy multiple candidates they have here."

"Marin, you talk nonsense," Mr. Dumbravescu said. "People have to have a choice."

"People are seldom able to make a good choice. Henrik Ibsen said, 'A majority is always wrong.' What does this say about the majority vote? Look around," Mr. Voicu insisted.

"Nobody denies that this system has imperfections, but in the end, it brings better results than the alternatives. We have discussed this before. I don't know why you're bringing it up again," Mr. Dumbravescu said, lying back on his seat.

"Because a candidate who is carefully checked by a professional group and is found able to perform the job, is better qualified than a smooth talker, better looking or better funded, who comes forward by his own will and whom people aren't able to properly evaluate. How can the public evaluate a candidate? From what the candidate says? Politicians are professional liars. From what the media say? Let's be serious."

"You know, we will never solve this issue," Mrs. Dumbravescu said. "Mrs. Ritivoi, Dr. Ritivoi, I am sure you haven't had *tschorba* since you left Romania. Do you want a bowl? I made it myself. If you want to try new tastes, Marin took care to order different kinds. Everybody, don't be shy."

"How can we? Marin's dinners are always a feast," Mr. Moraru said as he got up from his seat and picked up a new dish.

"If I may," I interfered, "the main problem I see is that the appointed candidates are meant to perpetuate the status quo. In our case, there is no merit in prolonging the communist regime. So I prefer the vote of majority. At least it provides the tools for change."

"Right," Mr. Moraru said, returning to his seat, "but even in a democratic election, people tend to vote for the incumbent, even if he is not the best choice. They seem to be more comfortable with continuity versus the change a less well-known character may bring."

"What did I tell you?" Mr. Voicu made a point with his right hand. "Continuity is the dream of any society. Propose the right candidate and let the system work its way. Give it time, and things will fall in place. Nobody wants to see things failing. The more tools the political system has at its disposal, the more successful it may be. Case closed."

Nobody argued. Everyone seemed busy with their plates. Mr. Voicu took a gulp of wine and turned to his food. The quietness was broken by Adriana:

"Mr. Voicu, why did you leave Romania? You did well there, and it seems that you like their ways of staying on top of things." She pensively separated vegetables on her plate.

"Yes, I did well. The problem was that I didn't join the Communist Party. I started to be asked why I didn't join. I told them I would think about it, and when it took a little too much thinking, I started to lose some of my positions. You know, we were supposed to be examples for all the employees, but I just didn't feel like joining. Then, with the Bistrita dam built, I wasn't as needed any longer. They had new people able to take over. I could feel an impending decline in my situation. So before being pinned down to a desk job, I used the influence I still had and arranged to participate in a conference on hydrodynamics in Belgrade. There, I got a visa from the Italian embassy, and to Italy I went. From there, like most refugees, I came to the United States, the most powerful country on earth.

By the way, in the refugee camp, at Latina, I met a Romanian dentist who made pretty good money working for an Italian dental technician. The technician had a small lab near the train station in Rome. He did all kinds of dentures and denture repairs to transients between two trains. You know, it was convenient. The only thing the technician couldn't do was extractions, so he hired dentists from the camp to do that. The technician would point out what teeth he wanted removed and the dentist would extract them. All was under the table."

"How do you interpret that?" I asked. "Is it good or tragic?"

"Easy money. Everyone was happy."

"That is communism in a nutshell: poor quality that satisfies those that don't know any better. No wonder the Italians have a strong communist party," Mr. Bumb said casually.

"That's not fair. All poor people would make the same choice no matter if they were aware of better alternatives or not. This is what they can afford: an extraction on a bench, using not-so-sterile pliers, next to the train station. It's better than nothing." Mr. Voicu looked down with the most serious face.

"This is not a simple issue," Mr. Filip said. "Did poverty induce materialism, or did materialism induce poverty?"

"It's not the right time to get philosophical. We simply have to admit that Marxism came as an answer to one-sided poverty. Now, of course, there is physical poverty, moral poverty, spiritual poverty, etc. I assume all played a role and not all belong to the working class. Unfortunately, communism addresses only the physical aspect. It conveniently dismissed morality and spirituality," Mr. Dumbravescu said pensively as he lay back in his chair contemplating his empty glass.

"It seems to me that Marx suffered from self-righteousness, which, in the end, supports the compulsion to control. You know, if he is right, then his ideas are those that solve the problem. We know from his biography that he was a control freak and injected the need for absolute control in his communist concept. Of course, if you want that kind of control, you have to dismiss the one that truly controls everything, which is God," Mr. Moraru said with his eyes sparkling.

"It's a real mess," Mrs. Dumbravescu said as she rose from her chair to bring more bread to the table.

"Abstract." Mr. Voicu objected undisturbed. "You can dissect those policies to no end and draw all the conclusions you want, but the fact is that communism offers undeniable advantages." He took a sip of wine.

"Marin, don't be silly," Mr. Filip muttered.

"No, no, no. In Romania, as I remember, the whole social structure was more organized; we had some healthy rules to follow. Here it is kind of chaotic to me. It appears that each does what he wants, and the government has nothing to say. I look at those girls who make babies in order to get government money. The more children they have, the more money they receive. The father is inconsequential. Even if the father is known, the mother has more control over her own life if she doesn't take him for a husband. If she doesn't marry, she has more money and more independence, and everybody is losing.

"You know, in my opinion, the government should get involved in this important social issue. In fact, there are many issues here. For example, those addicted to street drugs produce genetically damaged children, who are born addicted and prone to failure. Those children are then shifted to the taxpayers to take care of them without even asking if the taxpayers agree or not. I would sterilize the addicts to save society from this burden.

"Also, I wouldn't allow anyone who is on welfare to have more than two children. You don't deny them the joy of parenthood, but you don't allow them to make a business out of it. This is a civil issue. Not only do they reproduce for a gain, but they are also, most of the time, unfit to raise children. So we get a new generation of social parasites. This is a disgrace that no politician has the guts to deal with. Now, all those social parasites have the right to vote, and so are conveniently courted by the politicians. In my opinion, somebody who didn't contribute to the country's budget shouldn't have a say on how the budget is used, which is how the country is run. They shouldn't have the right to vote, God forbid. Talk about communists being bad." Mr. Voicu concluded with an angry face.

"Well, by your standards we are also social parasites. Our sponsor just brought us to apply for welfare." Adriana pointed out, straight in her chair.

"I am not talking about temporary help, which is okay. There are all kinds of characters on welfare for a lifetime, even for generations; people who can't even conceive to live any other way." Mr. Voicu paused for a moment, then said, "Excuse me for a moment," and left the room.

We sat quietly in our seats, with some still eating. Mr. Moraru tasted his wine.

"Isn't he a little extreme?" I asked.

Mr. Dumbravescu moved slowly in his chair. "He has his strong opinions. We're use to them. They make good topics of conversation and give us reasons to get together. Otherwise, it doesn't mean a thing."

"Wait until he starts blasting Churchill and Roosevelt for selling us to the Russians. That is his favorite rant." Mr. Filip smiled while arranging his silverware in perfect order. "You know, before the war, Greece and Romania had the same per capita income. In the mid-seventies, when our standard of living was still acceptable, a statistic broadcast by Radio Free Europe showed our per capita income as being two-and-a-half times lower than Greece's. Today, this economic difference should be much larger, thanks to communism. We have gone way down since."

"Communism or not, he gives great parties with good wine and great food ," Mr. Moraru said. His wife smiled.

"Well, he vents some frustration. We all know what our country went through." Mr. Bumb looked sweepingly across the table. "Mrs. Ritivoi, Dr. Ritivoi, don't be shy. There is plenty of food. This is not communism."

Mr. Voicu returned with a brisk walk, rubbing his hands. "All right, where did we leave off?"

"It seems that Dr. Ritivoi is not aware of the harm Winston Churchill and President Roosevelt did to the world," Mr. Filip said.

"Well, the way we had been taught modern history back home, it wasn't worth paying attention to," I said.

"Then you have a lot to learn," Mr. Voicu made himself comfortable in his seat. "To begin with, most of the problems we have today are due to Great Britain. Who was against the Romanian principalities coming together in a single country? Who divided the Arab land into artificially drawn countries? Who set the border between India and Pakistan through the middle of Kashmir? Great Britain. Why? It is the old Roman saying 'divide and conquer.' How much more humanitarian can they be? Then we got President Roosevelt, who had his own priorities. He got rid of Hitler to promote Stalin, an arguably better choice. This choice meant the division of Europe, the division of Germany, Korea, and Vietnam, with a subsequent fifty years Cold War, reunification hot wars, 'freedom wars,' Middle East drawn into the conflict, and the alienation of the Islamic world. The United States set the Taliban in power in the post-Soviet Afghanistan, with all its dire consequences, and so forth. As a result of the peace brokered by Roosevelt and Churchill, we finished with a "dark age" of Soviet-style communism spread over one-third of the world. This meant about two hundred million people killed and an untold number of people abused. Nobody talks about this. Right?"

"I thought you favour communism," Adriana said.

"I do, but not how the Russians applied it." Mr. Voicu said with a most serious face and turned in his chair with the left forearm on the table and the right one wrapped on the backrest.

"Well, that is the only communism there is and it followed Marx very closely," I said.

"There is such a thing as 'communism with a human face,' such as what the Hungarians and the Czechs tried to implement. I assume this is what some people in western European countries envisioned as communism." Mr. Dumbravescu took the challenge.

"We will never know if those ideas would have worked. Not one was allowed to unfold. The way I understand Marxism, it cannot amount to anything significant. Isn't there any debate in the American media on this subject?" I asked.

"Are you kidding? Did you pay any attention to the news?" Mr. Voicu asked with a spark of interest in the subject.

"No, my English is not that good," I answered.

"You aren't missing anything. It's mostly gossip. It seems that their only concern is to keep people entertained," Mr. Bumb said.

"True. Did you notice ABC's *World News Tonight*, the only network channel who claims to present world news, has mostly domestic news and even that is of a lower quality? Do you know why? It does so because uninformed people are easy to influence. Now, is this any better than what we had in Romania?" Mr. Voicu asked, his eyes sweeping the faces around the table.

"Well, I suppose, besides those free-of-charge channels, there are other sources of information that provide more substance." I extrapolated.

"There are, but this is what the common people watch every day. Nevertheless, even the cable channels are skimpy. Compare the quality of news reporting on equivalent channels in Europe with those in America, and you will see the difference. One way to regiment people behind your policies is to feed them poor and selective information," Mr. Voicu said.

VI

Wow! After so many years of simple, unstimulating, and safe conversations we've had in our communist past, I had gotten so many bold points of view all at once that I feared the FBI would pick all of us up in a van. This must be why some fellows back in the refugee camp asked, rhetorically, for another world in which to immigrate.

It wasn't the first time I had heard unusual opinions presented with such certitude. When suspecting and being suspected is a way of life, as it had been under communism, one has to feel right about his opinions in order to be able to live with himself. That is a strange system. It isolates those trained to think and brings together those who are not. Of course, those trained to think are the potential enemies; they can figure out the stupidity behind the glorious facade. Consequently, it became a matter of survival for the communist system to keep the more proficient thinkers docile, isolated, and as brainwashed as possible. This policy, as expected, made it difficult for intellectuals to sharpen their abilities and conditioned them to fall to self-righteousness as the only line of defense left to them. Don't underestimate it. In communism, the indoctrination is professionally handled. It is blatant and insidious, threatening and benevolent, constant and intermittent. Its basic purpose is to shape its citizens into a flock of followers of their dysfunctional system and to succumb to a faulty and alien way of thinking. Beyond that, we were left to contemplate a void. Being lonely, brainwashed, and lacking genuine guidance, we drifted away, lured by self-righteousness. As a matter of fact, self-righteousness itself was a mild form of political opposition. So it wasn't a small matter after all.

I believe that truth is self-evident and never needs clarification or explanation. The "truth" proclaimed by Marx had to be force-fed instead, which in turn disqualifies it as being valid. People spent most of their time and energy hiding that which became a liability: the truth itself. Everybody, some more than others, pretended to be as the system required of them. Marxism's flaws make communism attractive to flawed and self-centered people who cannot stand established rules and rush to establish their own. Whatever fits their own mentality seems right to them, then they impose it on the others, regardless of how appropriate or harmful they may be.

Even if Mr. Voicu's statements had been accurate, I knew I couldn't live looking for the bogeymen behind every corner. I couldn't expect to see in every patient a potential lawsuit and in every man a potential deceiver. I didn't think I *should* live that way now, after my escape from communism. I came to the United States for higher achievements, and this is what I will do. Nobody around me seemed to live in fear, including Mr. Voicu. As a matter of fact, he felt freer to criticize the United States than he had ever dared criticize communist Romania when he lived there.

It was surprising to me that after being exposed to the same information Mr. Voicu had, I had come to opposite conclusions. Most people I knew agreed that communism was a bad idea. Then I met Mr. Voicu, who, despite all the tragedies that affected his family, decided that communism is good. Of course, if he was right about it, that rightness should be universal or it couldn't be valid.

Mr. Voicu started to sample the universality of his opinions with his group of retirees. This worked pretty well for both sides. The older friends had limited prospects. They had left Romania with no money to speak of and with their pensions suspended. According to the communist law, while outside the country, retired people could not receive their benefits. The system was faithful to its materialist philosophy: if money is power, then by letting the retirees emigrate, the communist system gained while the capitalist enemy who picked up the tab lost. As an added bonus, this policy made a good, although deceiving, display of openness to emigration for the world to see. For these people, Mr. Voicu's dinners had been a rare entertainment where they could easily let him unfold all his theories. Just take it with a grain of salt and it may be fun.

Mr. Voicu, in his turn, had a captive audience of respectable people willing to be lenient. All was fine, except that righteousness had been conducive to loneliness. He never remarried, was always in a position of authority, and never managed to have a real friend. Inflexible as communism itself, he preferred to polish his prized opinions with his acquaintances and with the memoir he had planned to write. The memoir will allow him to vastly expand his audience and proclaim his opinions with no interruption and no discord. Mr. Voicu filled his life with all kinds of reasons to believe that he was fine, that he knew what others didn't, that he had found a solution to problems too big for anybody else . . . that he was special.

And he undoubtedly was. We all are. It is only that under communism, people had their specialness denied, and in reaction to that, many built their own kind of recognition. Mr. Voicu only did it with more vim than others. From this perspective, communism provided the right tool to a hypothetically enlightened leader to do marvels. His love for communism was in fact love for the means it could offer to someone like himself to correct the wrongs of the world.

Nevertheless, deep inside, he probably had doubts about his righteousness. Otherwise, he wouldn't try so hard to prove again and again the same points. If he would be confident, he wouldn't need anybody's approval.

4. Some Things Never Change

I

The next opportunity to debate over Mr. Voicu came five years later. It took me that long to get my dental license, build up a practice, buy a house, and go through a divorce, all of which had put me in debt like never before. On the bright side, those experiences allowed me to better understand my own condition as well as the world I was living in. I even got the time to reflect on communism's inner workings. I was also able to keep my office in the middle of a financial meltdown. It was then that Dr. Florea, one of the dentists who guided my first steps in the licensing process, invited me to his Christmas party. He knew how difficult my recent divorce had been and was no doubt glad to offer me this opportunity to relax a little.

When I arrived, the first thing I heard was Mr. Voicu's voice. He, Dr. Florea, and two other gentlemen were involved in an animated conversation in a cozy corner of the dining room not far from the kitchen. Contagiously well-disposed, each one had a cool bottle of beer in his hand. Dr. Florea spotted me at the door and guided me to their small group. I was then introduced to two gentlemen: Ion Muntean and Niculae Dirlea. When we came to Mr. Voicu, he said with a broad smile:

"Dr. Ritivoi, I almost thought you had disappeared from the face of the earth." He turned to Dr. Florea. "We have known each other since he arrived in California." He shook my hand and said, "We were talking about something I know would have been appealing to you. I have found it interesting that communism tries to implement what Jesus wanted all along: equality, social justice, fairness and dignity for all. Jesus asked the rich to give to the poor, and this is what communism did. Meanwhile, here in the cradle of Christianity everybody is for himself."

"No, Marin, the rich didn't give their businesses away; they were robbed at gunpoint. Don't glorify communism now," Ion Muntean said, making a large gesture with his hand holding the beer bottle.

"Communism doesn't have anything in common with Christianity." Niculae Dirlea added while shaking his head. "Any resemblance is superficial."

"As a matter of fact, they used a similar method," I said. The subject was of a particular interest to me.

"Don't be silly, Mihai. And what may that be?" Dr. Florea popped the cap from a cool bottle of beer and handed it to me.

"It does." I thanked him for the beer with an approving raising of the hand and a slight nod. "I don't know if Marx fully knew what he was doing but he copied a formula that nobody can beat: the communist heaven is always in the future and can be attained only if people obey the communist commandments."

"I don't know about that, but I know that communism tried to implement more social fairness than the Christian church or any other church . . . as far as I know," Mr. Voicu said. "Would God accept the injustices Christians have done in His name? He would rather accept an attempt to solve this problem even if only partly successful."

"Marin, a lot of people like the idea of helping others live with dignity, but you have to admit that communism drove this car into a wall. There is no dignity there. They had to redefine dignity in order to be able to claim it," Dr. Florea said with an eye on the party on the other side of the living room. "Excuse me guys, I'll be back." Then he charged toward a group which seemed to have lost their momentum.

"Let's step back for a moment," Mr. Voicu said. "When you see people hungry, poorly dressed, living in squalid conditions, unable to afford education or medical care, overworked and underpaid while others have money for everything imaginable, don't you feel it is unjust? Don't you feel there is more to life than earning and spending? Wouldn't you find self-respect in helping those who don't have a chance to get off the ground?" He looked inquisitively at each of us.

"If you don't already have self-respect, helping the poor would only be a temporary lift," Mr. Muntean said softly while watching the floor.

"Who can be indifferent to such tragedies?" I addressed Mr. Voicu.

"The surprise is, in order to fix those situations we need what Marxism discards, not what it upholds. How can I explain this? Fairness is a moral issue. It is an internal process which cannot be corrected through external laws and regulations. Of course, sensible laws help the situation but no legislation can resolve it. Only the individual's love for his neighbor can."

Mr. Muntean raised his eyes and smiled seemingly to himself. "That love has to come from both sides. How many times have we put the so-called 'underprivileged' into new housing and they trashed it? Put them in charge of a city and that city would be ruined. Communism brought down whole countries. Didn't it?"

We all looked at Mr. Voicu simultaneously.

"Doctor . . . ?" Mr. Dirlea hesitated with an inquisitive look.

"Dr. Ritivoi." Mr. Voicu helped.

"Dr. Ritivoi has a point," Mr. Dirlea continued. "Nobody can legislate love, least of all the communists. If people won't understand the need to change, nothing will change them. The communists understood that. This is why we had been subjected to so much propaganda and brainwashing." He tossed his bottle in the trashcan. We all took a moment.

"It seems that the law is for the unenlightened." Mr. Muntean sighed, casually resting against the counter. "It' s for the selfish ones."

"This is why it is written 'Christ is the end of the law' [Romans 10:4]," I said. "You know, there is a parallel between Phariseeism in Jesus' time and communism today. Both are based on following laws in order to qualify for heaven. The problem is that the law ignores the spirit. It is a poor substitute for the real thing. Jesus' fundamental message was love, and you don't have to obey any law. If you love, upholding the law becomes part of your nature and disappears as an external requirement. In a nutshell, love and law are two different things not necessarily connected. No law could bring victory over sin; only love can."

"All right, and how do you convince people to love? I tell you, we need control," Mr. Voicu said with conviction.

"The control is not ours. If we are believers, we have to accept control belongs to God." Mr. Muntean raised his eyebrows and looked at Mr. Voicu.

"You see, in our condition, these high ideals will never work," Mr. Voicu replied impatiently, his voice acquiring a higher tone. "People need direction, guidelines, and policies to keep them on track. Those ideas make a good subject for discussion, but they never work on earth. How can you love a criminal? How can you turn the other cheek to a guy who attacks you?"

"Turning the other cheek is a parable, like most of Jesus' teachings. It basically means not to retaliate. Retaliation perpetuates aggression to no avail. It's not necessary. It's proof that you had been deceived by appearances; you interpreted the slap as something more than it is. Avoid getting into trouble the best way you can." I said, and then turned to Mr. Voicu.

"And how do you explain that to an aggressor? I mean, how do you stop him? Isn't it legitimate to defend yourself?" He promptly replied.

"It is . . ." I tried to explain.

"No, let's not get into these things." Mr. Voicu continued. "I read the Bible in my time; I am familiar with all of it. To me it is all a bunch of nonsense. Abraham having children with several women while over the age of one hundred? No kidding. Then he misrepresented his wife to Pharaoh for his own personal gain, only to be praised by God above anybody else . . . ! Who can take such things seriously? To answer this question, think about those who wrote the Bible—priests and monks—who were no better than those of today. Seriously, Dr. Ritivoi, you are an intelligent man. How can you buy all these religious things? I believe in God, as I mentioned, but I also believe He is above all this religious nonsense. Be honest and fair and He will acknowledge that when the time comes. This is why I say that communism was well-intentioned, and it deserves credit for that.

I tell you, religion, particularly how they have mutilated it in this country, is a sham. It has nothing divine about it. I know priests and ministers, and I have seen how they don't practice what they preach. Obviously, they cannot be both for and against what they proclaim. That tells you what the quality of their beliefs are." Mr. Voicu's face colored and his eyes focused beyond the objects in front of him.

Once again, I lost Mr. Voicu to one of his monologues, this time about religion. All my fine, newly discovered spiritual insights were brushed away. Nevertheless, I didn't lose hope that someday I would be able to pick up from where we had left off and present him arguments he wouldn't be able to dismiss.

II

It's hard to believe that I won't be able to find a question too pointed for Mr. Voicu to evade the obvious answer. His praise of communism didn't make any sense. About six months later, I found a new restaurant in town, praising its fish recipes, something Mr. Voicu would never resist. He loved seafood. My invitation was accepted, and I anxiously anticipated to continue our conversation from where we left it, one-on-one.

We got comfortable in our seats. For hors d'oeuvres, Mr. Voicu ordered his favorite fresh oysters and a glass of red wine. He grounded pepper over each chilled oyster and ceremoniously swallowed its pulp with his eyes closed. That moment was as good as any other one for me to ask my first question.

"Mr. Voicu, if communism has so many good points, why do so many people living inside that system hate it? It seems that the only people who appreciate communism are those who didn't experience it first hand or those who benefited from it, of course."

"Naturally, those who haven't experienced it have idealistic expectations. The same thing happens to us who haven't experienced capitalism before. We thought it to be so great and that it offers everything communism can't. Then you emigrate, and you find that it's not so," Mr. Voicu said without letting the oysters out of his sight. "You should try these oysters sometime. They're excellent." Mr. Voicu tapped the corners of his mouth with his napkin.

"Are they alive?"

"Yes, but they don't cringe," he said with the peppershaker in his hand. "They're tasty."

"I suppose they may grow on you. For now, I will stick with bread and butter. Their time will come." I tried to look reassuring.

"All right. Well, capitalism improved itself in part because it had to face the communist system next door. If left to itself, it probably would have finished like in *Time Machine*: a polarized society with two human subspecies, one feeding upon the other." Mr. Voicu stopped speaking and watched the server arrive with the main dish.

"So this is where your acceptance of Marxism comes from. It is either one social class or the other who prevails, never an adjustment or a compromise," I said as I lay back on the chair to make more room for the waiter to organize the table.

"It's obvious that compromising only muddles things. If I were to compromise my abilities and work according to American laws, I wouldn't be anywhere financially. Do you know how I got all these real estate holdings?" Mr. Voicu asked.

"I have no idea."

"The bank manager asked me this question once. He knew me from when I first came here, and he couldn't figure out how I got from having nothing to having twenty homes. Of course, I couldn't tell him how. If he couldn't figure it out for himself then he wouldn't benefit from my advice either. For him, what I did would be illegal and unacceptable."

"Illegal?"

"Illegal according to this system, but in fact perfectly fair . I didn't harm anybody. On the contrary, I pay taxes, I provide employment, I create business, and I fulfill all my financial obligations. As you know, banks do not give you a loan unless you offer proof of income. This way, they feel pretty confident about your ability to pay them back. But what do they know about my abilities? Practically nothing. They only know what the average American does, and the average American is not as enduring and creative as we have had to be. I don't need them to tell me what I can and what I cannot do. If they want proof of income, I give them a beautiful one. I know an accountant who can write for me a first-class report. This is not legal, as I said, but I know the risks. I also know I can pay the bank back as agreed. Is there any harm done? No. What I did was to remove obstacles out of my way."

"Nevertheless what you did was illegal. Besides, you put the bank at potential risk. You were at risk too."

"Rubbish. I know what I'm doing. I know construction, I know the best suppliers, I know how to maximize a house with minimum investment, and I work the business myself. I've got all that I need, minimal overhead, and top expertise. I even got my own real estate license so I don't have to pay an agency to buy and sell for me. Can you imagine having to pay 6 percent of the purchase price to a real estate agent only for presenting my house to a buyer? For a $400,000 purchase, he gets $24,000. Do you know how much a regular Joe has to work for that kind of money? But who cares? This is capitalism."

Again, Mr. Voicu launched into one of his monologues about the evils of capitalism.

III

It seems so unfair to blame the society from which somebody achieved his greatest financial successes and which offered him the widest possibilities for not fulfilling all of his expectations. If Mr. Voicu had been one of the few with such propensity, I would probably have taken it as an idiosyncrasy and let him be. Unfortunately, I had met so many from ex-communist countries who expressed that similar thinking. Why? What is it from their communist experience that makes them so critical, unappreciative, uncomplimentary, and always on the lookout for the bogeyman?

I once met in California, a Romanian engineer who had figured out how to increase car mileage significantly without doing major changes to the engine. But he didn't want to patent his idea. He was afraid that if he were to try, the big oil companies would kill him in order to maintain their profits; a thought which put him back into communism. Probably, other thoughts held him back too. It seemed that he left communism only physically. In all probability, if his idea had been proven valuable, oil companies would rather buy it than commit murder. Nevertheless, he was afraid of a punishment that would never have happened, of rising above ordinary, of being himself. He even abandoned his engineering degree and lived the quiet life of a maintenance manager for as long as I knew him. He was a perfectly dutiful employee here as he had been in Romania. By coming to the U.S., he got little else than better living conditions while he could have achieved much more.

He had been equally afraid of the "dark secrets" behind the American democratic "façade" as he had been of communism. He, like so many others, was trained to be afraid. Fear pulls people apart, prevents sound judgment, induces guilt, anger, and condemnation, hampers love, blames, attacks, and breeds ignorance.

5. THE WIND OF CHANGE

I

Surprise! In December, 1989, Romanian communism fell as it did in the rest of Europe. One notable difference was that, while in the rest of Europe the fall was bloodless, in Romania, the leader of the communist party, Nicolae Ceausescu, was executed. His demise was brought about by his refusal to change. "We will change when the poplar tree produces apples." I remember him quoting this popular saying while in a public speech. He had no reason to change as long as he felt secure within the protective bubble he diligently had built for himself. Besides the 20,000 strong special units assigned for his personal safety, to various degrees, all the Securitate, police, and military worked for his protection. His handpicked inner circle constantly reassured him that he was both genial and loved. So why change? No reason, except that change is the biggest force in the universe.

These unexpected events made Mr. Voicu as proud as a peacock. He summoned his group of older supporters and a couple of closer acquaintances, me among them, for a grand celebration. Mrs. Dumbravescu took control of Mr. Voicu's seldom used kitchen and let her creativity loose to prepare all kinds of old Romanian dishes in a way that had never been seen before on that stove. Mrs. Moraru brought a large layered home made cake moist with Jamaican rum, loaded with homemade chocolate cream and fancy whipped cream decorations. Mr. Voicu updated his bar, and the spirit was there. We lived a historical moment. After so much humiliation and hopelessness, the Romanians showed enough resources to decidedly stop the communist madness. "We are the only former communist country who showed such a resolve," Mr. Voicu proudly said from the head of the table. "What other country solved the problem so decisively once and for all? If left alive, Ceausescu would have enough power to stage a comeback. The only way to change course was to eliminate him, and we did it with no hesitation."

"Now is the time to return to a democratic system and private enterprise," Mr. Bumb said prophetically with a smile that covered his whole face and a glass of wine in his hand. "It has to be either now, or we will have another long dark period."

"We have to be careful." Mr. Voicu intervened promptly. "We see the chaos democracy created in this country. A strong and enlightened leader—that is what we need; somebody who has all the power and uses it wisely for the country's good. Otherwise, we go from one compromise to another, to demagoguery and inefficiency."

"Well, Ceausescu had to go. As for this unique all powerful leader, I don't know. Historically, it has seldom worked, at least not in the long run," Mr. Moraru muttered with his eyebrows raised high.

"True, but in our situation, what I would really want to know is who did 'the job,'" Mr. Dumbravescu said. "The answer to this question answers a lot of other questions. How come the all-powerful and well-trained Securitate didn't intervene? How could the crowd organize so fast and so well? No matter how unhappy the population was, it couldn't spontaneously produce a cohesive rebellion against the highly organized communist state. You may object to this, but the popular resentment alone is not enough. It had to be worked out and led by an organized group in order to succeed. Just think about it: Ceausescu was captured, jailed in complete secrecy, tried by a specially created tribunal, sentenced, and executed within days. All was videotaped! Could the mob be that effective?"

"Be serious. Who could have such an effective organization inside Romania?" Mr. Voicu made a wide gesture of denial. "You know how efficient the Securitate was."

"I believe Ceausescu fell because he was the only European leader opposing the transition from communism to democracy." Mr. Dumbravescu marked his conclusion by pointing to a spot on the table. "He was an international spoiler smack in the middle of Europe, and this matters. There are enough organizations out there with the ability to handle this situation."

"And who could that be, KGB or CIA?" Mr. Voicu said with a dissatisfied face. "No. You have too much imagination." He shook his head. "This makes for a good novel, but no. Until further disclosure, I believe what I see. There was too much discontent at too many levels for people in a variety of positions not to spontaneously collaborate for Ceausescu's removal. We did it right."

"Right and smooth." Mr. Bumb rearranged in his chair. "Ceausescu didn't stand a chance with his stubbornness. You know, Russia is an interesting country. It went through two major revolutions with worldwide implications and both succeeded against much more powerful parties. The first one was the Communist Revolution of 1917, where the communists had been a minority. The second revolution was this 1989 anti-communist one against the mighty communist state, the Soviet Union, whose power had even the United States concerned."

"Well, in the 1989 uprising the communists hesitated during the crucial beginning; but otherwise, they resisted change all along. Gorbachev never intended to undermine his communist empire. On the contrary, his reforms had been meant to strengthen it. His downfall was that he believed his own propaganda. He thought that after three generations of indoctrination his subjects had assimilated the communist ways while they merely hid their discontent. Then we have this idiot, Iliescu, a personal acquaintance of Gorbachev, who tried to do in Romania what Gorbachev couldn't do in the Soviet Union. All he wanted to do was to lift the country from moroseness by offering freedom of speech and limited privatization, only to find out that people wanted more than he was willing to offer. People wanted freedom and democracy. So, when things didn't go his way, Iliescu unleashed the so-called "miners" to terrorize and disorganize the democratic movement, a stark reminder of communist vigilante groups from the communist takeover. Then, when the United States introduced a motion in the Security Council to deploy UN troops to Romania to secure a smooth transition to democracy, Red China vetoed the motion. You see, once again, communism boycotts democracy. It always did." Mr. Dumbravescu pleaded.

"Of course, those who pretend to represent the people couldn't rise against the people's demands. It would contradict their own validity. Several salvos of automatic rifles were all they could afford," I said. "Even if indifferent to validities, it would be unwise to mass kill."

The party got quiet for a moment. Mr. Muntean broke the silence.

"It's possible that the Securitate itself became the new ring master. As the political situation changed, they saw new opportunities for themselves."

"I cannot agree more." Mr. Filip shook his head. "With everything they did—shootings, the 'miners,' opposing early foreign intervention and foreign investments—Iliescu and his allies only bought time primarily to facilitate taking possession of most of the state properties by the Securitate officers and those politically connected. They had the money, the connections, and the know-how. The new business owners are exactly those who previously killed private businesses—the communists themselves. So much for the quality of their beliefs!"

"I cannot blame them for taking advantage of the new opportunities. The Securitate is still a government agency that has to keep the country safe. But regardless, I still believe Romanians did the right thing," Mr. Voicu said. "There is something special about doing it right. There is power in righteousness."

"Gentlemen, I believe the removal of communism is beneficial, but we shouldn't talk in terms of right or wrong." I dared to touch upon a point I had wanted to bring in for quite some time. "Those concepts are judgmental, subjected to personal interpretation and consequently cannot be expressed in absolute terms. Everybody does what he thinks he should do. What they do may be beneficial or not, but this is a different issue. Passing judgments prevents someone of having an open mind. It is dangerous to seek to be right all the time."

"I was expecting you to say that. You always avoid a firm conclusion: right or wrong. What's wrong with somebody being right and holding his ground? What's wrong with having some dignity?" Mr. Voicu answered, raising his voice a notch.

"I'm sorry. I don't believe there is anything wrong with having dignity. It's only that dignity doesn't require someone to be right," I answered with an even voice. "Keep in mind that righteousness comes with a hefty price. If you believe you're right, then you reject any new information that may change what you believe. And new information is always available. This is life; we need constant improvement. We should expect to change our minds when exposed to new information; we should be glad to change."

"I don't believe in relativism," Mr. Voicu said firmly. "This chair will always be a chair. There are some guidelines and firm laws we have to follow. There are principles we follow all our life. Otherwise, we have chaos. Even God, who you mention at times, gave us the Ten Commandments. Can you imagine the city traffic without traffic laws? I mean, you are too abstract. What you say doesn't apply to real life. Let me tell you . . ." and I lost him again to one of his monologues, which didn't take into consideration anything I had said.

How could I convince him that the Ten Commandments are not commandments but outcomes of love? How could I make sense of love to somebody groomed to be self-righteous? How could I convince him that being rational doesn't mean being right? How could I take away from Mr. Voicu the privilege of being right when being right was the pillar of his self-esteem? In our communist past, being right was the equivalent of being aware, knowledgeable, and worthy. The whole system was based on the righteousness it guarded with ferocity. That was our template for success and dignity.

II

Among other things, the fall of communism brought Mr. Voicu amnesty. He had judgment passed against him in absence for "running away" while on official duty. The Romanian government never informed him of his charges or his sentence, but this was nevertheless expected.

In my opinion, the main purpose of this sentencing wasn't so much a punishment as it was a means of preventing people like him from returning as successful visitors. This way he wouldn't be able to offer to those inside Romania a glimpse of what the West could provide. From an official point of view, it would be even better if, unaware of his charges in absentia, he would someday return to the Romanian border and there suffer the indignity of being denied entry. This kind of situation always had a way of becoming known in the community as a superior rejection of a fallen person.

All those communist tactics became history. He was free to return! The long suppressed nostalgia for old friends and places came back with a vengeance, and Mr. Voicu planned a long vacation back home. In order to secure a successful return, he tried to cover all angles and find goals that would make his investment of time and money worthwhile. His mother, in her late eighties, was in good health, but he argued that at her age, some attention would be appropriate. She was living alone in the provincial town of Tuza, where she and her late husband spent most of their lives. Nearby was the acreage they used to own, by then transformed into a state farm. Their home, from where her husband was picked up by the Securitate and sent to forced labor at the "Danube to the Black Sea Canal," had become the new town hall. This expropriation had happened in a different era long ago, long enough to cross the boundary between injustice and fate and thereby lose its painful meaning.

Mr. Voicu's father was never arrested. He had been taken with no given explanation. The party had little patience with the influential people of the old system. The official perspective was that the formerly rich would always resent those who had confiscated their holdings and forced them into poverty. So, from the communist point of view, forced labor was a preemptive strike in its fight against "the class enemy." The country had been in a state of war after all, the "class war."

All this had happened two revolutions ago. Old history. After so much damage, the country had the chance to flourish again. Mr. Voicu thought this was the right time to go back home and be useful. With his experience, he could do a lot. As a matter of fact, it was exciting to be there in such a moment and take part in the reconstruction process.

He could offer his expertise in new projects. He had already studied the possibilities for new hydroelectric plants while still in charge twenty years earlier. If the Construction Ministry would be willing to undertake those projects, then he could be a big winner. Even if he were to find himself out of the loop, there still could be other good investment opportunities in the new, untapped market. Exciting times! People he knew had been talking about all kinds of big possibilities.

Suppose none of these plans worked out, he argued, he should at least secure his aging mother's life. Ideally, he should bring her with him to California. Previous attempts hadn't worked out. Well, he would try again anyway; this time face-to-face. If unsuccessful, he would arrange for somebody to keep an eye on her and help with the chores. Money would boost her status in the community too.

At the very least, Mr. Voicu planned to meet former friends and revisit places of personal significance. So he had covered all the angles, mapped all the right reasons, and a month later, was on his way to Romania.

6. Back Home

Mr. Voicu had told me later that when he stepped outside of Tuza's train station, shortly after dusk, the town was so quiet that he could hear his thoughts. A couple of people passed him by. Their steps on the pebbled alley sounded strikingly loud. He smiled. After so many years in Los Angeles, he had forgotten the sound of quietness: it could make you see a different side of life. He felt as if it had healing powers. He walked slowly, enjoying every step. His mother's house was only two hundred yards away, down the main street and behind the first corner. It was close but also far enough to allow him to process those feelings. A dog barked unconvincing. The simple sounds of the sleepy town or the lack of them could bring so many thoughts! His mother showed a lot of common sense by not meeting him at the train. He needed that brief solitude.

Nobody was in the front yard but all the lights were on, and he could feel the excitement inside the house. He sauntered unobserved into the vestibule. Through the windowed door, he saw the room full of people talking and laughing. He put his luggage down and looked for his mother. It took a moment before she came forward from the middle of a group, where her small body seemed lost. She looked at the windowed door. Her face brightened, she clasped her hands, and her lips murmured "Marin." Nobody seemed to hear her. Nobody was supposed to. That was her private moment of joy. She ran forward, her eyes beaming. Marin opened the door and embraced her around her shoulders long and tenderly. Then he released his grip and kissed her forehead. She smiled like never before, pulled his head down, and kissed his cheek.

"You finally came back. I thought I'd never see you again," she murmured. "Marin, my son! Oh, how much I missed you." She wrapped her arms around his robust waist. "I am so happy to see you healthy." She took him by hand. "Come, let me introduce you to everybody. I let them all know you were coming. You may have forgotten some of them. Many were still children when you left."

"Mom, I love you, but you shouldn't have put yourself to so much trouble," Mr. Voicu said with love in his eyes, his hands still resting on her shoulders.

"Be nice. They want to see you. There's nothing wrong with that. Now, show them you're glad to see them too. It's not that difficult." She patted his back.

"Of course I will do my best. Don't worry."

"All right. Now you're talking." They stepped beyond the windowed door in the main room holding hands. People interrupted their small talk and turned their smiling faces to him.

"Welcome home, Mr. Marin."

"Good evening, Mr. Voicu."

"No place like home!"

Mr. Voicu shook hands left and right. There were about twenty people in that room. "Glad to see you again, Petre, Vasile, George, Costica. Oh, Mr. Popescu, do you still have your beehives?"

Mr. Popescu, a retired schoolteacher, answered modestly, "A few, only a few. I am not that young anymore. Those pesticides killed a lot of them. It's not like in the old days when your father was around. He loved nature and nature loved him."

"Thank you." Mr. Voicu hugged him with the tenderness someone would have over an unexpected, old and precious memory. "This is how I remember him . . . Look; I brought something for you all the way from America—a warm wool sweater." Mr. Voicu brought his luggage from the vestibule, opened one bag, and removed from it the sweater he brought for himself for just in case.

People smiled and looked at his open bag. Mr. Voicu caught the meaning of it. He knew people had been starved for Western goods. Under communism, the Romanian market was not only poorly supplied, but what had been available was of poor quality—products from communist countries. Quality was in the West. Everything from there symbolized freedom, class, thoughtfulness, and everything that we had been denied. People certainly idealized it. Anything from the West, even if not truly needed, was treasured. It meant specialness by association across a heavily guarded border, with a civilization we could only dream of.

Mr. Voicu had prepared gifts for several close friends but not for that many. To make things worse, his mother happily introduced everybody—friends, distant relatives, and neighbors—in ways that indicated each one's importance that qualified him or her for his "attention." Tough job. He gave away everything he had prepared to give, and then he gave away some of his personal belongings. Some people were disappointed, but there was only so much that he could do.

In the end, he zipped up his bag and set it aside. Then he took one of the small glasses of *tsuica* (poune brandy) from the table and raised it in front of everybody. "Good people, it is my joy to see you again after so many years. Many things have happened since, but let us hope for a better future. Good luck to you all."

"Good luck," said the older teacher.

"Good luck." The people cheered.

"Yes, it was hard. It was particularly hard after you left," said a hefty man in a black leather jacket.

"You're lucky. You got the better of the two worlds: a good job here and a good fortune there in California," said a man whose face Mr. Voicu vaguely remembered.

"I worked hard for both." Mr. Voicu looked attentively at his glass. "Possibly, I also had some good luck."

"We worked hard too, but for us it didn't turn out the same way. We're still poor," said the man in a leather jacket.

Mr. Voicu didn't miss the bitter tone. He felt sorry for their hardships as well as for their misplaced resentments. "The past is the past," he said. "Luckily you have the opportunity to start something new and different."

"I don't see anything being different." A man in a country attire raised his shoulders. "What opportunity? Those who deall the cards in this country have it all. We don't matter now just as we didn't matter in the past. We are still the used and abused ones at the bottom."

"You vote. That is not a little thing." Mr. Voicu put his glass back on the table.

"All right, and who should we vote for? What's the choice? They're all the same." The guests stopped what they were doing and looked at him.

"Choose one from among yourselves. I see some trustworthy faces right here."

Uneasiness spread around. "We are not politicians. We'd be like fish out of water," Vasile, the next-door neighbor, said.

"Everything has to start somewhere. All politicians have been something else before." Mr. Voicu swept their faces with an inquisitive eye.

"And look at them!" One smiled.

"So what would you do then?" Mr. Voicu asked.

"I don't know; provide for ourselves the best we can, I guess," the man in a country attire said, looking sideways.

Behind the others and quietly leaning against the wall with one shoulder was a man who used to be a technician but whom his mother had introduced as an engineer at the local factory. Mr. Voicu came to him. "Mr. Savu, you're so quiet! Congratulations on your professional progress. You look good after so many years . . . about twenty, I believe."

"Thank you, Mr. Voicu. It is a miracle we've made it at all. Lately, it had been very hard for us. You have no idea." He lowered the corners of his mouth in a display of self-pity.

"So I've read in the papers. I'm sorry for that."

"The papers . . . you had to be here to see . . . no food, no heat, no lights. We had only one street bulb in the whole town, the one in front of the city hall, and even that one was sickish."

"Why only one?"

"To save electricity. We got strict requirements from the top. From time to time, they even cut off the electricity altogether, unannounced; no schedule or anything. They just cut it for an unspecified duration," Mr. Savu said, still leaning against the wall.

"That was good for increasing the birthrate." Someone tried to joke.

"Ceausescu had all the angles covered ." One smiled.

"You don't have this problem there in America. You make love right there in broad daylight," said the man in the leather jacket.

"Well, whenever we find it appropriate," Mr. Voicu said.

"Don't tell me you can't make time when you want it."

"It's not that simple. A lot of times business takes priority." Mr. Voicu adjusted his voice to professional neutrality.

"Yes, we've heard about that. Over there, you'd rather lose your wife than your business," said the man in the leather jacket.

"But aren't you the owner of your business?" Another asked.

"I am, but this doesn't make it any easier. Business carries a lot of responsibilities."

"Yes, I know. Responsibility or not, it's much easier to get rich there," said the man in the leather jacket.

"You have to experience that system in order to understand it. From so far away and living under communism for so long, it's hard to figure it out. How shall I say . . . , let's just say it's entirely different," Mr. Voicu said.

"You know, we're not that misinformed here. You have a big house, I've heard. That is something nobody can take from you," Savu said.

"As a matter of fact, they can and quite easily."

"No, you don't have to say that," Savu mumbled and looked sideways like he was searching for something.

Mr. Voicu felt his credibility crumbling. "If you miss your payments to the bank . . ."

"You mean, you have difficulties in meeting those darn payments?" The man in the leather jacket asked.

"I don't, but it can easily happen. There are so many obligations you have besides the mortgage payments."

"Well, I follow the news. With the amount of money somebody makes there, there is no way to lose your house unless, of course, you lose your grip on reality. Anyway, let's not get into that. It's good to have you back!" Savu raised his glass.

Mr. Voicu picked up his refilled glass from the table and raised it in response. He noticed that no one from the whole gathering showed any interest in how he had made it in that far-away land or how life was there or how he was. They assumed they knew what advantages the West had to offer. A simple welfare check of $400 meant 12,000 Romanian leis a month, if calculated at the black market value of 30 leis for a dollar. An average professional salary in Romania was 2,400 lei; the difference was obvious. Consequently, it could be embarrassing if they had to listen to stories that differed from their perspective. If Mr. Voicu were to try to point out the toughness of his lonely beginning in the New World, he would be understood as looking for excuses not to share more with the fellows back home, or he could be understood as looking for pity, which would be a public relations disaster. So he kept his stories to himself. Nobody said "I am proud of you" or "You did well; bless your heart." There was none of that. He was among shifty eyes that pitied their own fortune. They wanted their sordid stories heard, not his.

Mr. Voicu went through the whole process with an uncharacteristic patience. Dealing with these friends and neighbours was like fast reading the book of their lives, and he read them effortlessly. He took another shot of tsuica as a nonverbal proof of camaraderie, and, to his mother's delight, fraternized with them until one by one they started to go home. Then Mr. Voicu took his bags and went into the room his mother had prepared for him. Two eternally optimistic children followed the bags, and, in the privacy of the room, approached him with boldness:

"Do you have anything for us?"

"Sorry children, all the gifts are gone. In these bags, I have only personal belongings. Anyway, I can give you these." He took out an apple and a banana, one in each hand.

One ran out with his banana while the other lingered for a while. After a short delay he said, "You know, a banana is more valuable than an apple. You should give the banana to your relative, who is closer to you and let the stranger have the apple."

Taken by surprise, Mr. Voicu couldn't reply for a moment. Both kids were equal to him, relatives or not. He understood where the boy was coming from, but wasn't this too much?

"May I have this pen?" the boy asked, aiming at his chest pocket.

"No, but I have something you may like even better. What about this marker?"

The boy didn't say anything, but he took the marker and followed his pal. It seemed he was satisfied he got something, but not as happy as he would have been if he had gotten what he had asked for. The fact that he received instead what Mr. Voicu wanted to give him raised the suspicion of getting something of a lesser value. Who in his right mind gives more than he has to? Mr. Voicu paused a moment. Had he experienced this before?

It had been a heavy day: a twelve-hour flight, the train from Bucuresti to Tuza, the party, and then the novelties! He took out his hygiene bag and slowly stepped into the bathroom. Only then did he notice that the house didn't have a shower or warm water. He washed his hands and face and returned to his room. It seemed less spacious than he remembered. He sat on the edge of the bed and listened to the quiet. Crickets sang their never-ending thrill in tune with his heartbeat. "Nature's harmony," he thought.

The wall in front of him had a single picture in the middle. Its old, skinny frame seemed like a relic from a previous life. The glass needed a good cleaning. He thought that memories fade away the same way records do. Both get outdated, weather-beaten, and taken for granted.

He let his sight cruise around the room. It felt like a museum—belonging to another time, dusty, cold, stale. He checked his bed: it didn't bounce and was the same old one that always felt cold. It was musty too, but he had no choice. Mr. Voicu sneaked in, pulled the comforter to his chin, and waited for it to warm up. Realities seldom match expectations, if ever. It crossed his mind that if he hadn't come, he would have continued enjoying his idyllic memories undisturbed.

The thoughtful and happy people he once knew had vanished. They had changed. None of those he saw that evening would defend a way of life or a principle any longer. Now it was all about making it.

His mother, on the other hand, seemed comfortable there. She had done well with the party, taking care of drinks and snacks. People treated her with respect and even volunteered to help her with an arm of firewood and other small chores. She fit in with them like a piece in a puzzle. Maybe the fitting puzzle was people's old self-image that had to match his mother's presence. Possibly, people had come to see him for the same reason he had come to see them: to revive idyllic memories that, at one time, had been their life. Yes, they came to remember the old and see the changes that a twenty-year lapse could provide. Their own changes had been too gradual to make an impact. He thought he should probably leave Tuza before the precious world of his memories would be irreversibly affected by new findings. Tired, he fell asleep.

He spent the next couple of days around the house. He strolled through the places where he had spent his early years, cleaned his mother's vegetable garden of occasional weeds, and in the evenings, watched how the flickering fire on the stove projected fantastic images on the walls. He listened to stories about her life and told her about California. She enjoyed his company, but in strange ways, she seemed to find more comfort in her undisturbed surroundings than in her son's presence with his exotic stories and his suggestions about how to change things.

His words "You need to rest after a lifetime of work and worries. It's time to take it easy" felt like a threat to her. She was fine; what is he talking about? In the end, when asked, she didn't want to consider coming with him to California. Going away for a while would upset her system. Not to mention, there was nothing for her to do there in America but sit idly in a pretty house all day long while her vegetable garden and her chickens would be denied her care. No, she belonged in Tuza! Her son, on the other hand, could come anytime. He was younger.

Her determination forced Mr. Voicu to switch to plan B. "Mother, you need hot water in this house. You cannot wash with cold water, particularly in the winter. It's a hassle to heat water on the stove every time you need it. I can arrange to have a water heating system in no time. Imagine how much easier it would be in the kitchen or in the bathroom."

"I do very well, thank you. I am comfortable with the way things are; besides, those things always break. I don't need that complication. Don't you have anything else to worry about?"

Mr. Voicu understood he had to switch to plan C: arrangements with neighbors to check on her and help with the chores. They were already part of her environment and interacted across the fence anytime they felt like it without being particularly conscious of it. Helping her when needed, here and there, already happened because it couldn't not happen. But Mr. Voicu wanted to make sure things would be taken care of in a more organized way. At her age, you never know . . . He thought, by hiring people to take care of her would improve her safety. Later, looking back, his efforts didn't improve things that much. On the contrary, by doing that, he further distanced himself from his old neighbors. From being "one of us," he became their remote employer in America. The help that used to flow naturally became an obligation.

Ioji, a young fellow in the neighborhood with no steady job, was happy to help with yard work, firewood, groceries, and whatever she might need. Mr. Voicu paid him in advance for a trial period and planned to come to a better-defined arrangement after that. With nothing more to buy or do, Mr. Voicu decided to use the rest of his time visiting other people and places. First on his list was Bucuresti, where he had met his wife and where he had reached the pinnacle of his career. He knew many people there with whom he could possibly do business. Then, he wanted to see again after so long his cousin and best friend, Tudor, and his wife, Lavinia. Mr. Voicu hadn't written much to them to protect their good standing with the communists; but that was in the past.

II

Mr. Voicu arrived in Bucurresti's Gara de Nord renewed with expectation. That train station used to be the place for enhanced emotions no matter if he was departing or arriving, going to search projects, vacations, or returning to the quiet comfort of his praised apartment. This time, the train station seemed smaller and more neglected than he had remembered. He advanced slowly along the platform, absorbing every impression, from the yellow pavement to the benches, to the people energized by the excitement of their arrival, and to those who anxiously came to greet. Several people asked him if he needed a taxi and followed him in disbelief when he declined. He was advised to use the marked taxies, not those "independents" who may take advantage of you.

Mr. Voicu took a leisurely walk toward the line of taxies next to the main entrance and asked a driver to take him to a hotel downtown, not the most expensive, but a good, centrally located one.

In the hotel lobby, the desk clerk asked for his identification card. Mr. Voicu took out his American passport.

"Do you have a Romanian ID?" the clerk asked.

"No. Is that important?"

"It is. Romanian citizens pay lower fares. Foreign citizens pay international prices. You know, Romanians don't have money." She rested her left elbow on the desk and lightly supported her temple with her fingertips. With her head slightly tilted, she looked at him upward.

"I have to pay like a foreigner, I guess." The receptionist took his passport without moving from her chair, put it on the lower counter to her left, gave Mr. Voicu the key of his room, and reclined in her chair.

He looked at her for a moment, then asked, "May I have the passport back?"

"I am not done with it. You may go upstairs, I will give it to you later," she said, looking at him impassively.

Mr. Voicu hesitated. What did she mean by "later"? She didn't have anything else to do. Why didn't she take the data and return his passport then and there? But then, in an unspoken way, she demanded a little importance and a little trust. Let her have them. He felt it would be safe and in a way charitable to do so and walked pensively to his room. Nevertheless, when spruced up, he pranced back to the lobby and asked for his passport. The lady behind the counter slightly moved on her chair, looked him in the eyes with a mixture of pride and reproach, and handed him the document. Mr. Voicu took it with a touch of guilt mixed with the anger that he so felt. This game had to stop, and he put the passport in his chest pocket before leaving the desk.

As soon as he stepped through the hotel door, his attention was captured by the life in the street. The fresh air and the stream of people in the always-dynamic downtown, where the best stores and the most appealing procommunist buildings had been located, immersed him in old, almost forgotten feelings. He had lived so many thoughts and emotions there. Each corner brought pieces of life gone by. Years of living distilled into seconds of quintessential memories, and his slow walk seemed a trip into the past.

Most street names had been changed from communist to democratic, which was obviously well-intended but was in fact an annoyance. He didn't care what the name meant; he simply found the change as another assault against his memories. On the other hand, he argued, changes should be expected. He sighed. There were signs of entrepreneurship: small firms here and there, kiosks, and vendors. In one window, somebody was affixing a poster with Ion Iliescu for president.

"Do you want the old communists back in power?" He casually asked the man.

"I don't take sides," the man answered. He quickened his work and avoided Mr. Voicu's eyes. "Somebody came and asked me to put this in the window; I put it in the window. I don't get involved." He picked up his tools, making an effort not to appear in a rush, and disappeared into his store.

"He had already taken sides," Mr. Voicu commented to himself. How could they want to go forward with such an attitude? Fear must run deep if the man with the poster took his attempt to chat as a threat.

"You don't ask these kinds of questions if you live here," a window shopper said while checking the display. "Communism is not over yet. So far, only the name has changed. Now they call it democracy, but it's still the same: the same people are in power, the same Securitate, the same shortages."

"These same people may look for a new way," Mr. Voicu said, glad to have engaged the man.

"New ways toward the same goal: personal enrichment," the window shopper said "Under Ceausescu, those highly employed couldn't attain this goal. He took it all for himself. His underlings, who stashed away a lot of money, couldn't use them because of Law 13 that punished people for illegal gains and because of all those internal investigations. So they killed him for their own benefit. They are the ones who used their influence to acquire state properties for peanuts and became rich in a way they couldn't have even dreamed of before. If nothing else, Ceausescu kept those vultures under control." He turned his head toward Mr. Voicu and asked, "Where do you live now?"

"In America. How did you know I don't live here?"

"Here nobody wears a light-colored coat. We all dress in shades of gray, the color of our lives."

The window shopper turned back toward the window and watched it for a moment before he swung away and sauntered along the street. He didn't care what Mr. Voicu may have had to say. Mr. Voicu noticed that, in general, those he talked to were not interested in replies. They knew what they knew and were not concerned with other people's opinions. If they were right, what others had to say would be superfluous, anyway. In that particular case, it seemed, the man already felt generous for sharing his honest opinion while knowing very well it's not safe to criticize the powers. He preferred to leave it there: generous, right, and unchallenged.

III

Mr. Voicu continued his walk along Ana Ipatescu boulevard toward his former office. Things hadn't changed much. A few stores had undergone a face-lift and brought in new inventory. A couple of blocks away, the Construction Ministry's building stood unchanged at the intersection of Ana Ipatescu and Chivu Stoica boulevard (Chivu Stoica boulevard had had its name changed to something he didn't bother to memorize). The same but seemingly smaller and dustier building dutifully bore its weight like a well-trained dog. Mr. Voicu entered the front door, as he always had, and walked through the lobby and up the stairs to the third floor. A plywood wall had been built at the second floor to isolate a small space in the far corner, probably for storage, judging by the flimsy, unpainted work. Most likely, the budget had been trimmed to the bone.

He knocked at the door of his former office, waited politely, and then, having no answer, opened the door. On the desk in front, facing the door, a man sat with a pen in his hand, looking up from his half glasses.

"Marin, what a surprise! I thought you had disappeared from the face of the earth. When did you return?" The man put his glasses on the desk and came toward Mr. Voicu with his right arm outstretched.

"Glad to see you, John." Mr. Voicu smiled and warmly shook the man's hand. "You look great after all these years. This place hasn't changed much." He looked around the simply furnished room. It never occurred to him how bare that office was: two chairs in front of that large old desk, another two chairs on the left side of the room, and a couple of bookcases filled with files. A poster hung where the portrait of Ceausescu used to be, maybe using the same old frame. "You have moved the desk, I see. Oh yes, I came into the country four days ago. I have spent all this time in Tuza, with my mother. I haven't seen her for almost twenty years. But tell me, should I congratulate you? Are you the new director here?"

"Yes, somebody had to be." John smiled with modesty. "I got this position only after the revolution. Before it was Vasile Popescu ; you know, that tall guy who divorced his wife and married the secretary."

"So he married her in the end."

"Well, he probably wouldn't have, but his wife kicked him out of the house. It was a whole circus." John showed a chair to his former boss and pulled for himself a similar chair from the other side of the desk. "If his wife would have left him alone, he would probably have cooled off and stuck to her."

Mr. Voicu sat down. "She loved him . . ."

"This is the irony. She didn't want to see him any longer because she loved him. If she weren't so heartbroken, they would probably still be together . . . I wish them well. But tell me, how are you? The last I heard, you where terminally ill somewhere in America." John smiled with a meaning.

"God forbid! No, I am fine. I have never had more than the flu. Now that things have changed here, I took advantage of the new freedom and came for a visit. Of course, I couldn't avoid seeing my old friends and my old office. I filled out a lot of forms on this desk."

"Yes, here it is, the same as you left it." John tapped the desk.

A pause followed. John was still smiling, but he had run short of words. Talking about other people was easy; not getting too deep into their problems was prudent; but the rest was difficult.

"Why did they replace Popescu? Not because of his divorce, I assume." Mr. Voicu tried to save the momentum.

"Oh, no! It was because of the embezzlement. Things got bad after you left. Those small liberties people used to take on the job, if you remember, got bigger. As a matter of fact, it became blatantly abusive. A leadership position started to be seen more like an opportunity to swindle than to do something constructive. With this democracy thing, some employees started to demand more professionalism and the removal of the most abusive figures. Popescu was on the top of the list. So he was replaced. He is retired now. As a matter of fact, I haven't seen him since." John pulled a pack of Marlboro from the desk and asked:

"Cigarette?"

"No, thank you."

John slid an ashtray from the middle of the desk within easy reach, lit a cigarette, and inhaled slowly and deeply. He leaned on the backrest, and, equally slowly, released a long stream of smoke. "I don't know if these abuses are the cause of our economic meltdown or the effect of deeper flaws. Maybe both. I don't know, and, as a matter of fact, it doesn't matter any longer."

"Well, things happen." Mr. Voicu felt he better avoid political debates and stick to business matters. "How is the work load now? Are there many projects under consideration?" he asked casually.

"Not really. It has been very quiet. The last big project we had was Ceausescu's People's House. You probably saw it. It is huge, almost as large as the Pentagon, with boulevards emerging from it in all directions—a match for his ego." John took another big puff and let the smoke cloud his eyes. "That building was supposed to be a center

241

for all government bodies, all kinds of international forums, both occasional and eventually permanent ones, and also his permanent residence and bunker all at the same time. Now they don't know what to do with the thing. With Ceausescu gone, his dreams went also. He was the only decision maker. Now, with no leader and no funds, we're left to shuffle papers, as you can see."

"This is only a temporary situation, obviously. Right now, the country goes through a period of transition. After this, things will probably get back on track."

"You've been gone for too long, Marin." John guided his attention to a point on the floor in front of him and stood silent for a moment. Then he continued. "Nobody thinks big any longer. After you left, we went through an austerity period so bad that our only goal was to make it through the day. All big projects and big political ideas failed us. It's time for smallness now. The country is tired."

"I understand, but didn't this revolution create any optimism, any excitement?" Mr. Voicu leaned forward in his chair.

"Excitement for personal gains in the old selfish ways, yes. The lid over the abuse cauldron has been blown. No more Law 13 with its control over someone's spending and no more limits on the number of properties somebody can have, no more internal investigations, and no more anonymous complaints. You remember how it was . . . Well, all is fair game now. This is a bad time to be honest. Everybody thought that democracy, the free market, would bring Western abundance just because we called ourselves "capitalists." The first freedom we are exercising is the freedom to openly use all the bad habits we had acquired under communism."

"I am afraid communism is blamed for more than its fair share. It upheld healthy principles as well," Mr. Voicu said cautiously.

"Healthy, but never applied . . . they couldn't be applied. How can someone combine individual freedom with central decision making?" John extinguished his cigarette in a slow, almost ceremonial way. "Everybody pretended to apply those principles. This falsity is at the origin of the failure we see today. How can I say it better? Well, for the common man, life is tougher than before. We are free, but this doesn't keep us warm and fed. It is difficult, and it will continue to be that way for only God knows how long. Personally, I don't see an end to it. The economic hardships will help the ex-communists in the next election when all those down and out will look for handouts, Iliescu will bring the country in debt more than ever before, and this will slow down any attempts at reform. It is hard." After a brief pause, John continued in a low voice. "What I tell you is confidential. Some things don't change, you know."

"Oh sure, it's understood. I appreciate your trust, but I would like to have a better understanding, if I may. If somebody comes from outside with money and wants to invest in a business here, what problems could he encounter?"

"Do you want to invest here?" John took a deep breath. "What can I tell you . . . Right now, those who make money in this country are the crooks. Nothing much is coming from honest work. Our situation right now is that our industry is not competitive, state-owned economic units are sold for pennies, work ethics are in shambles, and the bloated workforce is experiencing high unemployment. The few who became rich did it by gobbling state properties, most of them through connections and kickbacks. Others simply steal whatever can be stolen or ask for backdoor payments. Everything goes these days. Some industrious ones bring from Turkey things we craved for a long time and didn't have access to, like blue jeans, now that travel restrictions are lifted. The most disturbing to me is the fact that after so many years of "popular democracy", the disregard for the poor is astounding. Everybody wants to fulfill his long-denied material dreams. The goal of fairness and bringing dignity and freedom to the working class is completely gone. It's like these ideals never even existed. The desire to posess surfaced with a vengeance. This is how it is. Do you think you could fit into this picture?"

"I think that money talks. A good investment has to pay off." Mr. Voicu looked with hope into John's eyes.

"It usually does, but you pass as a foreigner now. You are not one of the boys any longer. If you come here with money, people will figure out ways to suck you dry unless, of course, you are big enough and set your own rules. How can I say it better? We are not communists and we are not capitalists. We are a combination of the worst from both. Our form of state is a hybrid with no name. I don't know, our bureaucracy is ferocious and our legal system is inadequate. As a friend, I would advise you to use your money there, in the West. Maybe in the future . . ."

"Some brag that they have made a lot of money in this emerging market." Mr. Voicu tried to pull for more information.

"Some did, but are you ready to lower yourself to the level of those 'successful' ones? Is money that important to you? I believe you can live a cleaner life in America than here, at least for the time being." John paused for a moment and continued while looking down. "Don't quote me on that. We still have to watch our backs."

"Certainly. I appreciate it, John. You gave me hope. The beginning is always confusing. Some people always take advantage of changing rules and so forth, but it will get better. You managed to hang on to your principles, and so did many others. Well, thank you again. I've taken already too much of your time."

Mr. Voicu was grateful to his former colleague. His memories of good people and good deeds had been revived, and truly, no matter how difficult the transition, the country could return to decency. He took time to ponder on John's words and on his whole experience of that trip. "To have or not to have, this is the mantra! Hmm, this is the core of capitalism. The only difference between one capitalist country and another is the moral standards on which each operates. The question is how you can make somebody moral. The country must have strong leadership able to keep them in line." He strolled through the streets for a long time, paying attention to people, gazing through stores, and looking for places that stuck in his mind for some reason or for no reason at all. From Magheru Boulevard he turned to Palace Square and crossed to Cismigiu Park. He used to take his dates on a rowboat ride there.

Passing through the park, Mr. Voicu noticed stray dogs slowly coming from different directions toward one of the intersections. He stopped to watch their strange migration, and then he noticed an older man, with a newspaper bundle under his arm and advancing toward the same place. The dogs started to wag their hanging tails and lower their snouts in a kind of bow. The old man took a bunch of bones with little meat from the paper wrap and gave them to the lean animals. He watched them eat for a while and then raised his eyes and noticed Mr. Voicu. He crumpled the newspaper in a ball and, apparently embarrassed to be seen feeding the stray dogs, left as slowly as he came with the paper ball under his arm. Why was he embarrassed?

The sun was setting behind the city's skyline; the time when lights inside homes are turned on. Close to the park, on Matei Millo, was his former apartment, on the third floor. He abandoned it when he emigrated. Many people had been fixated on emigration then. They thought happiness is found outside our borders, but is it? Mr. Voicu sauntered along the pathways waiting to see the light turned on in his former apartment, as it had when it belonged to him. Finally it happened. Yes! It cast that same warmth that he remembered. Those were the good old days; good indeed! This time, a stranger was enjoying it; hopefully a decent person, maybe a family.

IV

The next morning, Mr. Voicu got up with the anticipation of a better day. He would do some fun things: ride the streetcars, see places he used to enjoy, and see his cousin Tudor and his wife Lavinia. They had always been pleasant company. Besides, Tudor may have a different angle on investing in the new Romanian market. It should be an interesting day.

Spruced up and dressed, Mr. Voicu dialed his cousin's phone number.

"Marin, you're finally here!" Tudor answered. "I thought you changed your mind about coming. Man, you have made my day! You have to come tonight for dinner. Lavinia needs some time to prepare; you know how finicky she is."

"I deeply appreciate your intention, but food is the furthest thing on my mind. I want to see you and talk about our lives. This is all the food I need right now. No fancy preparations, please. A good wine from Cotnari would do it. As a matter of fact, I will provide the wine. Let me put it this way: if you promise no food, I will come."

"Done. I'm sure you haven't had *mititei* [Romanian skinless sausages] or *sarmale* [cabbage rolls] for years. Great, I will see you around six. I want complete stories."

Mr. Voicu put the phone down with a smile on his face. They will never change, he said to himself. Until six, he had the day to enjoy. He would probably take a tram, like in the old days, to Herastrau Park, where he used to walk during his many days of doubt and introspection. He hadn't ridden a tram since he left Romania. That particular feeling as the tram rumbled on its iron tracks, screeched on curves, with the conductor getting down from his cabin to switch lines—all those memories never left him. He couldn't forget those times when the students came out from their organized parties all at once, when the music was cut off, and would pull the trolley's rope to disconnect and prevent the tram from moving so they could all jump in. The conductor always took it with a grain of salt and let them have their fun. Mr. Voicu missed the look, the smell, the slow movement, and everything else that could transport him back twenty years. Then, he thought he should see again the National Art Museum, walk the short distance to the highly regarded Capsa café, and read a paper with a gourmet coffee and a fresh pastry in front of him. In the following days, he should visit a couple of resort towns in the mountains or the Black Sea, the coveted vacations spots of the country, or maybe both. From the information desk, he found that there were quite a few rapid trains throughout the day to those destinations.

He briskly came down the stairs to the hotel's restaurant for breakfast. As he weighed his options with his cup of coffee in hand, his attention was captured by two maids who, oblivious to the customers, argued over who was supposed to clean a spot on the carpet. In Mr. Voicu's opinion, the task wasn't worth the hassle, but for those girls this was a rather important issue. To transfer the task to the other would be a sign of victory, proof of authority, work dodged, everything to be proud of. Mr. Voicu had witnessed this kind of scene before, when he lived in Romania, but such an approach had never appeared to him so senseless. He felt like grabbing that cloth and cleaning that spot in no time. Case solved . Nevertheless, he wanted to see how it would all end up and poured himself another coffee. In the past, these conflicts seemed to die somehow, only to get resurrected later and wane again. This time, the supervisor came and tried to straighten things out.

"Florico, didn't I tell you girl so many times not to argue? You never listen to me."

This statement touched a chord with him. Instead of solving the problem, the supervisor elevated it to a new level. For Mr. Voicu, it was clear that Florica should only be reminded that cleaning that area was in her job description, nothing more. The supervisor should have reminded rebellious Florica that cleaning that spot was in her job description instead of demanding her to obey two persons and increase her resentment.

"This is how it is." Mr. Voicu concluded softly and got off his chair. Those girls were still living by the old communist ways when jobs had been secure and the main concern was how to dodge work. If I had to come back and live here, I would have a hard time dealing with these kinds of things.

Mr. Voicu hung the camera strap on his shoulder and stepped into the street. Early in the morning is a good time to take pictures. The sun is not yet that glaring. A short distance away, there used to be a tram station where he could get a ride to Casa Scinteii. From there, he only had to cross the Kiseleff boulevard and get to Herastrau Park.

Mr. Voicu walked a distance before he noticed the change. The iron tracks had been removed. Awakened from his thoughts, he stopped to strategize. "Where did they move the line?" he asked himself. "Better ask somebody who knows." He looked along the sidewalk to spot someone who didn't seem pressed for time. Coming his way, he noticed a man in his sixties, modestly dressed, with an empty bag in his hand. Mr. Voicu came closer to this man and asked, "Excuse me, Sir. Would you be so kind and tell me where I can find a tram station for Casa Scinteii?"

The man stopped, and his self-absorbed face started to redden. After a short pause, he said, "Do you know me? Why do you stop me in the middle of the street with such a question?"

"Sorry. I meant no offence. I hadn't seen this place for quite some time, with all these changes . . . I thought you may help me with directions, but if you find it inappropriate, I won't bother you any longer."

The man's face started to relax. "Where do you live now?"

It was Mr. Voicu's turn to feel uncomfortable. For these people, the United States may have sounded like another world. He didn't want to put this distance between himself and that simple man. Still, he couldn't lie. "I emigrated to America during Ceausescu's era."

The man's face seemed completely restored. Without removing his hands from his pockets, he said, "Many left, and probably it was the right thing to do. What is here to like?" He looked in the distance for a brief moment and continued. "Then, every country would accept you as an immigrant, but you couldn't get your hands on your passport. Now, the government gives you the passport, but no other country wants to let you in. The more things change, the more they stay the same." The man removed his hands from his pockets, turned ninety degrees to his left, and pointed in a general direction. "For Herastrau, it's better to take the metro. We have such a thing now, in case you didn't know. If you want a tram," the man turned to his right, "then you must take the first right until you meet the tracks. Number eleven will do it."

"Thank you. It was very kind to give me your time," Mr. Voicu said as he stretched his hand for a handshake.

"Petre Ionescu." The man shook his hand and nodded slightly. He had an agreeable demeanor after all.

"Marin Voicu. Pleased to meet you, Mr. Ionescu." He smiled.

Petre Ionescu stuck his hand back in his pocket and turned slowly back to his stroll down the street.

Mr. Voicu found the tram station with no difficulty and waited for number eleven. He expected to get in the streetcar, buy a ticket from the cashier inside, and enjoy the ride as he did in the past, but he had an uncomfortable feeling. Too many things had changed. He observed the people around him and noticed them stopping at a kiosk nearby before coming closer to the edge of the sidewalk and waiting to board the tram.

"Would you tell me, please, what they sell in that booth?" He asked a fellow traveler next to him.

"All kinds of things: papers, magazines, cigarettes," the man answered, surprised.

"I see people buying things that are not what you mentioned." Mr. Voicu insisted.

"Oh, those are tickets, of course."

"For the tram?"

"You can buy all kinds of tickets, but mostly for the tram, obviously."

"I apologize, but this is new to me. They used to have a cashier inside each wagon."

"That was long ago. You can buy these tickets anywhere in town. Don't forget it's not enough to have a ticket; you have to punch it once you get in."

"Punch it where? Does it still apply to get in through one door and exit through another?"

"No more. You get in through any door you want. Sorry, I have to take this one coming. Do what the others are doing." And the man rushed into the tram that had just arrived.

Mr. Voicu became embarrassed by the simple thought of what could have happened if he had stepped in with no ticket. From the vendor inside the kiosk, he found that the destination didn't matter. It was one flat fee no matter where you go. It was rather simple but unfamiliar. What if a particular station didn't have a kiosk?

The streetcar took off a little bumpily, enough that a passenger who just stuck his ticket into the puncher lost his balance and broke his ticket. He turned toward the person next to him and said firmly, "Now you have to buy me a ticket."

"Excuse me! Why should I do such a thing?" the other man asked, surprised, with a raised and uncertain voice.

"You pushed me and my ticket broke. If a ticket collector should ask to see my ticket, I will be fined." The first man held his ground.

"If the ticket collector stops you, you show the fragment. Nothing unusual."

"It is not punched, and I cannot punch it the way it is. It's too short. So you can give me your ticket and you can have the broken one if you believe it's worth anything."

"Sir, you don't punish me for something you did. This isn't my problem," the second man answered, visibly aggravated.

"I am fed up paying for others' mistakes. You pushed, you pay." The man with the broken ticket pumped his chest forward and came closer to the accused.

"Don't get stupid in your old age. If you want a fight, we'll get off and I'll knock your teeth out. All for a ticket, you fool." The second man's face became livid and his voice got as firm as it could.

"You are not going to bully me. We get out! With no ticket, I have to get off, anyway." The first man stood his ground.

"Sir, I would be more than happy to pay for this ticket and avoid all this aggravation." Mr. Voicu intervened.

"This is not for you to pay. He is the guilty one," the first man said loudly, pointing his finger.

"Why not hold the conductor guilty?" A passenger suggested.

Other passengers saw in this suggestion an opportunity to defuse the tension and jokingly proposed to hang the conductor. In the distraction created, Mr. Voicu stuck a dollar in the accuser's hand and said in his ear, "Buy it and put this issue behind you. You will do me a great favor."

"Thank you, but no. It's not the money." He refused to grab the dollar.

The next stop came soon enough and the two men got off. Mr. Voicu asked himself whether the two would fight for that ridiculous ticket. He couldn't believe they would. Probably, they just wanted out of that close confinement and release some steam.

How much that man wanted justice! Was it worth all the trouble? Mr. Voicu stood quietly, braced against a bar, until he reached his destination. He stepped off the streetcar pensively and crossed Kiseleff Boulevard with little concern of the heavy traffic. The tram incident still lingered in his mind. Isn't a small injustice as important as a big one? For a principled person, they are equal; for a practical one, they are not. Which one should we be? Nobody can be both.

The park opened in front of his eyes. A wide alley guided him straight to the lake. In that calm, sunny morning, Herastrau Lake stood still like a huge mirror reflecting the blue sky and its few fluffy clouds, framed by green lawns and weeping willows. Mr. Voicu allowed himself to be drawn into that serenity and started to search for sites to shoot. In one corner, he noticed a chain link fence separating the park, from the outdoor "Village's Museum". How could he have forgotten it? The museum had reassembled the most beautiful and creative homes from villages across the country. In the peaceful pace of village life, people had the time and the desire to customize their surroundings. They basically carved in wood their idea of functional beauty. That had been a time when villages had provided moral strength for the whole country. Then communism happened; it brought the rapid industrialization, which not only drained the most able workforce from villages but industrialized agriculture and turned around a whole lifestyle. In addition, this change was accompanied by the new communist questionable morality. There was no more time to get in touch with yourself, and inner values had been overrun by external and confusing ones. Communism shouldn't change what worked so well, but it earnestly did. Among other things, the new regime decided to place in the "Village's Museum" (created under King Carol I) the most sordid mud huts they could find in order to bring political correctness to that place, a reminder of communism's love for its people. Mr. Voicu pensively continued his walk.

The mild sun of that warm fall day felt so comforting. Yes, this was more like he remembered it. Mostly younger people were around, refreshingly few, enough to make him feel alone but not lonely. He sauntered along those alleys until he felt he saw everything he wanted. The coming dinner with Lavinia and Tudor started to feel more enticing than he had anticipated. Lavinia had always been a great cook. Now that he knew his way back, Mr. Voicu decided to return to the hotel the way he came, on tram number eleven. It should have been uneventful, and uneventful it was until a ticket collector came on board. He quietly did his job until he approached a woman who said with a straight face, "I don't have a ticket."

"Your Identification Card, please," the ticket collector asked with an even voice.

"I don't have an ID," she said with a touch of defiance.

"Everybody has an ID. Please present it."

"I don't have it."

"Madam, you are under legal obligation to do that."

"I am under legal obligation to present it to legal authorities. You are not a legal authority."

"Then, what am I, illegal?"

"You are a ticket collector."

"Leave her alone." A passenger intervened. "She probably cannot afford a ticket. What can you do in this situation?"

"No. I pay, you pay. She has to pay too," another passenger jumped in. "This is fair. If she doesn't pay her share, she has to suffer the consequences."

"Isn't there any mercy in you?" the first passenger asked. "What would you do? Put her in jail?"

"She has money to dress pretty decently, she must have some for a ticket too. For me and for many others it isn't easy either, but we do it. She can do it too," the second passenger said with conviction.

"You bring here a law enforcement authority and I will show him my ID," the lady passenger said, raising her left shoulder.

"It doesn't work that way," the ticket collector said, standing firm in front of her. "You come with me to the authority."

"I would leave her alone," the first passenger said with a softer voice.

"Bring her to the police." The second passenger stood by his opinion. "It's one law for all to obey."

The passenger with no ticket wasn't intimidated very easily. "The lawmakers are the biggest crooks. How much justice is in this country that you want to be just with me?" She raised her voice so she could be heard by the others. "Big sharks plunder the country freely and you want to sack me for several cents? Is this justice? All right, I will go to the police; see if they can do anything."

She was still talking when the tram approached the next station and she had to get off with the ticket collector. Mr. Voicu saw through the window the ticket collector holding the woman by her arm and guiding her away from the tram. He thought that she would probably have to listen to a good pep talk before being let go. The passengers had seen the law at work, and that was what mattered the most. Isn't that so? Those events used to conclude with an admission of guilt and the promise to obey the law in the future; and life went on. It's all an illusion of law!

V

Mr. Voicu felt drained when he reached the hotel. He was getting older. He unlocked the door to his room, removed his coat and his shoes, unbuttoned his shirt, and lay flat on the bed. In the quiet, he listened to the blood pulsing through his ears. Really, what should the ticket collector do to that passenger? What should anybody do? She could very well have been a professional freeloader, rather unemotional . . . who knows? His pulse was the only certain thing at that moment. He fell asleep listening to his heart beat.

When he opened his eyes, the sun was crossing the horizon and he didn't know whether it was dusk or dawn. Panicking, he jumped out of his bed and checked his watch. What luck; half an hour before the dinner date! Fully awake, he washed his face, checked his appearance in the bathroom mirror, and called a taxi. As the gypsies used to say, "You pay a buck but you sit in the front row." Better to avoid public transportation for a while.

He stopped in a couple of places for a case of *Cotnari* and a bouquet of freshly cut flowers and, happy with his performance, rang the bell at his cousin's door. They lived in an older neighborhood, with personalized, styled homes, built "before". In front of the house was an open trench, probably meant for some public works project that had dragged on for a long time, probably forgotten, judging from its eroded edges and the dust buildup. Tudor's family used to own that home before it became nationalized and divided to accommodate an additional family unknown to them. The building had only one front door and one vestibule, which the two families had to share. Tudor occupied the ground floor, which had two rooms and the original kitchen, while those living upstairs had another two rooms and the original bathroom.

Tudor opened the door. He was a man in his early sixties, slightly overweight, with thin, gray hair combed straight over this head. His brown eyes gleamed softly. He was clean shaven, with symmetric features . . . a pleasant face with nothing particular to grab anyone's attention. Tudor had been Mr. Voicu's closest relative in his age bracket and his best friend.

"Marin, come in man! It's so nice to see you after so long. You look great." Tudor put his hands on his shoulders, looked him in his eyes with a scrutiny that couldn't hide a prior approval, and hugged him. "Come in. You know the place. Our rooms are not as spacious as those you have there in California, but for us they are enough." Tudor took a step back on the side to let his cousin pass. "Oh! Lavinia will love those flowers. She is still in the kitchen. She will be here in a moment." Tudor guided him gently through the doorway into the vestibule. "My neighbors are always interested in what happens here," he said, giving a cold glance up the stairway and closing the door behind him.

"Lavinia, he's here!" Tudor shouted once the door to his private quarters closed.

"I heard it. I'll be there in a moment!" Before they could sit down, Lavinia appeared from the back door, still drying her hands with a kitchen towel. "Marin, you're finally here! I'm so glad to see you. Oooh, beautiful flowers. I love them, but you shouldn't waste your money. The most important thing is to see you. You two talk until I finish my cooking. It won't take long." She gave him a hug. "Sit down. Make yourself comfortable. I can't wait to hear all your stories."

"This is not part of our agreement," Mr. Voicu protested. "You turn the stove off and come here with us."

"Sure, I'll be there in a moment," Lavinia said as she disappeared through the backdoor.

In the dining room, the large table was set for a serious dinner. Their fine porcelain was set for soup, salad, the main dish, and the dessert all in their proper places and accompanied by proper silverwares and glasses for liqueur, wine, and water. There was a breadbasket set like a work of art. I Ironed napkins stood rolled in their holders. A crystal vase filled one-third with water was waiting for the freshly cut flowers. Mr. Voicu recognized the treasured set of crystal glasses handed down from their grandparents and lost his voice for a moment. So much attention! He had noticed in his walks that food was still sparse and very expensive for local incomes. Certainly, they must have made a major effort to receive him that well.

"Tudor, be serious. I came here to see you and have a talk." Marin objected with a smile.

"You forgot already how it is here. We talk with food in front of us. Words flow easier this way. Besides, you cannot disappoint Lavinia," Tudor said, raising his hands helplessly. "You didn't forget the wine, our favorite, I see. It has been hard to come by lately. Ceausescu exported it all."

Lavinia came through the backdoor with the flowers unpacked and trimmed for the crystal vase. "My dear, look how beautiful they are!" She set them in the crystal vase and fluffed them up.

Tudor showed her the bottles of Cotnari.

"Wow, what a real treat!" Lavinia glimpsed at the case of wine. " During the 'scientific diet,' it used to be impossible to touch a Cotnari. Democracy started on the right foot! Well, you two begin with the appetizers. I will be with you in no time." She rushed back to the kitchen.

Tudor showed Mr. Voicu his seat and took his place at the head of the table.

"Did you see your mother? It's amazing how well she does at her age, having to attend to that big house and take care of the animals and the vegetable garden. I believe that activity keeps her healthy."

"She does really well. I spent several days with her until we ran out of subjects of conversation. We spent too much time apart, I guess." Mr. Voicu looked down pensively. "Time and space do something to you."

"Now that you already speak like a philosopher, let's taste this homemade *tsuica*." Tudor picked a bottle from the buffet on his right and removed its plastic cork. "They're clean, pure prunes from Pitesti: no sugar or anything. We have some long term friends there." He filled two liqueur glasses. "Let's toast to good luck and welcome to our home." Tudor emptied his glass and set it on the table with an expression of a job well done.

Mr. Voicu did likewise slightly more slowly. "It tastes good. I could see the prunes." He paused briefly and changed the subject. "Tell me, the last years under Ceausescu, was it as bad as I heard? When I was still around, in the early seventies, life seemed manageable."

"The sixties, even the early seventies, were our golden years." Tudor refilled the glasses. "Then it started to deteriorate really fast. We had a shortage of food, and in the middle of it, Ceausescu started to tell us that we ate too much and introduced a form of rationing he called the 'scientific diet' [Kiss the Hand You Cannot Bite, p. 202]. Can you imagine such a thing?"

"Easily. Semantics is big with any government. In the U.S., any tax increase is called contribution, fee, surcharge or levy; janitors are called engineers; secretaries are called managers; salesmen are called company representatives or customer satisfaction specialists; and so forth. Everything is puffed up to look more glorious than it is."

"Well, this is benign by comparison. Ceausescu introduced a ration of 0.8 liters (1.4 pints) of cooking oil, 0.2 pounds of margarine, nine eggs, four pounds of fruits, 8.5 pounds of potatoes, and so forth per month per person. We had our coupons but even those couldn't be redeemed. Store managers either didn't receive the items or sold them under the table. Of course, the political system couldn't be held responsible. Ceausescu justified that situation by accusing the retired people of spending their time in lines and purchasing everything that was available while the hard working people toiled in factories. He and his wife called the elderly 'rats.' They hated them. Ambulances came late or didn't come at all when the patient was older. Seniors were accused of hoarding food, like in Stalin's old days. I don't know if this time anybody was punished for having small reserves of staples, but the rhetoric was there. There even had been created some vigilante workers teams. While depriving people, he exported all the food he could. Anyway, all the blame was put on the retirees. Didn't you get that information there in America?" Tudor picked up a bowl with carp caviar and placed it closer to his cousin. "Marin, you have to take some or I will get in trouble with Lavinia."

"Not in the American media, but the Romanian language papers did. Anyway, on the positive side, due to these austerity measures, Ceausescu paid the national debt." Mr. Voicu took a piece of toast and diligently spread on it caviar with the tip of his butter knife.

"He did pay, but our life got so much harder, and honestly, I didn't think it will ever get better. I don't believe the whole communist experience is worth the price we've paid," Tudor said. "It was so bad that people fell into a general state of depression. Streetlights dwindled to save energy, public works dragged on forever, and people went to work in order to punch the card and just lingered around. Throughout the economy, supplies were sporadic, and supervision lacked authority . . . There was a pervasive air of hopelessness. That ditch you saw on our street, in front of the house, has been there for years. I have even forgotten why they dug it. Last winter, it got covered by the first snow, so those not familiar with this area didn't know it was there. No signs of work in progress or warnings of any kind. That day, a motorcyclist fell into that ditch and broke his neck. People accepted the situation as a tragedy waiting to happen. The state couldn't possibly be held accountable, and life went on. This is where we are." Tudor emptied his second glass of tsuica looking distant, apparently unaware of what he had just done.

Mr. Voicu sipped from his and said, while looking at his glass, "Luckily, you have now a new chance, new hopes."

Tudor raised his eye, surprised. "What hopes? Be serious. With the same people, the same habits, the same mentality, what do you expect? A democracy?"

"You should expect some changes. Ceausescu is out, you've got the first free elections in forty-five years, the joys of private enterprise . . . these are something. The fact that there are some former communists in power is not all that bad. Communism deserves a new look," Mr. Voicu said.

"You've forgotten already that communism precludes private enterprise. By the way, where does this sympathy for communism come from?"

"Some elements of communism can be useful. It may sound silly, but after experiencing capitalism, I'm not sure a bolder quest for social equity should be abandoned."

"Some elements? Marin dear, you cannot mix oil and water. Somebody may conceive a new social system, an offshoot of socialism, maybe something similar with what the Chinese are doing or who knows what else, but capitalism with communist features is a contradiction. I don't know. This is too much for me." Tudor paused a moment, looking ahead. "I see no hope in the future. It's all a maze of selfish interests, intrigues, bribes, and lies. In the end, everything is nothing more than survival, as always." He turned his attention to the table and said tenderly, "Here. Marin, take more caviar spread. Lavinia prepared it her own way." He pushed closer the small bowl neatly decorated with green parsley, red slices of radish, and black olive halves.

Mr. Voicu scooped up some on the tip of his butter knife and spread it on another toast. It truly was a rare treat. He took another portion—nothing like home cooking—and checked the table for other goodies.

Tudor followed his cousin's eyes with interest. "Take for instance these tomatoes. They are organic, farm-ripened, and not green reddened with nitrogen like there in America. We know more than you credit us for." His eyes sparked with pride. "They go well with this feta cheese." Tudor put one tomato and a slice of cheese on his dish.

"Were you in town during the revolution?" Mr. Voicu asked as he started to slice the tomato.

"Not only in town, I was in the Palace's Square when Ceausescu made his famous last speech. I was there when he took the helicopter from the roof of the Central Committee and ran. I was in the middle of the action. People threw things at him. It was complete chaos."

Mr. Voicu looked attentively at his cousin and asked, "Did the Securitate truly shoot people in the square as I heard?" Then, he slowly placed the cheese on a buttered slice of bread.

"They did, but I didn't stay there to see. Once it started to look bad, I walked home. It wouldn't have helped anybody if I were dead. I have a retirement to enjoy. I understand . . ." Tudor was interrupted by Lavinia coming red-faced from the kitchen with a steaming porcelain bowl of chicken soup.

"Tudor, we need more activity here," she said, placing the bowl in the center of the table. "You didn't touch my chicken salad yet. You two are doing too much talking."

"My dear, we are having an intellectual conversation here. We tapped into higher values. Marin asked me about the revolution."

Lavinia sat in her chair with a sigh. "What revolution? I don't want to hear this word any longer. It is so misused that it has lost its meaning. Marin, let's change the subject."

"I apologize, Lavinia. I'm ignorant on this matter. What happened then if it cannot be called a revolution?" Mr. Voicu carved a portion of chicken salad and put it on his dish.

"I don't know what it was, and those who know don't say. Obviously, faithful to our tradition, nobody has the courage to challenge the leaders who are the ones who do know. They are also the beneficiaries of this change; so understandably, they paint everything in bright colors. The truth is an inconvenience to them. In conclusion, we don't know what happened."

"I am getting depressed. I thought it was a popular upheaval," Mr. Voicu said. Then he changed the tone. "In California, they sell this kind of salad in Middle Eastern stores, but it is not as rich as yours. I love it!"

"I'm glad you are enjoying it." Tudor pulled a smile. He watched Lavinia filling Marin's soup bowl with a detached look in his eyes. "Yes, let's change the subject. We changed our leaders from communists to former communists. How much of a change is that? The last political change—from democracy to communism—was a catastrophe. Now that we have gotten used to it, we change again. This is not an easy job. It means to destroy again the existing infrastructure; abandon familiarities, ways, and habits; more changes in the value system . . . Do you know how much disruption and hardship this creates?"

"The disruption, fortunately, is temporary. I am more concerned with getting rid of a system whose advantages we haven't yet had the opportunity to explore. We went from Stalinism to Ceausescuism. We only experienced the down side and missed what's good in this communist experiment." Mr. Voicu made his point with his fork in his hand.

"This is the trap of dictatorship. It's rare to find a good dictator. Even if they start doing well, the lack of counterbalances makes them go off the road. You know, nobody dares to correct a dictator. This is the problem." Pleased with his conclusion, Tudor looked wide-eyed from Lavinia to Tudor and back.

"The problem is that the food is getting cold," Lavinia said with a smile. "Marin, give me your dish." She garnished his dish with three steaming cabbage rolls and polenta and returned it. "I'm sure you haven't tasted *sarmale* [cabbage rolls] since you left."

Tudor remained quiet until the plate was filled. Then he continued. "If I understand it correctly, you don't have any objection to ex-communists being in power."

"Well, I don't believe it is important if they are ex-communists or not as long as they do the job right. Lavinia, you truly hit the spot. I didn't realize how much I missed this food," Mr. Voicu said between two bites. "You're a great cook."

"Thank you, Marin. You've changed," Lavinia said, looking at her plate.

Tudor stopped eating and gazed at his cousin. "Do you think a communist can do the job right? Can he be better suited for leadership than a properly educated, independent thinker?"

"Well, someone may have it in him regardless of his education or the lack thereof."

"So in your opinion, education is a waste?" Tudor asked with his eyebrows raised to there highest.

"No, of course not. It's just that common sense and education are independent entities," Mr. Voicu said slowly.

"To me, common sense appreciates education, which our communist leaders didn't. Well, not as they should have. You know Marin, you confuse me. What happened to you there in America? They ruined you." Tudor softened his words with a faint smile.

"I've seen the other side of the coin. That's all."

"Wow. I thought you'd be a capitalist by now." Tudor resumed eating.

"In a sense I am. I mean, capitalism is built from hard work and creativity, and this is fine. It is not fine when it's used to separate people rather than unite them." Mr. Voicu put his spoon down and looked at Tudor and Lavinia. "I have a proposal. Let's become capitalists! What about building a tsuica factory? Our Romanians have produced tsuica for centuries; they know how. Let them do on a larger scale what they already do in their small communal distilleries. Sound good?"

Tudor checked briefly Lavinia's face and answered, "Just a moment, this is not as simple as you put it. You need a lot of prunes; and then, we are not experienced in building a factory."

"I will buy a prunes orchard. As for the building, it's only four walls and a roof. We'll put inside a still and a source of heat, running water, and sewage, and that is pretty much it. The rest, we'll improve as we go."

"Lavinia, what do you say?" Tudor asked.

"I say nothing. This is your call. If you decide to go with it, I won't object. But don't involve me in any business. I have enough to do at home."

Tudor got some color in his face, and his eyes opened wider. "This is too much for two office workers like us. This is much too complex for us to get involved. You don't just start building it. There's so much bureaucracy, red tape, and kickbacks that in the end you lose all your motivation. But besides that, we don't know the technology. Let the professionals do a professional job. It's too much; let's be realistic," he said, agitated.

Mr. Voicu finished his sarmale, tapped the corners of his mouth, and pushed his plate slightly forward. Lavinia picked up the dishes and took them in the kitchen. "Let's say then, what if we start a washing and ironing business? We buy a bunch of washers and dryers, hire a couple of fellows handy with ironing, and we are set. As the business grows, we grow. We'll improve the equipment as needed and we'll be set."

"You talk like an American. You forget this is Romania. No. I appreciate your interests, but this is not for me."

"Tudor, you don't lose anything. I'll do all the investments; you have to only manage it. We'll keep in touch. I'll come here every so often. It's not like I would abandon you in the middle of nowhere." Mr. Voicu tried to motivate his cousin.

Lavinia came with a platter heaped with mashed potatoes, sauerkraut, and pork chops. She put it quietly in the middle of the table and started to serve. They ate for a while without saying anything. Mr. Voicu broke the silence.

"May I ask you then, what are your plans for the future?"

"Our future is in God's hands," Tudor said as he turned and picked up a bottle of wine from the credenza behind him and uncorked it.

"I didn't know you were religious. How did that happen?" Mr. Voicu paused to catch the answer.

"It didn't happen," Lavinia answered. "God comes into discussion when we have no other answer. We don't have a plan for our future. We hope that Tudor will keep his job for as long as possible and will retire with a good pension. They are still about 80% of the last salary, but it seems they will be lowered substantially." She moved her empty wine glass to make it more accessible to Tudor.

"Pensions are never generous enough. Sorry, but this is the time to make your move." Mr. Voicu raised his glass. "For a better life!"

"For a better life!" Lavinia and Tudor said in one voice, and all clinked their glasses.

"We don't ask for much. If we can have decent food, time to rest, and good company we can consider ourselves fulfilled, right?" Tudor asked while looking at Lavinia.

"At this time, in this country, you cannot make money from decent work." Lavinia said and savored the taste of the wine.

"That's right," Tudor chipped in. "Those who make money today do it from perks and bribes and taking state properties for themselves. Under communism, we all chipped away at state property. Now the whole thing is being plundered. This is the difference between then and now . . . this is the only difference. Honesty is only a slogan."

"Plundering is a sure way to bring the country down." Mr. Voicu observed.

"A country cannot go away; it stays and endures," Tudor said while playing with his glass. "If foreign powers would leave us alone, our country will pull itself up from its boot straps. We have always survived, and we always will. The current situation has, nevertheless, its particular twist: we have lost our sense of self-worth. Those forty-five years of criticism, mistrust, underperformance, fear, backwardness . . . all of that took its toll. If we don't value ourselves, nobody will. This is part of the communist tragedy. There is no value in the communist goal, no value in what we managed to achieve in our lives, no value in what we have been allowed to know, nothing to be proud of in our condition as slaves to a system run by slaves. We are shadows of what we could have been if left alone." He emptied his glass in sad conclusion.

Mr. Voicu made an effort to rise above the unhappiness that permeated the air. "Come on, Tudor. Lamentation doesn't bring us anywhere. Europe went through an endless chain of wars and tragedies, and it is still at the top. It has been hard, but we can overcome it."

"It's too late for me. Let the young and idealistic ones do it," Tudor said, scrutinizing his napkin. "I wish them good luck."

Mr. Voicu felt he should do all he could to stop that kind of talk; the sooner the better. "Well, let's drink to the success of the young and idealistic people." He raised his glass.

"For the young idealists!" Lavinia and Tudor raised their glasses and forced a smile.

Mr. Voicu detected for the first time a touch of despair in their brave attempt to revive the good, old times. This impression struck him too hard to acknowledge it. "Lavinia, you have given me the most pleasant surprise since I've stepped out of the airplane. Your cooking has no match," he said with a smile.

"It's not over until it's over." Lavinia returned the smile. "You still have to have a sour cherry pie and a cup of Turkish coffee."

"How can I refuse? I always loved sour cherry pies. I didn't have any since I left the country," Mr. Voicu said and changed the tone. "Guess what? I am planning to go to Predeal tomorrow."

"Good idea. That area has improved a lot. Do you have a ticket? "

"Not yet. In your company, time is losing its meaning. I didn't want to commit."

"Look what I have for you. We are well prepared here." Tudor got off his chair and opened a drawer in his small desk at the other end of the room. "I have the railroad schedule." He returned flipping through the booklet. "Let's see . . . There are some good non-stop routes in the morning. There is an eight thirty, then you have another one at ten."

""It all depends when I'll wake up. After such a feast, I expect to oversleep. Your dinners are always memorable. I'm not worried. I'm with friends."

7. A Simple Question

I

In the main hall of Gara de Nord train station, Mr. Voicu stopped to take a look at the old, oversized boards with listings of arrivals and departures. They were refreshingly concise and clear. While checking the availabilities, he noticed next to him a foreign-looking young lady staring at those boards with the utmost confusion. She probably cannot read them, he thought, and gladly offered to help.

"Excuse me, miss. Is there anything I can help you with? I speak Romanian fluently."

"Actually, there is something I cannot understand; maybe you can. I asked for a ticket to Constanta, and the lady from the ticket counter told me to come back in an hour. No explanation given. I don't understand why I have to come back in an hour. Is she going to have the tickets then? Why then and not now? I don't understand this system."

"It truly seems confusing, but let me ask. Which window is it?"

She pointed to one of the several small windows in a row, all placed in such a way that one could not make eye contact with the clerk inside unless he bowed down. The window indicated by the lady had a thick glass covered inside by a small green curtain of heavy material with a CFR [Romanian Iron Roads] logo. Mr. Voicu assumed the clerk was still at her desk behind the curtain and knocked. No answer. He knocked again and again. A visibly upset employee pulled the curtain swiftly and, without a word, pointed upward. Then, equally swiftly, she pulled the curtain back. Mr. Voicu glimpsed at the "closed" sign above, but still, he wanted the clerk to clarify her previously made statement. He knocked again and again. The employee pulled the small green curtain again and said angrily:

"Don't you know how to read?"

"The issue is not if I know how to read . . ."

And before he could come to the issue, the employee jerked the curtain back, angrier than before. For God's sake, couldn't he ask a simple question? He knocked on the window again, and again, and again. This time, the curtain didn't move. Instead, a side door opened and a security guard came through, who was as angry as the clerk behind the green curtain. With the determination of an angel of justice, he walked to Mr. Voicu and grabbed him by the back of his shirt.

"Tell me, handsome, did you read that sign up there? It says 'closed.' Do you know what closed means or are you an idiot? Ha? Tell me! You're certainly an idiot. Otherwise, I wouldn't have to teach you how to behave in public places. We don't need you around here. Take your baggage and get out before I lose my temper."

While holding Mr. Voicu by the back of his shirt with one hand, he slapped the back of his head with the other. Then he pushed him toward the exit, alternating jerks with kicks on his butt, and slaps on the nape of his neck in a show of disgust.

"I am an American citizen . . ." Mr. Voicu tried to defend himself. Instead of getting some consideration, his words managed to aggravate the guard.

"Now you are an American! Strange that this doesn't make you more intelligent. You still look like a worthless piece of sh..! You don't fool me. I know who you are. You are one of those "Jehovians" who come here to confuse people with religious bigotry. Get out of here! Go back to America! Preach to your cows and leave us alone. We always get somebody who comes to teach us something. Go and make the Americans happy and leave us alone. Get out, you mother f . . . . r, before I kick your ass in."

The security man kicked, jolted, and slapped Mr. Voicu through the gate and across Gara de Nord's Square to the far side, away from his jurisdiction.

"Go in your mother's . . . I don't want to see you around here again. Got it?"

Then he turned around still mumbling, slightly bent like under a burden.

Mr. Voicu walked the walk, pushed and humiliated, with no opportunity to say anything of substance. His mind was ravished by thoughts and feelings none of which had the time to come into expression. What he was subjected to wasn't physically painful or damaging, but it hurt deeply. All he had wanted was simple information in that hall which had no information booth. How could it have degenerated into such an abuse? How could his good intentions towards that girl as well as towards the country have been interpreted as disruptive, even harmful? How could he be accused of proselytizing for Jehovah Witnesses when in fact he didn't respect any religion? But regardless, his dignity was violated. His love was rejected. His good intentions were misinterpreted and dismissed, all in the most vulgar way.

He expected the passersby to be revolted by so much brutality, but no one did. Where was the Romanian compassionate spirit? Where was that surge of dignity that had slashed communism and executed the entrenched and arrogant dictator? Where was their pride and kindness . . . ? People on the street were totally indifferent to the way he was treated, as if nothing unusual had happened.

In fact, it was nothing unusual. In the forty-five years of communism, they had been subjected to much worse. In comparison to starvation, freezing, permanent fear, and repression, a kick in the butt was tender. People's dignity had become so abused that a few angry words didn't mean anything any longer. Besides, in their state of permanent suspicion, who could be sure he didn't deserve that treatment? Who had the time to get involved into something that didn't pertain to him and that he didn't know anything about? It could backfire. After all, each one has his own cross to carry. Each one is responsible for himself only.

Mr. Voicu realized that Romania was no longer the country he thought he knew. It was not the home he had expected. It wasn't his home any longer. In the twenty years since he had left, so many things had changed. He felt abandoned like a child whose parents had disappeared while he was looking the other way. Loneliness was such a frightening thing! A breeze ruffled his thin hair. He didn't notice it. It didn't matter.

Standing on the sidewalk, Mr. Voicu felt the need to do something as big as his heartache, but he couldn't move. Hundreds of thoughts were rushing through his mind, but none seemed appropriate. The only suitable solution seemed to be to cover his wounds and move on like those around him, bent inward to protect their souls. He thought, "Perhaps this is the right thing to do under these particular circumstances." Romanians, as a matter of fact, had the perfect answer to their particular condition. It was like a cocoon, perfect for protection but unable to fly. He realized that because his life in California was different than theirs, his answer to daily trials had become different as well. In fact, he had become so different that he didn't belong any longer to his own country. He didn't have Romanian problems and he didn't share in the Romanian answers.

For the first time he felt humbled. If ever in charge of the country, as he used to dream, he realized he wouldn't be able to change anything nor could anybody else. If he would try hypothetically to fix the country's problems, as he had previously imagined, he would appear out of touch, more like a weirdo. Nature had to follow its own course, not his. The best he could do was, like everybody else around him, tend to his wounds, adjust to the times, and move on.

Those who understand forgive, so Mr. Voicu found himself the forgiving victim of an unforgiving aggressor. In fact, he turned the other cheek without being aware of doing it.

The people who had witnessed his indignity had already moved on to their destinations. The embarrassment of being seen humiliated moved on with the crowd. Only the pain remained. He picked up his luggage and walked back across the square toward the line of taxies. Numbly, he watched the driver put his bag in the trunk, and then, as in an automatic chronological sequence, he got into the backseat and asked the driver to take him to the airport.

II

Mr. Voicu didn't hope to find a seat available on the next flight to the United States. Those flights were few and suddenly popular. Nevertheless, he trusted that he could arrange something. From his past Romanian experiences, there were always some seats reserved for special situations, seats that could be made available right before departure.

The next flight posted was about three hours away. The agent hadn't arrived yet at his desk, so he used the time to call his mother. The chance of her changing her mind and agreeing to come with him was slim to none, but it was good to renew the offer before saying good-bye. He told her that some urgent business called him back to California and that he had to leave.

"You go and take care of your things over there and don't worry about me. I am fine. You live in a violent place, not me. I have all I need: a household to keep me busy, good neighbors, food, and heat. There is nothing for you to worry about. You should be careful in that country. It always comes on television with weird things. I watch your movies all the time."

"Those are only movies, Mom; make-believe, entertainment."

"You call that entertainment? Where do they get those ideas from?"

"Mother, that is Hollywood, not America."

"Isn't Hollywood in America? Don't talk nonsense."

"Yes, but they live by their own standards there. America is a free country. Don't worry, nobody takes it seriously there."

"I hope not. Anyway, take care of yourself and write more often. If you take it easier, you may find a good girl and get settled."

"All right, Mom. I talked to Ioji to help you with groceries and whatever chores you may need. He seems a young nice fellow, unemployed though. It is all arranged; you only tell him what you need and he will do it."

"Very well, I will tell him. Now, have a good trip, and call me when you get there."

When he returned to the ticket counter, a small line had already formed. Even with prior reservations, people still had uneasy feelings before they actually saw the ticket in their hands. Mr. Voicu patiently got in line. He felt their apprehension; it always had been that way. These poor people had few and hard-earned opportunities to travel across the border. They were always afraid that the opportunity could be snatched from them at any moment.

Mr. Voicu put his reservation on the counter and said, "I would like to exchange this ticket for today's flight. A change in my schedule has made it necessary to leave earlier."

"I'm sorry, Sir. We have no seats available for today. The earliest available is for next Thursday."

"Oh! It is very important for me to go back today. I really have to change a reservation I made sometime ago. Is there any possibility to update it for this flight?"

"Not likely. If you had called a week earlier, you could have, but now there is no way. All seats are sold out."

"Who knows, you may get a last-minute cancellation," Mr. Voicu said while slowly pushing forward his passport with a one hundred dollar bill showing discreetly through the side.

"Wait here." The clerk said while pushing the passport out of sight. Then she took the next one in line.

Mr. Voicu moved aside enough to allow the next customer to the window and yet to maintain his priority place at the same time. After serving the next customer, the clerk left her seat, picked up the passport, and disappeared somewhere in the back. When returned, she handed Mr. Voicu his passport with the ticket inside. The one hundred dollar bill was gone.

One hundred dollars was a small fortune in the aftermath of the revolution, something close to that girl's monthly salary. Of course, a moralist would argue that bribery is wrong, but is it? Political lobbying is bribery and it is an acceptable practice everywhere. The big investors have access to the best stocks while the small ones get the crumbs. When the supply is limited, some get their goods and some don't. You either elbow in and get one of the limited number of items you want or you get moral and leave it up to chance. This is how those who have always win. They know how to be one step ahead of those who don't have. "Isn't this the way it is?" he argued with himself.

The issue being resolved, he bought a paper and sat down to read it in peace. Departure was more than an hour away, so he had plenty of time. He picked an article, and after a couple of paragraphs, he started to feel uncomfortable. The writing was so much less than expected. Instead of relying on facts, it abounded in lamentations and accusations. To Mr. Voicu, it seemed that the author mistook his own opinions for standards of righteousness. He was supposed to report the facts, not to pass judgment or to describe his own feelings. The columnist could eventually offer a brief comment but nothing more. Other articles where written the same way. He didn't remember the papers being that badly written when he had lived there.

Some noise from the ticket counter distracted him for a while. An English-speaking lady had a bad temper:

"This is impossible. I have this seat reserved in my name. This seat is mine. Understand? You cannot tell me it is taken. I want to talk to your supervisor. It's incredible!"

"Look, you are not in my computer. What do you want me to do? Expand the airplane?"

"I don't care about your computer. Get me your boss."

"It's always something," Mr. Voicu thought and got back to his reading. Regardless of the writer's style, he still could get a feel for the issues at stake. When the speaker announced the boarding for the New York flight, he had about had it with that paper. He tossed it in a trashcan and walked towards his terminal. He stepped onto the airplane with the feeling of entering another world. Everything he had experienced in Romania started to fade rapidly into a past that felt more distant than it was. What he had been through became more and more like a fading memory, and he quietly enjoyed putting his experiences behind while getting comfortable in his seat.

III

Once the plane was up in the air and the passengers were allowed to remove their seat belts, a lady came to him and asked with an English accent. "Excuse me, Sir. How did you get this seat?"

"From the ticket counter, of course."

"Obviously. I don't want to imply anything, but this seat was reserved for me until somebody gave it to you. I am only curious why. This is the first time such a thing has happened to me."

"If this seat means anything to you, I will be more than happy to exchange it." Mr. Voicu answered with a huge effort to appear in control of himself. The misdeed he initially had covered with convenient explanations hit him in his face with its whole ugliness. His faceless victim, who, in his wishful thinking hadn't suffered any inequity, had taken a human face and came forward to challenge him. More than that, if that lady had gotten a seat, then somebody else was stripped of his rights instead; somebody who didn't demand his or her prerogatives forcefully enough . . . probably a more submissive Romanian. For them, abuse is nothing new. This time, the abuser was Mr. Voicu himself, the one who thought he had a solution for all abuses.

What could he tell her? Should he be as honest as he thought he was? No, he couldn't. This would start a whole chain reaction of blame and punishment, which would create a lot of pain and solve nothing. It takes more than a complaint to change the way things work. Better leave it as it was and bear his own guilt.

"No, thank you," the lady replied. "My other seat is equally as good. I only wanted to understand how this change happened."

Mr. Voicu felt a strong desire to confess and regain some dignity in his own eyes, but then he would unveil an ugliness which would stain his country's image, while, in fact, his country was a victim rather than a perpetrator; a victim of abuse by other countries that had forced these people to find ways to survive. Then, survival compromises dignity. It is easy for these Anglo—Saxons to claim purity, but are they? They, with their spheres of influence and perpetual wars, all orchestrated outside their borders. Regardless, this was his doing. He had better swallow the bitter consequences. What a surprise it was! In the end, he was no different than those around him.

"I wish I could help you, I am sorry," he said.

"Well, I won't take your time any longer. Enjoy your trip."

"I'll do my best. You take care."

He looked through the window and watched the clouds underneath like white cotton candy. No wonder people imagine the angels living in the clouds. How can anybody live on earth and be an angel?

IV

Back in California, it was my turn to ask Mr. Voicu of the news and trends from back home. This time, he was more introspective and less inclined to pass judgments, which made our meeting more intimate and pleasantly friendly. But then, he got involved with his business and willfully put his Romanian experiences behind. He continued to believe that communism could be superior to capitalism, if properly applied. I could never convince him that communism has built-in flaws that will always prevent it from delivering. It cannot be any other way. Still, communism remains attractive to a lot of people for a lot of reasons. I assume, most of the sympathizers like the idea but are ignorant of its fine print or like it for selfish reasons. I see communism as the last Tower of Babel, the last coordinated attempt to build a fulfilling society to the exclusion of God and the dismissal of his eternal values. I believe that this exclusion of God offered Mr. Voicu the exciting perspective of full control over public affairs, an excitement he couldn't miss. He anticipated how much could be done if . . . and he embraced the same thought the communists had!

This latest Romanian experience, like his American experiences and all the experiences before that, didn't change much of his opinions. His self-righteousness survived unscratched, as did his disappointments with both Romania and the United States. After all, self-righteousness entails blame, guilt, and close-mindedness, which in and of themselves excludes growth, love and peace. But then, what is life without growth, love and peace? The communist system itself failed to succeed because it relied on self-righteousness and suffered all its consequences.

Unfortunately, Mr. Voicu's disappointments didn't stop there. Several months later, he received a call from the Romanian Consulate in Los Angeles. His mother had been murdered. The investigation concluded it was a robbery gone wrong. The suspect, apprehended in a town hundreds of miles away, was Ioji.

This latest incident, like the death of his father and of his wife, didn't cause him more than sorrow. He interpreted the Romanian occurrences as consequence of individual behavior unrelated to the values acquired under communism. As for American capitalism, he still understood it as a poorly managed society. These beliefs justified him to live his life by his own "right" rules. Capitalist leniency allowed him the freedom to do so until he collided with the law of the land. Then, he lost all he had.

Most of his building improvements had been done without city approval in order to avoid higher property taxes. It was only a matter of time until the city found out and levied rather stiff penalties. Mr. Voicu decided to fight in court. About the same time, one of his female tenants claimed she had slipped on a wet concrete alley in the building's backyard, and cracked her tailbone. Mr. Voicu found it hard to believe and asked her to show him her tailbone. Words passed between them, and from there, Mr. Voicu found himself sued for sexual harassment. The case became more serious when another tenant joined the first one. This time he was accused of looking at her improperly, which made her lose sleep and have flashbacks of him winking at her. She then had to take sleeping pills for a period long enough to cause addiction.

Mr. Voicu asked his insurance company for legal assistance, but the company declined to defend him because the claim was of a personal nature and, consequently, not covered by his business policy. He felt disappointed but not discouraged. Who could believe such fabrications as these ladies alleged? He didn't see any difficulty in proving his innocence. For his legal defense, he chose an attorney he had used along the years, for all kinds of small business matters. Unfortunately, this attorney had no court experience. Subsequently, Mr. Voicu lost his case. Only then did he hire a skilled attorney to repair the damages, but not much could be done. To make things worse, another woman came forward and filed a law suit, frivolous in his opinion, for sexual harassment. Discouraged, Mr. Voicu sold his properties, sold his loans and his attorney, took the little cash remaining, and fled to Romania. There, he bought under Tudor's name the apartment where I had visited him, next to that tiny square park. To the very end, he maintained his appreciation for the communist doctrine, disappointment over how it had been implemented, and disdain for capitalism. All my arguments on these issues didn't mean a thing to him. His self-righteousness survived unshaken.

I would never know if this attitude of his was inspired by the communist environment during his formative years or if he had this tendency from birth. Regardless, he replicated in his personal life the self-righteousness that failed the whole communist system. He could otherwise have had a fulfilling and happy life.

BIBLIOGRAPHY

The Barnes Review November / December 2001

TBR March / April 2005.

TBR July / August 2006.

TBR July / August 2008.

TBR March / April 2009.

Alexandru, Doina. Corneliu Coposu, Confesiuni. Anastasia House, 1996.

Axworthy, Mark. Third Axis Forth Ally: Romanian Armed Forces in the European War, 1941-1945. Arms & Armour, 1995.

Behr, Edward. Kiss the Hand You Cannot Bite: The Rise and Fall of the Ceausescus. Villard, 1991.

Charen, Mona. Useful Idiots. Regnery Publishing, Inc. 2003

Coposu, Corneliu. Confesiuni. Editura Anastasia, Bucuvesti, 1996.

Deletant, Dennis. Ceausescu and the Securitate: Coercion and Descent in Romania, 1965-1989. M.E. Sharpe, 1996.

Deletant, Dennis. Romania Under Communist Rule. Civic Academy Foundation. Bucharest, 2006.

Dutu Alec. Sub Povara Armistitiului 1944-1947. Tritonic, 2003.

Dutu Alec., Dobre Florica. Drama Generalilor Romani (1944-1964). Editura Enciclopedica Bucuresti, 1997.

Femia V. Joseph. Marxism and Democracy. Clarendon Press. Oxford 1993.

Figes, Orlando. <u>The Crimean War</u>. Metropolitan Book Henry Holt and Company, New York 2010.

Gaddis, John Lewis. <u>The Cold War: A New History</u>. Penguin, 2005.

Gardener C. Lloyd. <u>Spheres of Influence</u>. Elephant Paperbacks, 1993.

Hitchins, Keith. <u>Rumania 1866-1947</u>. Oxford University Press, 1994.

Ionescu, Ghita. <u>Comunismul in Romania</u>. Bucuresti: Litera, 1964.

Kenez, Peter. <u>A History of the Soviet Unoin from the Beginning to the End.</u> Cambridge University Press, 2006.

King, R. Robert. <u>History of the Romanian Communist Party</u>. Hoover Institution Press, 1980.

Lukes, Steven. <u>Marxism and Morality</u>. Oxford University Press, 1987.

Lungu B. Dov. <u>Romania and the Great Powers, 1933-1940</u>. Duke University Press, 1989.

Manuel E. Frank. <u>A Requiem for Karl Marx</u>. Harvard University Press, 1995.

Pacepa I. Mihai, Lt. General. <u>Red Horizons</u>. Regnery Gateway, 1987.

Romascanu Gr. Mihail. <u>Tezaurul Romanesc de la Moscova</u>. Editura Seculum I.O. Bucuresti, 2000.

Scurtu Ion, Almas Dumitru, Gosu Armand, Pavelescu Ion, Ionita I. Gheorghe. <u>Istoria Basarabiei de la Inceputuri pina in 1994</u>. Editura Tempus, Bucuresti, 1994.

Van Meurs, Wirn. <u>The Bassarabian Question</u>. Columbia University Press, 1994.

CPSIA information can be obtained
at www.ICGtesting.com
Printed in the USA
LVHW090107050320
649021LV00001B/2